...afraid to ask awk...

...ar joy for a teenage reader, to ... ...enged

... than instructed' Patrick Ness, *Guardian*

'Poignant and powerful . . . A heartwarming, bittersweet
story of the deep and lasting bond between a boy and his
little brother' *Canadian Children's Book News*

'Incredibly thought-provoking' *Sun*

'Funny and involving . . . very believable' *Flipside*

'A moving, original novel' *Booklist*

'O... ...s story is filled with compassion and has no easy
answers' *Publishers Weekly*

...i utterly engaging read . . . Highly recommended'
The Bookbag

www.**davidficklingbooks**.co.uk

Also by Kenneth Oppel

Starclimber
Skybreaker
Airborn
Dusk
Firewing
Sunwing
Silverwing
Dead Water Zone

Coming soon:
This Dark Endeavour

www.kennethoppel.ca

Half Brother

KENNETH OPPEL

David Fickling Books

HALF BROTHER
A DAVID FICKLING BOOK 978 1 849 92000 1

Published in Great Britain by David Fickling Books,
a division of Random House Children's Books
A Random House Group Company

Hardback edition published 2011
This edition published 2011

1 3 5 7 9 10 8 6 4 2

The Random House Group Limited supports the Forest Stewardship Council
(FSC), the leading international forest certification organization. All our titles that
are printed on Greenpeace-approved FSC-certified paper carry the FSC logo. Our
paper procurement policy can be found at www.randomhouse.co.uk/environment.

Mixed Sources
Product group from well-managed
forests and other controlled sources
www.fsc.org Cert no. TT-COC-002139
© 1996 Forest Stewardship Council
FSC

Set in Goudy by Falcon Oast Graphic Art Ltd.

DAVID FICKLING BOOKS
31 Beaumont Street, Oxford, OX1 2NP

www.kidsatrandomhouse.co.uk
www.totallyrandombooks.co.uk
www.randomhouse.co.uk

Addresses for companies within The Random House Group Limited can be found
at: www.randomhouse.co.uk/offices.htm

THE RANDOM HOUSE GROUP Limited Reg. No. 954009

A CIP catalogue record for this book is available from the British Library.

Printed and bound in Great Britain by CPI Bookmarque, Croydon, CR0 4TD

For my whole family

PART I

This is how we got Zan.

He was eight days old and his mother was holding him, nursing him. He was cuddled against her and she made comforting sounds, waving the flies away with her free hand. Her back was turned so she didn't see the gun when it fired the dart into her leg. She looked round with a grunt. She saw a man and a woman on the other side of the cage. She stared at them long and hard, still feeding her baby. She knew. It had happened once before, and she knew it was about to happen again. She shuffled deeper into the corner, held her baby tight. Then the tranquillizers kicked in and she slumped clumsily against the wall. Her eyes were still open, but had a glassy look.

The man opened the cage and moved swiftly towards her. He wanted to get to her before she dropped the baby, or rolled over and crushed it. The mother sat, paralysed, watching as the man pulled her whimpering baby away from her body. Outside the cage, the man passed the baby to the woman. She wrapped it gently in a soft blanket and cradled it in her arms, making shushing sounds.

This was my mother.

As she walked away from the cage with the baby, she sang to him, songs she'd used with me when I was little. After a few days she got on a plane with her new baby, and flew home to us.

Chapter 1

Zan

I woke up, a teenager.

It was six a.m., June 30th, and I was in a sleeping bag on the floor of my empty bedroom, in our ugly new house on the other side of the country. When you didn't have curtains, the dawn was your alarm clock.

I didn't care. It was my birthday and I was thirteen years old, and there was something exciting about being up so early, seeing the first light slant across your walls, hearing the birds make a racket, and knowing you were the only one awake in the house. The day seemed huge.

Dad had promised to take me for a swim at the lake, and then out to a pizza place for dinner. I hoped he hadn't forgotten. Because, with Mom away, I wasn't too sure he'd remember to get me anything. I'd mentioned a new bike, but he'd never been much good at things like birthdays, especially when he was busy. And right now he was super busy, getting ready for his new project.

I sighed. If I was lucky, the movers would come, and I'd get a bed for my birthday. I looked around my new room, trying to decide where I was going to put all my stuff when it finally arrived.

Scattered beside me on the floor were a bunch of magazines and comics, and I started paging through the latest issue of *Popular Mechanics*. There was a really cool article about how you could live in your own helicopter, and the pictures showed this big double-decker chopper on pontoons, tied up at a lake-side dock. Inside the helicopter was this super happy family. There was the mom and daughter being happy in the kitchen and the father being happy in the shower, and the two sons being happy playing with toys in their bedroom. The chopper was surprisingly spacious. The family could fly away when-ever they wanted and live all over the world, but still be at home.

I wished we could've moved like that.

All we had was an ancient Volvo, and it had taken Dad and me six days to drive from Toronto to Victoria.

We could've flown, but Dad had wanted me to see my own country. He'd told me a bit about the Canadian Shield and the Prairies and the Rockies. A road trip, he'd said, just the two boys, while Mom was away in New Mexico, picking up the baby. We'd see all the cool sites, eat burgers and drink milkshakes, stay in motels with swimming pools, and have a blast.

I was suspicious right away. I knew the whole thing was

cooked up to distract me – like giving someone a handful of Smarties on a crashing plane. But Dad was a really good talker. When he was enthusiastic, *you* got enthusiastic. He made you feel like you were the only person in the world, and he was sharing these things with you alone.

So I got pretty excited, and the day after school was out, we packed up the car and headed off. At first we talked a lot – actually, Dad did most of the talking, but I didn't mind, because he usually didn't talk this much to me. Normally he spent his days at the university, lecturing, or working on his research, and when he came home, he was all talked out, and didn't have much left to say – not to me anyway.

I really liked being with him the first couple of days. He'd already been out to Victoria for the job interview, and he told me how beautiful it was. Mountains and sea practically everywhere you looked. The house we were going to live in was huge. The climate was the best in Canada. He told me how exciting it was going to be for me, starting at a new school. New teachers, new friends. It was going to be a big change, but Dad said change was wonderful and invigorating and the best thing that could happen to us as human beings. I'd love it, he said. He'd already decided, so there was no point asking *me* how *I* felt.

But not even Dad could talk for the entire eight hours we spent each day in the car – and every day he got a little quieter. Turned out we didn't stop at as many tourist sites as he'd promised, because he had everything scheduled very tightly, and he knew exactly where he wanted to be at the end of each day. So mostly what I saw of Canada was moving at fifty-five miles an hour.

Sometimes, instead of sitting up front, I sprawled across the back seat, reading Spider-Man comics and Ray Bradbury, or just listening to the radio. Dad let me choose the stations at least, tuning in to new ones when the old ones evaporated with the cities, and provinces, and time zones we left behind. The Rolling Stones belted out 'Angie' over and over again, and Dad watched the road, lost in his own thoughts. I sucked on orange Freezies, and the car smelled like French fries and ketchup, and the Fresca I'd spilled outside Thunder Bay.

On the fourth night, we were back in our motel room after dinner. Dad had hardly talked to me all day. Things had gone completely back to normal. I was just cargo.

Dad picked up one of his big books – on linguistics or primates, they all looked equally huge and terrifying – then glanced up like he'd just noticed me. Maybe he was feeling sorry for me, because he gave me a handful of change and said I could buy us something from the vending machines.

I went down to the end of the hall. I put in some nickels and dimes and got Dad a bag of his favourite potato chips. Then I decided on a Mars bar. I pressed the button, and watched the big corkscrew coil turn. But it stopped too soon and my Mars bar was just hanging there. I thumped the machine, but it wouldn't fall.

And suddenly I was angry. It happened to me like that sometimes, a big solar flare of fury inside my head.

Dad got his chips. That was typical. Dad always got what he

wanted. But me, no. I hadn't wanted to move. I liked Toronto. I liked my friends, and I'd wanted to stay, and Dad hadn't even *asked*. He just talked and talked and told me how great it was going to be.

And now I couldn't even get a stupid Mars bar. I grabbed the machine by the sides and tried to shake it. It moved a little. I put my weight into it. I was furious. I was like one of those mothers who sees her kid trapped under a car and suddenly has the strength to lift the whole thing. I figured if I could just tilt the machine forward an inch or so, my chocolate bar would fall loose.

I got the machine rocking, and then it was rocking too much, and I felt the huge refrigerator weight of the thing pushing back, and I knew it was going to fall on me.

Two huge hands slammed against the machine and I looked over and saw this enormous guy putting his shoulder to it and pushing it back into place.

'You coulda been killed, buddy!' he puffed.

'Jeez,' I said, staring stupidly at the machine.

'These things crush you, you know,' said the guy. 'Happened to a cousin of mine in Red Deer.'

'Really?' I said numbly.

'Oh yeah, big time. That your Mars bar?'

I nodded. He reached through the flap, grabbed it, and handed it to me.

'Have a good night now,' he said, and started plugging his own coins into the machine.

'Thanks,' I said.

I went back to our room. It took Dad a few seconds to glance up from his book. He probably had a paragraph to finish. 'That took a long time,' he said.

'The vending machine almost fell on me.'

Dad put down his book. 'Were you pushing it?'

'A bit.' I felt sick. Not just about the close call, but about how furious I'd been.

'Ben, you should never, *never* do that!' he said. 'Those things can kill you!'

'You don't have to get so mad!' I said. Maybe it was delayed shock, but my knees went wobbly and tears came into my eyes. Dad came over and hugged me.

I was glad he was hugging me, but at the same time I didn't want his hug because I still felt angry with him.

Later, after he was asleep, I lay awake for a bit, watching the headlights of the passing cars through the curtains and wondering what life was going to be like in Victoria.

The next day, instead of leaving at the crack of dawn, Dad let us have a long swim in the pool and then we took a detour off the Trans-Canada to a place called Drumheller where they'd discovered dinosaur bones. After that, it was up into the Rockies. The views were fantastic, and Dad made plenty of stops so I could take pictures.

On day six, we got to Vancouver and took the ferry across to Victoria. Our house, it turned out, wasn't actually in the city itself. It was on the outskirts, in the country, because we didn't want neighbours. Or, as Dad said with a wink, the neighbours didn't want us.

The university had found us a place off West Saanich Road. It was mostly farmland, with some pastures where you'd see cows and horses. You could drive a few minutes without seeing a single house.

'And here we are,' said Dad, pulling into a gravel driveway.

The place looked kind of sullen and dingy to me. On our old street in Toronto, the houses were red brick, skinny and three storeys tall. This one was wide, but just two storeys. The bottom was wood, painted dark green, and the top floor had some kind of pebbly stuff that Dad called stucco.

'It's perfect for us,' he said enthusiastically, as we walked to the front door. 'Come on, wait till you see your new room.'

My bedroom really was much bigger than my old one, and there were two bathrooms upstairs, so I wouldn't have to share with Mom and Dad any more. It was strange, and a bit lonely, walking through all the empty rooms. They had nothing to do with me.

The only part that wasn't empty was the downstairs extension, which the university had just finished before we arrived. It still smelled of wood and fresh paint. It was like a little guest house, connected to the kitchen by a door. You walked in and there was a playroom with cushions and a wooden box of blocks and toys and picture books. There was a little red table with matching chairs. There was a kitchenette with its own sink, fridge, hot-plate and high chair. Beyond that was the bedroom. The chest of drawers was already filled with colourful little T-shirts and shorts, and there were packs of diapers and a pail for the dirty ones. There was a comfy chair, and even a shelf with stuffed animals.

A colourful mobile hung above the empty crib.

I was still in my sleeping bag flipping through *Popular Mechanics* when I heard the sound of a big truck pulling up outside the house, then honking as it backed down our driveway. I ran to my window just to make sure it was really them, then out into the hallway in my pyjamas.

'Our stuff!' I hollered.

Dad staggered out in his boxers. 'The truck's here?'

'Yeah!' I was thinking: *My camera equipment, my records, my bed.*

Dad lurched back into his bedroom and pulled on some pants and a T-shirt. I did the same, and then we were both running down the stairs, throwing open the front door, and rushing out to greet the movers. They already had the back of the truck open and the ramp down.

We didn't bother with breakfast. We were too busy telling the guys where our stuff should go. I was watching for my boxes. It seemed like for ever since I'd helped pack up my room in Toronto. The guys worked pretty fast, and I was amazed how quickly our entire life was moving from the truck into the new house.

After a few hours they were done with most of the big stuff and were working on the rest of the boxes. I was unpacking in my room. I'd been worried about my photo enlarger and records, but nothing was broken. And I'd have a bed for my birthday after all! Better still, the movers would be gone in an hour or so, and Dad and I would definitely have time for a swim, and dinner at the pizza place.

Outside, a car horn gave a couple of honks. I went to the window and saw a taxi pulled up behind the moving van. The driver was taking a suitcase out of the trunk, and then he came round and opened the back door. Inside was Mom.

'Dad!' I yelled. 'Mom's home!'

'What?' I heard him call out in surprise.

I ran downstairs and outside. Mom was walking towards me, beaming. In her arms was a little bundle of blankets. I'd been missing her, but I hadn't realized just how much until I saw her. With her free hand she pulled me close.

'Ben,' she said, kissing the top of my head. 'Happy birthday, sweetie.'

'Thanks.' Dad hadn't even mentioned it yet.

'You're early!' Dad said, striding out of the house and kissing her.

'They thought he was ready, so I got an earlier flight,' Mom said. 'I left a message at the department, but I guess you didn't get it.'

'I didn't. Our phone's not hooked up yet either. So how's our little gentleman?' Dad asked.

Mom pulled back the blankets, and there in her arms was a sleeping baby chimpanzee.

He was ugly. His tiny body fitted in the crook of Mom's arm, his head resting on three of her fingers. His skin was all wrinkly. His nose was squashed flat and his jaw stuck way out. Frizzy black hair covered his whole body, except for his face and fingers, chest and toes. He had long skinny arms. His short legs were pulled up, and his toes were so long they looked more like fingers. He wore a little white T-shirt and a diaper and smelled like shampoo and Mom's perfume. As we watched, he stirred and opened his eyes. They were brown and seemed huge in his small face. He stared at me and Dad, and then up at Mom, as if for reassurance. Mom held him closer.

'He was a little angel on the plane,' she said. 'Not a peep, even when he was awake.'

'He'll do just fine,' said Dad, smiling. 'If he's this agreeable all the time, we'll have no problem with this little guy.'

I looked from Dad to Mom. They seemed really happy. And I suddenly wondered: *Was this how they brought me home when I was born? When Dad first set eyes on me, had he smiled, just like he was smiling now?*

I looked at the chimp. He was the reason we'd come.

I'd moved all the way across the country so my parents could be with him.

So they could teach him how to talk.

Dad was a behavioural psychologist. That meant he studied the way people acted. Animals too. Professor Richard Tomlin. In Toronto he taught at the university. A few years back, he did something clever with rats and published lots of articles, which led to invitations to other universities to show people what his rats could do. Everyone got very excited about it.

Then he got bored with rats and got interested in whether humans were the only animals who could learn language. Dad said there were some scientists in the 1930s who actually tried to teach chimps to speak, but it turned out chimps didn't have the right kind of tongue or larynx or something, so they couldn't form human words.

But Dad knew how smart chimps were, and wanted to see if they could learn American Sign Language, just like deaf people.

So for the past couple of years he'd been asking the university to get him a chimp and fund the experiment. But even though Dad was a bit of a hotshot, and very good with rats, the university wasn't so sure it was interested. I knew Dad had been getting frustrated because he talked a lot about how short-sighted the psychology department was, dragging its feet like this.

But then he got a job offer from the university out here in Victoria. Not only would they give him a big promotion and make him a full professor, but they'd get him a chimp. Dad said yes. I didn't think he even asked Mom. He certainly didn't ask me. He would've moved us to Tibet if they'd given him a chimp.

It turned out finding one wasn't all that easy. You couldn't just buy one at a pet store. *I'll take the cute little one over there.* And it couldn't be some scraggly old chimp from a zoo. Dad wanted a brand-new chimpanzee. A fresh slate; that's what he'd called it.

It took about six months. When he finally got the call, I could tell just from his voice that it was good news. After he hung up, I'd never seen him so excited.

'Borroway has a baby they don't want!'

He'd talked about this place lots before. Borroway was an Air Force base in New Mexico. They had lots of chimps. In the fifties and sixties they brought a whole bunch into the country to use them for the American space programme. But that was twenty years ago, and now it seemed like they didn't need as many. One of their adult females was about to have another baby and they didn't want to take care of it.

It was perfect for Dad. He needed a baby chimp that could be taken away from its mother, days after birth.

He wanted a baby he could raise like a human.

We ordered in pizza that night, and ate it in the living room, on the orange shag carpet. We had our sofas now, but it seemed more relaxing – and kind of decadent – to sprawl out on the floor with our shoes and socks off, like hippies. Mom especially looked like a hippie, with her long hair, bell-bottoms, fringed vest and the Native medallion hanging from a leather necklace.

Dad was pretty strait-laced. I'd seen some of the other professors in Toronto wear jeans, but Dad always liked a proper suit and tie for work. His hair was short. He didn't go in for all this touchy-feely stuff; he preferred facts. Like Mom, though, he was good-looking, even though he was getting close to forty. They were certainly a lot younger than most of the other parents I knew, because they got married so early, when Dad was a grad student and Mom was still in undergrad. Mom was just twenty-one when she had me.

And now she had another baby.

I looked over at the little bassinet, where the baby chimp was fast asleep, his tiny fingers twitching every now and then. I'd never even had a pet before. No cats or dogs in our house. Dad hated the idea of pets.

'What're you going to call it?' I asked.

'Well,' said Mom, pouring herself some more red wine, 'they'd already named him Chuck at the base, after Chuck Yeager.'

'The guy who broke the sound barrier?' I said.

She nodded. 'But I don't think he looks much like a Chuck.'

'The name's not important,' Dad said. 'He just needs one.'

'Well, I think the name's important,' said Mom. 'How about naming him after where he came from?'

'New Mexico?' I asked.

'No, the place he would've been born in the wild.'

'A bit sentimental, don't you think?' said Dad. He hated sentimentality. He said it got in the way of the truth. It was the enemy of science. He wanted to strip it all away and show things and people as they really were. It was better that way, he said. Healthier and more honest.

'Congo,' said Mom.

I frowned, trying to remember my map of Africa. 'Isn't the country called something else now? Zaire?'

She nodded. 'But the Congo's also the river that runs through central Africa. There's a theory that the river separated two different groups of chimps. And that's why they evolved into different species.'

Dad shook his head. 'Congo sounds a bit too much like Bonzo – the chimp in that awful Ronald Reagan movie. I don't want the association.'

'How about Kong?' I suggested. It was sort of fun, thinking up names.

Mom chuckled. 'King Kong? For this tiny little thing?'

'Tarzan, then!' I said.

This time Dad laughed. 'Keep in mind, I have to use this name in all the scientific papers. It's a bit hard to take Tarzan seriously.'

'For someone who said the name didn't matter, you're being awfully picky!' Mom said, giving Dad a playful jab with her finger.

I thought some more. 'Just the last bit, then. Zan!'

'I like it,' said Mom right away. 'Does that meet with your approval, Richard?'

'Sounds like something out of *Star Trek*,' said Dad, 'but sure, I can live with Zan.'

I wonder if I can, I thought, looking at the sleeping chimp.

Mom poured a little splash of wine into my empty cup.

'You're old enough to have a sip,' she said. She raised her glass. 'To our new teenager.'

We all clinked glasses and drank. It was probably the worst thing I'd ever tasted.

'Sorry we didn't get you to the lake or the pizza place,' Dad said.

'It's OK,' I lied. It had been a crazy day, with the movers and Mom arriving all at once, and getting the house in order, and making sure the chimpanzee had everything he needed. At least Dad had remembered to get me the bike – he'd been keeping it hidden in the garage. And it really was an excellent bike.

'Let me get you some more ginger ale,' Mom said, after I'd choked down another sip of wine.

She went to the kitchen and when she came back she was holding a birthday cake, thirteen candles lit up. She and Dad launched into 'Happy Birthday to you'. Normally it made me kind of embarrassed when they sang, but this time I couldn't help smiling, because I honestly hadn't thought there'd be cake. Mom must have made a special trip earlier to get one.

I blew out the candles and made a wish. I wished that we'd be happy in our new home.

Then I looked over at baby Zan, all swaddled in his bassinet, and thought:

We are the weirdest family in the world.

Chapter 2

Freaky Little Brother

Over the next few days Zan mostly slept, and Mom kept him in his little bassinet while we unpacked boxes and shifted furniture and put our books on the shelves. I could tell that Mom wasn't thrilled with the house. She said things like: 'Well, it's no beauty, but it's very spacious.' She liked the back yard (even if it was enclosed with a high chain-link fence) and the trees, and the farms all around.

I was pretty excited about setting up my new room with my posters and big floor cushions. Even better, the walk-in closet was big enough for a table to hold my enlarger and trays, so I had my own personal darkroom.

When Zan wasn't sleeping he wanted to be held. He needed bottles every two hours. Mom carried him everywhere with her in one of those colourful African slings. She changed Zan's diapers and bathed him and dressed him – I didn't think I'd ever seen her so happy.

'Would you like to hold him?' she sometimes asked me.

I shook my head. I didn't want to touch him.

When Mom held Zan it looked completely natural; when Dad held him it never looked quite right, even when he made cooing sounds and rocked him. Usually Zan would start whimpering, and Dad would look at Mom and go, 'Am I doing something wrong?' and she'd say, 'No, no, he's probably just hungry or wet. Let me see.' And Dad would hand him over, looking relieved.

I rode my bike a lot.

Dad spent most of the time on the university campus, getting his office ready, and preparing for the courses he had to teach in the fall. And Mom was busy taking care of Zan and, when he was asleep, working on her thesis. Unlike Dad, she still had to get her PhD, and to do that, she had to write a thesis – a really long book. She was going to write it on Zan, while running the research project with Dad.

My favourite time to go for a ride was in the evening right after supper, with the sun slanting through the tops of the trees and the shadows all long on the road. Toronto got so hot and humid in the summer sometimes, you just felt soaked stepping outside, no matter what time of day it was. Here, there always seemed to be a breeze, and in the mornings and evenings, the air cooled down so you didn't get hot or thirsty.

The road smelled like tar and dust and cut grass. It smelled like a promise. Whenever I passed a cluster of houses I'd slow down, hoping to see some other kids hanging out in the front yards. I guess I was hoping they'd wave me over and we'd all go tooling around on our bikes and buy Freezies at the local corner store. So far, no luck.

Not far from our house was a construction site, and a big sign facing the road, showing what the houses in the new subdivison would look like. Right now it was just big machines perched crookedly on piles of rubble and lots of concrete cylinders. One evening I thought I saw a couple of kids moving around near the machinery, but it was dusk by then, and I didn't feel like wandering out there.

So I headed for home. In the distance I saw the lights of the city, and felt a hunger to be down there, to be a part of that light. Back home in Toronto, Mom and Dad had just started letting me go downtown with my friends on the streetcar. I wondered how long it would be until I had someone to do that with here.

A few days ago, Mom had let me call up Will and Blake on the phone. It was good to hear their voices, but sometimes it got awkward and we didn't know what to say. Sometimes the line was crackly and there were delays in our voices and it made them seem even farther away. I'd probably never see them again, thanks to Dad.

'I think we should start using sign language with Zan now,' Dad said over breakfast one morning in mid-July.

I looked at him over my spoonful of cornflakes. 'He's only, like, three weeks old.'

'I think it's a good idea,' said Mom. 'Just so he gets used to seeing the signs.'

'We'll have the whole team of research students by fall,' said Dad, 'and that's when we'll start teaching him properly. But for now I've drawn up a short list of high-frequency words. These'll be his first words, so if we can give him a head start, so much the better.' He nodded at the big kitchen bulletin board, where he'd tacked up a list.

Up. Drink. Give. More. Eat. You. Me.

'Hang on,' I said. '*I'm* supposed to learn sign language, too?'

'It's pretty easy, Ben,' said Dad. 'And it would really help Zan. And the project.'

I shrugged. 'It's not *my* project.' I shovelled more cornflakes into my mouth, staring down into my bowl. Mom and Dad didn't say anything, but from the corner of my eye I saw them glance at each other, then back at me. Dad had his calm, psychologist expression on.

'I know all this change has been tough on you, Ben,' he said, 'and it's perfectly normal to feel jealous of—'

'I'm *not* jealous of Zan!' I said, looking at him, sucking happily on a bottle in Mom's arms. Zan was fine: I didn't feel much about him, one way or another. But I was sick to death of the *project.* I'd been hearing about it for months and months back in Toronto and, for the past two weeks, it was pretty much all Mom and Dad talked about. They'd dragged me across the country for it, I had no friends – and now I was supposed to help them out?

'I don't ask you guys to do my homework,' I muttered.

Mom laughed. 'He's got a point,' she said to Dad.

Dad nodded patiently. 'It is an unusual project, Ben, I know. But Mom and I wouldn't be doing this if we didn't think it was going to be something truly remarkable. Think about it,' he said, and I couldn't help looking up from my cereal to meet his gaze. 'This isn't a typical animal behaviour study. This is the first proper human attempt to talk, actually *talk*, with another species. Chimps are our closest relatives, and they're extremely smart, but we've never had a conversation with them! If we can give them the tools of language, imagine what they might tell us, teach us! It's incredible.'

Some of this I'd heard before, but it did sound exciting. It was like something from a sci-fi movie. One day people would read about it in *Popular Science*, and I could be a part of it. I caught myself nodding as Dad carried on, his eyes bright, his hands grasping at the air for emphasis.

'And that's why the project's whole design is so radical,' he said. 'We're trying to teach another species our language. Human language. So we need to raise Zan like a human baby, so he can learn language just like a human would. No cages. No labs. He's one of us now. He has a crib and clothes and toys. And most important he has a family. He has a mother and a father – and a big brother, too.'

'Ben,' Mom called up the stairs, later that morning. 'There's someone here for you.'

'Who?' I asked as I went down.

'I don't know,' she whispered.

I reached the bottom of the stairs and looked out through the open front door. A kid about my age was riding around on his bike in the driveway.

I went to the door. 'Hi,' I said.

'Hey. You just moved in, right?' the kid asked.

'Yeah, about a month ago.'

'I live up the road,' he said. 'I've seen you cycle by.'

He coasted a bit closer to the door, keeping his bike balanced without putting down his feet. He was pretty good. He had shaggy blond hair and was fairly big without being huge. He smiled a lot.

'So, you coming out?' he asked.

'Yeah, sure, hang on.'

I went and told Mom I was going out. She seemed pleased.

'I'm Ben,' I said as I wheeled my bike out from the garage.

'Tim,' he said. 'What grade are you in?'

'Going into eight. You?'

'Same. Are you going to Brentwood?'

'Yeah.' That was the local school. 'Is it pretty good?'

'Awful,' he said, grinning.

We charged around on our bikes. I let him lead the way, pumping hard to keep up. We went past where they were building the new subdivision, and Tim slowed down so we were alongside each other.

'It's really cool in there,' he said. 'We go there sometimes when they're not working.'

I remembered the figures I'd seen once at dusk. Then Tim sped up again and took me down some roads I didn't know, and we ended up at a little plaza where there was a bakery that had a big cooler with all different kinds of pop.

We sat outside on the edge of the sidewalk and drank from the sweaty bottles.

'You play soccer?' Tim asked.

'Not much.'

'Football?'

I shook my head.

'Any sports?'

'I run. Cross-country,' I said.

He grimaced, like that didn't count.

'I do a lot of photography,' I said, feeling I needed to make myself look better. 'I wouldn't mind making movies one day maybe.'

'That's cool,' he said. 'Where you from?'

'Toronto.'

'What'd you come here for?'

'A stupid monkey,' I said.

He laughed and sprayed out some pop. '*What?*'

'Well, a chimp actually,' I said, and told him about the project.

'That's crazy,' he said. 'You like pinball?'

'Yeah!'

'We've got a pinball machine in our rec room.'

I looked at him in amazement. 'Really?'

'Yeah. Dad got it used from one of his customers. It's pretty good. You've got a second set of flippers up the ramp. C'mon.'

It turned out Tim lived just a couple of minutes up the road from us, in a small blue house. I'd passed it lots of times on my bike but never seen him. We went in the side door, straight

25

down to the basement. The rec room had a low ceiling, and wood panelling. The carpet was dingy. There was a TV and a couple of beat-up sofas and some coffee tables and a floor lamp. On the wall was a truck calendar. The whole room smelled like old shoes.

Blinking quietly in one corner was a *Planet of the Apes* pinball machine. On the back panel were pictures of angry-looking gorillas in helmets and armour and rifles, chasing humans in tattered rags. I'd seen the movie, and it was pretty exciting.

I'd never known anyone who had a pinball machine in their house. In Toronto there was an Italian coffee place near the school where we sometimes played at lunchtime, and it cost a quarter. Tim just pushed the red start button on the side, and the machine burbled into life, popping out the first ball. Tim was excellent, no surprise, since he had the thing in his house. He played the first ball for about ten minutes before losing it. Then it was my turn.

We talked a bit as we played. He loved soccer and was on a local rep team. His dad was a plumber. He had a brother two years older than him. His favourite subject at school was gym. He liked Charlton Heston movies. He liked Led Zeppelin and hated the Osmonds, especially Donny.

'Want to see something?' he asked after we'd been playing for about half an hour.

'Sure,' I said.

He took me through a doorway into the unfinished part of the basement. There were a couple of bashed-up deep freezes, only one of which was humming. Tim went to the quiet one and hefted up the lid. A musty smell of paper wafted out and I looked down at pile after pile of magazines with naked women on the covers. The sheer number of them, and all that skin, stunned me. The sudden heat in my cheeks travelled all the way down between my legs.

'Wow,' I said, swallowing and looking over at Tim. Even he looked kind of awestruck, gazing at them like the contents of a treasure chest.

'Yeah,' he said.

Overhead we heard his mother's footsteps in the kitchen.

'We'd better not look at them now,' he said, letting the lid drop.

Walking back to the rec room, I saw a wall rack with four rifles in it.

'Those are Dad's,' he said. 'He goes hunting. I'd let you hold one, but he keeps them locked up.'

I'd never held a gun, and wasn't sure I wanted to. 'That's OK.'

'I've got a BB gun,' Tim told me, as though this would cheer me up. He grabbed a lightweight rifle tipped against the wall and held it up for me to see. 'Model 105 Buck. Come on.'

In the back yard he set up some paper cups along the fence that bordered the fields and we took turns shooting at them. The ammunition was these tiny steel balls. To load, you pumped a lever, then held the gun to your eye to aim through the cross-hairs. Tim was a good shot. He could knock the paper cups off the fence almost every time. By the end, I'd gotten a couple. It was fun, actually.

Towards the end, I went to put the cups back on the fence and felt a sharp pain in the back of my jeans. It was like getting stung by a wasp.

I swore and gripped my bum and looked round. Tim was laughing. He was holding the gun.

'Jeez,' I said. 'That hurt!'

'Yeah, it does,' he said. 'Sorry. Couldn't resist.'

I looked at my hand to see if there was any blood, but there wasn't. It hadn't even torn my jeans. It just stung like heck. I was kind of angry with him, but he was smiling and laughing so good-naturedly it was hard to stay mad.

I figured I'd made a friend.

When I got back home, I walked into the living room and Mom was sitting in an armchair, holding Zan. Her blouse was unbuttoned and folded back on one side, and Zan was sucking at her breast. She and Zan both turned to look at me at the same time, Zan's face brown against my mother's pale skin. I instantly looked away, feeling like I'd done something wrong, like I'd seen something I was never meant to see.

'Sorry,' I said, and headed out of the room.

'Ben, wait,' I heard my mother say. 'I'm sorry, I didn't hear you come in.'

'It's OK,' I said, stopping in the doorway, staring down at the carpet. From the corner of my eye I saw Mom put Zan down on her knee. He started whimpering and pawing her as she buttoned up her blouse.

'Even with the bottle, Zan still seems to want to nurse,' she said. 'Your father thought it might be a good idea. To try and make sure he gets everything he'd get from his own mother.'

'Right,' I said, nodding. I didn't want to think about it – not at all, really. 'It's sort of weird to see.'

'I know,' she said. 'I have mixed feelings about it, too. And it's not like I have any milk to give him anyway.'

'You don't?' I asked.

She smiled and gave a little laugh. 'You need to have your own baby to produce milk.'

'Oh,' I said, blushing. 'Right.'

'Anyway, I can't keep it up for too long; it's getting painful.'

I nodded and made a *hmm* sound, like I was all calm and interested in what she was saying. Mom was always very big on everyone talking openly, and sharing everything, and not being embarrassed about our bodies especially. She said it was unhealthy to be embarrassed about the human body, and that it was beautiful and honest and natural.

But I'd had about as much nature and honesty as I could handle right now.

It was another week or so before I held Zan for the first time.

I was sort of nervous. I sat down on the couch and Mom put him in my arms. He was awake and he just settled against me, gazing up into my eyes and occasionally making a soft panting sound. It was a really intense look, like he expected something.

I remembered Mom saying that chimps spent a lot of time grooming one other. So I combed through Zan's hair with my fingers, kind of patting him and stroking him, and he got very quiet and looked at me even more intently. Then I pretended to find something interesting in his hair, pick it out, and pop it into my mouth. I made a satisfied smacking sound. Zan looked very interested at that and hooted softly.

Without even realizing it, I was stroking him, and before long his eyes started to look sleepy, and he dozed off. Mom asked if I wanted to give him back, but I said it was OK, and stayed there like that for a little longer, Zan sleeping in my arms.

Mom took a picture of us with my camera.

It was hard to know what Zan thought of all the signs we made as we talked with him. But his eyes were alert and curious and he seemed to watch everything.

He always wanted to be held, so before I picked him up, I'd sign *Up* – just pointing my index finger skyward – and then lift him. And he loved being hugged, so I thought it would be a good idea to teach him that sign as well. Before I gave him a hug, I'd do the *Hug* sign, which was simple, just crossing your arms across your chest, like you were giving yourself a hug.

The first time Dad saw me doing it he asked me to stop. 'We need to start slowly with him,' he said. 'We don't want to confuse him.'

'I think Ben's got the right idea, though,' Mom said. 'Shouldn't we be stressing the things that are most part of his life?'

'I suppose it's fine for now,' said Dad. 'But when we start teaching him properly, we'll need to stick to the signs we choose. It's got to be very methodical.'

In the first week of August, when Zan was about five weeks old, Dad decided it was time to introduce names. We picked the morning, so he was good and alert. It was Sunday. We all gathered around him in the living room and, for some reason, I thought of church. We never really went ourselves, but I'd been to a few baptisms.

In sign language, you get to invent your own name for yourself. A lot of the time it's just the first letter of your name, signed somewhere on the upper part of your body, maybe the middle of your chest, or somewhere on your arm.

For Z you stuck out your index finger and traced a zigzag shape in the air.

Mom worried it might be a bit complicated for Zan, so I said maybe we could do it big across his entire chest, so the sign wasn't too small and fiddly.

'Good idea,' said Mom.

Dad looked intently at Zan. '*You . . .*' He pointed at him. '*Zan.*'

And he touched him with his index finger, slowly tracing the Z across Zan's chest. He did it several times, and then Mom and I did it as well, to reinforce it.

'Zan,' I said. 'You're Zan.'

'We've got to show him our names too,' Dad said, and made the sign for *father*: hand held with all fingers straight out, tapping the thumb twice against his forehead.

'Dad,' he said, over and over again as he made the sign.

It was weird watching him do it, calling himself Zan's father. Part of me felt it was wrong.

31

The sign for *mother* was almost the same as *father*, only you tapped your thumb against your chin twice.

Somehow, when Mom did it for Zan, it didn't seem quite so fake – maybe because she spent so much time with him, and did everything a real mother would do for him in the wild.

'Now show him the sign for *brother*,' Dad said to me.

I suddenly felt sick. 'I don't want to,' I told him.

'This is a very important aspect of the project,' Dad reminded me.

I shook my head. 'It's a lie, though.'

I caught a glimmer of impatience in Dad's eyes. But I wasn't doing this just to get at him; I really couldn't bring myself to call myself Zan's brother.

'You know,' Mom said quietly to Dad, 'the sign for *brother* is quite complicated. I'm wondering if it might confuse Zan anyway. Maybe Ben should just make up his own name for himself.'

I saw Dad take a breath, then nod. 'That OK with you, Ben?'

'Yeah,' I said gratefully. That I could do.

I thought about it a second and then made the letter B sign against my heart.

'Ben,' I said to Zan. 'I'm Ben.'

CHAPTER 3

LIFE OF THE PARTY

A wooden sign surrounded by flower beds told me we'd just entered *Windermere*. Right away I could tell it was a fancy neighbourhood. It wasn't so far from where we lived, but it looked like it had been all planned out. It was a bit like being in the forest, there were so many trees and plants. All the houses were very nice, with bay windows and perfect lawns and flower beds and stone paths everywhere. I wouldn't have been surprised if little gnomes in red caps had appeared to wash the windows, sweep the big wide driveways and polish all the new cars in them.

It was the second week of August, and the chair of the psychology department, Professor Godwin, had invited us all over for a barbecue. Apparently he had a son close to my age named David. I was sitting up front with Dad, and in the back, Mom was holding Zan.

'Do you wish we lived here?' Dad asked Mom.

'It shrieks new money,' said Mom.

Mom came from old money, which meant a family in Rosedale that had been rich for a long time. She hated old money because it was snobby and lazy and rigid; but she hated new money too because it was about showing off and proved that people had their priorities in the wrong place – and if the new money people weren't careful they could turn out to be just as bad as old money.

Dad came from *no* money. He got through school on scholarships and student loans.

'Aren't *we* new money now?' I asked, confused. 'Since Dad's full professor and making tons of money?'

'I wouldn't call it *tons* of money,' said Dad.

'We'd be new money if we lived here,' said Mom.

Dad sniffed, but I wondered if he was a bit envious, maybe regretting that he had to live in an ugly house out in the boonies. I kind of was. I saw lots of kids on bikes, and there was a big field where some teenagers were playing Frisbee.

We found the right house. It was like something from a fairy tale. The outside was white plaster, criss-crossed with dark beams.

'Fake Tudor,' said Mom disdainfully.

'Be good,' Dad said to her.

'What do you mean?' Mom said. 'I'm bringing a chimp. I'm going to be the life of the party.'

We parked, and as we got out of the car, I caught Dad glancing at our beat-up old Volvo, then at the shiny new Mercedes in the driveway.

We could hear the chatter of the other guests coming from the back yard, so Dad led us down the side of the house, through the gate and into the garden. It was a bit like one of those scenes from a Western when the hero walks into the saloon and everyone goes quiet and turns to stare. All eyes were on us, then Mom, holding Zan in her baby-sling.

After six weeks of living with Zan, I'd almost stopped thinking of him as unusual. Now, I realized again how weird it was to be carrying around a little chimp in diapers like a new baby. We must have looked like a circus act. What would they say if they knew Mom had tried breastfeeding the chimp? My cheeks burned.

But then Professor Godwin and his wife were hurrying over to greet us, and people started talking again.

It turned out Mom was right. She *was* the life of the party – or at least Zan was. There were more people than I'd expected, and they all made a fuss of Zan, especially the women. They all wanted to hold and cuddle him. Zan was pretty happy about it all. He liked it better when women held him. With one man he started hooting and making his unhappy face, where he curled out his lips like he was crying. I didn't blame him; the man smelled so strongly of cigarette smoke, I would've cried too.

I saw some other kids loafing around out in the yard, but I didn't feel like going over and introducing myself, so I stood around for a bit with Mom while she talked to Mrs Godwin.

'So where have you got Ben going to school?' she asked.

'We've registered him at his local school, Brentwood.'

Mrs Godwin nodded and made a little sound in her throat. 'You know, I've heard mixed things about it.'

'Is that right?' said Mom.

'It's fine, of course, but a bright boy like Ben should really be going to Windermere.'

'I'm not that bright,' I said.

She looked at me blankly for a moment.

'Ben's joking,' said my mother.

Mrs Godwin smiled weakly and looked back at Mom. 'They've got an amazing accelerated programme there, and the teachers are fantastic.'

I didn't want to be in an accelerated programme. I was having enough trouble in the *decelerated* programme. I wasn't exactly kidding about not being bright. I was a lousy student. Most subjects I struggled with, math especially.

'We know Ted Lancaster, the headmaster, quite well,' said Mrs Godwin, putting her hand confidentially on Mom's arm. 'If you're interested, we can put you in touch with him. I'm sure they could fit Ben in.'

'That's very kind of you, thank you,' said Mom, in the formal voice she used when she was trying hard to be polite.

I wandered off, but realized I was keeping an eye on Zan, just making sure everyone was treating him all right as they passed him around. There wasn't much chance of him coming to harm, as long as people held him properly and didn't drop him. And it was pretty hard to drop Zan – impossible, really. Even if you let go, he wouldn't. His grip had been strong from the very beginning. Baby chimps weren't like humans –

they had to be able to hold onto their moms right away.

I saw Dad talking to a group of other men, and wandered over, hanging back a little so I could listen in. I guessed they were all professors at the university, because Dad seemed to know some of them already. He had them all laughing.

People loved my father. They were always telling me what a great guy he was, how dynamic and funny and smart. Even my own friends seemed charmed by him. I could tell just by looking at the professors' faces that Dad was doing his hypnotist thing, getting them all enthusiastic.

A silver-haired fellow with a pipe was saying, 'It's a fascinating journey you're embarking on. I've done a little reading on chimpanzee cognition, and it seems they're very good at imitating.'

The way he said it made me think it wasn't just a comment, but a question, maybe even a challenge. I watched Dad carefully.

'Absolutely,' said Dad. 'So the key is to make sure they're not just imitating the signs, but making them independently.'

The silver-haired guy took a thoughtful pull on his pipe. 'Of course it also depends on how you're defining language. As opposed to mere communication.'

'Theo, you've put your finger right on a key question,' Dad said, and he wasn't Dad any more – he was Professor Richard Tomlin and it was like the few times I'd watched him lecturing his class. Energy and authority seemed to waft off him like a heat mirage. 'This was one of the areas I focused on when designing the project. We need to see word acquisition, yes, but then we need to see Zan using language in a structured way. Ideally he'd be able to initiate conversation, grasp basic grammar, syntax, an understanding of tense.'

'And what of Noam Chomsky?'

Dad chuckled and nodded. 'Well, I think we all know Mr Chomsky's position – that language is something only humans have; that animals can't learn language any more than we can learn to spin spider-webs. I'm a huge admirer of his work. But I think he's dead wrong on this one.'

Everyone in his little group was quiet for a moment, as if Dad had said something very controversial – even obscene – but I could tell they were also impressed with how he'd just come out and said it, fearless.

'Of course,' Dad said with a nonchalant smile, 'I could be wrong. We'll have to wait and see. Zan might turn out to be a complete moron.' His group erupted into laughter again. 'As scientists, all we can do is test our hypotheses.'

Someone touched me on the shoulder, and I turned to see a tall kid with freckles.

'Hey, are you Ben Tomlin?' he asked.

'Yeah, I'm Ben.'

He offered his hand and we shook. 'David Godwin.'

His mother had probably told him to look out for me and make me feel welcome.

'We were going to start a game of Risk. You interested?'

I loved Risk, and nodded.

I took a last look over the back yard, just to make sure Zan was OK, and then followed David towards the house. Their rec room was a lot nicer than Tim Borden's. Big sliding doors led out onto the back yard. There was thick carpeting and lots of pole lights, and orange egg chairs and a ping-pong table, as well as a pool table and, on the walls, framed vintage travel posters with trains and steamships in exotic locations. I doubted the head of the psych department had a collection of girlie mags in the freezer.

There were two other kids already sitting around the big wagon-wheel coffee table where the board was set up. David introduced me to Hugh and Evan, and then we sat down and I started counting out my pieces.

'So,' David asked quietly, 'did your dad do experiments on you when you were little?'

'No,' I said, taken aback – then saw he was joking. 'You?'

'Big time,' he said. 'Electrodes.' He put his fingers to his temples and delivered a high-voltage jolt. Everyone snorted with laughter.

'That explains the psychotic episodes,' quipped Hugh.

'Completely fried my brain,' David said to me. 'You sure he didn't do anything to you?'

'Well, there were days in a dark box, but I thought that was normal,' I said.

The other guys laughed some more. 'Good one,' David said.

Right away I felt comfortable with these guys. They reminded me a bit of my friends back in Toronto.

The four of us played happily for about three-quarters of an hour, talking about the CN Tower going up, and the space probe NASA had just launched, and the Skylab space station.

It seemed to me that pretty much anything was possible these days. It was 1973, and if we could build space stations, and the world's tallest structure, why couldn't we teach a chimp to talk?

I was doing pretty well at Risk – mostly because I'd had some lucky dice rolls. I controlled North America and was close to taking over all of Europe, so I wasn't particularly happy when I heard someone at the sliding doors say, 'The burgers are ready, you guys.'

I looked up and couldn't stop looking.

The girl was about my age. She wore a sleeveless white shirt tucked into beige shorts. Her legs were tanned a pale brown, and in the sunlight I could see the downy blonde hairs of her thighs. She had a white hairband in her long brown hair. Across the bridge of her nose was a dusting of freckles. When her eyes met mine, I forced myself to stop staring.

'Yeah, we'll be out in a minute, Jen,' said David, not even glancing at her.

She turned and walked back into the garden.

'Who's she?' I asked casually.

'My sister. OK, I'm attacking Kamchatka. Roll.'

'I'm kind of hungry,' I said. 'You mind if we call it quits?'

'And foil my plans of world domination?' David said. 'How dare you.'

But he dropped the dice, stood up, and started for the doors. We all followed.

The barbecue was about one hundred per cent more interesting now. I found out Jennifer was exactly my age. David was actually older than us by a year and a half. I didn't want to talk to her or anything – that was too scary. I just wanted to look at her.

I ate with the other guys, while the adults sat around a couple of big tables on the patio and drank cocktails with their burgers and baked potatoes. Jennifer was sitting on a low stone wall bordering the patio, with a couple of other girls.

After dinner, Mom came over with Zan and asked me to hold him for a while.

'Do I have to?' I whispered. I felt myself starting to blush. Things were going well with these other guys and I didn't want them to think I was a freak or a sissy. Mom just gave me a look and put Zan into my arms.

And then all the guys were looking at him and asking questions.

'So he's going to talk?' said David.

'Well, not talk exactly,' I said. 'Chimps can't talk. But he can learn ASL. American Sign Language.'

'That's pretty wild,' said Hugh. 'Talking with a chimp.'

'What'll they talk about?' Evan asked.

David snorted into his pop. '*Give me another friggin' banana. And make it quick.* Stuff like that.'

'Are you going to help teach him?' Hugh asked.

'Yeah. Sure. He's part of the family now.'

Suddenly I felt proud to be holding him, and to know so much about chimps.

'Can I hold him?'

Startled, I looked over and saw Jennifer beside me.

'Oh, hey, sure, yeah, hi,' I said idiotically. 'Yeah, sure.'

Carefully I transferred Zan into her slender, waiting arms.

'Oh my God, he is *so* adorable,' she said. 'How old is he?'

'Just under six weeks.'

She was wearing some kind of perfume. It smelled like the incense Mom burned in the house sometimes. Sandalwood. I wanted to breathe it for ever.

'So, is he like your pet?' she asked.

'More like my baby brother,' I said, surprising myself.

'That is so cool.'

'He's pretty cool, yeah.'

Zan seemed to like her too. He nuzzled right up against her breasts. She caught me looking and gave a little embarrassed laugh.

'So are you going to Windermere next year?' she asked me.

I shook my head. 'Do you go there?'

'We both do,' she said, nodding at her brother.

I decided that Windermere was the school I'd wanted to go to my entire life.

'Don't you have to be really smart to go there?' I asked.

David shook his head. 'Nah. Jennifer got in.'

'Goof,' she said.

Then she handed Zan back to me and returned to her friends.

The rest of the barbecue I kept hoping she'd come back and talk to us, but she didn't. I sneaked looks at her whenever I could. I didn't want to be too obvious. Still, I must have spent about twenty minutes total just staring, and I never caught her glancing in my direction.

On the way home, I sat in the back seat with Zan asleep in my arms. Mom was talking about Mrs Godwin.

'She certainly has firm opinions about the right schools. She kept telling me Ben should go to Windermere University School.'

She looked over at Dad, like she was expecting him to snort and shake his head and say how ridiculous that was.

'It's not such a bad idea,' Dad said. 'We probably should have put a little more thought into schools before we moved.'

'The local school is perfectly fine,' said Mom.

Dad said, 'I think Ben might benefit from a more rigorous environment.'

'The specimen is in the back seat,' I reminded them.

Mom turned round to look at me. 'You'd have to wear a uniform, Ben.'

I shrugged. 'Wouldn't be so bad.'

'I'm against the whole idea of private schools,' she said.

'*You* went to private schools,' I pointed out.

'So I should know what a breeding ground for privilege they are.'

'You got an excellent education,' Dad said.

'You'd put him in private school just because the Godwin kids go?' Mom asked, chin lifted.

'I'm *thinking* of putting him in, if it's good for him.'

'Hey, I'm open to the idea,' I said. 'David and his friends were cool.'

'We'll see,' said Dad.

Mom shook her head and stared out of the window.

I looked down at Zan. 'Dad, what you said at the party, about how Zan might be a moron and the whole thing wouldn't work. You didn't really mean that, did you?'

Dad didn't reply for a second. 'You're not supposed to go into an experiment with any particular bias, or it can affect how you structure your experiment – and how you see the results.'

'But it's impossible to be completely unbiased,' Mom added. 'You wouldn't have embarked on it if you didn't think there was a good chance something interesting would happen.'

'I've got to be very careful with this project, though,' Dad said. 'Some of the people in the department have their doubts.'

'Who?' I asked. All those men around him at the party, hanging on his every word, laughing.

'Theo Schaffter for one,' Dad said.

'The guy with the pipe?'

'He thinks I'm crazy. He's probably not the only one.'

'But they just hired you!' I said. 'Why would they do that if they thought you were crazy?'

'The university wants a big splashy project that'll get funding and a lot of attention,' Dad explained. 'Godwin likes me, but just because he's head of the department doesn't mean everyone else has to like me. We'll win them over soon enough, though, once they see what Zan can do.'

'You think he can learn to talk, right?' I said.

'Absolutely,' Dad said. 'Zan's going to go all the way, right into the history books.'

CHAPTER 4

DOMINANT MALE

'Zan, stay still!'

I hated changing Zan's diaper. It was fine the first few weeks, when he'd just lie there on the changing mat. But at four weeks he'd started grabbing at the diaper with his fingers – and his toes, which were just as nimble. It was like he had four hands. At five weeks, he'd discovered he could roll over. Now, at over six weeks, he could crawl. It was almost impossible to keep him still.

It was a few days after the barbecue at the Godwins', and I was babysitting. Mom had had to go out and she'd asked me to watch Zan for a couple of hours. Dad was home, but upstairs in his study, working. He was too busy with graphs and charts and making phone calls to other important people to actually take care of his own chimp – which was pretty typical. Dad was a big fan of the hands-off approach when it came to parenting.

I managed to get Zan's poopy diaper off and was crazily

wiping his bottom clean as fast as I could. He looked at me solemnly and, with a hoot, flipped over onto his stomach.

'Come on, Zan!' I pleaded. I grabbed him firmly around his furry hips and turned him back over.

'Hey, Dad,' I muttered to myself, 'how about *you* change him now and then? How's that grab you?'

I wanted to get the new diaper on Zan before he peed all over me. I'd seen it happen to Mom, a big golden arc splashing everywhere.

I unfolded the new diaper, but before I could slide it under his bum, he snatched it with his toes and was waving it wildly all around, panting softly, the way he did whenever he was excited and wanted to play. I grabbed the diaper, but just as quickly it was back in his toes again.

'OK, fine, you play with that one,' I told him, taking another diaper from the pile. I could feel myself getting angry. I didn't want to be babysitting Zan right now. I didn't *want* to change his diapers. This was *Dad's* project.

I slid the new diaper under Zan but he rolled towards me, and grabbed hold of my shirt. Before I could get him off, he'd climbed around to my back and was lowering himself down my right leg.

One of his favourite blankets was there on the floor and he grabbed it in his hands and slid across the floor, pushing with his legs.

'No way, Zan!' I said, catching him up in my arms.

He peed all over me. All down my chest and pants. He had lots of pee.

I swore and put him back down on the floor.

'That's bad, Zan!' I shouted. 'Bad boy!'

I grabbed a towel and dried myself off. Zan made a little playful pant-hoot up at me.

'Oh, you think it's funny?' I said. 'How about if I pee on you? Would you like that?'

I was undoing my zipper when Dad came into the room.

'What's going on?' he asked, looking at me sternly.

'Zan peed all over me!'

Dad looked at my open zipper. 'Were you going to pee on him, Ben?'

'Maybe,' I muttered, pulling up my pants.

'Ben, he's just a baby. Of course he's going to pee on you sometimes.'

'I don't see him peeing on *you*! Why don't you change your freaky little son once in a while?'

'Ben, you're shouting,' Dad said calmly.

Zan was watching all this, looking solemnly from me to Dad, like he was trying to figure out what was going on.

'Mom asked you to babysit for just a couple of hours,' Dad went on. 'Does that seem so unreasonable? Two hours?'

'Two hours more than you,' I shot back.

'You need to work on controlling your temper, young man.'

Control. Another one of Dad's favourite words.

I looked back at Zan and felt my anger wash away. His eyes were huge. Above his backside he had this little white tuft of hair, which all babies had for the first few years. It was very cute. He rolled over and I dropped down beside him and started

47

tickling him. His eyebrows shot up and he grinned, and his arms and legs pulled in with excitement. He never got tired of this, and the harder you tickled, the more he seemed to like it. He shrieked with glee. Pretty soon I was laughing too. Whenever I stopped and held my hands over him, he'd freeze, silent, and look at me with his eyes wide and expectant. Then, when my hands dived back down, he'd start panting and kicking again.

'Get him in a diaper, pronto,' Dad told me.

'It's not so easy,' I said.

'Don't let him get away with it, Ben. You've got to be firm.'

'I *was* firm.'

'He's only going to get more stubborn. The way we treat him now is going to affect his behaviour the rest of his life. Show him you mean business.'

And with that, Dad bent down, grabbed Zan from behind, and picked him up.

I think Zan must have been startled, because he gave a little shriek, turned, and bit Dad on the wrist.

It wasn't a real bite – because Zan's baby teeth hadn't even come in yet. But Dad's expression darkened. He held Zan up so they were face to face.

'No, Zan!' he said, with a stern shake of his head. 'No!'

Zan's eyes got so big his body seemed to shrink.

'You're scaring him, Dad!' I said.

'Good,' said Dad. 'He needs to know that's unacceptable. We can't have him biting. Just wait till his teeth come. Now get him in a diaper, please.' He passed Zan to me and left the room.

Zan lay very, very still on the diaper mat and just watched me while I changed him. Dad was right: being strict seemed to do the trick, but I couldn't help feeling sorry for Zan. We could put him in diapers and pretend he was a baby, but he was still a chimp, and chimps bit sometimes. I'd read in one of Mom's books that they bit each other in play. Their skin was so much thicker than ours, they didn't feel it as much.

I'd even let Zan nip me a few times when he was over-excited, but I guess I should have been harsher with him when he did it.

He wasn't allowed to be a chimp. He had to be a human.

That night after dinner, Tim Borden dropped by and we went out on our bikes.

I'd been spending a fair amount of time with him over the summer, which surprised me, because we didn't really have a ton in common. Maybe we were both just bored. It didn't matter. It got me out of the house, away from poopy diapers.

We'd mostly ride around, or hang out in his basement, play-ing pinball and Monopoly and Risk and taking peeks at his father's magazines. We spent time at my place too. I was a bit nervous the first time I showed him Zan. I guess I was worried he would laugh or think Zan was some kind of goofy pet.

But instead he'd asked if he could hold him. He was very careful when I put Zan in his arms, and Zan seemed to like him – which made me like Tim all the more. Mom liked Tim, but I'm not sure Dad did. I got the feeling he thought Tim wasn't the kind of kid I should be hanging out with.

It was another one of those perfect summer nights as we cycled in the direction of the construction site. At the entrance were two other guys, waiting astride their bikes. Tim called out to them, and we pulled off onto the gravel.

'Hey,' Tim said, 'this is Ben.'

It was the first time I'd met Tim's friends. Jamie was on his soccer team. He had red hair and a chipped front tooth, and seemed like a good-natured guy. Mike, I wasn't so sure about. He had scary eyes. They were intelligent, but they stared really hard, and I couldn't tell what was going on behind them. It didn't look like there was a lot of sunlight and chirping birds back there. He didn't talk much.

'You want to go in?' Tim asked me. Obviously he'd planned this with the other two, and I didn't want to look like a wimp.

'Sure,' I said.

There was a chain across the entrance, but we just hopped off our bikes, ducked under, and wheeled our bikes in a ways, out of sight of the main road.

The site was how I imagined a battlefield from World War One. All rubble and mud and pools of oily water and lots of metal debris and oil drums and wire. There weren't any houses going up yet. It looked like they were still working on the underground stuff, because there were big trenches, and beside them huge cement cylinders on their sides. They were so big we could walk right through them, barely stooping.

'These are the storm drains,' Tim explained.

The massive digging machinery sat crooked on the uneven earth, casting long shadows. In a sci-fi movie it would've all come to life and made a grab for us. Mike and Jamie climbed up into one of the excavators and sat in the cabin, pushing at the controls for a bit. After they came down, Mike lit a cigarette and passed it around. I took a puff and held the smoke in my mouth for a second before blowing it out.

'So you're the guy with the monkey,' Jamie said.

'Chimpanzee,' I corrected.

'What's the difference?' asked Mike, turning his dark eyes on me.

'Different animals. Different species.' I might've told him that the chimp was the closest ancestor to humans, but I wasn't sure he'd be interested.

'You should bring him here,' said Mike, looking around. 'He'd go nuts playing out here.'

'Hmm,' I said. I couldn't think of a worse idea. All I saw were the sharp things Zan could cut himself on. All the holes and puddles he might fall into.

Near the big trench and storm drain segments, Mike found an old spray-paint can on the ground. He picked it up, gave it a shake.

'Check it out,' he said.

Around the inside of one of the cement cylinders, he sprayed a big circle, then quickly took his lighter and lit it. The flame took right away, licking hungrily all around.

'Wicked!' said Tim.

'Mike, you freaking pyro!' said Jamie.

'Watch this,' Mike said. He stepped back, then took a run and jumped right through the ring of fire, landing in a crouch

51

inside the cement tube. I let out my breath. I'd half expected him to catch fire.

Inside the tube, he stepped closer to the circle of flame, shook the can and sprayed some more onto the fire. The aerosol ignited in a long cone.

Even Tim looked a bit nervous now. 'The can's gonna blow up in your hand!' he said.

But Mike just laughed and fed the fire some more. I imagined an explosion. I imagined him aflame, screaming. He took a few steps back, then jumped on out.

'Easy,' he said, then looked at me. 'You go.'

I was about to say no, but for some reason I didn't. Back in Toronto I would've said no. But maybe here I could be the crazy kid for a change. I'd never been that kid before.

I took a run and hunched over as I leaped through. I hardly even felt the heat of the fire. It was just like passing your finger fast through a candle flame. I was inside the tube now, and I felt good. I'd done it. The flames smelled greasy. The other three were watching me, and behind them I could see the road and the entrance to the construction site –

And a pickup that hadn't been there before.

'Hey, get out of there!' someone shouted, and I spotted a man, hurrying towards us.

'Crap!' I said, and the other guys all turned at the same time, then started running. I ran out the back end of the tube and kept going, cutting across the construction site towards the road, veering around machinery and piles of steel and crates, skirting sludgy pools. It was pretty dark by now. I could still hear the man shouting, but I couldn't see Tim and the others anywhere.

I staggered on through some tall grass, vaulted over a low wooden fence, and was back on West Saanich Road. I didn't know what had happened to the other guys. I wanted my bike, but there was no way I was going back right now. What could I do? Miserably, I started home on foot. I'd come back later for my bike. I walked way off to the side of the road, near the trees, so I could hide in case the guy in the truck came past.

When I got back home it was really dark, and Mom opened the front door as I came down the driveway.

'Where've you been?' she demanded, not looking at all happy. Then: 'Where's your bike?'

'I just left it,' I said vaguely.

'What happened?'

There was no way out. In the kitchen I told her and Dad what we'd been doing at the construction site.

'That was very foolish behaviour, Ben,' Dad said.

Mom shook her head in horror. 'Jumping through *fire*?'

'Well, let's see if we get a call from the police,' said Dad.

'The police?' I said, feeling wobbly. 'I don't think he was a policeman.'

'No, he was probably a security guard. But he might call the police. Trespassing. Destruction of property. Setting a fire . . . this is serious stuff.'

'It won't come to that,' Mom said, frowning at Dad.

'He didn't see any of us,' I said. 'We all ran.'

But what if he'd caught Tim or one of the others? Would they tell on me?

'I can't say I think much of the company you're keeping,' Dad said.

'Tim's OK,' I told him hesitantly.

'He's got a good heart,' Mom said.

Dad raised an eyebrow. 'I wouldn't say it's a friendship that has much of a future.'

''Cause his dad's a plumber?' I asked. I don't know why I said it exactly, except that it was the kind of thing Mom and Dad argued about sometimes, with Mom accusing Dad of being a snob, or too uptight. It just came out.

'That kid's going nowhere,' Dad said.

'Richard! Don't tell him that! He's going to be at school with these boys.'

'I don't think so,' said Dad. 'I talked to the headmaster of Windermere today, and he offered Ben a place.'

Mom looked at Dad in astonishment. 'You didn't tell me about this.'

'I was going to tell you both tonight.'

'No, but you didn't even tell me you were *pursuing* this,' said Mom firmly.

'I think it's a better fit for Ben—'

'Ben might've liked a say—'

'I'm OK with it,' I said, thinking of Jennifer Godwin's legs.

'Good,' said Dad. 'I don't think the Windermere kids spend too much time setting fires at construction sites.'

There was a knock at the door.

I looked at Mom and Dad, my heart racing.

'Well, let's see who it is,' said Dad.

I trailed after him and Mom. It was Tim. He'd walked my bike back for me. He looked pretty sheepish when he saw Dad.

'Sounds like you boys were up to no good,' Dad said.

Tim just hung his head and nodded.

'Thank you very much for bringing Ben's bike back,' Mom said.

'It's OK,' he mumbled.

Dad just walked away, like he was too disgusted by the whole thing to say any more. I went out to Tim and took my bike. Mom left us alone.

'So what happened?' I asked. 'Anyone going to jail?'

Tim gave me a little grin. 'Nah. We just ran off. That guy didn't even chase us. He just stood there shouting. Said if he ever saw us again, there'd be big trouble. Is your dad gonna call my dad?'

'I doubt it.' He'd never done anything like that before.

'Good. I should get home. See you.'

'See you. Thanks.'

That night, I couldn't sleep. My mind was still swirling with all that had happened. Leaping through rings of flame like some circus performer. Running for my life through a construction site. Going to Windermere. Going to Windermere with Jennifer Godwin.

Later, I heard Mom and Dad talking in their bedroom. I heard my name a few times, so I crept closer to my door to listen.

'Can we even afford it?' Mom was saying.

'Oh, sure,' said Dad. 'On my new salary, that's not a problem.'

'I just don't see why it's necessary,' Mom said.

'Even after tonight?' Dad said.

'He's a thirteen-year-old boy. You never did foolish things when you were that age?'

'You know it's not just that,' Dad said. 'I don't want a repeat of last year. And I think he'd benefit from a more disciplined school environment.'

Mom's voice was angry. 'The way you talk about him sometimes. He's a good boy, Richard.'

'I know he is. But he also needs a good kick in the pants. I want him with the right sort of kids, and I want him to start taking school more seriously. Windermere will sort him out.'

The next morning, Mom and I were in the kitchen, feeding Zan mashed-up banana in his high chair. I sat beside him, spooning it into his mouth. He loved banana. He loved pretty much everything we fed him – hot cereals and mashed vegetables and Jell-O.

'Eat,' I said, and made the sign, touching the tips of my fingers to my mouth. 'Zan eats.'

Not that he needed any encouragement. His mouth would open for more even before I'd loaded up the spoon. If I was taking too long he'd make an impatient high-pitched bark.

He was tiny in his high chair, much smaller than a human baby of the same age. His little head was barely above the tray, but his coffee-coloured eyes were, as always, incredibly alert and eager.

So far Zan hadn't made any signs, but he was sure good at imitating us. When I widened my eyes, he widened his. If I stuck out my tongue, he did the same. And if I patted my head, he sometimes patted his own.

'Drink?' Mom said, when he was done with his food. She made the sign, touching her thumb to her lips. Zan's hands shot out, as if to hold a bottle, even though Mom hadn't shown it to him yet.

'He certainly understands a lot of things,' said Mom, screwing on the top of the bottle and bringing it over. She took Zan out of the high chair and held him as he drank. He loved being close to people, and was still almost always attached to one of us.

'In the wild,' Mom said to me, 'the babies stay with their mothers for four or five years. They get carried everywhere for the first year or so.'

'You know way more about chimps than Dad,' I said.

She had piles of books everywhere, by people like Jane Goodall, who studied chimps in the wild. I read bits of them sometimes. It was really interesting.

'Well, Dad's been busy designing the whole experiment, but someone has to learn about them as animals.'

Dad was in charge of Project Zan, but Mom was in charge of actually taking care of him. Which was perfect, because Mom's thesis was about cross-fostering. That's what they called it when you raised one species as a different one. There were lots of cases of kittens growing up thinking they were dogs, or chicks identifying more closely with sheep than other chickens. Zan was being cross-fostered as a human, and Mom wanted to find out just how similar the two species were. What made a chimp a chimp, and what made a human a human? She figured there might be some things that were purely chimp-like, and even if we raised Zan as a human, he'd never lose them.

Dad wasn't very interested in this part. What he cared about was whether we could teach Zan language.

Zan finished his bottle and Mom put him down on the kitchen floor. He liked to walk around on all fours, pulling up on the chairs and cupboards. He still wasn't strong enough to climb onto things yet. After a while he scampered over to Mom's foot and sat on it, his long arms tight around her leg.

Mom walked around for a while like that, laughing, and then reached down and lifted Zan up, where he snuggled happily against her chest.

We talked about Windermere and the uniform and what private schools were like, and how I shouldn't ever think the kids there were smarter or better than other kids. I loved talking to Mom because I never felt like she was trying to study me. With Dad I sometimes got the feeling he wanted me to think something, or realize something, or admit something. Mom and I just talked.

When Dad got home from the university he called out hello from the front door and came into the kitchen. He gave Mom a big hug and kiss, and Zan went really weird. He started hooting and pushing at Dad's arms – like he didn't want him to be touching Mom. At first Dad laughed and Mom did too, but then Zan seemed to get even more upset, and I saw his mouth open and before I knew it, he bit Dad on the wrist.

Dad pulled his arm back. Zan shrieked at him.

'No, Zan!' said Dad. 'No biting!'

But Zan ducked his head lower, trying to bite Dad's hand again.

As I watched in astonishment, Dad leaned down swiftly, grabbed Zan's shoulders and bit him on the ear.

Zan squealed and flung himself against Mom, clinging tight, peeing through his diaper all over Mom's shirt.

'You bit him!' I yelled.

'Yeah, I bit him,' said Dad. 'Now he'll know not to bite me ever again. It's a tip I got from the chimp handler at the Chicago Zoo.'

I rushed over and looked at Zan's ear. There wasn't any blood. There wasn't even any mark.

'He's fine,' Dad said. 'A bit of a shock, that's all.'

Mom frowned at Dad. 'They're very protective, Richard. He might have thought you were attacking me.'

'We can't have him biting,' said Dad.

'He's terrified of you now!' I exclaimed.

'He *needs* to be scared of me,' said Dad. 'He needs to know I'm the dominant male.'

I shook my head, not understanding. 'But you said we were raising him like a human. When I was a baby you didn't bite *me* on the ear.' I looked over at Mom. 'Did he?'

'Of course not,' Dad said. 'But he's not human, Ben, all

right? We can raise him like a human for the purposes of the study, but he's still a chimp, and we need to be able to manage him.'

'You didn't need to bite him,' I muttered, and looked at Mom, hoping she'd come to my defence. She looked sad, but not angry.

'Your dad's right, Ben,' she said. 'If we let Zan bite now, it'll be harder to get him to stop later, when his teeth come in. Chimps want to dominate. Dad needs to be the dominant male. Now, I need to change my shirt.'

She tried to pass Zan to me, but he clung tight and wouldn't let go. I felt a little hurt that he wouldn't let me comfort him, but I guess it was natural he'd want his mother right now. She went upstairs with him.

Dad put his hand on my shoulder. 'It's all right, Ben,' he said.

But I didn't want to look at him, and the Dominant Male went off to mix himself a drink.

CHAPTER 5

BEAVER LAKE

Jennifer Godwin and I lay side by side on the sand.

It was the day after Dad had bitten Zan. David had called me up and asked if I wanted to go to Beaver Lake with him and Jennifer. Maybe his father had put him up to it. I didn't know. I didn't care. I was here. Beside Jennifer.

David's older brother, Cal, had picked me up in the station wagon. He was seventeen and had his licence. He'd brought one of his own school friends, and they didn't have much to say to us. At the lake, they didn't even want to put their towels near us. Right now they were down in the water, throwing a football around, showing off how hairy their chests were.

David was stretched out on my other side, tanning his front.

I was pretty nervous, being in my bathing suit around Jennifer Godwin. She was wearing a red one-piece. I was relieved to see she didn't have really large breasts; I think that would have finished me off. She wore her hair in a ponytail.

Being so near her, I couldn't really relax. I had a magazine, but I was just staring at it, not reading. It was all just letters and colours on the page. I couldn't get over all her bare skin, all of her, stretched out on her stomach. She was reading a book called *I Capture the Castle*.

'Is it good?' I asked.

She nodded. 'Pretty good.'

'What's it about?'

'These two sisters who live with their crazy writer father in a castle. They both fall in love with the same guy.'

'Your back's getting a bit red,' I told her.

She raised herself up on her elbows and looked over one shoulder to see. 'Where?'

'Just near the middle, where it, uh, scoops down.'

She passed me her bottle of suntan lotion. 'Could you put some more on, please?' she asked politely.

'Yep,' I said, trying to sound like girls asked me this practically every day.

I squirted some lotion onto my hands and rubbed them. I didn't want my hands to be cold on her skin. When I touched her back it felt really hot, and amazingly soft and smooth. I didn't push too hard. I rubbed the lotion in carefully. I wanted to make sure I covered every inch of exposed skin.

'I think that's good,' she said. She was reading again.

'Yeah, I didn't want to miss any spots,' I said. 'It really is pretty red.'

'Thanks,' she said, and turned the page of her book. She seemed pretty involved in it.

David and I did most of the talking. He told me stuff about Windermere, which teachers were cool and which ones were total goofs. I was looking forward to going there now. I liked David, and Hugh and Evan had seemed nice too. It was good knowing I already had a couple of sort-of friends.

Later, when Jennifer went down to take a dip, I said to David, 'Is your sister going out with anyone?'

'Why, thinking of asking her out?' he asked.

The way his lips curled told me I'd made a mistake.

'No, no, I was just wondering.'

'She's not allowed to date till she's sixteen. House rules.'

'Oh, sure – that's a pretty good rule,' I said.

I didn't care. I'd put suntan lotion on her back. We were practically dating.

A couple of days later, I woke up with the feeling something was wrong. I checked my clock radio and saw it was 7:20 a.m. Since Zan had arrived, I'd been waking up whenever he did, because the university had hooked up this radio monitor between Zan's bedroom and Mom and Dad's. When Zan woke up in the night, or in the morning, we'd hear him crying out for us, and someone would go down to him.

He was usually awake by seven, but I hadn't heard a peep from the monitor. It was Saturday, and Mom and Dad were sleeping in.

I waited another ten minutes and then went downstairs and let myself into his suite.

He was still asleep, which was unusual. Before I even

touched his little body I could feel the heat coming off it. He stirred and made a moaning sound. When I picked him up he was limp, and trembling. Right away I carried him upstairs to Mom and Dad.

'I think Zan's sick,' I said.

Mom and Dad sat up in bed, and I passed Zan to Mom.

'He's got a fever,' said Mom. 'A big one.'

Dad was looking really worried, and he almost never looked worried. That made me freak out big time.

'Call the vet!' I said.

'No, the university arranged to have a medical doctor for him,' said Dad, hopping out of bed. 'I've got the number . . .'

He went to his study, and I heard him talking on the phone.

Mom and I got dressed. We tried to give Zan a bottle but he seemed too dopey to take much of it.

It seemed for ever before the doctor arrived, but when I looked at the clock I saw it was only forty-five minutes. He examined Zan in the living room.

'Pneumonia,' he said. 'He'll need antibiotics.'

It seemed strange that he could have pneumonia in the summertime.

'I can give a liquid form,' said Dr Jakes. 'Is he taking his bottle?'

Mom shook her head. 'Not properly.'

'We'll need to set him up with an IV, then. It's in my car.'

'Is it serious?' I asked him, my voice shaking.

'Yes,' said Dr Jakes, 'but he'll be OK.'

He had a hard time getting a needle into Zan's thick skin; I winced every time I saw the tip jabbing him. Zan was too sick to do more than whimper. Finally the doctor managed to get the needle into the vein, and he set up the IV stand. Soon a plastic bag of antibiotics was dripping into Zan.

'I'll come back at the end of the afternoon,' said the doctor. 'Call me if there's any big change, though.'

I couldn't eat my breakfast. I felt guilty. Maybe we should've been dressing Zan more warmly when we took him outside into the back yard. His body was made for the tropics, not for Victoria, even though it was a nice warm summer.

Dad stayed home all that day, and seemed just as concerned as Mom and me. Zan kept sleeping, which Mom said was good, because he wouldn't be ripping out the IV, and the drugs could do their work making him better.

Mom held him on the sofa and I held him too. His little body was hot and limp. I was worried he'd die. He was so help-less. He didn't have a real mother or father any more, or brothers or sisters. He really needed us. I looked at him and I didn't think: *Chimp*. I just thought: *Zan*.

The next morning, Zan seemed more alert when he woke up. By noon he'd ripped out his IV. I got really worried then, because how was he going to get his medicine – every drop counted. But when the doctor came by an hour later, he was delighted, and said Zan was obviously on the mend. He left us with some liquid antibiotics to put in his milk.

Mom went into the kitchen right away to fix him a bottle and a dose. When she came back to the sofa to feed him, Zan took the bottle eagerly in his feet, sucked for a minute, and then reached out for me with his arms.

Mom smiled. 'I think he wants you to feed him.'

'Really?' I said, smiling.

She passed him into my lap, where he sat, happily sucking away.

And then I did something I'd never done before: I kissed him on the head.

CHAPTER 6

SCHOOL BEGINS

In the last week of August, Dad and Mom started interviewing students to work with Zan. The idea was that Zan would have someone with him from eight in the morning till six in the evening, taking care of him and playing with him, but all the while teaching him sign language.

Even though it was Dad's project, he wasn't going to be spending much time with Zan. He'd be at the university, teaching courses, and going through the data everyone collected. Day by day it was Mom who'd be running the show, doing a five-hour shift, training and overseeing the students, and working on her doctoral thesis. Mom and Dad figured they'd need at least ten research students.

Mom wanted the interviews to be at our house, so the applicants could meet Zan. And Zan was picky. There were lots of people he didn't like, especially guys. He wouldn't come close to them, or he'd be aggressive and pull at them and shriek.

A couple, he tried to bite. Maybe he saw them all as trespassers. Chimps were very territorial, and Zan seemed to think the house was his to rule. He didn't want any more males in it.

And Dad was almost as picky. He thought most of the students were flakes he wouldn't trust to fill up the car. Luckily there didn't seem to be any shortage of people wanting to work with Zan. Dad said the entire university was buzzing about the experiment, and lots of students were eager to play with a baby chimp, and earn some extra money and course credit.

But as September crept closer, they'd hired only six people.

Peter McIvor arrived for his interview on a Tuesday afternoon, fifteen minutes late. I was the one who opened the door. He had long brown hair in a ponytail and a beard, and his clothes were very hippyish. He actually wore a Peace button. He looked rumpled, and smelled musty.

'Hey!' he said with a smile so big and friendly I smiled back right away.

'Hi,' I said.

'I'm Peter McIvor. Sorry I'm late. I sort of . . . got lost. Had to ask for directions.'

He looked back vaguely at his car, like he was amazed he'd made it here. I was amazed too. His car was the most beat-up thing I'd ever seen. I felt kind of sorry for him. I knew Dad wouldn't like him.

'Listen,' I whispered, and he leaned in closer. 'When he asks you why you want to work for the project, tell him you think Chomsky is dead wrong. Chimps do have the cognitive ability to acquire language. Tell him you want to be part of the world's first study to communicate with another species.'

I'd eavesdropped on enough of these interviews to know the questions Dad asked, and the kinds of answers he liked.

'Uh-huh,' said Peter. 'Cool.'

'Come on in,' I said, and showed him into the living room, where Dad was waiting with all these notebooks around him, looking terrifying and stern. I headed upstairs. But just at the top, I stopped and waited so I could hear what happened.

At first, Dad did the talking: his usual spiel about the project and its aims. I heard some papers rustling, and knew he was reading through Peter's resumé and transcripts.

'So,' said Dad, 'you're going into your third year . . . majoring in psychology. You've got some linguistics courses under your belt, that's good.' There was a pause. 'Your second-year marks are a bit sloppy.'

It was the same kind of thing Dad said to me about my report cards.

'Yeah,' said Peter. 'I didn't have a great year last year, but I'm much more organized this year, more focused, you know?'

'Do you know any ASL?' Dad asked.

'What's ASL?'

I winced. This was not going so well.

'American Sign Language. That's what we'll be using to teach Zan.'

'No, but I'm good with languages. I grew up in Montreal and my French is still pretty good. I could pick ALS up like that.' He snapped his fingers.

69

'ASL,' corrected my father. 'And you'd have to pick it up fast. So why do you want to work with Zan?'

I smiled in relief. I'd given Peter the perfect answer for this one.

'Well, OK, I'm going to be honest about this,' Peter said. 'I really liked *Planet of the Apes* – not the movie, but the book, you know, the original French novel? I mean, I didn't *read* it in French – but it was written in French, originally. The movie was all right – did you see the movie?'

'I didn't, no,' I heard Dad say tersely.

My mouth was hanging open. I couldn't believe it. What was Peter doing?

'Anyway,' he went on, 'I just ... It was really thought-provoking, and it made me think about ape intelligence and human intelligence and, yeah, I'm curious about how smart they are. Because in the book they evolve way beyond us. We like to think we're the smartest thing going, but maybe we aren't, you know?'

'Well, in this world we are,' said Dad.

'And I love animals,' Peter hurried on. 'I had tons of pets growing up.'

'This isn't about pets,' said Dad. 'This is about finding out how language begins, and whether humans are the only creatures capable of it.'

'Oh,' said Peter. 'But you'd want someone who was good with animals, wouldn't you? If you wanted to teach the chimp.'

I came downstairs and went to the kitchen to get a drink. As I passed the living room I caught Peter's eye. He looked

70

defeated, slouched in his chair. In the kitchen I opened the fridge and took out the bottle of Coke, listening.

'I don't know if you're ready for this, Peter,' I heard Dad say. 'Seems to me you need to be concentrating on pulling up your marks.'

'Well, I'll definitely be doing that,' Peter replied. 'But I'd also love to be part of this project. I mean, Chomsky is just way out of line on this, you know? Humans aren't the only animals on the planet that can have language. I know Zan could learn.'

I paused, mid-pour, for Dad's reaction.

'Interesting,' he said. 'So you're more a proponent of B. F. Skinner?'

'Absolutely,' said Peter. 'I think his ideas about behavioural conditioning are far more persuasive.'

'Right on,' I murmured to myself.

I turned as the sliding door to the back yard opened and Mom came in, carrying Zan. During an interview, she would always take Zan outside so Dad could conduct the session in peace, and then she'd bring him in at the end.

'How's it going?' Mom whispered to me.

'I like him,' I whispered back. 'Dad might be coming round.'

Mom nodded and went through to the living room. I hung back in the doorway, watching.

'Hey, there's the little man,' said Peter when he caught sight of Zan.

Mom put Zan down on the carpet. A lot of the time, Zan would just scamper back to her, but not this time. He looked at Dad, then Peter – and made a happy pant-hoot and scampered straight for him. He grabbed hold of Peter's leg and stared up at him beseechingly.

'I think he wants a hug,' said Mom.

Without hesitation, Peter reached down and lifted Zan onto his lap. It was the first time I'd seen Zan so eager to meet someone outside our family.

'Hello, Zan,' said Peter, smiling.

Zan pulled on Peter's beard.

'He likes you,' Mom told Peter.

'And I like him,' said Peter, chuckling as Zan tried to pull off his Peace button. 'Wow,' Peter said. 'His eyes.'

'What about them?' Dad asked.

'It's just – you look into them and there's a real person there looking right back at you.'

I liked Peter even more. Zan was now climbing up his chest to his shoulders, and trying to swing on his ponytail.

'OK, Peter, we'll let you know by the end of the week,' said Dad. 'Thanks for coming.'

'Why bother keeping him in suspense?' said Mom. 'He's hired.'

Dad looked at her in surprise, and I did too. They'd never told any of the other candidates right away. I could see Dad wasn't happy, but he wasn't going to make a scene in front of Peter. Dad hated scenes; he thought they were 'inappropriate'.

'Honest?' Peter said, his face alight, looking from Mom to Dad.

I think he was as confused as I was.

Mom walked towards him with her hand extended. 'I'm

Sarah Tomlin. I'll be the chief researcher on the project. We'll be in touch with your schedule next week.'

'Hey, thanks a ton, thanks so much!' said Peter. 'OK, this is great.'

Zan climbed off Peter and into Mom's arms.

Dad smiled tightly. 'See you next week, then, Peter.'

Two weeks later, Dad dropped me off at Windermere University School on his way to work. I'd been at the school once before, last week, to attend an orientation meeting for new students and their families. We'd met some of the teachers, and taken a tour. But this was the first day of school, for real, and the parking lot was crammed and there were uniformed kids everywhere. My breakfast was doing a slow swirl in my stomach.

Windermere was a bit like a British boarding school – the kind you read about in books, anyway. It had its own campus, with three classroom blocks around a large quadrangle, and a huge playing field (rugby was a big deal, apparently) and a dining hall and residences for the boarders. About half the kids were boarders, and the other half were day students like me. When Mom had first seen the school she'd called some of the buildings fake-Tudor. It made me smile now, as I got out of the car.

'Hey,' said Dad from the driver's seat. 'You're going to love it here.'

'Yep,' I said, and slammed the door, shouldering my knapsack.

I knew where I was going at least. I headed across the quad

towards the main classroom block, keeping my eyes open for the Godwins, or Hugh or Evan, but I didn't see them.

The school smelled like my old school. Floor wax and chalk dust and shoes. I thought I looked like a goof in my uniform, even though Mom and Dad had said I looked fine. Handsome, Mom said. I hated how the shirt and tie felt all tight around my neck.

I found my homeroom, and Mr Davies was already there.

'Welcome, Mr Tomlin,' he said, shaking my hand. Like a lot of teachers at the school, he had an English accent.

'Good morning, sir,' I said. You were supposed to call everyone sir and ma'am here.

'This is Henry Gardner,' Mr Davies said, introducing me to another grade eight boy. He was short and sandy-haired, with glasses. 'He's going to be your guide today, just to make sure you know where to find everything. We don't want you wandering off into the bog.'

'OK, great, hi,' I said, shaking Henry's hand. I took a seat beside him and some of his friends. Back behind a desk, running my fingers over the gouged pen marks, I felt the same vague panic I always felt before a test.

'So, do you know David Godwin?' I asked Henry.

'He's grade nine,' he replied, like there wasn't much else to say. 'Why, do you know him?'

'Sort of. Our dads work together at the university. He seems like a nice guy.'

Henry looked at me doubtfully and shrugged. 'I stay away from those guys. Their idea of fun is shoving people in lockers and throwing their clothes into the swimming pool.'

'There's a swimming pool here?' I said.

'Yeah, but I wouldn't advise swimming in it,' Henry said, and laughed a bit.

I laughed politely. I'd already decided Henry and I would not be spending much time together. As more and more kids filed into homeroom, I could tell that Henry and his pals were definitely low-ranking. I knew, because in my last school, *I* was a class nerd, and I wasn't planning on being one again.

I had it all figured out for this year.

New city.

New school.

New Ben.

I could be whatever I wanted here. And what I wanted was to be a dominant male. No one messed around with the dominant male. He submitted to no one. Everyone submitted to *him*.

This was my plan, and I kept repeating it in my head like a mantra, as the room filled.

Just before the bell rang, Jennifer Godwin walked in, talking excitedly with two other girls. The blonde one was almost as good-looking as Jennifer; the other one was kind of plain, and she was doing most of the talking. Before Jennifer sat down near the front, she saw me, and I said hi, and she gave a little smile and a nod and then she was back in conversation with her friends. I'd been hoping she'd come sit near me, but that was expecting too much, I guess.

She looked younger in her uniform than she had in her

bathing suit. I thought about lotioning her back, and my face felt hot.

Mr Davies took attendance and handed out our timetables. After that there were some announcements and the bell went again and we were off, Henry at my side, talking to me really fast and explaining everything. He was like that pesky little dog in the Looney Tunes cartoon – the one the bigger dog is always swatting and telling to shut up. I'd spend the day with him, let him show me around – and then ditch him. I didn't want people to think we were friends. I figured that would pretty much finish me off at Windermere.

I guess one of the reasons Henry had been picked as my guide was that we were in all the same classes. Math. English. History.

All the guys seemed to be calling one another by their last names. 'Hendricks!' 'Thompson!' 'Burns!' But I didn't catch the girls doing this to each other. I guessed I would be Tomlin.

All morning I kept looking around for David Godwin, but couldn't see him anywhere. I passed his hairy brother, Cal, in the quad, and he just grunted at me without stopping.

This was the first school I'd been to where you could get a hot lunch. The dining hall had a high-raftered ceiling (fake-Tudor), and long wooden tables with benches on either side. The noise of people eating and talking swooped from table to table.

I looked around and hoped Henry would lead me to the table where Jennifer Godwin was sitting. There were definitely girls' tables and boys' tables, and not a ton of mixing. Henry took me to the farthest corner of the dining hall where a bunch of small, bespectacled kids sat near the end of a table. They looked like hobbits.

There was obviously a system here. The oldest kids sat at the end nearest the kitchen, and everyone else sat farther away. I soon realized why. The grade twelves came back from the kitchen carrying big metal trays of food. They helped themselves first, then passed the trays on down the table until they were empty.

'You kill it, you fill it,' chanted someone to the person who'd taken the last of the lasagne. Then that person took the tray back to the kitchen for a refill.

Way down at the hobbit end of the table, I could see it would take a while to get some food.

To my surprise, David Godwin and Hugh arrived at our table and, near the middle, kids made room for them. Clearly, they were higher-ranking males than the usual grade nines.

'Hey, David! Hugh!' I said.

David looked at me coolly. 'Tom-lin,' he said slowly, drawing out each syllable.

'That the chimp kid?' the guy across from him asked.

'He is indeed the chimp kid,' said David, helping himself to some lasagne.

'Was he raised by chimps or something?'

'He *looks* like he was raised by chimps,' Hugh said.

'That's me,' I said. 'Chimp boy.'

I nodded and tried to laugh along with everyone else, looking at David and trying to figure out if he was laughing with me or at me.

At me.

Everyone at the table started jibbering and *eeking*, the way they thought chimpanzees sounded. I took a deep breath. A dominant male did not submit.

'They don't sound like that,' I said. 'You guys sound like monkeys. Little teeny-weeny monkey boys.'

'What's the difference?' someone asked gruffly.

'Chimps are bigger and much more powerful,' I said.

'So how do they sound, Tomlin?' David asked.

'More like this.' I started doing deep pant-hoots, faster and faster, until they were almost barks, rocking up and down in my seat. Everyone was looking at me like I was crazy, so I went a little further. I jumped off the bench onto the floor and, hunched over, moved on all fours towards David. I shoved my way onto the bench beside him and started grooming his hair.

'Tomlin, you freakin' weirdo!' he said, trying to push me away.

I smacked his hands away and pretended to find something really exciting in his hair. I let loose with a shriek of excitement as I popped it into my mouth. I gave a few more contented pant-hoots, and then stopped.

'Tomlin, you are seriously twisted,' said David, giving me a shove, but he was sort of smiling.

'*That's* how chimps *really* sound,' I said, and started back to my seat. All across the dining hall, people were looking my way, including a male teacher, who was walking over with a frown.

'Sit down,' he told me. 'This is not a zoo.'

78

'Sorry, sir,' I said. 'But I *am* chimp boy.'

I heard the other guys at the table laugh.

The teacher didn't think this was funny. 'Detention on the first day is no way to start the school year,' he said.

'No, sir,' I said.

'He just can't control himself, sir,' David told the teacher. 'He was raised among jungle apes.'

'You can join him if you like, Godwin,' the teacher said. 'Now settle down.'

I took my seat. I wondered if Jennifer had heard all this commotion. Henry Gardner and the other hobbits were looking at me differently, and so were the other kids farther up the table. I wasn't sure if they were impressed or freaked out.

It didn't matter. I'd made an *impression*.

I was pretty glad when the school bus dropped me off at the end of the day.

After my chimp-boy routine at lunch, I'd started worrying I'd done the wrong thing, and people would just see me as a complete head case.

It was stupid to think that David would want to hang out with me at school. Grade nines didn't hang out with grade eights. As for Jennifer, she was obviously super popular. She was too busy to talk to me, even though we were in the same English and history classes.

Inside our house it was quiet. It was one of the days both Mom and Dad were on campus. Peter McIvor and another student named Cheryl Tobin were on the afternoon shift with

Zan. Through the sliding doors in the kitchen I could see the three of them outside, playing in the sandbox.

I wanted to be with them, but Dad had told me that I wasn't to distract Zan when he was with the students. Just as I was about to turn away, though, Zan must've seen me. He scampered across the lawn, with Peter not far behind, towards the sliding doors. He knocked on the glass with his little fists.

I waved at him. It was an overcast day, and kind of cool for early September. Zan wore a T-shirt and shorts, and kept gripping himself like he was chilly.

'I think he's cold,' I told Peter through the glass.

'What?' he said.

'Cold. He's cold. He's shivering.'

It seemed mean to ignore Zan, now that he'd seen me, so I opened the door, and he rushed in and climbed into my arms. Then, holding on with his legs around my left hip, he leaned back and slapped his arms across his chest again.

'Holy cow,' said Peter quietly. 'He's not cold. I think he's signing!'

'Hug!' I exclaimed. And then to Zan: 'Hug?' And I did the sign back to him. I put my arms around him and hugged him. 'Hug. Hug. Hug!' I said.

He hugged me even tighter. That hug felt good.

I looked at Peter and we both shook our heads.

It had been only two weeks since the project officially started.

'His first word,' I said.

'*You* taught him his first word,' said Peter, clapping me on the shoulder. 'Way to go, man.'

It was like Zan and I had both started school on the same day.

PART II

I'm a slow learner.

Letters. Numbers. They've never come easily to me.

When I was nine, Mom and Dad had me tested. They wondered if maybe there was something wrong with my brain. A learning disability. A psychologist came to the house and asked me questions and looked at me and timed me and examined all my answers and wrote up a big report.

He didn't find anything wrong with me.

I just wasn't that smart, I guess.

Mom said it would all come in time: all the words and numbers would start to make sense, when I was ready. But I always got the feeling Dad thought I wasn't trying hard enough.

He thought I had a bad attitude. He thought I was lazy. He got angry when my report cards came home.

I thought I was trying, but I just wasn't very good at school.

I wasn't good at a lot of things, like controlling my temper.

But I was good at loving Zan.

CHAPTER 7

PROJECT ZAN

Drink, Zan said to me.

I shook my head and pointed at the food on his tray.

Eat, I said.

We were talking with our hands.

Zan was in his high chair in the kitchen, and I sat in front of him, trying to feed him cereal with a spoon. He was over eight months old now, and could hold his own spoon and fork perfectly well, but he still liked throwing them more than putting food in his mouth.

Drink! Zan signed, jabbing his thumb urgently at his lips.

He wouldn't get his drink until he'd eaten some food. Mom was very firm about that; she worried he'd fill up on milk and ruin his appetite.

Off to the side, the photographer was moving around, taking pictures. *Time* magazine was doing a feature story on Project Zan and they'd sent a reporter and photographer to spend the day with us. At first, Dad hadn't been sure he wanted them to come. He didn't think we were far enough along. He wanted to wait. But the university was keen, and I think they'd pressed Dad into it. It was an international magazine, and it would get the university a lot of attention.

And us too, Mom had said. She'd spent all of yesterday frantically cleaning the house and Zan's suite, and worrying about what we'd all wear. She had me in cords and a vest, and had slicked my curly hair down with this cold, slimy stuff that was actually called Slik. I hated it, but I could tell everyone was stressed out about *Time*, so I just did what she wanted.

Today was like Zan's first public performance, and we didn't really know how he'd react to having strangers in the house, watching him all day. I kept thinking about that Bugs Bunny cartoon where the guy discovers this frog that can dance and sing. But whenever he tries to show other people, the frog just sits there stupidly and goes *ribbit*.

We all wanted Zan to be our dancing frog today and show everyone how smart he was. In the six months we'd been teaching him, he could already make eight signs, and understand dozens more.

I still had trouble believing it. A chimp learning human language? Every time he mastered a new sign it was like he was learning to name the world, bit by bit. No other chimp had ever done anything like this before. For the first time in human history we could talk, really talk, to another species. Sometimes it really did seem like something from a sci-fi movie.

Dad had carefully planned out the whole day so Zan would

be doing things that would encourage him to sign. I'd been a little worried earlier, because when the reporter and photographer first arrived, Zan was pretty wild. He bounded around on all fours, he climbed furniture and bounced off walls. He was really interested in all of the photographer's gear, the lighting stands and the shiny umbrella things and the camera itself. He wanted to shriek at everyone, and touch everything. Luckily Peter and I had managed to distract him with one of his dolls. After a few minutes, he seemed to lose interest in the strangers, and just wanted to get on with his regular Saturday.

Now, in his high chair, he signed *drink* to me once more, a little half heartedly, and when I signed *no* he just stared at me reproachfully for a few seconds.

Out, he signed, gripping his long brown fingers in one hand, then pulling them free.

I couldn't help smiling. If Zan liked his food, he'd stay and eat contentedly until it was gone. If he didn't, he got restless within minutes. This particular cereal and vegetable blend wasn't his favourite, but it was good for him, so we tried to get it down him.

Eat, I signed again.

Zan looked down at his food miserably, then back at me.

Hug, he signed.

I laughed. He was hoping I'd take him out to hug him – another favourite ploy of his to end a mealtime.

'Incredible,' I heard the reporter murmur behind me. He'd been watching the whole thing, taking notes. Dad and Peter had been quietly translating the ASL signs for him.

Hug, I signed to Zan, and leaned closer so I could put my hands around his little shoulders and touch my face to his. I felt his long skinny arms around my neck, but when I tried to pull back, they tightened.

'Zan,' I said aloud, 'let go, please.'

He didn't let go. I heard the soft hooting sounds he made when he thought something was funny. I tried to pull back but his grip was surprisingly strong and I couldn't help giggling. And the more I giggled, the louder his pant-hoots became, until we were both laughing. I could smell his food in the bowl below me, and I had to admit, I wouldn't have wanted it either.

I started tickling Zan. The tray was in the way, and I couldn't get to his most ticklish spots under his ribs, so I went for the armpits. He shrieked with delight, and his arms flew free of my neck. I pulled away.

He frowned at me, curling his lips out in displeasure.

More, he signed.

More what? I signed.

Hug!

I looked back over my shoulder at the reporter and Dad and Mom, who were both beaming with pride. Really, it couldn't be going any better. In the last five minutes, Zan had used four of his signs, and had formed them perfectly.

After lunch we all moved out into the back yard. It was early March, sunny and surprisingly warm. In Toronto we would've been staggering through grimy grey snow, but here we'd just cut the grass, and there were flowers in bloom and green things on the trees, and you were comfortable in a sweater. Zan wore shorts and a fleecy sweatshirt with the sleeves cut off so he could move his arms freely.

Zan loved the back yard, no matter what the weather was like. The first few times we'd taken him out, I was surprised he wasn't more interested in the trees. He pretty much ignored them. A couple of months ago, I held him up to a low branch and tried to get him to grab hold. I assumed he'd just swing himself up and start sailing through the branches, like chimps in the wild. Zan held onto the branch for a second, but was trembling, and looked so frightened that I took him down right away. He clung to me for a long time. I guess it shouldn't have surprised me, since he'd been born in a lab and raised in a house. Why would he know anything about trees?

His favourite place was the big sandbox. When he was younger he just wanted to dig his feet and hands into the sand, over and over. Then he tried eating it. He'd cram handfuls into his mouth and swill it and crunch it around and dribble it out. Then what he liked to do was watch *me* dig with the shovel. Before long he was grabbing it from me and digging on his own, hurling all the sand onto the lawn. We needed to buy a lot of extra sand. After a while he started filling the buckets and dumping them out. He could do this for a long time, really concentrating.

Lately what he most liked was to play hide-and-seek in the sand with his dolls. He'd hand them to me one at a time and want me to bury them, and then he'd dig around and find them all in about two seconds. Dad had decided that's what we'd be doing today for the journalists, because we were trying to teach him the sign for *hide*.

He already knew how to sign *baby*. That's what he called his dolls. Most of them were human babies, although he also had a little chimp, a kitten, and a GI Joe action figure bulging with muscles and guns. I got him that one because I thought he needed some boy toys. He called that one *baby* too.

Peter and Dad got themselves settled in the sandbox with Zan's dolls. Dad wanted to be in some of the pictures with Zan too, since the project was his. I just hoped it wouldn't throw Zan, because I wasn't sure Dad had ever played in the sandbox with him before. Dad let Peter do the signing.

Hide was a complicated one. It started out a bit like *drink*, which I thought was confusing. You had to put your right thumb to your lips and then move it down and hide it under your left hand. Zan was pretty good about putting his thumb to his lips, but not about the second part.

Zan handed Peter the doll and he held onto it, looking at him expectantly.

Impatiently, Zan made the *baby* sign.

Hide baby, Peter signed back to him.

Baby, Zan signed and made a little pant-hoot.

Hide baby, Peter signed.

Baby, Zan signed, very slowly and carefully, as if Peter wasn't very bright and might not have understood him.

Peter signed just *hide* this time, and Zan hurriedly touched his thumb to his mouth – the first part of the sign.

'Good, Zan!' Dad said. 'Very good.'

Zan's eyes widened, not understanding what all the fuss was about.

'Now show him the rest, Peter,' Dad said quietly. The photographer clicked away from all angles.

Peter gently took Zan's right hand and touched it to his mouth, then brought it down and covered it with his left hand. Most of the time, Zan didn't like his hands being held and would pull them away. Today, he put up with it long enough for Peter to guide him through the sign twice. Then Zan picked up the doll and shoved it at Peter in exasperation.

Peter and Dad then got on with the game, and hid all the dolls, signing *hide* as often as they could. Zan didn't put the whole sign together, but it would come. He was fast, and getting faster, at learning.

After a good long session of hide-and-seek, Mom and Dad spent some more time playing with him, and showing him things around the yard, holding his hands and letting him swing between them. I remembered them doing that with me, but I didn't think we had a picture of it. Who would've taken the picture? There was no *Time* photographer taking shots of me when I was little.

I watched them from across the yard, and for a moment it was like seeing some strange beautiful family that wasn't mine. Mom was going down the slide with Zan between her legs, Dad waiting for them at the bottom. The photographer was loving it, and so was Zan. He didn't usually get this much attention from so many people all at once. Dad hardly ever played with him. It was mostly me and Mom, or Peter and the other research assistants, in pairs.

'I hear you taught him his first sign,' said Norman Sayles, the reporter, walking over.

I nodded, feeling proud and kind of embarrassed. 'Well, it was more like I was the first person he signed to.'

'Incredible. *Hug*, wasn't it?'

'It was *hug*.'

'It must be quite something, having a baby chimp in the house,' said Mr Sayles.

'Yeah, it's great,' I said, my eyes wandering over to Mom and Dad, wondering if it was OK for me to be talking to the reporter. He didn't have his notebook open or the tape recorder going, so I figured he was just making conversation while the photographer got his shots.

'Keeps your parents pretty busy, I bet,' he said.

'Well, we have a lot of help. There're students from the university who come.'

'I bet he can be quite a handful sometimes, hey?'

I grinned. 'He can be pretty messy.' I told him about how he got upstairs to my room once and trashed it.

He chuckled. 'It's remarkable watching you two together. The way you communicate so easily. Do you think of him as a pet or a little brother?'

My reply came instantly – and somewhat angrily. 'A little brother. He's way smarter than a pet. He's like a real person. He's one of the family.'

The reporter nodded and smiled.

'Can't imagine life without him now, I bet,' he said.

'Nope.'

Dad was coming towards us now, and Mr Sayles walked off to meet him.

At the end of the day, when the magazine people had left, Dad asked what Sayles had been asking me. I told him.

'There'll be more reporters,' he said. 'Best not to talk to them. They all want a story.'

'What do you mean?' I asked. I thought Zan *was* the story. What else did there need to be? We were teaching a chimpanzee how to talk!

'Oh, he was probably hoping you'd say something about how hard it was to raise a chimp, and how jealous you were, and how much strain it was putting on the family.'

'I didn't say anything like that,' I said defensively.

'I know. That's just the kind of thing they'll be hoping for, though. Best to let Mom and me do the talking. The project doesn't need any negative publicity.'

'How could there be?' I asked. What could be wrong with teaching language to an intelligent animal? We were making Zan's life *better*, and maybe we could make the lives of all the chimps better. I said so to Mom.

'Not everyone will agree, Ben,' she said ruefully. 'We've opened Pandora's box. We're going to get all kinds of publicity, and we won't be able to control whether it's good or bad. Get ready.'

CHAPTER 8

PROJECT JENNIFER

We didn't make the cover of *Time*, but we got six pages inside, with tons of photos of us playing and signing with Zan. We all looked incredibly happy. The headline was THE REAL DOCTOR DOOLITTLE? and focused on how chimps were our closest relatives, and one day we might just be able to talk to them. I thought it was a pretty positive article, and was surprised Dad was annoyed by it.

Norman Sayles, the reporter, had also talked to some psychologists from other universities, some of whom didn't say very nice things about Project Zan. One guy said we shouldn't be wasting our time on chimps, when there were so many ways we could be helping humans have better lives.

I didn't get any of that, and I really didn't care much. What I cared about was how I looked in the pictures. People at school were going to see them. Jennifer was going to see them. There was one photo where I thought my smile looked goofy and my hair looked way too greasy (stupid Slik), but in the other two I looked pretty good – my hair had loosened up a bit. One of Mom's friends had once told me I looked like the young actor Michael York, and he was famous and a sex symbol, so I was hoping maybe Jennifer would think so too.

It was a Tuesday when the magazine came out, and that night, as usual, I slogged through my homework. I needed Dad's help with algebra – again. I guess he was generous to help me, but he always seemed impatient, like he couldn't quite believe I was having trouble with such easy stuff.

There was a lot of work at Windermere and it was way harder than what I was used to. My first term I'd felt buried under homework. I'd made the cross-country team, and Dad wasn't thrilled because he said I should be concentrating on my classes, but Mom stood up for me, and let me stay on the team. I even won third place at the regional finals. I liked running. I felt strong. I felt like I was in control.

I couldn't say the same for French and math and grammar. I didn't struggle as much as I used to with words and numbers, but it was still an effort. My Christmas marks had not been great. Dad had called them 'sloppy'.

When I was finally done with my homework that night, I found one of Mom's blank logbooks, took it upstairs to my room, and closed the door. In neat scientific writing, on the cover I wrote:

Project Jennifer.

Since September I'd been trying to get to know her better. But it wasn't easy. We were in only two classes together, our lockers weren't close together, we ate at different tables at lunch time – and she was always, *always*, with her two best friends. Shannon was the one with shoulder-length blonde hair, big blue eyes, a neat little nose and a neat little mouth. She was definitely pretty, but not as pretty as Jennifer. Shannon was quiet. You didn't hear a lot out of Shannon.

Jane was the loudmouth – and she terrified me. She had short brown hair, a long face, and she laughed a lot, but not in a nice way. Her smile sometimes looked more like a sneer. There was no way I could get near Jennifer when she was with Jane. I'd see Jane talking and looking around and laughing, and I was always worried she was talking about me. The few times I'd worked up the courage to pass by and say hi, I could hear Jane giggling right afterwards. Everything seemed to make her giggle and snort and sneer.

Jennifer hardly ever came over to talk to me. Once, she actually said goodbye to me at the end of the day, and I smiled all the way home on the bus, nearly missed my stop, and smiled all through doing my homework and eating dinner.

I guess I could've asked David about her, but it was risky. Ask too many questions about his sister and he'd be on to me. He probably already was. So I tried to be patient and listen, and observe her from afar.

With Project Zan, every researcher kept a logbook. What Zan ate, what he didn't eat. What games he liked to play. What made him grumpy. What made him happy. What signs he used, how often, and how accurately. When he peed and when he pooed.

I figured I didn't need to know *quite* so much about Jennifer, but I did need to get serious. I needed to get scientific. And a scientist needed data. The more findings I wrote down, the better luck I'd have getting to know her – and getting her to like me.

I opened the logbook to the first page and took a deep breath.

I had a lot to learn. Girls were very different from guys. They seemed to hug each other a lot and get all excited about seeing each other in the morning, or seeing a new scarf or a new bag or something. Sometimes there were big dramatic scenes and someone would be crying and someone else would be comforting her and giving dirty looks to someone else. They already knew the names they were going to give their kids, and how many they were going to have. It was pretty freaky.

I wrote the day's date at the top of the page, then underneath:

What she likes:

Then I just started writing whatever came to mind:

Parker pens.

Horses.

Colourful erasers at the ends of her pencils.

ABBA.

Stickers on her school binders with a) funny sayings on them; and b) rock band logos.

Glam rock from England.

I looked at my list. It was pathetic. I'd have to come up with way more than this. I thought harder.

I Capture the Castle (note: check out author, find out what else he's written).

Zan (she liked holding him at barbecue. Might want to learn more about chimps).

I put stars beside these last two items because I thought they might make good topics of conversation.

I was starting to feel a little better. This was scientific. I could even write down funny lines to use with her. Based on my data, we'd soon be having all these great conversations, and she'd be smiling and laughing at everything I said.

As it turned out, the *Time* piece gave me a huge boost. The day after the magazine came out, the headmaster mentioned it in Chapel (we went to Chapel Monday, Wednesday and Friday mornings), and afterwards, crossing the quad, Jennifer walked up to *me*. She actually walked up to *me*, without Shannon or Jane in tow.

'So you're totally famous now,' she said.

'Yeah, right.' I nodded, rolling my eyes. I didn't want to seem conceited. 'Phone ringing off the hook.'

'*Time* magazine,' she said. 'That's really cool. Congratulations.'

'Thanks. Hey, did you know ABBA's got a new album out? They mentioned it on *American Bandstand* last night.'

Her face lit up. 'I know! I can't wait. Do you like them?'

'Are you kidding? I *love* them,' I said. I'd never actually heard one of their songs.

Then the bell went and we had to hurry off to class. It was the longest conversation we'd had all year. Pump me full of helium, I couldn't have felt lighter. The logbook was already paying off.

At lunch, when I went into the dining hall, David Godwin waved me over. 'Hey, Tarzan,' he said.

A nickname – I loved it! I hoped it stuck. It sure beat chimp boy.

When David and Hugh made room for me at the table, I could barely believe it. I'd been promoted. I glanced down at the hobbits, and saw their hungry looks of envy.

I'd barely sat down before the tray of pork chops was being pushed into my hands.

'The food comes so much faster here,' I said.

'Life is good here,' said Hugh, chewing.

'Groovy hair in *Time*,' David said. 'It was practically *gleaming*.'

'My mom's got some Slik left over if you want it,' I said, and he laughed.

'I hate that stuff,' Hugh chimed in. 'If I see it, I pour it down the sink.'

After lunch I headed to English class, feeling as mighty as the real Tarzan. Jennifer smiled at me as I walked in, and I tried to give her my best dominant male smile. The bad news was we were doing Shakespeare right now. *Twelfth Night*. I spent more time looking at the footnotes than the actual lines, just trying to figure out what was going on. These people and their crazy lives made almost no sense to me.

I liked Mr Stotsky, but he often got people to read aloud in class, and I was lousy at it. The two times I'd done it before, he kept telling me to slow down and 'take my time with the language', and I'd been really embarrassed, especially with Jennifer in the class. I was hoping he'd skip me today.

But he didn't. 'Mr Tomlin, would you like to be our Orsino this afternoon, please.'

'No thank you, sir,' I said impulsively.

That got a good laugh, and I started to feel pretty cocky. The dominant male always took charge.

Mr Stotsky raised an eyebrow at me. 'You see yourself in a different starring role, perhaps, Mr Tomlin?'

That was a good one, and the kids were laughing with him now.

The dominant male never backed down. 'I'm just not in a reading kind of mood today, sir, sorry.'

Everyone laughed, but a little nervously.

'I'm sorry, too, Mr Tomlin. You can report for detention after school.'

I could feel myself start to flush, and fought it, tried to exhale quietly and let the blood flow away from my cool, careless cheeks. I'd got a detention, so what? A detention was a sign you were a scrapper. I was marking out my territory as an alpha male.

I felt like I was in control.

On Friday, when the bus dropped me off in front of the house, there was a brand-new Mercedes in our driveway. I thought Professor Godwin must be visiting, or someone else from the university, but it was just Mom and Dad in the living room.

They looked like I'd caught them in the middle of a fairly lively conversation. Beyond the kitchen, I could hear Zan playing in his suite with the students.

'Is that a student's car out there?' I asked in surprise.

Dad shook his head and gave me a mischievous smile I'd never seen before.

'*You* bought a Mercedes?' I exclaimed.

'Oh yeah,' he said. He looked like a kid who'd done something reckless but was defiant and totally happy.

I saw Mom roll her eyes.

'Oh, come on, Sarah,' Dad said. 'The Volvo was hanging by a thread. The drive across Canada pretty much finished it off. We needed a new car.'

'But not a Mercedes.'

I thought Mom was coming down kind of hard on him. Dad had a big new job now, and he was practically famous. We'd had that Volvo for ever anyway, and Dad hardly ever bought anything, probably because he'd grown up with so little money.

'Your father got a new car practically every year of his life,' Dad said to Mom.

'Yes, and it was disgusting.'

Dad shrugged. 'Well, you know what? I've wanted a Mercedes for a long time, so why not now? What's wrong with that?'

Mom shook her head. 'Fine. But we both know what this is about. It's so you can have the same car as the department chair.'

'No,' said Dad. 'Mine's actually quite a lot nicer.' He looked at me with this wicked smile, and winked. I couldn't help laughing. I *liked* Dad this way. I didn't think I'd ever seen him enjoy himself so much.

'Well, your timing's uncanny,' said Mom, smiling herself now, 'with the Godwins coming to dinner tonight.'

'That *is* funny how that worked out,' said Dad, kissing her mouth.

'The Godwins are coming for dinner?' I said.

'David and Jennifer too,' said Mom.

For a second I couldn't take a breath. 'Really?'

Mom said, 'I've got to pick up a few things at the plaza. You want to come give me a hand?'

Dad jingled the new car keys in front of her. 'This is your set.'

'Thank you, Alpha Male,' Mom said.

To me, Dad said, 'Make sure she doesn't scratch up my new car.'

We drove down to Cordova Plaza. The Mercedes was really nice. It had leather seats, electric windows and an amazing stereo, and it didn't smell like ketchup and Fresca. I felt rich just sitting in it. Mom parked the car very carefully. At Safeway I helped her buy some food and load it into the trunk. Then she wanted to go to the florist and pick up some fresh flowers, so I waited for her in the hobby shop.

I was nervous about David and Jennifer coming. What would Jennifer think of our house, and what would we talk about all evening? I'd better review my logbook for some ideas.

I walked up and down the aisles of the shop, pausing to look at all the rockets – the ones with solid fuel engines that you ignited with a car battery. I was wondering if it was worth saving up for one. There was lots of room in the back yard to blast it off.

'Hey,' someone said, and I looked round and saw Tim Borden.

'Hey, Tim,' I said, and suddenly felt self-conscious because I realized I was still in my school uniform.

'What happened to you?' said Tim. 'You just disappeared.'

I felt guilty about the way I'd dropped him. After the construction-site incident, we'd hung out a bit together, but then I'd just started making lame excuses whenever he came by or called. I'd never even told him I wouldn't be going to his school in the fall.

'My parents wanted me to go to Windermere,' I said, as if that explained everything.

I looked over as Mike appeared at the end of the aisle. He smirked when he saw me in my uniform.

'Aren't you just the sweetest little thing,' he said.

Automatically, I loosened my tie and undid my top button – as if that made me look any cooler.

'Windermere. That private school on the other side of the Pat Bay highway, right?' said Tim.

'Yeah, it's OK. Too much homework.'

'Windyqueer,' Mike said.

I wasn't looking at Mike, but was aware of him staring at me the whole time with those scary dark eyes of his. It actually made me feel a little sick, he seemed to hate me so much.

Tim asked, 'How's Zan?'

'He's good, yeah.'

'My dad said he saw you guys in the papers or something.'

'*Time* magazine.'

'Man, that's cool,' said Tim.

'Come on, Tim,' said Mike.

'Well, see you around,' said Tim, and he honestly looked a bit sad.

'Yeah, see you,' I said.

'Loser,' muttered Mike as he walked off with Tim.

I tried on a lot of pants and shirts before I figured out what to wear. I wanted to look good for Jennifer. I had a shower and blow-dried my hair, brushing it out to make it straighter. I hated my curly hair. It never looked cool. On the counter I saw Dad's Old Spice aftershave. I'd always liked the smell; it seemed kind of manly and it worked for that guy in the TV ads, the guy in the sailor's cap with the hot girlfriend. I sluiced a whole bunch onto my hands and then splashed it over my face and neck. I wished I had straight hair; then I'd look really good in a sailor's cap.

When I came downstairs, Mom looked across the living room at me and said, 'Are you wearing Old Spice?'

'Yep.'

'You might want to rinse off just a little.'

I felt stupid. 'Really?'

She nodded. 'A bit strong.'

The doorbell rang and I rushed back upstairs and splashed water all over my face, scrubbing my skin with my hands. I patted myself dry with a towel, but now my neck was red and chafed. I could hear the Godwins coming in. I couldn't go downstairs like this – I looked sunburned. I hurried to my bedroom and dragged out a black turtleneck. I hated turtlenecks; I knew they were supposed to be all artsy and beatniky, but I still thought they were kind of uptight. But Mom was always saying I looked sharp in them. I just hoped she was right.

When I came down, the Godwins were all standing around in the living room and Dad was making cocktails for the grown-ups.

'Hey,' I said casually to Jennifer and David. Their older brother Cal wasn't coming. He had better things to do than hang out with his parents' friends. He could drive. I didn't know a lot about what seventeen-year-olds did on Friday nights, but I guessed there'd be dancing and girls and making out.

David was wearing a really cool orange shirt with the collar way open. Jennifer had this tight dress with a crazy design all over it and a thick green belt. There was lip gloss on her lips. She looked fantastic, and I felt a surge of excitement and hope. She'd done that for me. She'd dressed up for *me* because she liked me and wanted me to think she was pretty. Maybe I was wrong, but that was my assumption. Scientists had to have assumptions.

In her hand was a portable record player in its pink plastic case. She saw me looking at it and said, 'I didn't know if you had a hi-fi in the rec room, so I brought mine.'

'We don't actually have a rec room,' I said.

'You don't have a *rec room?*' she said, looking horrified.

'Isn't that against the law or something?' David said, shaking his head at his sister.

'The basement's unfinished.' I lowered my voice. 'It's kind of gross. It's where Dad keeps all his experiments that go wrong.' I put my arms out and took a few clunky Frankenstein steps.

Jennifer and David laughed. I saw Dad glance over from talking to Professor Godwin, but I didn't think he'd heard what I said.

David tapped the army surplus satchel hanging from his shoulder. 'Jennifer picked out some albums, and I brought some *real* music.'

Jennifer rolled her eyes.

'We can play them upstairs in my room,' I said.

'I've got the new ABBA album,' she said. 'It's really good.'

'Can't wait,' I said.

'Liar,' said David, shaking his head in disgust.

'They do that cool "Waterloo" song.' A couple of nights ago I'd heard it on the radio for the first time.

Jennifer's face completely lit up. 'That's got to be my favourite song!'

'We're going upstairs to listen to some music,' I told Mom.

She broke off from talking to Mrs Godwin long enough to smile and nod and say she'd call when dinner was ready.

I was really relieved they'd brought a turntable and records – I'd been worried about what we were going to do all evening.

I didn't want them to think our place was boring. Especially since we didn't have a rec room. Good thing Mom had gotten me to tidy up my room in case we ended up there. The whole time I was tidying I kept thinking of what would make me look coolest, and I'd left out little things that I thought were interesting. My cross country ribbons on the bulletin board, my camera, some artistic black and white photos I'd developed recently.

'Where's Zan?' Jennifer asked as we walked upstairs.

'In his suite, with Peter.'

'Can we go visit him?' she asked.

'Probably not a good idea. We'd just get him all excited,' I said. I could see Zan making a run for the door and getting into the living room and jumping on the dinner table. Dad would freak out.

'What time does he go to bed?' David asked.

'Usually about eight.'

'Beddy-bye time for little chimps,' Jennifer said.

I chuckled. 'Yep. Beddy-bye for little chimps.'

'He is so cute,' she said.

I led them into my bedroom and helped Jennifer find an outlet for her record player. We were down on our hands and knees, underneath the desk, and I was aware of how close she was to me, her arms and shoulders and hair. I'd imagined her in my bedroom lots of times – and the things we might get up to – and it made me blush to think of it right now. She passed me the cord and I plugged it in and backed out.

'Is that Old Spice?' she said, sniffing.

'Hmm?' I said.

'I didn't know you were shaving,' David said mockingly.

'Tarzan shave every day,' I said in my Tarzan voice, and when I saw Jennifer's eyebrows lift sceptically, I said, 'Twice a day – me very hairy,' and she laughed.

David spread the albums out on the floor. I knew which ones were his. Pink Floyd, The Who, Led Zeppelin. Jennifer had brought Bay City Rollers, Elton John, ABBA, and a single called 'Seasons in the Sun' that they were playing about every twenty minutes on the radio.

'I call first pick,' said Jennifer.

David sighed and handed her the ABBA album. 'I've only heard this, like, a hundred times.'

We put on the record. David and I sprawled out on the floor, and Jennifer sat on the edge of my bed – which I thought was pretty cool: she was on my bed – and mouthed the words of the songs. I watched her eyes travel around my room – the Hitchcock poster, the Truffaut poster – hoping maybe she'd ask me something about them, so I could be all hip and fascinating, but she didn't say anything, not even when she saw my camera on the desk. We all talked a bit about school and teachers and TV, but we only got through about four or five songs before Mom called us down for dinner.

Mom was pouring the wine and gave me half a glass and asked the Godwins if it was all right if their two had a small glass, as well.

Professor Godwin sort of snuffled and said, 'Yes, yes, of course,' but I could tell Mrs Godwin was a bit shocked.

'Do you like wine?' I asked Jennifer. We were all three of us together at the end of the table.

'I don't know yet,' she said, taking a sip. She wrinkled her nose, but then took another sip.

I was feeling pretty suave now, the big-city boy with the cool bohemian mom who let me drink wine. I was wearing Old Spice and there were pictures of me in *Time* magazine.

'Your parents let you drink all the time?' David whispered beside me.

'Oh sure,' I lied. The grown-ups were already yakking away, so I explained to David how Mom's parents were European and had let her drink when she was a teenager. And how it was better that way, because then she didn't go crazy and get drunk all the time when she turned nineteen.

'Man,' David said. 'Wow.'

The truth was, I still wasn't that used to wine. Since that first taste on my birthday, I'd had maybe a couple of tiny glasses, and the one Mom had poured me now was bigger than usual. But it didn't taste so bad to me any more, and with every sip I felt warmer and more relaxed. David and Jennifer and I were talking and eating and drinking our wine, and the conversation was moving so fast it was hard to keep up.

The meal seemed to accelerate. Occasionally I tuned in to Dad and Professor Godwin's conversation. Dad had the charm at two hundred watts, and was talking about Project Zan and how the big grant application was coming together. Whenever I checked in with Mom and Mrs Godwin, it was usually Mrs Godwin droning about the trouble they'd had with their new electric oven, or how they were getting their patio stone replaced, and Mom trying her best not to look bored. If Mom was talking, she was very dramatic and her hands were going, and she was talking about American foreign policy or the art show at the university gallery, and Mrs Godwin was just nodding and looking at Mom like she was an alien life-form.

After dessert we went back upstairs and David put on *Led Zeppelin II* and pretended he was playing guitar, while Jennifer and I laughed at him.

'They shout too much,' Jennifer said when the song was finished. 'Your pick,' she said to me.

'I must be crazy,' I said, 'but I'm ready for more ABBA.' I was still feeling pleasantly hot and speedy. My body wanted to move.

'No!' howled David, then he threw back his head and said, 'Oh, all right! Spin those crazy Swedes!'

Jennifer put on 'Waterloo' and cranked it. My room throbbed with sound. Jennifer started singing along and sometimes she'd look right at me and swing her hair, and it was the most electrifying thing I'd ever experienced. Her cheeks were flushed and her eyes were amazing and if she'd dangled a leash I would have bowed my head so she could slip it around my neck. I couldn't look away. Then I heard David singing out the chorus, and before long I was on my feet and we were all belting out the words so loud we couldn't even hear Björn and Björk, or whatever they were called, any more. When it was over, Jennifer just picked up the needle and dropped it back at the beginning of the song, and we did it again.

After that we burned through 'Crocodile Rock' and 'Rocket Man' and then, when we needed a breather, Jennifer put on 'Seasons in the Sun'.

'This,' she said, 'is the saddest song.'

It was a super sappy tune about this guy dying, and David and I started singing along in these really schmaltzy voices and pretending we were breaking down and weeping and clutching each other's arms. At first Jennifer kept shushing us, but by the end she was giggling too.

'Goofballs,' she said.

After that, David put on *Dark Side of the Moon*, which was not a sing-along kind of album, so we just listened and talked a bit.

After a while Jennifer said, 'Teach me some sign language.'

'Which signs do you want to know?'

'Start with *hi* and *bye*.'

Those were easy, and I showed her.

'What are the ones you use with Zan?' David wanted to know.

I felt like I had something special and rare to give them. I taught them *up* and *drink*, *give* and *more* and *eat*.

'Cool,' said David. 'Hey, where's your bathroom?'

When he opened the door to go out, the sounds of our parents laughing downstairs swirled in, along with the slightly skunky smell of the Godwins' cigarette smoke. It seemed they were having a good time.

Jennifer said, 'Did you really teach him his first sign?'

'Yeah, sort of,' I told her, pleased. She must have gotten

that from *Time*. It meant she'd read the whole article. Maybe she'd stared a while at the pictures of me.

'So what's *hug*?' she asked.

I showed her.

'That's so cute,' she said, gripping herself with her arms. 'Like really hugging someone.'

'Yep,' I said, wishing her arms were around me. 'And *tickle*'s pretty close, only you tickle yourself right there.'

I wiggled my fingers to show her.

'Right *here*?' she said, reaching over and tickling me under my arms.

I laughed in total surprise. 'Or down here – that's where Zan likes it,' and I went for her under her ribs.

She squealed and giggled and tried to twist away and I could've held her tighter, but I let go. She stepped back, just a little, still breathing hard.

'What other signs do you know?' she asked.

I put my fingers to my lips and then moved them to my cheek.

'What's that?'

'*Kiss*,' I said.

She repeated the sign, smiling at me in a playful kind of way.

I was staring at her glossy lips and I wanted to kiss them for real, but I heard David coming back from the bathroom. Probably I wouldn't have done it anyway, because I was afraid she wouldn't like it, and maybe David would see, and Jennifer would be upset and run downstairs in tears and I'd be humiliated.

I totally had the hots for her. She probably didn't have the hots for me. Not yet. But I wanted her to. I wouldn't rest until she did. I'd do *anything*.

If I could teach a chimp sign language, I could probably teach Jennifer Godwin to fall for me.

CHAPTER 9

GIVE HUG

Zan loved washing up. Sunday night after dinner he sat right up on the counter beside the sink, holding a dish in one hand and the scrubber brush in another. Sometimes he just cleaned the same plate over and over again, but it kept him happy, and we all signed to him while we washed. It was a good way of teaching him *water* and *dirty* and *soap*, which he was pretty interested in. We had to make sure to lock the bottle of soap up right after using it, because Zan liked squeezing it into the water and making more and more bubbles.

All weekend I'd been thinking about Jennifer. I kept remembering the feel of her fingers tickling me. I could still feel her waist in my hands as I tickled her back. Project Jennifer had taken a big leap forward, but part of me was worried tomorrow at school everything would go back to normal, and she'd hardly notice me. It made me shrivel up inside just to think about it. I wanted my hands on her again. I wanted her hands on me . . .

'Mom and I were talking,' Dad was saying, 'and it seems unfair that we pay all the students working with Zan – but not you.'

'I checked the budget,' said Mom, 'and we have enough money to pay you too.'

'Really?' I was surprised.

'Absolutely,' said Dad. 'You've put in a lot of shifts.'

I didn't think of them as shifts at all. That made it sound like work, and mostly I loved spending time with Zan. It was best when Mom and Dad weren't around, because they were always watching Zan and taking notes, or wanting me to do educational things with him. To me he wasn't the subject of an experiment, or a famous chimp; he was just my little brother and we were goofing around.

I glanced at Zan, dunking his dish back into the soapy water and seeing how many bubbles he could get on it. He made me happy. I missed him when I was at school all day. Sitting in class, I'd sometimes think about the funny things he did, and smile.

I did love the idea of making money, but it seemed weird to get paid just for spending time with one of the family, and I told this to Mom and Dad.

'My parents paid me for babysitting my little sister,' said Mom with a shrug. 'I don't see the difference.'

I nodded. That made me feel a lot better.

'It's only fair,' said Dad. 'And you're also a really good teacher for him, Ben. You're a big part of this project.'

'Yeah?' I asked, smiling. Dad sounded proud of me. Maybe

my name would end up alongside his and Mom's in the science textbooks.

'So I'd get to come to the weekly meeting, then, right?' I said.

Dad chuckled. 'Haven't you already?'

He knew I was usually listening in from the top of the stairs, or the kitchen, where I'd take about an hour to pour myself a drink. Every Sunday night, Peter and all the other students came to our house to talk about how Project Zan was going, and discuss the week's events. Which techniques were working and which weren't. Good things Zan had done. Bad things he'd done. What new words they should work on next. Even though it was a meeting, it looked more like a party to me, because there were so many students that people ended up sitting on the floor.

I looked over at Zan and noticed he wasn't washing his dish quite as enthusiastically as usual. He kept glancing at something. I turned and saw the bottle of dish soap. Somehow we'd forgotten to lock it up. I reached for it, but Zan leaped over the sink at the same time and got it first.

'Zan, give me the soap!' I shouted.

He was off the counter and scooting across the floor, a big golden arc of liquid soap spraying over his shoulder.

'Zan, stop!' Mom cried.

'Grab him!' Dad bellowed.

Zan was shaking the bottle like crazy and squeezing it at the same time, and soap was jetting everywhere in crazy curves. I made a grab for him, but he was so soapy he just squirted through my fingers.

117

Dad lunged, slipped on the floor, and went down cursing. Zan darted through the doorway into his suite, and I skidded after him. He was hooting enthusiastically and squirting soap for all he was worth. He'd probably been dreaming of this moment for a long time, and the look of glee on his face – I couldn't resist it. I started laughing too, as I chased him into his bedroom. He leaped onto his bed and as I drew closer he squeezed the bottle and got me right in the middle of the chest. I tussled with him on the bed and somehow managed to wrestle the bottle from his slippery grasp. Then I gave him a squirt and he shrieked with delight.

'Enough!' Dad shouted behind me.

When I saw the look on his face, I stopped smiling. He was really pissed off.

'It's like a goddamn circus!'

'The Tomlin Circus,' Mom said, coming in with dish towels, looking amused. 'And a circus of your very own making, Richard. You're the ringmaster.'

'A ringmaster usually has a bit more control,' Dad said, and some of the grimness in his face disappeared. 'What a mess! Zan! That was very naughty!'

Zan looked pretty stricken, and immediately turned to me. *Hug*, he signed.

'Don't smile at him, Ben,' Dad snapped. 'Look strict so he understands.'

I tried to frown and look severe, but it was hard when he kept hugging himself, his brown eyes huge and beseeching.

Give hug! Zan signed to me.

118

'Did you see that?' I shouted.

'What?' Dad said.

'He signed *Give hug*!' Mom exclaimed.

'Two signs!' I said. 'That's the first time he's put two signs together!'

'You saw it?' Dad asked Mom, who nodded, beaming. 'You'll need to document it in your log. I missed it.' Now he sounded annoyed.

'Don't worry about that now,' Mom said. 'Two signs after only six months! He just made his first sentence. Do you realize that?'

During all this Zan was looking around at us – Mom, Dad and me – like he was wondering what he had to do to get a hug around here.

I reached down and took him into my arms and squeezed him tight.

'Give hug,' I said into his ear. 'You're a genius, Zan.'

The lights went down, the curtains opened, and the movie began.

I was sitting beside Hugh and David, popcorn balanced on our laps. Right in front of us, in the next row, were Jennifer, Shannon and Jane. It was Saturday and we were at the Coronet for a matinée of *The Golden Voyage of Sinbad*. It was my idea. A few days ago I'd called up David and asked if he wanted to go.

'Ask Hugh too,' I'd said casually. 'And, hey, if Jennifer wants to come too, that's cool.'

She'd come – just as I'd hoped – but unfortunately she'd

also brought the rest of her cult. Still, my plan was mostly a success. I had Jennifer in front of me, so close I could see the little mole under her left ear. I wanted to taste it.

Project Jennifer had made a lot of progress in the three weeks since the Godwins had been to our house for dinner. Jennifer was much friendlier now, and we talked a lot more at school. It still wasn't easy, especially with Jane around. I kept hoping Jane would come down with mono, or some sickness that would keep her bed-ridden at home, just for a little while, like three or four months. But no such luck. Jane was like an alien force field, trying to keep me away from Jennifer. At school, whenever I started walking towards their group, Jane would spot me coming and wave and call, 'Hey, *Ben!*' in this super mocking way.

At first, that alone was powerful enough to repel me. But after pondering it for a few days, and jotting ideas in my logbook, I just clenched my teeth into a big smile, waved back, and said in an even louder voice, 'Hey, *Jane!*' And somehow that seemed to confuse and silence her for a few moments – long enough for me to get into the inner circle and start talking to Jennifer.

By now, my logbook was filling up, so I usually had something pretty interesting to talk about. Even so, I had a lot of competition. She was very popular, and there were a bunch of other guys in our grade who talked to her. It seemed so effortless for them. Most of them had been at the school for ever, like her. I'd just been dropped in, like a paratrooper behind enemy lines.

But I had something over these other guys: I was friends

with Jennifer's brother, a grade nine, a high-ranking male. Twice he'd invited me over to his house, just to hang out, play Risk, kick a soccer ball around in the park. Sometimes Hugh would be there too. Sometimes Jennifer. One time she'd even played Risk with us (we made a secret pact and wiped David off the face of the planet).

And here we were now, all together, thanks to the plan I'd formulated in my Project Jennifer logbook, line by line, like a scientific experiment. We were having a group date.

Actually, Jennifer and I were having a date, and everyone else was just cover – but no one knew this except me.

The movie was a lot of fun. David, Hugh and I cheered the sword fights, and hooted at the corny dialogue. Afterwards we walked out, blinking, into the bright sunlight of early April.

'That was so cheesy,' said Hugh.

'I liked it,' said Shannon shyly.

'No way!' sneered Jane.

It was unusual for Shannon to say anything, ever, and when I saw her face fall, I felt sorry for her.

'I liked it too,' I said. 'It was a blast. What's not to like? Exotic locations, monsters, sword fights.'

'I thought it was magical,' said Shannon, giving me a grateful smile.

'That evil chick was pretty foxy,' said David, finishing the last of his popcorn and tossing the carton into a trash can. 'Six arms. That could come in handy.'

'I couldn't get over their hair,' said Jennifer. 'Sinbad looked like one of the Bee Gees.'

We still had an hour before our parents were supposed to pick us up.

'You want to go look at the record shops on Johnson?' I said, following Step Six of my plan.

'Sounds good,' said Jennifer, giving me an approving nod. Jennifer liked shopping. I had more than fifty references to shopping in the logbook.

As we walked down the street we stopped at a bunch of places, and I casually watched Jennifer: the clothes she touched, the jewellery she pointed out to Shannon and Jane, the records she pulled off the shelf. I filed it all away.

'Oh my God,' I heard her say. 'Check this out.' She was holding up an ABBA album I hadn't seen before.

'This is their live recording from their big Stockholm concert,' she said. 'I didn't even think you could get this here.' She flipped it over. 'It's not even in English!'

'That would be Swedish,' said Hugh, glancing over her shoulder.

'I know it's Swedish, Hugh, thanks,' she said sarcastically.

'Buy it,' said Jane.

She shook her head. 'I haven't got enough. Anyway, it's way too much.'

'That's a bummer,' I said, giving an inner shout of triumph.

And then we had to get going so our parents could pick us up.

'We need to start filming him,' Dad said at the Sunday meeting.

There I was, sitting on the living-room floor near Peter, my own little notepad open, pen at the ready. It was my third meeting and I was still feeling pretty pleased with myself. Just me and the university students, in one of the world's most groundbreaking experiments in linguistics and primatology.

'Up till now we've just been recording his signs in our daily logs,' Dad continued. 'But our grant proposal's coming up, and I want it as strong as possible.'

Everyone knew about the grant. The big one. It came from the Canadian government, and it was supposed to be a ton of money. Dad wanted it. The university wanted it, too – not just because it would save them money, but because it was prestigious.

'So,' Dad said, 'I want unassailable data. I want everyone to be able to *see* Zan signing. And that means video, so it can be interpreted by impartial third parties.'

'I think that's a really excellent idea, Professor Tomlin,' said Susan Wilkes, one of the student researchers. She agreed with everything Dad said. She was pretty, in a bland, thin-lipped kind of way, but the worshipful gaze she always fixed on Dad creeped me out. I think it creeped Mom out a bit too, because sometimes I'd catch her giving Susan a look.

'Who's going to do the filming?' asked Ryan Cross, one of the other students.

Ryan was Dad's star graduate student. Dad was always talking about how promising he was and how brilliant his last term paper was, and how he had all the right stuff to become a real scientist. I wished he'd praise Peter a bit more too, since he was by far the best at teaching Zan.

'We're going to install several cameras in his suite,' Mom said. 'And they'll film continuously during the day.'

It was weird to imagine surveillance cameras in Zan's room. It made it seem a bit like a laboratory – or a prison.

Ryan was nodding and making notes. I could see why Dad liked him. He was very calm and confident.

Peter cleared his throat. 'A lot of the signing happens spontaneously,' he said, 'just when we're playing with him. You know, just fooling around, especially out in the back yard.'

Dad nodded. 'I appreciate that. It just means we'll have to keep Zan in the playroom more. The cameras will be virtually hidden, so he won't notice them and get distracted. And we'll set the cameras at three different angles, so they should capture most of his signing, as long as he's at his desk.'

Desk? I looked at Peter and our eyes met. I knew what he was thinking. If Dad spent just a fraction more time with Zan, he'd know what a bad idea this was. Mom should have known better, though. I wondered if she'd talked about it with Dad, or maybe he'd just over-ruled her. I glanced around at the other students. A lot of them were looking at their shoes and scratching their noses awkwardly, but no one said anything.

Susan nodded enthusiastically. 'At a desk it'll be much easier for us to monitor and record his signing.'

Peter said, 'I think it might cut down on how much Zan actually signs.'

Dad looked up from his notepad. 'Why's that, Peter?'

Dad had this terrifying stare. I wasn't sure if he *knew* he was doing it, but he'd look over the top of his glasses and just lift his eyebrows a bit and wait. I was pretty impressed with Peter, standing up to Dad. I didn't think I could've done it.

'He doesn't really like sitting at the desk,' Peter answered. 'It's probably, like, his least favourite place. In fact, he hates the desk.' He looked around at the other students. 'Come on, guys, let's be honest. How long can you get him to sit in a chair?'

Dad smiled pleasantly. 'I'm sure we can think of ways to modify his behaviour at the table. He's making significant progress, and I wouldn't want to see that change.'

Dad was in full Doctor mode, using all his scientific words. *Significant* progress? I would've said *fantastic* or *amazing*, but to Dad it was just something to note down and chart on a graph.

'The desk might actually *enhance* his progress,' Ryan commented.

'We've brought him to two-word phrases,' Dad said, 'and his rate of sign acquisition is increasing sharply. He's smart. And he's older now too, so I think he should be able to work at the table for an hour in the morning, and an hour in the afternoon, after a good long break.'

Zan wasn't even a year old and Dad wanted him to sit at a table for a whole hour? But I shouldn't have been surprised. Zan wasn't allowed to just be Zan. He needed to produce data.

I looked over at Susan, who was still nodding and smiling. Peter said nothing more, but he was busy making notes. He seemed to be writing an awful lot, and he looked angry.

'Zan's at twelve signs now,' Dad was saying. 'If he continues at his current trajectory, he should be at twenty, twenty-five signs by his birthday. Twenty-five words for a one-year-old. That's pretty good for a *human* child. You're doing great work, everyone. Well done. Any other questions?'

No one had any.

On Wednesday morning, I got to homeroom early and left the record on her desk, wrapped up with a little note inside that just said: *For your listening pleasure. Happy Birthday. Ben.*

And then I sat down and waited, with my history binder open so it looked like I was studying. From the corner of my eye I watched as she came in and saw the present. Her eyes went all wide. She unwrapped the record, gave a gasp, said, 'No way!' and then read my note. She turned and gave me the best smile.

'You are so nice!' she said.

I'd gone back to the store and bought the live ABBA album she'd admired. Now that I was getting paid for Project Zan, I had some money to throw around. I couldn't think of a better way to blow it.

'Hey, no problem,' I said. 'The guy said it was probably the only copy in Canada.'

'You're kidding!' she said, clutching the record.

'That's what he said. A friend of his bought it in Sweden.'

'This is so cool. Thanks, Ben!'

And right there in class she looked at me and made the sign for *kiss*, just like I'd taught her.

CHAPTER 10

REMARKABLE RESULTS

'How do you feel about your math marks, Ben?' Dad asked.

It was Saturday. Mr Greensmith had sent home a letter yesterday, because I'd nearly failed two tests in a row. Dad had been out late at some work thing, and hadn't seen the letter until this morning. We were getting Zan's room ready for a teaching session, moving the table and chairs into position for the cameras, loading up the fun box.

How did I feel about my math marks?

It wasn't Dad's style to come right out and say he was disappointed or angry. It was some kind of psychologist thing, I guessed. He wanted to know how I *felt* about the marks – as a self-improving exercise. He wanted me to look deep into myself and make the startling discovery that my marks were crap, that I'd messed up, and needed to try harder next time.

I took a breath and said, 'Well, to be honest, they exceeded my expectations.'

He looked up at me sharply. 'They did, did they?'

'I was pretty sure I was going to flunk both of them. But I scraped through.'

'And you feel OK about a C minus?'

I shrugged. 'I'm no good at math.'

'No. You don't *care* about math. Honestly, Ben, a chimp could get better marks than this.'

'Why don't you teach Zan, then?'

'If you need help, you just have to ask me,' he said.

That made me angry. Dad did sometimes help, but he wasn't around much, even in the evenings. He had meetings and a night class, and he was all tied up with his own work. Anyway, I didn't like the way he helped me. He'd sit there and tell me I was messy and get me to erase things and start again more neatly. And he almost always shouted.

'It's not like your second-term report card was any great shakes either,' Dad said.

'I guess no one cares about the A I got in gym,' I mumbled.

'You're a smart kid, Ben. You should be getting much better marks.'

I wasn't convinced I was that smart; and I didn't know how much better I could do. Or even how hard I wanted to try.

'Maybe we're asking too much of you with Project Zan,' Dad said.

I looked at him, wondering if this was a threat. 'No, I like doing it,' I said.

'I know you like doing it. But your schoolwork should take priority.'

'OK, yeah,' I said miserably. 'I'll try harder.'

'And what about all these detentions? Six this term. What's that about?'

I just shrugged. There was no way I could tell him about my strategy of being a dominant male. It was working, but sometimes there was a price to pay.

'We're going to keep a very close eye on your grades,' Dad said.

He kept saying 'we', but I wondered if Mom was really in on this too.

'And if we don't see an improvement, we're going to scale back your time with Zan.'

Suddenly I was furious. He was using Zan like a reward! Zan wasn't something that you could take away or give. He was part of the family. Just because my marks were crappy, he couldn't separate me from Zan.

I said, 'You're the one who wanted me to go to Windermere.'

'You didn't seem to mind the idea,' he said.

He was right about that, but I wasn't going to admit it. 'It was more important to you. So you could look good with your boss.'

One of the things I'd learned from Dad was how to watch and listen and figure out how to get under someone's skin. It worked.

For the first time, Dad looked angry. But he managed to keep his voice calm.

'Ben, I am not paying these fees so you can goof off. If I

don't see some major progress I'm taking you out. You can say goodbye to David and Jennifer Godwin, and go straight to Brentwood school and *hang out* with your construction-site pals.'

'Maybe you should accept you've got a stupid son,' I said, and wanted to add: *But there's probably an experiment you can do to make me smarter.*

'That's enough, Ben,' he snapped, and I knew it was time to stop.

Just then Mom came in with Zan, walking hand in hand. He'd finished his breakfast, and was all cleaned up.

'You guys all ready?' Mom asked.

'All ready,' Dad replied.

Zan looked from me to Dad, then back to me again, and it was like he knew exactly what had passed between us. Maybe he could sense or smell it. He reached out his arms to me for a hug. I picked him up.

'Don't pick him up unless he signs,' Dad told me.

I put him back down.

Dad flicked a switch on the wall and started the cameras. It had been two weeks since we'd started filming everything, and Zan was signing less. Peter had noticed it, and everyone else had too. So Dad wanted to take Zan through a session himself and evaluate the situation.

We got Zan seated on his chair, opposite me and Dad. Dad wanted me around because Zan usually misbehaved when he was alone with him, and Dad knew I'd help keep him seated and happy. I thought it was pretty rich that Dad ticked me off for not doing better at school, and then expected me to help him with his research.

Zan always looked a bit forlorn sitting in his chair. He was still so small and his head barely cleared the table. He signed *out* to me, but I shook my head and told him to wait.

From the fun box on the floor, Dad took out Zan's favourite baby doll and put it on the table. Usually this would trigger all sorts of signs. You could *give* the baby and *hide* the baby and put the baby *up* and put the baby *down* and *hug* the baby.

But Zan just looked at it like he'd never seen it before in his life.

He turned to me and signed *out* again. He wanted to play outside.

Dad waited a minute and then signed *baby* himself, trying to cue Zan.

Zan stared at him blankly. And suddenly I wondered if he was punishing Dad for being mean to me. Was he saying, *I'm not doing squat unless you start being nicer to Ben?* It was crazy, probably, but thinking it made me feel kind of happy.

Then Zan got off his chair. Dad picked him up and put him back on.

'Sit, Zan,' he said, making the signs.

Dad put the baby away. From the fun box, he took a cup and a bottle of ginger ale – Zan's favourite drink. Usually just the sight of the bottle was enough to start him begging. Today he stared at it without any interest. Dad poured himself a drink, raised it to his mouth, and had a sip, making appreciative smacking noises.

Zan scampered off his chair.

Dad put him back on and said sternly, 'Sit, Zan!'

Zan sat.

Dad got out the music box, which we were using to teach Zan the sign for *listen*. Zan loved it when we wound it up and the tune came scrolling out from somewhere inside the box. But today, Zan couldn't have looked more bored.

'I don't think he's in the mood,' I told Dad.

'Clearly not,' said Dad, looking at me like I was somehow responsible, like it was something Zan and I had cooked up just to annoy him.

Part of me wanted Zan to perform, because I was suddenly scared that if he didn't, Dad might punish him. Make him sit in the chair all morning, or go without lunch.

And the other part of me was full of admiration. Zan could talk, but he was choosing not to.

He was saying he didn't feel like it. He was saying no.

He was giving my father the finger.

I wished I had Zan's courage.

A couple of days later, Peter called in sick, so Mom had to fill in for him. When I got home after school, she was wiped out. She'd done a double shift, and Zan had been acting up all day. He'd thrown his food and ripped off his diaper and peed on the floor, and he'd been aggressive with one of the new students.

That night I put him to bed, and he was so exhausted he was asleep the moment he was in his pyjamas and had the bottle to his lips. Looking at his small, sleeping

132

body, it was hard to imagine he was capable of such mischief.

Later that night, I woke up to Mom and Dad having an argument in their bedroom. They always seemed to have them at night, I guess so I wouldn't hear. But usually I woke up anyway, and stood by my door so I could hear better.

Sometimes I wondered if they liked fighting. Mom was pretty dramatic and usually did most of the talking. Dad was calm and soft spoken. When I was younger, I used to feel sorry for Dad, because I'd hear him talking less and less, and I'd imagine him getting kind of worn out and saggy. But I was wrong. Dad was like a camel. He paced himself. He could go on for ever with very little food or water and save his energy and stay strong. It was hard to know who won most of the fights, but I figured it was usually Dad.

'You never play with him,' Mom was saying.

'He doesn't need me to play with him,' Dad said.

I was confused. Were they talking about me?

'And when you do,' Mom went on, 'it's to test him. I don't think that's healthy for the relationship.'

'What's this really about?' said Dad, in his infuriating psychologist's voice. 'You had a hard day. I appreciate that, Sarah. Zan acted up and you had to take an extra shift, and you're exhausted.'

'You can't dismiss it that easily, Richard,' Mom argued. 'You set this thing in motion, you can't just walk away from it.'

'How on earth am I walking away?' he said. 'I'm overseeing this entire experiment. I don't need to be in the trenches every day collecting data. That's what the students do.'

In the *trenches*? Was that really how Dad saw spending time with Zan?

'This experiment,' said Mom, 'relies on cross-fostering. Raising Zan human. You are supposed to be his *father*. Now, how would you describe being a father – I'm just interested to know. What kind of obligations and responsibilities and activities does that entail? In your esteemed opinion?'

She was sounding pretty sarcastic, and I heard Dad give an impatient sigh. 'In the wild, the fathers don't have anything to do with the babies. They don't even know who the fathers are mostly. Zan gravitates more naturally to his mother and siblings. Ben, Peter, the others – they're surrogate siblings and playmates. And he's got you. That's what he needs. That's natural.'

'But teaching him human language is not. You can't have it both ways, Richard. Are we raising him like a chimp or a human?'

'You're suggesting I'm a weak father figure for him.' Was that amusement in Dad's voice?

Mom said, 'He certainly hasn't bonded with you. That doesn't bother you?'

'No,' said Dad.

Mom muttered something that sounded like 'No surprise there.'

'Look, I'm sorry you had a hard day.'

There was a pause and I was hoping he'd say something nice – not so much about Mom, but about Zan. What he said next was, 'I regret not getting a female.'

Mom said nothing.

Dad went on. 'I heard they were more compliant – but what could I do? All they had available was a male, and we couldn't wait for ever.'

I felt sick. Didn't Dad feel *anything* for Zan? How could he just wish for another chimp – an easier chimp – just like that?

'Zan's not the problem,' said Mom. 'You've got to be more involved.'

'I don't have time. Anyway, I'm not an animal person, you know that.'

'Zan thinks he's human.'

'We talked about this at the outset,' Dad said. 'We talked about the risks of getting sentimental about the subject.'

'Sentimental,' said Mom disdainfully. 'Is every kind of emotion *sentimental* for you?'

'We knew it would interfere with the experiment,' Dad persisted.

Mom snorted. 'I don't think that was ever a risk for you, Richard. But, yes, it's a risk for me, and it's certainly a risk for Ben.'

'Ben will adjust,' Dad said.

I wasn't quite sure what they were talking about now, and I frowned, listening hard. But they must have moved off into the bathroom, or they were talking more quietly now, because I couldn't hear any more.

I went back to bed, but it took me a long time to get to sleep.

* * *

135

The next morning I woke up early. It was six thirty and the house was quiet. I didn't hear any hooting noises coming from the baby monitor, so Zan must've been asleep too.

But I remembered how he'd been sick in the summer, and I felt anxious after all of Mom and Dad's arguing in the night. Still in my pyjamas, I went downstairs, unlocked the door to Zan's suite, and quietly went in. I thought he'd like it if I was there when he woke up. It would be a surprise, and I could imagine his eyes going all wide and how he'd give an excited pant-hoot and fling himself into my arms. I wanted his body against me.

I walked through the playroom and silently opened the door to his bedroom. The sun was on the rise and, even though the curtains were still drawn, there was plenty of gentle light in the room.

I was surprised to see Zan already awake, sitting up in his bed, his back to me. He was playing with his dolls. He'd arranged them in a semicircle around himself: the baby, the chimp, the chick, GI Joe.

He was *signing* to them.

With one hand he offered the chick his empty bottle of milk, and with his free hand he signed *drink*. He held the bottle to the chick's mouth for a moment, then dropped it impatiently and signed *hug*. He picked up the chick and clutched it to his chest.

As I stood there, watching in wonder, Zan turned to look at me. His expression said: *Can I help you?*

I almost felt like I should apologize for interrupting, and

come back later. I was hoping he'd turn back to his toys and keep signing. But now that Zan had seen me, he lost interest in his dolls. With a hoot he stood and scampered towards me, arms raised to be picked up. I waited until he signed *hug* before I lifted him.

I changed his puffy diaper, my mind buzzing the whole time with what I'd just seen. He'd been talking to his toys, trying to teach them language!

I heard Mom in the kitchen, and right away carried Zan out to tell her. She seemed as excited as I was, and we hurried upstairs to tell Dad. He was in his boxer shorts, buttoning up his shirt, when we all barged in.

'I'd love to get that on film,' he said. 'I wonder if we can rig up a camera in his room.'

'It means he's not just imitating us,' said Mom.

'Or doing it for reward,' he added excitedly. 'He's applying it spontaneously, in different contexts.'

'He really is remarkable,' I said to Dad. 'Isn't he?'

Dad looked at me for a moment, then winked. 'He is, Ben. He's remarkable.'

CHAPTER 11

NEW DATA

She let me kiss her.

It's weird, but that's how I thought about it.

Not *we kissed* or *she kissed me back* but: *she let me kiss her.*

It was at the dance, Friday night.

Earlier, when Mom had dropped me at the Cordova Heights Rec Centre, I'd spotted Jennifer way back in the parking lot, with David and Hugh and some of their other friends. Maybe they were doing a bit of drinking before they came inside. I thought about going over, but I didn't want it to look like I was squeezing in on them, uninvited. I wondered why they hadn't mentioned anything to me. *Hey, Tarzan, meet us back in the parking lot for some liquid refreshment.* So I just headed for the main doors and went inside.

There were a bunch of other private schools at the dance, and it was crowded. I milled around trying to find people I knew, and it seemed to take ages before I finally spotted

Jennifer, dancing with Hugh. It was a great song and she looked like she was having a really good time, and I wished it was me out there with her.

I found David standing on the sidelines with Evan.

'Tarzan, hey!' he said, waving me over.

We talked a bit, but the music was so loud we were shouting into each other's ears. His eyes kept darting all over the place. I smelled booze on his breath.

'You tanked up, Tarzan?' he asked. 'You imbibe some European cocktails with your *très* groovy parents?'

I shook my head. I didn't feel like I needed *anything* to drink. The music pulsed through me, up through the floor, the bass thumping in the centre of my chest like a bigger, better heart. I was in this fabulous cave of sound and shadow and light. I wanted to get out there on the dance floor.

When ABBA's 'Waterloo' came on I started walking out towards Jennifer to ask her, but she didn't see me, and kept dancing with Hugh. So I spotted Selena Grove, who was pretty cute, and asked her to dance. I caught Jennifer's eye and she waved at me and beamed, which made me feel great.

The song went fast, these big bright, loud moments all jammed together. Dancing, sound swirling, shouting to be heard, arms pumping, light everywhere like confetti, the acrid smell of dry ice, a whiff of shampoo as a girl whirled past. And the music hurtling you through it all.

After Selena, I danced with Jennifer a few times. I wondered if she'd had something to drink too, because she seemed more affectionate than usual, grabbing my arms and jumping up and down.

Afterwards, she went back to Shannon and Jane and they all hugged each other. I hung out with them for a bit, but it was frustrating because it was really hard to hear, and mostly they seemed to be laughing at bad dancers or complaining about the square music the DJ was playing.

I didn't want to look like a barnacle on Jennifer, so I went off to get a drink and then danced with some other girls, and talked to some of the guys from my grade. On one side of the hall was a kind of observation gallery and I could see people up there in the near-dark, making out. I wished I could take Jennifer's hand and lead her up there too – but maybe not. Maybe that was more for professional making out, and I wouldn't know what I was doing. It looked pretty intense.

As I stood around in the shadows I ran into David again. I got the feeling he didn't like dancing that much.

'Where's Hugh?' I shouted into his ear.

He pointed at the observation gallery.

'Up there?' I said, surprised. 'Who with?'

'Kelly Browne.'

She was a grade nine girl. 'He likes Kelly Browne?'

David shrugged. 'He does tonight.'

Towards the end, the DJ was pumping out some really far-out music, and the dry-ice machine was belching fog so the auditorium looked like a scene from a Dracula movie. Coloured searchlights swept the room. Civilization had totally broken down and you could get away with anything.

140

As the strobe lights started going I found Jennifer and pulled her into the thickest part of the fog. She was laughing and her eyes were super bright and her cheeks were flushed and I just wanted to stare and stare.

She said something to me that I couldn't hear.

'What?' I shouted, leaning closer.

'Stop staring at me!' she shouted back.

'OK,' I said, and kissed her.

I didn't know how good a kiss it was, because it was my first. Her mouth was moving a little bit against mine, but I wasn't sure if it was excited moving or just polite moving. Her lips were soft and warm and tasted like lemonade, and something hotter and harsher underneath.

'Whoa, tiger,' she said, grabbing me gently by the hair and pushing my head back. 'Is my lip gloss smushed?'

'I don't care about your lip gloss.'

'I do,' she said, running her index finger round the edges of her lips.

I saw her glance off to the sides, like she was wondering if anyone had seen. The fast song ended and they started playing 'Stairway to Heaven'.

'You going to ask me to dance?' she said, tilting her head.

'You want to dance?' I asked.

I held her and we moved back and forth. I didn't kiss her any more because the fog was seeping away and I felt self-conscious.

'Stairway to Heaven' is eight minutes, two seconds long. I know because when I got home later that night, I took out the album and checked, then played the song very quietly into the headphones so I wouldn't wake Mom and Dad. Just over eight minutes.

I'd held her for every second.

Saturday was my morning with Zan – and today, Peter was sharing the shift with me. We got Zan up and fed him and took him outside to play, our logbooks and pens always at the ready. I was getting pretty good at recording information. I'd found it hard at first, because a lot of things could happen really close together, but over the weeks Mom and Peter had given me some pointers, and the pages of my logbook weren't a total mess any more.

Right now, Zan was watching the birds come and eat from the feeders hanging from a couple of our trees.

I kept stretching and yawning and muttering 'Man,' over and over again.

'You tired?' Peter finally asked.

I looked over. 'Hmm? I didn't get much sleep. There was a dance last night.'

'Any good?'

'Pretty good,' I said. I'd been hoping he'd ask. I liked Peter a lot, and imagined he had an exciting life with lots of girls and parties.

'Jennifer Godwin and I made out a bit.'

'Well, well, well,' he said, nodding. I'd already told him a little about her. 'Quite the ladykiller.'

'Not really.' I couldn't imagine talking about this with Dad

– especially since Jennifer was the daughter of his boss. There might be a rule against that. Peter was only seven years older than me; he was a guy and he'd understand. 'Hey, can I ask you something?'

'Shoot,' he said.

'What I don't get,' I said, 'is what happens next.'

'What do you mean?'

'Well, like, should I be getting her flowers or chocolates and stuff?'

Peter stared at me. 'Are you *marrying* her?'

'No!'

'I don't think you need to send her flowers. Why not just take her out on a date?'

'She's not allowed to go out until she's sixteen.'

'Ah.'

'We go out as a group sometimes,' I said. 'Did you have a girlfriend in grade eight?'

He looked shocked. 'Me? No way. At your age I was a nerd.'

Now it was my turn to look shocked. Peter was my idea of cool. He was relaxed and smart and he was really good with Zan, and I thought the way he dressed was right on too. After some of the Sunday meetings, Dad and Mom (Mom's idea, for sure) usually let the students have a drink and stay and smoke and talk, and Peter sometimes brought his guitar. He could play pretty much any song you wanted, and could do it by ear. When I watched him, I wished I could play a musical instrument. Guitar looked hard. How could he not be cool?

'No way,' I said.

'Yes way,' he said. 'Thirteen, I was a disaster zone. Yellow police tape all around me. *Do Not Enter.*'

'Why?'

'I was *weird*, man.'

'What did you do?'

'I had ant farms and stuff. And newts. And two iguanas. My room smelled. No one wanted to come in. Especially girls. Not that I invited any.'

'Are you going out with someone now?'

I'd always assumed Peter was going steady with one of those really smart, sultry girls you saw on campus. They had long hair, and John Lennon glasses – the glasses just made you want to take them off so you could see how super amazing they were underneath.

Peter shook his head. 'Not at the moment, alas. Couple of years back I went out with this girl named Suzanne. But that wasn't really anything – well, nothing good.' He kind of shuddered. 'Not for either of us. My advice to you is to play it cool. Just, you know, hang out together. Get to know her. You're *thirteen*, man!'

Playing it cool. That seemed like good advice. I wondered if I could take it.

That night at dinner, Zan was awful.

He wailed in his high chair and threw his food and spilled his water. Mom and I tried our best to make him happy, but nothing worked. It was impossible to talk: Zan was making so much noise. I could hardly eat my own food, I was so busy picking up spoons and forks and wiping vegetable goo off my arm and cheek. Across the table Dad got grumpier and angrier until his face looked hard as concrete.

'Maybe we should give him Jell-O,' I said to Mom.

Someone had told us that chimps loved Jell-O, and it turned out they were right. Zan was crazy about it. We often served it to him as dessert.

'But he's eaten nothing,' said Mom, shaking her head in dismay.

Very slowly, Dad said, 'Give. Him. The frickin' Jell-O.'

I went to the fridge and scooped some green Jell-O into a plastic bowl. I put it in front of Zan.

He fell silent, looking at it jiggle. I exhaled. The Jell-O never let us down.

But before I could spoon some into his mouth, Zan grabbed the entire quivering blob and whipped it across the table. It hit Dad right in the face and kind of exploded over his forehead and hair.

We all sat there, staring. Even Zan seemed a little stunned, but only for a second, and then he was hooting and rocking his high chair back and forth. Mom and I started laughing. Dad chuckled as he mopped up his face with his napkin – but it sounded forced.

'I guess Zan didn't like his Jell-O,' Mom said.

Zan brushed the tip of his nose with his index finger, twice, then twice more.

Funny.

He'd signed *funny!*

'Yes!' I said to him. 'Funny!'

We'd been using that sign with him for months now, whenever we were laughing together. We'd told him that tickling was funny. Putting his doll in the toilet was funny. Making silly faces was funny. This was something he'd never seen before – Jell-O on Dad. But, instinctively, he knew this was funny too.

Funny! I signed back to him.

'You should sign it too,' I said to Dad, who was still wiping Jell-O out of his eyes. 'To reinforce it.'

'Our little scientist,' said Mom with a smile.

'Yes, of course. *Funny*,' Dad signed. His big, fake smile finally turned into a real one as we all started laughing, and I felt a rush of happiness.

After Mom had put Zan to sleep, we were all in the living room. Mom was reading some scientific journal, and Dad was looking over a ream of computer printouts. I was finishing some homework, but kept wondering what Jennifer was doing. Was she at home, or out with her friends? Was she thinking of me? Was she thinking of our kiss?

After a while Dad said, 'Zan's signing has definitely taken a sharp decrease over the past three weeks.'

'He doesn't like sitting at the desk,' I told him. This was old news. The only person who claimed Zan signed better at the desk was Ryan Cross, but I was pretty sure he was lying.

'It's the most controlled way of teaching him, Ben,' said Dad. 'The most effective way. There's no way around it. The real issue is his behaviour.'

'What do you mean?' said Mom, frowning.

146

'Discipline,' Dad said. 'We've got to be firmer, or he's going to think he runs the place. He's a male chimp and he's already starting to exhibit all the characteristics of an alpha male.'

'How can *he* be the alpha male if *you're* the alpha male?' Mom asked, and there was an amused and slightly challenging tone to her voice.

'We need to be firmer with him,' Dad repeated.

'I do, you mean,' she said.

'*All* of us have to be firmer,' said Dad. 'Or else his behaviour, and his learning, will deteriorate. Dinner tonight was *appalling*.'

Mom rolled her eyes. 'He's only ten months old, Richard.'

'I bet I was pretty noisy when I was that old,' I said, looking hopefully at Mom. 'Wasn't I?' I hated to think Dad thought Zan was really bad.

'You certainly were,' said Mom, giving me a kind smile.

'The issue's a larger one,' said Dad. 'I think it's time to add another shift during the day, and include Sundays. We can get the students to give Zan a separate dinner in his suite and put him to bed at night.'

In alarm I looked from Dad to Mom. 'But I *want* Zan to have dinner with us,' I said. 'During the week, I don't see him that much because of school.' And when I got home there were students with him until six. 'The evenings are the only time we're all together – and Sundays.'

'Zan takes a lot of energy,' Dad said. 'Especially for your mother. We need more help.'

'I don't think it's necessary,' said Mom.

'We talked about this at the outset,' Dad said. 'It was always the plan to increase the shifts to provide total care for Zan.'

I didn't remember any mention of this. I guessed this was just one of the many things they'd decided without me.

'But I'll hardly get to see him!' I protested.

Dad just said, 'We're scientists, Ben, not zookeepers.'

'That's not the way it is, though,' I said. I was really angry and trying to keep my thoughts straight, but my head was jumbled with images of the day Mom brought Zan home, and we were all looking at him asleep in her arms, and he was like a baby come home from the hospital. How Dad said he was more my little brother than my pet. Mom letting him suck at her breast . . .

'We're supposed to raise him like a human, for the good of the experiment.' I threw that last bit in for Dad, so it didn't sound like I was being sentimental. So it sounded scientific. 'Human kids eat with their parents.'

Dad sniffed and shook his head. 'Ben, when I was a kid I had a separate dinner. Your mom too. When we got more civilized, then we ate at the table with the adults. Zan's not there yet – as we saw from the Jell-O incident. At the end of the day, I think I'm entitled to a civilized meal.'

I said nothing, I was still too angry.

Mom was watching me. 'I think we could work out a schedule so we have Zan with us some nights, and other nights we get the students to feed him separately. But I think it's important we're the ones to put him to bed at night. At night he needs us.'

Dad grunted. But he didn't say no, and I realized we'd scored a little victory.

But I also knew something had changed. Maybe not for Dad, but for me. I finally realized something. As far as Dad was concerned, Zan had never been a beloved little baby. Zan was, and only ever would be, a specimen.

Monday when I arrived at school, I was so nervous my joints felt like Jell-O.

'Hey, *Ben*!' Jane said with more of a sneer than usual. I supposed Jane and Shannon knew. Jennifer would have told them right away. It took all my determination to keep walking towards their little group in the hallway – Jane's force field was very powerful today.

'Hey,' I said casually to Jennifer, and then our eyes went elsewhere. I'd hoped that, after our kiss, we'd have this amazing unspoken bond, and electricity would be coursing between us. But things seemed worse now, much worse. All the good opening lines I'd prepared in my logbook evaporated inside my head. I just stood there listening to her talk to her friends, and wishing the bell would hurry up and go.

As I made my way to homeroom, I suddenly felt paranoid. Everyone was looking at me. How many people knew? Had she told David? She didn't need to. All it would take was one person to spread it through the whole school. Jane would do that, no problem.

Over the weekend, I'd thought I wanted everyone to know I kissed her. But what if she'd told her friends I was a bad kisser?

Or she hadn't wanted to kiss me but she was just being polite and now everyone would think I was a total nerd?

Later that morning, as I was changing for gym, Mike Heaman said, 'So, you and Jennifer Godwin. Good going, Tomlin.' He didn't sound sarcastic, but genuinely admiring.

'Yeah, well,' I said, tying my shoelaces. Playing it cool.

'So are you two going out now?'

'Nah. I mean, she's not allowed to go out till she's sixteen. Parents.'

'Oh yeah?' He didn't look convinced by this.

I was kind of late getting to lunch that day, and David and Hugh were just leaving. David nodded his head in greeting but didn't say anything. Maybe it was best that way. A big group of grade tens came in and filled up the middle of the table, so I sighed and headed down to hobbit-town.

'Hey, Ben,' said Henry Gardner, handing me a platter. There was one French fry left. I put it on my plate.

'Kill it, you fill it,' said one of his nerdy friends, and guffawed.

'Yep,' I said, getting up.

After lunch, I was on the way to math class when Andrew Rees said, 'Hey, Tomlin, nice work,' and winked at me.

Between geography and science, Mark Curtis said, 'She's quite the babe, Tomlin.'

My alpha-male pride was feeling pretty stoked by the end of the day.

After final period, as I was getting stuff from my locker, Jennifer came up to me without Jane or Shannon attached to her.

'Hey,' she said, smiling, and I felt this wave of happiness crest over me. Palm trees sprang up and sand spread out to the blue sea.

'Hey,' I said, and had to fight hard not to mention the dance. I wasn't going to be the first to do it. I was going to play it cool, just like Peter said.

'So, like, at the dance?' she said.

'Uh-huh,' I said helpfully.

A couple of people passed by, looking at us, and I felt pretty important, just hanging out and talking with Jennifer.

'That was fun, right?' she said.

'Oh yeah, it was fun,' I agreed, nodding.

'Just 'cause . . . well, it's not like we're going out or anything—'

'– because you can't go out till you're sixteen yeah – I know.'

'Right,' she said, looking surprised and almost relieved. 'OK, cool.'

'Absolutely,' I said.

'Great. You're the *best*, Ben!'

And she gave me a little hug, the kind she gave to her friends when they were all excited to see each other after a whole period apart.

'OK, see you!' she said brightly.

'See you!'

I went back to getting my books, trying to figure out what we'd just said to each other.

I decided I really had no idea what was going on.

* * *

When I got home, Dad's Mercedes was in the driveway, which was unusual. Normally he didn't get back from university until at least six. He was sitting in the living room with Mom, and he had a drink in his hand.

'What's wrong?' I asked, my heart thumping. 'Is Zan OK?'

'Zan's fine,' said Mom, and looked over at Dad. 'We just had some disappointing news about the project.'

'We didn't get our grant,' Dad said.

'The big one?' I said, and Mom nodded. I didn't understand. The way Dad had talked about it, it sounded like a sure thing. I remembered him and Professor Godwin discussing it at our place over dinner, laughing and drinking.

'What went wrong?' I asked.

Dad shook his head, his eyebrows lifting wearily. 'They saw the merit in the project but didn't find our initial data extensive enough.'

'But Zan's *talking*!' I said. What more did they want? We were teaching a chimpanzee to talk! He'd learned twenty-five words now. We had proof.

'I think they just wanted more data,' Mom said. 'And a slightly different design for the experiment.'

'So what's this mean?' I asked.

'It's a blow,' said Dad, taking another slug of his drink. 'We were counting on that money to keep the project running.'

'Can't the university just pay for it?' I asked.

There was an uncomfortable pause. 'Well,' said Mom, 'the university agreed to do it at the beginning—'

'But the understanding,' Dad said, 'was that we'd

152

win this grant that would cover pretty much everything.'

This sounded bad. 'Are we going to be poor?' I asked.

Mom laughed. 'No, no. It's not like *that*.'

Dad put down his glass and gave a sigh, but looked more determined. I could see a flame kindling in his eyes. 'We'll just have to do a lot more door-knocking. There're some smaller grants I can trigger, and the department will certainly tide us over until we can reapply for the big one. That's nine months. We'll need to have a fair amount of new supporting material to push it through.'

'You guys can do it,' I said. 'Zan's smart. He'll keep learning new words. He'll make a ton of progress.'

'Of course he will,' said Mom.

Dad grinned and lifted his glass. 'Here's to Zan,' he said.

Listen, Zan signed to me a few days later.

We were out in the back yard together after dinner. At first I heard nothing, then I heard the birdsong. I just nodded.

Bird, I signed absently. I was thinking of something else – my stupid math homework still waiting to be done, and Jennifer, always hovering in my thoughts: how to please her, how to make her crazy about me. How I should look. What I needed to say. How I had to be.

That stuff she'd said to me at my locker, I thought I got it. When she said, *We're not going out*, she hadn't meant she was *glad* we weren't. I figured she meant, since she wasn't sixteen, that we *had* to keep it secret. It was a *secret* romance. We just had to play it cool. Under the radar. If anything, it made it even more exciting.

Listen, Zan told me again, and with that one word, he seemed to be asking me to do more than just listen.

His gaze was intent. He often watched the birds in their feeders, flitting from branch to branch. It was like he really wanted me to understand how beautiful the birds were, and how happy it made him to hear them. He loved the birdsong and wanted to share it with me.

So I tried to listen like a chimp. I tried to imagine myself in his world, with his sharper eyes and ears, and keener sense of smell. And I sat beside him and just listened to the birds for a while.

Listen, said Zan once more, glancing over at me, as if he was worried I'd get distracted – like humans did – but I was still listening, noticing now how different all the bird sounds were, the notes, the tempo, the patterns.

We stared up at the trees for a long time, Zan and I, just listening.

CHAPTER 12

THE LEARNING CHAIR

Sunday afternoon the handyman came to set up the learning chair.

It had a wooden seat and back, but the rest was metal. It looked big and strong, and had a harness that buckled across the hips and shoulders. It was a chair that didn't take no for an answer. The handyman bolted it right into the floor of Zan's playroom – which was really more like his classroom now.

Afterwards Zan was happily climbing all over the chair like it was a new piece of playground equipment.

'You're going to strap him in there?' I asked Dad.

'Only when he's uncooperative.'

'But he's like a prisoner then!' I objected.

'Not at all,' said Dad. 'It's a consequence of bad behaviour. If he sits properly in the chair and does his work, we don't need to strap him in. The choice is his. He's a smart animal. He'll learn quickly.'

I looked over at Mom, wondering how she felt about this.

A lot of the time, Zan didn't want to learn. When we tried to shape his hands into the right signs, he'd often pull away, or think we were playing a game and start hooting softly with delight, tickling us back. Sometimes he'd just run off and do something else. I didn't blame him. I hated school too.

'Maybe some days he just doesn't want to be taught,' I said. 'He's not even a year old!'

Mom had said the same kind of thing once, in Zan's defence, so I was shocked now when she replied, 'We're going to try it, Ben.'

I could see Dad doing this, but not Mom. She looked very calm and matter-of-fact, but a bit strained. I bet she'd argued with Dad about this beforehand, and he'd talked her into it.

'The straps won't hurt him,' she said. 'Look, they're nice and padded. And Dad's right, he'll figure out pretty fast how to avoid them.'

I turned away from Mom, angry. Just looking at the chair made me feel sick.

'Ben,' she said gently. 'We all care about Zan. But this is a scientific experiment, and we need the grant to keep it going. Unless we get really good data from Zan, we might not get it.'

'You wouldn't do this to a human,' I said. 'You wouldn't do this to *me*.'

'Might be good for your marks,' Dad said, and he laughed and slapped me on the shoulder, but I didn't feel one bit better.

That evening at the weekly meeting, Dad told everyone about

not getting the grant. He was all energetic and enthusiastic and he made it sound like it was just a temporary setback. He talked about how it gave them a fabulous opportunity to strengthen their proposal. Then everyone filed into the playroom really quietly, because Zan was asleep, and Dad showed them the learning chair.

Back in the living room, Dad explained the need for the chair. As usual he was persuasive.

'Now, the harness is only to be used if Zan keeps getting up from the chair,' he said. 'Give him three warnings, and only after that do you strap him in.'

'Keep him in for just two minutes,' said Mom. 'Then let him out.'

'But if he gets up again,' Dad said, 'the harness goes back on, for an additional minute each time.'

None of the students said anything, not even Peter, which really surprised me. I kept watching him, hoping he'd protest. Mom and Dad already knew what I thought, so there was no point in me talking. It was Peter's turn now. But Peter kept staring at his notebook, writing – not even writing, I saw when I craned my neck. He was doodling over and over again until the lines were so dark the paper started to shred.

'OK,' said Dad, 'let's go over the new shift schedule . . .'

'Sorry, Professor Tomlin,' said Peter. 'Um, about the new chair.'

Dad looked up with that overly patient look he had when he was impatient. 'Yes, Peter.'

'I'm wondering if . . . my impression is . . .'

He faltered, and I suddenly knew why he hadn't said any-thing earlier. His voice was hoarse and kind of wobbly, like he was almost too angry to talk.

'Do you think,' he managed to get out, 'that the chair may be taking us in the wrong direction?'

'No, I don't,' said Dad. 'It's the right direction.'

'What I mean is, he's been signing less since we started working at the desk. That's, um, already been established. So I don't think Zan's going to want to sign any more just because he's strapped in.'

Dad's eyes widened. 'It's not my wish for him to be strapped in, Peter. I'd rather he's not. Give Zan the *guidance* he needs and he'll learn that the straps are unnecessary.' He looked around at his students earnestly. 'But that's up to each one of you.'

I thought it was a pretty dirty trick. Dad was making it sound like it was their fault if Zan didn't want to cooperate. Like they were bad babysitters and needed to pull their socks up.

'Zan trusts all of us,' said Peter. 'He might think of us as teachers, but way more like friends or brothers and sisters. Once we start strapping him in, it'll change the relationship.'

'Yes, but the relationship *needs* to change. You're not play-mates, you're caregivers. If he understands that, he'll respect you more.'

Peter said nothing for a moment, then, 'I don't think I'll be able to strap him in.'

Dad nodded. 'Well, you have an excellent relationship with Zan. Let's hope it's not necessary.'

'I mean,' Peter said, 'I won't put him in the straps.' His voice was firm now.

I counted the terrible seconds of silence. Ten . . . eleven . . . twelve.

To my surprise, Mom spoke before Dad.

'It's understandable some of you might feel uncomfortable about the straps. But I think we need to remember that Zan is a small child – *like* a small child,' she corrected, glancing at Dad, 'and sometimes they need a firm hand. If they know what's expected of them, they feel more secure.'

'The key is *consistency*,' Dad said, smiling at everyone. 'We need to make sure that Zan receives the same treatment from all of us. Then he'll know the rules, and what's expected of him, and we can get rid of the learning chair altogether. It's good for Zan and it's good for the project. Are you all right with that?'

'No, I'm not sure I am,' said Peter.

I really admired him, standing up to them like that. I thought he was super brave.

'Peter,' Dad said calmly, 'we're all scientists here. We are in pursuit of the truth, a truth that might have any number of benefits for humanity. Zan is a smart animal, but he's still an animal. He is not human, and he's not a person. Zan belongs to science. And for our experiment to proceed, we need results. I have no time for the sentimentality of animal activism, but if this is a question of conscience for you, I respect that, and you can resign from the project at any time.'

I held my breath – I think everyone in the room did – watching Peter. He couldn't quit. He was the best at working with Zan. He was the best at taking care of him. Zan loved him; he'd be devastated if Peter stopped coming. And so would I.

I looked at Dad. He was very composed. He looked like someone who knew he was going to win.

Peter just muttered that he'd need to think about it.

Before I went to bed, I got out the dictionary.

Dad had said Zan wasn't human. There was no arguing with that.

But not even a *person*? I was pretty sure that couldn't be right, and was disappointed when I read the definition.

An individual human being.

So you had to be human to be a person. It didn't seem fair. I tried to think of what *made* someone a person, the unique things. And it seemed like Zan had all of them. He had a distinct personality. He had favourite toys and games and food and drinks. He liked to play. Sometimes he liked to learn. He had friends. He had a family. He loved me and Mom and Peter. And he could *talk* to us, or was starting to, anyway. Day by day he could name more of the things around him, and tell us what he wanted – and even what he was thinking about. Like the birds in the back yard: *Listen.*

Weren't these the same kinds of things that made *me* a person? How was I any different? Maybe I was smarter and I could talk better, but I bet Zan was smarter about some things. He had better eyesight and smell, and one day he'd be stronger than me. Put me in a jungle and I'd seem like a total idiot. Being a person couldn't be just about how smart or strong you were.

But the dictionary said you had to be human to be a person.

Maybe the dictionary was wrong.

Tuesday after school, Peter and I were doing a four-to-eight shift together in the back yard. Dad had compromised about the new schedule. Four evenings a week, we had Zan on our own; three evenings, other students were with him and would give him his dinner and put him to bed. On Sunday no students came at all. Dad wasn't happy about it, but Mom had insisted. This time, she'd won.

It was May and the days were pretty warm now. Zan liked to play in the sandbox for a bit before we gave him his dinner.

Peter was still fuming about the learning chair. 'Why not just run some high voltage through it and call it an electric chair?' he said. 'Yeah, I'd learn really well, bolted into a chair like that.'

'You won't quit, will you?' I'd been worrying about it constantly the past couple days.

He sighed and filled another bucket of sand for Zan, signing *bucket*. 'I don't want to,' he said to me. 'But that chair . . .'

So far, it hadn't been a success. But Dad, and even Mom, had warned us it would be rocky at first. Zan hated being strapped in. He'd hated it on Monday, and he'd hated it earlier today. Apparently he hooted and then shrieked. He struggled. He wouldn't sign.

Peter said, 'I wonder if the whole project's screwed up.' He looked at me carefully. 'We're pals, right? You wouldn't rat me out to your dad?'

161

I shook my head.

'Yeah, I trust you. You're a good kid. I've just been reading a bunch of stuff on animal testing lately. And it's pretty awful. I mean, I used to think the space chimps were really cool. You've heard of them, right?'

I nodded. 'Ham and Enos. NASA blasted them up in rockets before humans.'

'The chimponauts,' said Peter.

'They were on the cover of *Life* magazine,' I said.

'But you know how they got those chimps?' he asked.

I shook my head.

'Well,' said Peter, 'African hunters would track down chimp mothers who had new babies. The chimps would be up in the trees and the hunters would shoot them down. The mothers would clutch their babies as they fell. Most of them died together when they hit the ground. But apparently some of the mothers tried to fall backwards so their bodies would shield the babies from the impact.'

I didn't say anything. It was too horrible.

'Any babies that survived,' Peter went on, 'the hunters tied up to a pole by their hands and feet. They'd walk them through the jungle to sell to European traders. Then they'd crate them up and ship them to the United States. I read that only one in ten babies survived the voyage. And those got to be guinea pigs for the astronauts.'

He told me about one test where they put the chimp to sleep, glued an oxygen mask over his face and crammed him in a capsule filled with water. Then they blasted him along the ground in a rocket sled, just to see how the body would react. That chimp never woke up. And Peter said there were lots of other tests they put the chimps through before NASA sent up Alan Shepard, the first man in space.

Peter shook his head. 'Everyone says, "Oh, but isn't it better the chimps died than the humans?" And I know we're all supposed to agree. But it's not like the chimps had a *choice*. Ham and Enos didn't have a way to say yes or no. Zan *does*. And maybe when he says *no*, we should listen. Otherwise it's a kind of slavery.'

'Slavery?' The word seemed so extreme. 'You don't think we treat Zan well?'

'Sure, we mostly treat him well,' Peter said. 'But he's here for a reason. And it's not because your parents wanted a chimp.'

'I know that,' I said. 'But apart from the learning chair, it's pretty good for him.'

'Better than a zoo, anyway,' said Peter. 'Still, he doesn't really have any kind of freedom. Not like he would in the wild.'

'In the wild he could get eaten or starve to death,' I pointed out. I'd heard that one from Dad, and it seemed like a pretty good argument. I didn't know why I was suddenly using Dad's lines, thinking from his point of view. I guess we were still a family, and I wanted it to be a happy one. It made me nervous when someone outside criticized it.

'Look,' Peter said, 'I don't know if you're interested, but there's this guy coming to give a talk at the university next week. I guess you'd call him an animal rights activist. He thinks we shouldn't be using animals in any kind of experiments.'

'Even one like ours?' I said.

'Maybe. I don't know. That's why I'm going to hear him. You want to come?'

'Dad wouldn't like it,' I said.

'No, your dad thinks this guy's a lunatic.'

'I'll go,' I said.

'You want to come over after school?' Jennifer asked me on Thursday.

Lunch was almost over and we were standing in the quad with David and Shannon and Hugh – and Kelly Browne, who hadn't been far from Hugh since the last dance. I guess they were technically going out now.

'Sure,' I said, trying to sound all casual. Jennifer had never invited me to her house before, and I felt a rush of excitement. 'Who's coming?'

'Not me,' said Hugh. 'I've got rugby practice.'

'Yes, we all know you have *rugby* practice,' Jennifer said, rolling her eyes. Hugh had just been promoted to the grade nine A team. And he'd been working it into conversation quite a bit.

'You sticking around?' Hugh asked Kelly.

Her mouth turned down at the corners. 'To watch you practise? It's kind of muddy out there.'

'Nice team spirit,' said Jennifer.

Kelly gave her a sour smile.

'I've got piano,' said Shannon.

'Oh, right,' said Jennifer, like it had slipped her mind. 'And Jane's got a doctor's appointment, right?'

Mono, I thought hopefully.

'Oh well,' Jennifer said, with a careless shrug. She looked from Hugh to me, then brushed my hand. 'Looks like it's just us, then.'

The Godwins lived really close to the school, and I walked home with David and Jennifer.

The last two periods had passed in a blur. It was like the teachers were speaking in a variety of different languages, only some of which existed on Earth. I had no idea what we covered. All I could think was: *Jennifer has invited me over to her house.*

She knew Hugh couldn't come. She knew Jane couldn't come. I was pretty sure she knew Shannon couldn't come either, because Shannon always had piano lessons after school on Thursday.

So really she was inviting just me.

Her father would not be home yet. Her mother was out playing golf until six. Yes, David would be there, but he said he had a ton of homework, so maybe he'd disappear to his room to work.

We walked down the shady streets, talking about the glam rock scene in the UK, and Evel Knievel trying to jump his car across the Grand Canyon.

'Hasn't he already broken every bone in his body?' Jennifer said.

'Except his neck,' I said.

'Actually, I think he broke his neck once,' said David. 'This time he's got a jet engine to help him make the jump.'

'The guy's nuts,' I said. But if Jennifer had been waiting

on the other side of the Grand Canyon, I would've done it.

David let us into the house. I called Mom and told her I was over at the Godwins' and would catch the bus home later.

We hung around the kitchen a bit, getting drinks and toasting Pop-Tarts. Then we went down to the rec room. David clicked on the TV and we all slumped in a row on the chesterfield. We caught the tail end of *Happy Days*, and then *The Flintstones* came on.

David sighed and stood up. 'As much as I'd like to watch cartoons with you kids,' he said, 'I've got an essay on fascism to write.' He trudged upstairs.

We were alone. Sitting side by side on the sofa. I tried to think up lines from my logbook, but couldn't.

'You want me to change the channel?' Jennifer asked.

'Absolutely not,' I said. The dominant male took charge. 'I love *The Flintstones*.'

'Really? Me too!'

'I had a crush on Betty when I was younger,' I admitted.

She looked at me, lips parted in surprise. 'You're kidding.'

'No. She's a fox. I like her cave dress, too. Have you noticed she never changes it? Same one every episode.'

Jennifer wrinkled her nose. 'I'd never thought of that.'

'Come on,' I said, 'be honest. You probably had a thing for Barney.'

She gasped in outrage. 'I *never* had a thing for Barney!'

'OK, he is a bit short. How about Fred, then?'

She was laughing pretty hard. 'You are such a *weirdo*! Did you have a thing for Wilma too?'

'Nope. Just Betty. I like brunettes.'

She was still laughing when I kissed her, but then her mouth relaxed into mine and we turned towards each other on the chesterfield. Fred Flintstone was shouting, 'Yabba-dabba-do!' At first she tasted like cherry Pop-Tart but as we kept kissing, I stopped noticing. I felt like some desert wanderer who'd finally reached a well. My hands grazed her cheeks, her hair. She had both hands around my neck. When my tongue touched hers, I wanted more – wanted everything about her.

She pulled back and, for the first time, I felt I could really look at her – without having to worry about being rude, or her friends noticing. The freckles across her nose made her more beautiful. Her mouth looked swollen and delicious.

'Your lip gloss is definitely smushed,' I said.

She shrugged. 'Oh well.'

We talked for a bit, and then we heard David coming downstairs, already tired of fascism and wanting to watch *I Dream of Jeannie*.

Next week, on Tuesday, I signed myself out of school early and took the bus to the university campus. I was worried I'd run into Dad, or even Mom, so I kept an eye out as I made my way to the Tenney Auditorium. Peter was waiting for me in the lobby and we went in to get seats.

It was a pretty upsetting talk. The guy's name was William Eckler and he showed slides of all sorts of tests being done on animals. Mostly they were small animals like mice and rats and rabbits. He was very calm and matter-of-fact. He said a lot of the time the tests were for things like makeup, and not medicines that might cure people.

'But even if they were,' he said, 'should we be torturing animals so we can heal humans? Is that fair?'

I guess I'd always assumed humans were more important than animals. We killed and ate animals all the time – unless you were vegetarian, which I wasn't – so it seemed hypocritical to start worrying about animals' feelings or how we treated them. I found it hard to worry too much about a rat or a mouse.

At the end of his talk, Eckler showed a movie of the inside of a medical research facility. It was called the Thurston Foundation. The movie had no sound and it was black and white. The picture was all shaky, like they'd smuggled a hidden camera inside, and filmed in a hurry.

I saw rows and rows of cages filled with all sorts of animals. The camera got in really close to one of the cages, and inside was a chimpanzee. He was little, maybe three months old, and much skinnier than Zan was at that age. It looked like some of his hair had fallen out. He was rocking back and forth really fast, his huge eyes blank.

I felt my stomach start churning, and was glad when the film ended.

'Scientists like experimenting on chimps,' said Eckler. 'They're the closest species to us on the planet, so they think if a drug works on them, it'll work on us. That little cage you saw is called an isolette. It's so small the animal can hardly turn round and it's kept in strict isolation. The animals have usually been injected with some kind of virus so scientists can test a new drug or vaccine. They might not develop any symptoms, or they might get really sick. Sometimes they die. Now, that little chimp you just saw – you lock up a living creature, especially one as smart as a chimp, and it suffers not just physically, but psychologically. It was hugging and rocking itself for some kind of stimulation. Chimps are very social. They need company.'

I'd read that too. Something like: 'One chimp is no chimp.'

There were some pamphlets you could take at the end, and I shoved some into my knapsack.

Peter walked with me to the bus stop. I kept thinking of that little face behind the bars of the cage.

'Zan has a way better life than that,' I said.

'He sure does,' Peter agreed.

It was strange, but the talk actually made me feel better about Zan. We were worried about strapping him into a chair – but in the lab they were locking them in boxes and poking them with needles and giving them diseases.

'That lab they showed,' I said. 'Was that the kind of place Zan was born?'

Peter shook his head. 'Borroway's not a biomedical facility,' he said. 'They're Air Force. They don't do medical tests, not exactly. Just stuff to see how chimps will react to certain conditions.'

'Like that rocket-sled test you told me about.'

'Right. So maybe it's not so different.'

'It was a good thing we rescued him, then,' I said.

Peter shrugged. 'Well, he was taken from his own mother when he was eight days old.'

'I know that,' I said, 'but if he'd stayed at the base, he might've ended up dead in some experiment.'

'Yep.'

'So we rescued him, really,' I said.

'He's still a prisoner, though,' Peter said. 'Zan's just lucky his prison guards are nice.'

'I'm not one of his *prison* guards,' I said, annoyed. 'He's more like my brother.'

Peter just looked at me. 'People don't usually get paid for playing with their little brothers.'

A few weeks ago I'd told him I was getting paid for my shifts with Zan, and now I wished I hadn't.

'Kids get paid for babysitting their little brothers and sisters,' I said, using Mom's argument. 'Anyway,' I added after a few seconds, '*you* don't work for free.'

Peter chuckled. 'Nope. I've gotta pay my way through school.'

'So only I shouldn't get paid?' I said.

Peter smiled apologetically. 'Hey, I'm sorry, man. I know you love him. I love him, too. My head's just full of this stuff and . . . I'm just thinking out loud. Forget it, OK?'

'OK.' I couldn't really get mad at Peter; I liked him too much, and he was always kind to me.

We reached the bus stop and I could see my bus coming from down the street.

'Do you think Zan should have some chimp friends?' I said.

Peter laughed. 'Yeah, I'm sure your dad would be thrilled to have another one in the house. That's not the main thing I worry about,' he said. 'You know what I worry about? What's going to happen to Zan when this experiment's over?'

All the way home, I mulled over what Peter had said.

I'd never really thought about an afterwards with Zan. When a baby arrived at your house all tiny and wrapped up, and you bottle-fed him and took care of him, you assumed he was part of the family and there to stay. That's what I'd thought. And that's sure what Zan thought: we were his family.

I'd never had a pet. But it seemed like when people brought home a puppy or kitten, it stayed with them until it died. And Zan was so much more than a pet. You couldn't send him away just because the experiment was *over*.

I had to change buses at Cordova Plaza. As I waited I could see the Bank of Montreal, where I'd been depositing all the money from my shifts with Zan. I wondered if I should go and take it all out and give it back, and make a little speech about how I didn't want to be a prison guard any more.

But I was selfish. I liked having my own money. I could buy stuff for Jennifer, and take her out someday, when she was allowed. Which was three years away. In the meantime, I was saving up for a new camera.

But I started thinking maybe I should be saving up for something else.

Maybe I should be saving up so I could take care of Zan.

CHAPTER 13

KILLER CHIMP

Tonight was one of our dinners without Zan, so Dad was in a pretty good mood. It was certainly calmer without Zan, but the room felt empty to me. Right now the high chair was in his playroom, where he'd been fed by the students. Occasionally I heard a faint pant-hoot from his suite, and it made me sad. I picked at my food. It took me until dessert before I could bring myself to ask the question.

'What'll happen to Zan when the project's over?'

I was looking at Mom, and saw her eyes go to Dad, so I knew this was something they'd already talked about. She was worried how I'd react. Dad must've planned something; he was such a planner.

'The project was designed to go on for years and years, Ben,' Mom said. 'Indefinitely, really.'

'OK,' I said. Indefinitely was good. It was practically for ever. 'But what if you don't get the grant?'

'Very, very unlikely,' said Dad.

'Just say. What if you have to end the experiment?'

Dad was about to speak, but Mom talked first.

'This is a ground-breaking experiment, Ben. The whole world's watching. No one wants it to end.'

'Absolutely,' said Dad. 'As long as Zan can keep learning, the project will go on.'

I let out a breath. I felt a lot better and suddenly wanted another helping of dessert. Maybe I'd been worrying about nothing. Zan had been in *Time* magazine. He was famous. The first chimp to talk. As long as we kept teaching him, he'd keep learning. He wasn't going anywhere.

I woke up the next day with my throat hot and gummy, and by the time I got home from school I felt really lousy. I didn't sleep very well that night, and in my head was this movie about Zan in a hotel, and no one was very happy to see him. It just went on and on, keeping me twitching and turning, trying to get comfortable in bed. When I woke up, I was parched and my throat crackled with pain.

'Stay home and rest,' Mom said. 'I've got to give a tutorial this morning, but I'll be back by noon.'

Before she left, she brought me lots of orange juice, and a piece of toast and peanut butter, which I choked down. Then I took some aspirin and slept a bit more. I dreamed upsetting sounds, and when I woke, I still heard them. Zan was having a temper tantrum in his suite. I looked at my clock. Ten. School time for him. I wondered if he was strapped into the learning chair.

173

I threw on my dressing gown and went out into the hall. Zan was shrieking and hooting. I heard a man speak sharply to him, but Zan kept it up. He didn't sound just upset – he sounded terrified. I sat at the top of the stairs. I'd never heard him like this before, and it made me queasy.

Dad had always told me not to interfere with the students. So I sat, praying for Zan's crying to stop. The sound was like a gripping pain in my chest, and it made me want to cry.

It didn't stop.

I counted to ten and it didn't stop.

I counted to twenty and it didn't stop.

I ran downstairs, the sounds getting louder as I neared the kitchen. I unlocked the door to Zan's suite and went into the playroom.

Ryan Cross and Susan Wilkes were with Zan, and looked over at me in surprise.

Zan was buckled into the learning chair, struggling and screaming. It smelled bad in the room, like he'd had a big poo. When he caught sight of me he became even more frantic.

'Let him out,' I said.

'He had three warnings,' said Ryan calmly.

Susan looked kind of stunned, just watching the whole scene.

'He's too upset!' I said.

'He's only been in there five minutes,' Ryan replied, checking his watch and making a note on his clipboard. 'Also, Ben, this is not your shift.'

He reminded me so much of my father just then.

174

'Let him out,' I said again.

'He's always like this for the first little bit,' said Ryan. 'Then he quiets down.'

'It's always this bad?' I demanded.

Ryan shrugged. 'We're just following your father's protocol, little man.'

Had Zan been crying like this *every* day? I was usually at school, but Mom worked from home most of the time. She would've heard. She hadn't said anything about this. Didn't it bother *her*?

I walked towards the chair. Ryan put out his hand to stop me, but I pushed past and started undoing the buckles.

Zan was so upset he lunged at my hands as if he wanted to bite me. Maybe he thought I was going to tighten the straps or something.

'Zan,' I said calmly, 'I'm going to take you out.'

Out, I signed for him, over and over again until he calmed down a little and began to sign back to me – *out*, *out* – and hoot eagerly.

'Your dad's not going to be happy about this,' Ryan said.

'Too bad.'

Zan sprang out of the chair into my arms and wouldn't let go of my neck. He was kissing my cheek over and over again and signing *kiss* and *hug* and *go out*.

'Enough is enough!' Ryan snapped. He stepped forward and put out his hands to take Zan from me.

Zan bit him. Hard.

'Shit!' bellowed Ryan, pulling his hand away. Zan's baby

teeth had come in long ago and they were sharp. Blood welled from Ryan's third finger. It looked bad.

'You're going to need stitches,' said Susan, her face pale. 'I can drive you to the hospital.'

Ryan grabbed a dish towel and wrapped it tight around his finger. He swallowed. 'Goddamn monkey,' he muttered.

'You OK with Zan alone?' Susan asked me.

'Yeah, fine,' I said, even though I felt kind of woozy, and my throat was ragingly sore.

'Probably a good idea to call your dad,' she said. 'Tell him I'm taking Ryan to the emergency room at the Jubilee.'

I was glad to see them both go. Ryan deserved what he got, but there was going to be a lot of trouble. I sighed and, with Zan still hugging me tight, I went to the phone to call Dad.

Dad was frighteningly calm when I told him. He just wanted the facts. He asked if I was OK, told me to take care of Zan, then hung up to drive to the hospital.

When Mom got home at noon, I told her everything. She didn't say very much either, but she looked worried. Zan was good as gold over lunch. He knew he'd done something very bad and was trying to make up for it by being extra obedient, and making his signs very, *very* clearly.

At around three o'clock Dad came home and called me downstairs. I was still in my pyjamas, feeling rotten. Mom and Dad were waiting for me in the living room. Zan was out back with the new shift of students.

'Ben, you have created a huge amount of trouble,' Dad said.

'Me?' I exclaimed. 'What about Ryan?'

'Ryan said Zan was starting to calm down when you barged in and got him all riled up.'

'That's a lie!' I said. 'Zan was screaming. You could hear him all over the house. He woke me up.'

'How many times have I told you not to interfere?' Dad demanded.

I looked at Mom. 'I'd never heard him sound so upset!'

'It wasn't your responsibility, Ben,' Dad told me.

'Yeah it was!' I said. 'If I heard Mom screaming I'd try to help her.' I left Dad out of my example on purpose.

He started to say something, then shook his head. 'Ryan's going to be in the hospital overnight. Zan's bite went all the way to the bone. The doctor said if it had gone just a bit deeper he would've lost the tip of his finger. As it is, Ryan's got an IV full of antibiotics in his arm to prevent an infection.'

'Will there be any permanent damage?' Mom asked.

'Just the scar,' said Dad. 'We're lucky he's not suing us.'

'Thank God,' murmured Mom.

'But he is quitting,' said Dad.

'Good!' I said. 'He didn't care about Zan.'

'Ryan's one of my best students,' Dad said. 'He was methodical and rigorous and he was an asset to the team.'

I shrugged.

'You're off the project, Ben.'

It was like being punched in the centre of the chest. My body suddenly felt airless. 'Why?' I gasped, like some little kid.

'Your attachment to Zan's getting in the way.'

'But . . . you said I was good with him—'

'It's too emotional for you now,' said Dad. 'Probably it was never the greatest idea. That was my fault. Having my own son as one of the assistants – it throws the reliability of the data into question. I'm sorry, Ben, but it's not in the best interests of the project.'

'What about *my* interests?' I shouted. 'What about *Zan's*? We want to spend time together!'

'You'll still see Zan, evenings and Sundays,' Mom pointed out.

'Frankly, you could use the extra time for your own school work,' Dad added.

I just stared at both of them, and no words came, just the drumbeat of my heart. When words finally did come, they were stupid and childish, but out they rushed.

'You are so mean,' I yelled, and burst into tears.

Mom tried to hug me, but I didn't want her touching me and trying to make me feel better, so I pushed past her and ran upstairs to my room.

I felt crappy all Saturday, so I stayed in bed reading, watching TV, and thinking about Jennifer. Sometimes I stood at the bedroom window and looked at Zan in the back yard with the students. Mom tried to be really nice to me, but Dad didn't talk to me much. He was in a really bad mood because a reporter from the local paper had called this morning to ask about the biting incident. Someone from the hospital must have blabbed, and now it was going to be in the papers.

The story ran Sunday. It wasn't a big piece, not front page or anything, but they did call it 'a chimp attack'.

'Let's just hope it doesn't get picked up in the nationals,' Dad said darkly.

I didn't have a fever any more, and even though I still felt wiped out, I wanted to be with Zan. I think he was glad to see me. We spent a lot of time just tickling and hugging. It was good to feel the squeeze of his arms around my neck, his hair warm against my cheek.

Mom made me bundle up before I took Zan outside to play. I hid his dolls all over the back yard and tried to get him to close his eyes while I did it. He tended to peek. Then he'd scamper all round, looking for them. It was almost impossible to find hiding places he couldn't discover in less than two seconds.

'Hey, it's the killer chimp,' said a voice.

I looked over and saw Mike, with Tim Borden beside him, standing on the other side of the chain-link fence.

'Hi, Ben,' said Tim, lifting his hand.

'Hey,' I said warily.

'Doesn't look very scary,' said Mike, watching Zan as he scampered down the jungle gym and made his way to the fence.

I went over with him. 'He just bit someone's finger,' I said. 'It's not a big deal.'

'How do you know he doesn't have rabies?' Mike asked.

'He's had shots.'

Zan looked the opposite of ferocious as he stared up at Mike with his big brown eyes. He made the *hug* sign, but I didn't feel like telling them what he was saying. Mike didn't deserve it.

179

'Are you still teaching him sign language?' Tim asked.

'Oh yeah,' I said. 'He knows forty signs now. He's pretty smart.'

'Can we come in and see him?' Tim asked.

I remembered how gentle Tim had been with Zan whenever he'd seen him last summer, but I didn't trust Mike. Anyway, Dad would probably freak out if he found out. He didn't want to risk any more biting incidents.

'Maybe another time,' I said, and felt kind of mean. I still liked Tim.

'Fetch,' said Mike, and he lobbed a stick over the fence. It came down about five feet from Zan. Zan looked at it without much interest.

'Jeez, my dog's smarter,' said Mike. He bent down and picked up another stick and lobbed it over, staring defiantly at me. That one landed a bit closer to us this time.

'Careful, Mike,' said Tim.

'Just trying to make it easy for him,' Mike said.

Zan picked the stick up and shoved it back through the fence.

'Good boy!' Mike said sarcastically. 'Maybe you're not so stupid.' He started poking his fingers through the chain link near Zan's head, wiggling them and then jerking them back.

'Come on!' said Mike. 'Try it! Try to bite me!'

Zan tried to grab Mike's fingers, but Mike kept pulling them out of reach. Zan looked at me and signed *funny*.

'Is that sign language?' said Tim. 'What's he saying?'

'He's saying Mike's funny,' I told him.

Tim laughed. 'Yeah. Funny in the head, for sure.'

Mike got bored of the finger game and picked up another stick. He chucked it high over the fence, and this time it almost hit Zan.

'Knock it off, Mike,' I said.

'I'm just playing with him,' Mike said. And he picked up another stick.

Zan hooted excitedly.

I lifted Zan into my arms and started carrying him back to the house.

'See you, Tim,' I said.

I was halfway across the yard when I saw a rock skitter across the grass near my feet. Then one hit me in the back. I whirled round. Mike was standing there, whipping rocks through the fence at me.

'Don't be a goof, Mike,' Tim was saying to him.

'I want to play with the killer chimp!' said Mike.

'Get lost, you idiot!' I said, and he threw another rock.

It hit Zan in the shoulder and he gave a shriek. On his fur was a tiny bead of blood. I'd never felt such fury. It had a sound, and a colour and it tasted like blood in my mouth. I slid open the patio doors and got Zan safely inside. Then I ran for the gate in the fence, flung it open, and bolted towards Mike, shouting at him.

'Hey,' he said, kind of smirking. 'Hey, bad shot, OK?'

He was way more solid than me, but I had a lot of momentum and I put my hands up and shoved him hard, sending him staggering backwards.

181

'If. You. Ever. Hurt. Him. Again – you're *dead*!' I shouted.

Then he hit me in the face and I was punching him back, but it seemed like I was mostly just getting clobbered. I didn't care. I was so mad, it felt good just to be lashing out at Mike and hurting him as best I could. Dimly I was aware of Tim telling Mike to stop, and saw him trying to push Mike away. But Mike just kept at it, his scary, calm eyes fixed on me. We were both down on the ground now, kicking and punching – and suddenly I was pulled up and Dad was there.

'Stop it!' he shouted.

Mike scrambled up, and the look on his face was so scary I thought he was going to have a go at Dad. Then he just turned and started walking away.

'If I see you boys here again, I'll call the police,' Dad told them. 'Your parents'll be hearing from me.'

'Tim didn't do anything,' I panted, wiping blood from my nose. I was only now starting to realize where I'd been hit. My face and chest really hurt.

'Come on inside,' Dad said to me, taking me by the arm.

He'd stopped the fight, saved me from getting totally pulverized, but the weird thing was, I barely felt grateful.

It was pretty great showing up at school on Monday with a big bruise on my face.

'Oh my God!' Jennifer exclaimed when she saw me in homeroom. 'What happened to you?'

I shrugged nonchalantly. 'Got in a fight,' and told her the

182

story, which I'd carefully written down and revised many times in my logbook.

Shannon, and even Jane, looked genuinely shocked.

'That guy's a psycho,' said Shannon. 'Does it still hurt, your face?'

Jane said sarcastically, 'Yeah, Shannon, I think it probably hurts.'

'It's not so bad,' I said to Shannon with a smile. 'I'm just glad Zan wasn't hurt any worse.'

'Poor you,' said Jennifer, and she touched my cheek gently.

It was a very good day. I felt my status as dominant male couldn't get much higher. I was a fighter. Project Jennifer was in excellent shape. If there was a grant I could apply for, I was pretty sure I'd nail it.

When I got home from school, I went to the kitchen for a drink. In the back yard, Peter saw me and hurried inside, leaving Zan with the other student. He was grinning ear to ear.

'Take a look,' he said, leading me into Zan's suite.

I walked into the playroom.

The learning chair was gone.

'Hey!' I exclaimed. 'All right! What happened?'

Maybe I'd been too hard on Dad. Or maybe Mom had convinced him the chair had to go.

Peter grinned. 'Your dad decided it was counter-productive.'

I snorted. *Counter-productive*. That was so like Dad.

'He was right,' said Peter. 'Zan's daily signing was way down. His behaviour was terrible. Also, I told your dad I'd quit if he didn't get rid of it.'

'Wow! Did you really?'

Peter nodded. 'Yup. I told him I just couldn't keep going with the project. I said I'd be leaving at the end of the week. I don't know if it made any difference.'

'I bet it did,' I said. 'You're the best with Zan. He wouldn't want to lose you.'

'Well, he already lost Ryan, so maybe he was worried about someone else taking off. Anyway, the main thing is, that freaking chair's gone!'

'Thanks, Peter,' I said, and then frowned. 'Would you really have quit?'

He shook his head. 'No way. And not because of the money,' he added quickly. 'Not entirely, anyway.'

'So why?'

'I just think Zan needs as many allies as possible. People who care about him – as more than just a specimen.'

CHAPTER 14

SUMMER

There was no way we would've been invited to the party if it weren't for David's brother, Cal. He was on the 1st XV rugby team, and they'd just won the Howard Rees Cup this afternoon, which was this huge deal. The school always won. The main hall was filled with trophies. I think they might have lost once, back in the 1950s, but only because three of their best players had polio or something.

It was Saturday night, second week of June, and there was a bonfire going on the beach, and lots of beer, and people with painted faces bellowing rugby chants and jumping into the lake. Most of the kids were seniors, so I hardly knew anyone. I was sitting on the sand with Jennifer, Jane and Shannon.

'I think we're the only grade eights here,' I said.

'It's pretty cool,' said Jennifer. 'This is, like, *the* party of the year.'

'Some beverages?' said David and Hugh, grinning. Dripping bottles of beer dangled from their fingers.

'My parents made me promise I wouldn't,' said Shannon.

'Mine too,' said Jane, and took a beer.

'I'll share yours,' Jennifer said to me, when I took one.

Beer was disgusting, even worse than wine, but David and Hugh were drinking it, so I figured I had to, also.

The shadows got deeper and more jagged. Kelly Browne appeared suddenly from the darkness and then she and Hugh disappeared together, hand in hand.

'She's like a vampire,' said Jane. 'It's like she wants to suck out every last ounce of his blood.'

'Ugh,' said Jennifer.

Then, a few minutes later, Shannon said she needed to go to the bathroom, grabbed Jane and Jennifer by the hands, and they all went off together.

'We won't be seeing them for several hours,' said David, slouched against a tree. 'So, Tarzan. Good year for you?'

One of the best things about private school was that it finished earlier than regular schools. Classes had ended yesterday. Next week was exams, then it was summer.

'Great year,' I said. 'As long as I don't flunk finals.'

He snorted. 'You'll be fine. But how're you going to cope this summer without us?'

I laughed. 'What do you mean?'

'The entire Godwin family is going to Europe, my friend.'

'Are you serious? How long for?'

He held up all five fingers of his free hand, then put down his beer and held up his thumb.

'Six weeks?' I exclaimed.

186

'Yep. They're calling it the trip of a lifetime.'

'Are you seeing every country or something?'

'One every two days, I think, yeah.'

I took a big gulp of beer. In my Project Jennifer logbook, I'd already written down a list of all the fun things we could do this summer. And I had a whole schedule drawn up of how I was going to get to second base with her. Third base wasn't even under consideration yet. I thought it was important to set reasonable goals.

'So you get back when?' I asked.

'Early August.'

'Oh man!' I said.

'Yeah, I know.' He smirked. 'Watching *The Flintstones* alone isn't much fun.'

I looked at him, wondering how much he knew. Everything, probably.

'I need another beer,' he said, and ambled off.

I waited for him a while, and then felt like a goof sitting all alone. Empty beer bottle clutched in my hand, I wandered along the beach, looking for Jennifer. The bonfire had burned down and the only light came from the occasional blinding flare of car headlights up in the parking lot. I nearly tripped over a couple making out. I thought I caught a glimpse of Hugh and Kelly Browne all tangled up, groping furiously. A group of people with their faces painted blue ran past me, screaming towards the water. I kept walking until there was no one around.

Six weeks in Europe. Jennifer hadn't mentioned anything. Maybe they just found out.

'Ben?' said someone, walking towards me.

I squinted. It was Shannon. 'Hey,' I said.

'Oh, thank God!' She actually grabbed me and leaned her head against my shoulder. 'I thought I was lost. The bathroom is a million miles away.'

'Where're the others?'

'They took off. Jane said she saw a black widow outside.'

'Hilarious.' I could see Jane doing something like that.

As we kept walking, I realized this was the first time I'd ever talked to Shannon alone. She hardly ever talked when she was around Jane and Jennifer. Maybe Shannon was afraid of being mocked too.

'I hope I get to meet Zan one day,' she said.

I looked at her and smiled. 'Yeah, he's great. He's turning one next week.'

'It must be amazing, what you guys are doing.'

'It's pretty neat, yeah.'

'This sounds stupid, but I loved those *Curious George* books when I was little – you know those books?'

'Sure. I loved them too.'

'I thought having a monkey as a pet would be the best thing in the world. I mean, I know Zan isn't a monkey. Is he as naughty as George?'

'Much naughtier sometimes.' I laughed. I always liked talking about Zan, so I told her a bit about him as we headed back towards the party.

Jane and Jennifer were there at our old spot with David.

Hugh had returned with Kelly, both of them looking pretty rumpled.

'You guys are *such* good friends,' Shannon said sarcastically to Jane and Jennifer.

'She said there was a black widow spider!' Jennifer protested. 'Someone got bitten last month – didn't you hear about that?'

Jane snickered into her beer bottle.

I sat down beside Jennifer, and waited until the others were talking about something. I leaned in closer. 'I can't believe you're going away,' I whispered.

'Dad kind of sprang it on us,' she said.

'Six weeks!' I said.

She looked at me gravely. 'Yes. But I will return, Tarzan, I promise.'

And she kissed me in front of everyone.

On June 20th we celebrated Zan's first birthday in the back yard. Peter was there, and lots of the other students. I'd wanted to invite David and Jennifer – it was my last chance to see them before they left for Europe – but Dad said it should just be people Zan was very familiar with; he didn't want Zan to get overexcited. As it was, he was pretty darn excited.

I didn't know if he understood what was going on, but he wolfed down three huge pieces of Mom's banana cake, had more glasses of ginger ale than was good for him, and ripped the wrapping paper off his presents with lots of hoots and shrieks.

Mom and Dad got him a new ball, and I got him another

birdfeeder that we could hang up in the back yard to attract even more birds. (*Listen bird*, he signed to me when he opened the box.)

Peter got him a pair of his own sneakers, because Zan was fascinated by people's shoes and was always pulling them off and trying them on himself.

Dad invited the local paper, and they sent a photographer to take some pictures of Zan surrounded by all of us, singing 'Happy Birthday to You' before we cut the cake. Dad figured it might undo some of the bad publicity we got after the biting incident. *See, he's adorable and no one lost a finger!*

My own birthday, ten days later, was pretty good too – much better than last year's. This time we actually made it to Beaver Lake, leaving Zan at home with Peter. I really liked it just being the three of us. When Zan was around, all eyes, including my own, were on him. He was the star of the family, the celebrity. I wondered if I was still a bit jealous of him sometimes.

But it was strange being without him. When he was little, we'd sometimes taken him with us shopping and even to restaurants, but now that he was so active, we couldn't take him out in public. He wasn't used to cars or big crowds. He might get freaked out and bite someone or – and this was scariest to me – he might run off into the forest and decide he didn't want to live with us any more. Dad had once said that if we ever took him out in public we'd have to put him in a collar and leash, but I'd hate to see that – even if it was for his own safety.

I stretched out on my beach towel. School was all over now.

My final marks weren't the greatest, but I'd improved a bit, and that seemed enough to satisfy Dad. He wasn't going to pull me out of Windermere. I closed my eyes and thought of Jennifer, somewhere in Europe. I thought of smoothing suntan lotion on her perfect back.

When we got home, Mom and Dad gave me a great new photo enlarger as my main present. And in the evening, instead of going out to a restaurant, we just ordered in Chinese food, because that way, Zan could be with us. It wouldn't have felt right without him.

Just knowing Jennifer was on the other side of the world made everything feel less like summer.

I thought about her all the time, wrote about her in my bulging logbook, and re-read the old bits. It wasn't only notes and observations. It was also a diary. Our after-school make-out session took up about ten pages – I hadn't wanted to leave anything out. Sometimes I just described how I felt about her. Or I'd imagine things we might say to each other, and do together. I wouldn't say it ever got dirty exactly, but there was some pretty personal stuff in there.

The only picture I had of her was our class photo. But in my head she got more fabulous and luscious with every day, until she was so overwhelmingly beautiful, I could barely stand it.

So I wouldn't go crazy with boredom, Mom and Dad signed me up for these summer day camps at the university. I wasn't wild about them, but Mom said she wasn't having me loafing around the house all July. So I'd go in with Dad in the

191

mornings, and while he worked in his office, I swam and did team-building stuff and made tie-dyed T-shirts with a bunch of other thirteen- and fourteen-year-olds. Probably I should've seen it as an opportunity to make some friends and meet cute girls. But there was only one girl I was interested in.

I got a couple of postcards from David, and one from Jennifer. Hers was from Italy and had a picture of the Roman Colosseum. At the end she wrote *Wish you were here*, followed by two exclamation marks and a heart.

The world should have been in Technicolour, but seemed more like black and white.

Towards the end of July, Peter asked if I wanted to catch a matinée of *Conquest of the Planet of the Apes*. I was pleased he thought I was cool enough to hang out with.

He drove me downtown in his beat-up Corvair. Near the passenger seat there was actually a little hole in the floor where you could see the road. We had the windows rolled down and the radio going. I decided I wanted a car just like this when I got my licence.

The university year had ended back in May, and Project Zan had lost a few of its students for the holidays, but Peter had stayed on and was doing a lot more shifts over the summer. I got to help out more too. I wasn't collecting data any more, but I didn't care. I just wanted to be with Zan. With the learning chair gone, Zan seemed much happier. The temper tantrums had fizzled out; he'd started signing more, and learning faster.

We were in the cinema with our popcorn, waiting for the

movie to start, when Peter slouched down in his seat. 'Oh man,' he said in a whisper. He tilted his chin. 'Creepy Susan Wilkes.'

She was sitting near the front with some guy. She didn't work with Zan any more. I wasn't sure if she'd quit, or Mom had fired her. I once overheard Mom saying to Dad, 'She has designs on you.' Whatever the reason, she was gone, and I was glad. Zan had never liked her much, and I hadn't either.

Then the lights went down and the movie started. It wasn't as good as some of the others in the series, but it was still pretty entertaining. The apes led a revolt against the humans who'd been enslaving them.

'Those damn apes, huh?' said Peter as we walked out – quickly, so we wouldn't run into Susan Wilkes. 'Rising up against us like that.'

'That's what happens when you make them cook for you,' I said.

Peter chuckled. 'Yeah, I guess we had it coming.'

'Hey, you don't think Zan has a plot to take over our house, do you?'

'Ben,' said Peter, 'he's already done that. Wake up!'

We headed down past The Empress, got ice cream, and walked around the inner harbour, looking at the boats and craft stands, listening to the buskers. With an aching intensity I suddenly wished I were with Jennifer.

'So, what do you think of this new guy your dad's bringing in?' Peter asked.

I turned to him in surprise. 'What guy?'

'He didn't tell you? This hotshot linguist from Berkeley. Greg Jaworski.'

Now that I wasn't going to the weekly meetings any more, I wasn't that up on the official Project Zan; everything I learned was from Mom and Dad over the dinner table, or more often from Peter.

'Where's Berkeley?' I asked. I'd heard Dad talk about it, but I couldn't remember.

'California. He's going to make sure Zan's learning language properly.'

We sat down on a bench, and looked back at the ivy-covered Empress.

'I don't get it. We all know Zan's learning language properly. What do we need this guy for?'

'Well, your dad's not technically a linguistics expert, so I think Godwin put some pressure on him to bring one aboard.'

It was strange, thinking of someone telling my father what to do. To me, Dad always seemed like the guy who knew everything and gave the orders. Other people scrambled. It was especially uncomfortable to imagine him being bossed around by David's father.

'It's probably good for the project,' Peter said. 'You know, its credibility and everything. There's a lot of linguists who don't even think ASL is a proper language.'

'Really?'

'Yeah, but Jaworksi does, and he's big. So with two experts heading it up, Project Zan looks pretty hot now. I don't think your dad was crazy about sharing credit, but it's not like he has a lot of choices right now.'

'What d'you mean, *choices?*'

'Just that he's got to make the project work *here*. There aren't too many universities that would sponsor something like this.' He must've seen the confusion in my face. 'Teaching chimps sign language is not something most big old universities would take seriously. It's pretty far-out. U of T wouldn't touch it. Harvard and MIT probably wouldn't either.'

'How would you know?' I said. But I remembered Dad grumbling about how U of T wouldn't get a chimp for him. I'd thought it was because the university was stupid, not because the whole idea of the project was crazy. 'Anyway,' I added defensively. 'Dad just got another grant a couple of weeks ago.'

It was only a small one, apparently, not like the biggie he was still hoping for, but it would help. And now Dad seemed more relaxed.

'I know,' said Peter. 'Look, I think it's totally radical and ground-breaking. And it's good news for everyone, Jaworksi joining the project. It's bound to win that big grant. And it might open up some US funding too.'

'That's good,' I said.

As long as the project kept going, Zan would be safe. He'd stay part of the family.

August 5th had been marked on my calendar all summer, and when it finally arrived, I wanted to call Jennifer that very afternoon, but didn't. She'd be tired from their trip back.

The next day I thought about calling, but decided I'd look

too eager. *Play it cool.* When I called the day after, there was no answer, and I lost my nerve and didn't call again.

Next morning, the phone rang, and Mom answered and called out that it was for me. My heart was pounding. I hoped it was Jennifer.

It was David.

'Bonjour, Benjamin,' he said.

'You speak French now, I see.'

'I speak many languages now,' he replied.

'How was your trip?'

He grunted. 'It was OK – kinda boring. So you want to go to the beach? A bunch of us are going. And, yes, that includes my little sister.'

'Sounds good,' I said. 'Thanks for the postcards.'

'No problem. We'll swing by and get you around ten-thirty.'

The beach. Fantastic. Just like last summer. I'd made sure to get tanned over July, so my chest and legs didn't look all pasty. I put on my bathing suit and stood in front of the mirror for a while, checking out how I looked from different angles.

When the Godwins' station wagon pulled into the driveway, I could see it was just full of guys. Cal was driving, and another one of his hairy rugby friends was in the front, shirtless, looking muscular. David was in the back with Hugh.

'The girls are coming in a different car,' David explained as I got in. 'Jane's older sister is driving.'

'*Jane's* coming?' I moaned.

David screwed his face up into his best Jane impersonation. 'What's your prawblem, Ben? *Gawd!*'

'She scares me,' said Hugh.

'She's crazy about you, though, man,' David said to me. 'It's obvious.'

'You're kidding me.' The only thing obvious was that she hated me, and loved seeing me squirm.

'Jennifer told me, Tarzan.'

I nodded, hoping David would keep going and tell me Jennifer was crazy about me, too. But he didn't.

'Is Kelly coming?' I asked Hugh.

'Ah, Kelly, Kelly, Kelly,' said Hugh. 'We split up.'

'What happened?' I asked.

'She didn't like *Gilligan's Island*,' he said.

David snorted, like he knew something I didn't. But Hugh didn't say anything else, and I wasn't going to be a pain and ask more questions, so I let it drop.

We drove all the way out to Willows Beach in Oak Bay. I'd never been there before. There was a field and a playground and a snack bar that was pumping out the smell of French fries and vinegar. The beach was nice and long, and the tide was way out so there was lots of sand. Across the water was a little island and beyond that you could see the mountains rising up on the American side, snow-capped.

The girls were already there, lying side by side on their towels, Jennifer in the middle, looking at a photo album.

I sucked in my breath as we drew closer. My entire focus was on Jennifer. She was wearing short shorts and a halter top and these really glam sunglasses.

All morning I'd wondered how she'd greet me. Throwing

herself into my arms and kissing me crazily was my first choice, but unlikely, I thought, especially in public. She wasn't getting up from her towel, so I just said, 'Hey, welcome back!'

'Thanks!' she said.

'Did you get the shades in Europe?' I asked.

'Paris,' she said. 'Pretty fab, huh?'

'Very Brigitte Bardot,' I said, which seemed to please her. 'So are these your pictures from Europe?'

'No, Ben,' said Jane, 'they're her pictures from Disneyland. Duh.'

I ignored Jane. Now that I knew she liked me, suddenly she didn't have as much power. I felt like Superman after the kryptonite has been taken away.

'Hey, I want to see these too.'

No one was exactly shifting to make room, so I plonked myself down on the sand in front of Shannon's towel. The album was kind of upside down, but that was as good as I was going to get. Jane made a big sighing sound.

'Ooh, who's that?' Shannon said, pointing at a photo of Jennifer with some guy.

'Oh. He was our tour guide in Berlin,' said Jennifer.

'What a hunk!' said Jane.

'European guys are really good-looking,' said Jennifer in this casual way. 'And do they *ever* know how to dress.'

I thought he was kind of weaselly, but I didn't say anything because it would sound like sour grapes. I started to worry she'd had some kind of fling with him. Mom sometimes talked about her trip to Europe after high school and it sounded pretty wild. Crazy romances happened in Europe all the time. Luckily I didn't see any more pictures of the Berlin tour guide, and I figured it was unlikely Jennifer had had a torrid affair right under her parents' noses.

Anyway, according to David, who flopped down beside us with Hugh, they were only in Berlin twenty-four hours. Jennifer went through the pictures, taking us from country to country. David chipped in with his own funny commentary, sounding like a voice-over from those old newsreels.

'Bustling Trafalgar Square in the heart of London! Look at all the tourists feeding the pigeons! Look at all the pigeons crapping all over the tourists! Delightful fun!'

There were tons of pictures of the Godwin family in front of statues and historic buildings. Lots of pictures of Jennifer looking gorgeous on cobbled streets and on riverboats and old stone bridges. I didn't like thinking of all these other people getting to see her while I was way over here.

By the time the last page of the photo album was turned, I hated the entire continent of Europe, and all the well-dressed people in it.

Jennifer took off her halter top and shorts, and her bikini was underneath. I tried not to stare. It looked like her breasts had gotten bigger since the last time I'd seen her in a bathing suit – exactly a year ago. And she seemed different, a little more aloof. She'd gone to Europe and gotten all sophisticated and Europeanized.

She was sandwiched between Shannon and Jane, like they were bodyguards. When she needed lotion on her back, she asked them, not me.

I kept hoping she'd wander off meaningfully along the beach, and I could walk with her, but she seemed happy gabbing to her friends. A few times I walked down to the water alone and stood looking heroically into the distance, but she never joined me, so I gave up and started throwing the Frisbee around with David and Hugh.

After a while the girls came and wanted to join us, so we made teams and started a game of Frisbee tag.

'Let's see those muscles ripple, *Ben*,' said Jane.

I tried to whip the Frisbee at her head a couple of times, but kept missing.

I noticed that Hugh had no problem making body contact with Jennifer, and a couple of times he ploughed into her pretty hard. He'd been David's friend for so long, I guess they'd all grown up playing together. I was always worried I was going to nudge her breasts – as much as I wanted to – or hurt her, so I was always kind of skimming past her.

Once Hugh knocked her right over onto the sand and when he helped her up I heard her give a little shriek.

'Did you just slap my butt?' she demanded.

She didn't seem that upset, and Hugh just laughed and ran off with the Frisbee.

I started looking at Hugh more closely. I'd never thought of him as handsome. But he was a year older than me, and he was big and played rugby on the A team. Did that automatically make him cooler than me?

I started thinking backwards, fusing scenes together in my head like some crazy movie flashback. Hugh danced with her at the dance. He talked with her at school and made her laugh sometimes. But I'd just thought they were pals. David had never mentioned anything about Hugh liking Jennifer, or vice versa.

When it was time to go home, I was hoping Jennifer would come back in the station wagon with me, but Jane's older sister had come to pick her up, and Jennifer wanted to go with the other girls. Hugh lived really close to Jane, so he went with them.

The day hadn't turned out at all the way I'd imagined it.

Greg Jaworski, the hotshot from Berkeley, showed up in mid-August. He was going to stay in our spare room for two weeks, working on Project Zan with Dad and Mom.

He was wiry and bearded and smiled a lot. His eyes behind his glasses were just the tiniest bit buggy and he talked really fast. Everything seemed to excite him. He was excited about meeting Dad and Mom and me. Excited about meeting Zan. Excited by the hidden cameras. And he was really excited when he watched us signing with Zan for the first time. He used the word *fascinating* a lot.

At first Zan didn't know what to make of him, and hung back. But by the end of the first afternoon, Zan was climbing into his lap and taking off his glasses. He seemed to like Greg, and that made me like him too.

'What a fascinating little fellow he is,' Greg said.

I wasn't sure how Project Jennifer was going, but Project Zan was going to be just fine.

CHAPTER 15

UNEXPECTED FINDINGS

It was the Wednesday before the Labour Day weekend, and CBS television was all over our house, setting up cameras and lights.

Peter and I were out in the back yard with Zan, playing with him until the film crew was ready.

'I hope he doesn't freak out when he gets in there,' I said.

'Every celebrity's entitled to a few tantrums,' Peter joked, but I could tell he was nervous too.

The university had been contacted just last week by a show called *60 Minutes*, which was huge apparently, a much bigger deal than *Time* magazine. They'd wanted to send a film crew to Victoria to do a piece on Project Zan. Dad had been hesitant about the whole thing, but the university wanted the publicity, and Greg Jaworksi agreed, saying it would focus the eyes of the world on our research.

Every so often, Mom would come out into the back yard

with just one or two members of the film crew, so Zan had a chance to get used to everyone gradually. It seemed to work, because when we finally took him inside, Zan seemed pretty calm – which was amazing, since our house was totally transformed.

The furniture was all moved around and there were cables taped to the floor and big lights on stands and a boom mike dangling like a giant fishing rod over the living room. It was like they were shooting a movie in our own house and we were all actors.

But Zan was the star.

Nervously I watched him look around at everything and everyone with wide eyes. Our house was hot with all the lights, and crammed with strangers: the lighting guys and sound operators and cameramen and the show producers and the interviewer himself, who was famous and very distinguished-looking.

I would've freaked out, but Zan was a complete charmer. Dad and Greg Jaworski had the fun box set up in the middle of the living room and Zan promptly sat down beside it and signed *Come play* to Peter and me.

So we sat down on the floor and played and signed as the cameras rolled, and then Dad and Greg took over for a while. Mom and Peter and I stayed close the whole time. I couldn't believe how well-behaved Zan was. He seemed to forget all about the lights and the camera pointed at him.

The crew stayed for three days, shooting tons of footage of Zan, and interviewing Dad and Greg and Professor Godwin. It couldn't have gone better. Dad said so himself after they'd finally packed up and left.

Two days later, Greg left too. He was going back to California with boxes of logbooks and videotape of Zan to review. He seemed genuinely fond of Zan, and even more excited by the project than when he'd arrived two weeks before.

I wasn't surprised. It had been a full year since we'd started teaching Zan ASL. He used about forty-five signs reliably. Sometimes he combined two signs. He signed to his toys when he played with them. I'd even seen him sign to the birds in the back yard. Once I caught him sneaking into the kitchen and heading for the fridge, signing *drink* to himself when he thought no one was watching.

What's more, he was learning faster than ever. During August he'd learned two new signs every week. *Mine. Come. Good. There. Hurt. Dirty.* It was almost impossible to believe, watching the new words formed by his swift hands.

It was like they'd always been ready, eagerly waiting for us to give them a voice.

First day of grade nine, and I was *ready*.

After Dad dropped me off, I walked across the quad, Led Zeppelin's 'Good Times Bad Times' blaring in my head, my personal dominant male soundtrack.

Project Jennifer had definitely lost ground over the summer. It wasn't surprising, since she'd been away for most of it. But there was certainly no progress in August. After the beach, we went out a couple of times in a big group, once to a movie, once just to hang out in Beacon Hill Park. She was perfectly nice to me, but she always seemed kind of distracted. And there'd been no more kissing.

I was ready to get things back on track. I'd been doing research.

The previous week I'd taken my logbook down to the local library and checked out the women's magazines, like *Vogue* and *Cosmopolitan*. I slipped them inside *Popular Mechanics*, so no one would see. They were filled with all sorts of informative articles about how to hook a man and drive him crazy with desire – and what kind of man was the best man to drive crazy.

According to the articles, women liked men who made them feel good about themselves. They liked men who complimented them, and admired them, and made them feel like the centre of the universe. But they didn't want to be smothered. In fact, they liked confident men who were a bit mysterious, even a bit distant. It seemed men had to do a lot of stuff – but I figured I could handle it.

As I crossed the school quad, I passed Jennifer with her little cult and noticed her hair was different.

'Jennifer Godwin,' I said, '*love* the new hair!' Not stopping to talk, just walking by, playing it cool. *Places to go, people to see.* Jane didn't even have time to give me a sneer.

The first obstacle came pretty fast, though. It turned out Jennifer and I weren't in the same homeroom any more. In fact we were in only one class together. History. When I came into the room, she was already there, and waved at me like she wanted me to come sit beside her. I casually lifted a hand, ambled over, and sat down between her and Selena Grove. I made sure to start talking to Selena, who'd been to Toronto over the summer holidays. *A bit mysterious. A bit distant.*

During the day I kept an eye on Hugh, trying to figure out if he liked Jennifer too. And did Jennifer like *him?* It was hard to tell. Mostly Hugh seemed to ignore her. I wondered if Hugh had read the same magazines as me.

I wasn't intending to ignore her. I'd still talk to her and joke with her, but I just wouldn't smother her. It would take discipline, but a good scientist didn't deviate from his methodology.

Friday afternoon, at the end of the second week of school, I was talking with David at my locker, cramming stuff into my knapsack.

'So what are you up to this weekend?' I asked. By 'you' I meant him and Jennifer, and I was hoping they had something planned and would invite me along.

He shrugged. 'Nothing much.'

'Want to do something?' I said.

'Yeah, maybe.' He didn't seem terribly enthusiastic. 'I'll call you later.'

A whole bunch of stuff tumbled out of my locker onto the floor.

At the top of the pile was my Project Jennifer logbook.

I had no idea how it got there. I always kept it at home.

Always. Somehow it must've gotten stuck inside one of my schoolbooks.

And there it was, face up on the floor: *Project Jennifer* in big letters.

I looked at David. He was staring down at it. I bent to snatch it up, but he grabbed it first.

'David,' I said.

I tried to swipe it out of his hand, but he turned his back on me, laughing, and flipped it open.

'Man,' he said, 'this thing is *full*!'

Again I tried to snatch it back, but he shoulder-checked me and kept looking.

I was terrified he'd find something really embarrassing, and suddenly I felt a flare of my old anger. I grabbed him by the shoulders and shoved him hard against the locker. His eyes narrowed.

'Take it easy, Tarzan,' he said, tossing the logbook at me. 'As if I care about your stupid diary.'

I glanced around the hallway. Had anyone seen this? Just a couple of upper-years.

'Sorry,' I muttered. 'It's just . . . it's private, man, all right?'

'Forget it.' He walked off.

I felt like I was going to throw up. David was a good friend to me. I just hoped he was a loyal one, too.

'So, after he has lunch,' Peter said, 'he usually likes some quiet time for an hour or so. You can read him a book, or play with his dolls, nothing too rambunctious.'

It was the weekend, and I was in Zan's suite helping Peter train one of the new research students, Joyce Lenardon.

'OK,' she said, noting it in her binder. She was very organized. She had the same kind of haircut as Jennifer.

'. . . right, Ben?' Peter was suddenly saying to me.

'Sorry, what?' I said.

'Zan also likes watching the birds outside if it's nice.'

'Oh, yeah. He loves that.'

I'd been distracted all day, worrying about whether David would tell Jennifer about the logbook. I'd thought about calling him up and asking him – begging him – not to, but I was worried he'd still be too angry with me. I'd really blown it.

Zan was walking around his playroom with us, holding Peter's hand. I noticed Peter's grip was good and tight. We'd had a lot of new students start in the past few weeks, and I thought Zan was getting tired of it. Sometimes if he didn't like them, he'd really act up.

Since we'd gotten rid of the learning chair, mostly his behaviour had been excellent. But he was also getting bigger, and stronger, and – when he felt like it – more aggressive. He'd start tickling someone and then his tickles would get too rough, or he'd grab hold of the student's leg and refuse to let go, and just squeeze and squeeze. We'd had a couple of people quit after their very first shift with him.

Luckily, Zan seemed to like Joyce. She was very calm, and that seemed to make Zan calm.

'Why don't you just sit down with us on the floor,' Peter said to Joyce, 'and I'll read him a book and—'

Peter had opened a book to read to Zan, but Zan took it from his hand and carried it over to Joyce.

'Wow,' said Peter. 'He must really like you.'

Joyce smiled as Zan climbed into her lap.

Book, Zan signed.

'Oh, that's the sign for *book*, right?' said Joyce.

'That's it,' said Peter.

Joyce started reading, pointing out all the pictures. If Zan knew the word, he'd sometimes sign it to himself.

Then he suddenly turned to Joyce and signed, *Drink*.

'What's that one?' Joyce said.

'Drink,' I said.

Sweet drink, Zan signed at Joyce, who looked at me again for an explanation.

'No, Zan,' I said, signing back. 'No sweet drink. He had enough at lunch,' I told Joyce.

But Zan ignored me and kept signing only to Joyce.

Sweet drink.

Get drink.

Me drink.

And Joyce just kept smiling kindly and looking a bit confused, because she didn't know much ASL yet. Zan's signs got faster and sloppier, and I looked over at Peter, worried.

'Do you think he's getting a bit frustr—' I began, and then I heard Joyce cry out and saw Peter lunge at Zan. Joyce was holding him back with her hands, and Peter grabbed Zan under the arms and wrenched him away.

'No, Zan!' said Peter. 'No!'

'What happened?' I asked, bewildered.

'He tried to bite her,' Peter said, and then Zan twisted free of his grip and jumped up onto the table and shrieked at Joyce.

'Joyce,' said Peter, 'go to the kitchen while we get him calmed down.'

Pale, Joyce stood up and left the playroom.

'Why'd he do that?' I asked Peter.

'Maybe he felt insulted she didn't sign back – I don't know,' said Peter.

But we didn't have any more time to talk because Zan was having a nuclear temper tantrum now. He ripped off his shirt and diaper.

'Zan,' I said, signing. 'Stop!'

We chased after him into his bedroom, where he peed and pooed on the floor. Then he hurled himself back into the playroom and jumped up onto the kitchenette counter. He shrieked and hooted, and I wasn't sure if he was happy or furious.

He grabbed hold of two cupboard handles and pulled. Luckily they were locked, but before we could get to him, he pulled so hard the doors ripped off their flimsy hinges. Zan flung them to the floor and swiped his hands into the cupboards, bringing down a cascade of glassware and dishes.

'Zan!' I shouted, as he threw a glass at the wall.

It was one of the first times I didn't understand him.

I looked at him, having his temper tantrum, and thought:

Animal.

* * *

210

On the Sunday night that the 60 *Minutes* piece was airing, the Godwins invited us to dinner so we could all watch it on their huge wood-panelled colour TV.

I was pretty nervous about going over. It had been two weeks since the logbook incident. At school, David and I would nod and say hello as we passed in the hallways, but we weren't talking much.

Had he told Jennifer? Maybe he hadn't even read anything – he hadn't had it in his hands that long. Maybe all he'd really seen was the cover. But what would Jennifer think if she knew I'd written an entire book about her? Would I be the mysterious man that made her feel admired and complimented? Would she be flattered – or just think I was a psychopath?

There was another problem too. I worried I'd made a mistake with Project Jennifer. I couldn't help noticing that the more distant I was with her, the more distant she seemed to be with me. I was starting to have doubts about how effective my current methods were. I'd have to reassess the data.

It was David who opened the door when we arrived.

'Hey, Tarzan!' he said.

He gave me a big smile, and I felt such relief. He was still my friend. He wouldn't have told Jennifer. Professor and Mrs Godwin ushered us into the living room, where they uncorked a bottle of champagne.

'Where's Jennifer?' Mom asked.

Everyone else was there, even Hairy Cal, with almost all his chest hair buttoned up inside a shirt.

'She's a little under the weather,' said Mrs Godwin, giving

Mom a significant look. Mom nodded sympathetically. 'But she said she'd come down for dinner.'

Was Jennifer sick? No one seemed that concerned. Or was she just hiding in her room because she didn't want to see me?

But a few minutes later she came downstairs. She looked fine, maybe a tiny bit pale, which I thought made her look even sexier, like she'd been up all night, gazing out of the window, listening to music – maybe thinking about me.

'Hey,' she said to me. 'Are you excited about seeing yourself on TV?'

'I don't even know if I'll be in it,' I said. 'They shot a ton of stuff, but they said it was only going to be ten minutes, so who knows.'

I shrugged like I didn't really care, but I was figuring there'd be at least one or two shots of me. I'd never been on TV before, and this was *international* TV. I was hoping this would give me a big boost – maybe the final push I needed to complete Project Jennifer. Being on CBS was way better than being European.

'Want to go downstairs?' David asked me before dinner.

'Sure.' I looked over at Jennifer, who was sitting on the chesterfield with her mom.

'I'll be down in a bit,' she said to us.

I was hoping we could go and blast some music. If I could get her alone, even for a few seconds, I was going to kiss her again. One of the other things I'd learned from the women's magazines was tips on kissing. I didn't think I was a total disaster – I'd never drooled on her or bitten her – but I had a lot of room for improvement. 'Five Kisses to Make Your

Man Swoon', the article had promised. I really wanted to try them out.

But Jennifer never showed up, and Mrs Godwin was calling us up for dinner. The Godwins did not serve the kids wine.

'School tomorrow,' Professor Godwin said. 'Can't have you staggering into Windermere hungover.'

Jennifer didn't seem very hungry. I pulled out a couple of my best lines (from the logbook) to get a conversation going, but she wasn't playing along tonight. I talked mostly to David.

After dessert it was almost time for 60 *Minutes*, and we all settled around the TV. It turned out our segment was near the end, so we had to get through the rest of the show first. My heart was thumping away, faster and faster with each minute.

I glanced at Mom and Dad and they seemed excited, but kind of tense too. There was a sort of blue waxy look to their faces, or maybe that was just the light spilling out from the huge TV screen.

Suddenly I thought it was weird that Zan wasn't here to see this. Peter was back home babysitting and he said they'd try to watch it on our little black-and-white TV, but Zan probably wouldn't care. I'd never seen him watch TV with any interest.

Finally our piece started. I could barely concentrate on what the host was saying. There were some nice shots of Victoria – described as a small picturesque city in the Pacific Northwest – and the university, which they described as a small university whose psych department was quickly building a worldwide name for itself with cutting-edge research.

I glanced over at Professor Godwin and he looked fairly pleased with himself. His wife squeezed his hand.

Then it moved to our house. They started in the kitchen, with a shot of the high chair from behind, and for a second, you would've thought it was just a regular kid sitting in it. But then as the camera moved closer and around, you saw it was actually a chimp. It was Zan, in his sweatshirt and shorts, holding a spoon and feeding himself Froot Loops. I was helping him.

I looked pretty good on TV. I was tanned and my hair was sandy blond. But it was strange, watching myself. It was like looking at someone *pretending* to be me. I'd had no idea my mouth moved like that when I talked.

'Hey, that Tomlin kid's quite the stud,' said David.

'Shush, David,' said his mother.

I glanced over at Jennifer. She was blushing. That was a good sign. If she didn't like me, why would she blush?

There were interviews with Dad and Greg Jaworski and Mom, and one with Professor Godwin in his office, and then lots of footage of Zan at our house, playing and signing. I was in quite a few of the shots. They described me as Zan's 'big brother'. Then there was Peter, reading Zan a bedtime story.

'Is Peter a major toker?' David asked.

'David,' said his father warningly.

'He *looks* like a major pothead,' David whispered to me.

Jennifer was looking over and nodding, so I laughed, but right away felt mean, like I'd betrayed Peter.

And then, suddenly, filling the screen:

The learning chair.

214

It was a black-and-white photo, and I don't know if they'd touched it up or something, but it looked huge and terrifying and cruel.

Zan was strapped into it, small and totally defeated.

I was so shocked I scarcely heard what the host was saying in the voice-over. Something about strict methods and controversial teaching techniques.

'I thought you'd gotten rid of that thing,' Professor Godwin said sharply to Dad.

'We did,' Dad said, eyes fixed on the TV. 'I have no idea how they got that picture.'

It seemed like it was up on screen for ever. It was terrible. It made Zan look like a prisoner. I'd hated that chair from the first moment I'd seen it, and now everyone in North America was looking at it too.

Then up came William Eckler, the animal rights guy, and he was saying that human beings had a very poor record of treating apes and chimps with the respect they deserved. He said that people who performed experiments on these animals were little better than slave owners.

'Crackpot!' said Professor Godwin. 'Honestly, why did they get him on?'

'At least they said we don't use the chair any more,' Mom pointed out.

There was another minute or so of Zan playing and signing with us, and he looked perfectly happy in his sandbox and on the jungle gym. But the whole mood of the piece had been changed now.

Afterwards, it was pretty uncomfortable in the Godwins' living room. Everyone said nice things and talked about how it was very positive overall, and would really attract the scientific community's attention to the project, and the university. But it was sort of like having someone throw up at a birthday party. You tried to make the best of it, but the smell was hard to ignore. By the time we left, I felt like I might throw up myself.

We got into the car and Dad drove in total silence until we were a couple of blocks away. It was like he wanted to make sure the Godwins couldn't hear.

'Ben,' he said. 'Do you have any idea how they got that picture?'

'Why are you asking him?' Mom asked, sounding surprised.

'I didn't take it!' I exclaimed.

'You telling me the truth, Ben?'

'Richard!' Mom said. 'Ben wouldn't lie to us!'

'Fine,' said Dad, but he didn't sound convinced. 'Well, do you know who *did* take it, then?'

'No!' I said.

'What about Peter?' Dad asked.

'Why would Peter do that?' I demanded.

'He was against the chair from the start, just like you.'

'Yes,' said Mom, 'but what he wanted was for you to get rid of it. And you did. What would he gain by giving a picture to CBS?'

I was insulted they were even talking like it was a possibility.

'Lots of people took pictures,' I reminded them. It was true. Most of the students at some point had brought a camera and taken snaps of themselves with Zan. He was famous. A talking chimp. Everyone wanted their own memento.

'It could've been anyone,' Mom said. 'It's probably someone who quit or left.'

'I intend to find out who it was,' said Dad. He sounded furious. 'CBS never told me they were putting any of that in.'

'They didn't need your permission,' Mom said. Her voice was strangely calm. 'They're reporters, after a story.'

'We were way too lax,' Dad fumed. 'Letting students take pictures.'

'What's going to happen now?' I asked, suddenly worried. 'Is someone going to take Zan away from us?'

Dad actually gave a snort of laughter. 'We've done nothing wrong, Ben. People like William Eckler, frankly, are voices crying out in the wilderness. They're bleeding hearts who live in a dream world. We meet and exceed every single guideline on how to treat animal test subjects.'

'Is that how you think of him?' I said, shocked.

'Who?'

'Zan. An *animal test subject*?' It was the first time I'd heard him use that term.

Dad blew out his breath in exasperation. 'Not right now, Ben. Tomorrow is going to be a very bad day. We're going to be deluged with phone calls from people worried about the welfare of that poor little chimp.'

I was glad Zan wasn't going to be taken away. And part of

me was glad CBS had shown the chair. I didn't think Dad was embarrassed about it, or thought it was cruel, but maybe now, with so many people watching, he'd be even more careful about how he treated Zan.

The next morning I half expected people with signs to be demonstrating outside our house, chanting: 'Free Zan! Free Zan!'

At school, when I got to homeroom, someone had put a stuffed chimp on my chair, all tied up in string, with a note saying, *Somebody help me!* It made me feel really sad, and even though I tried hard to think of something funny or outrageous to say or do, nothing came to me. So I just threw the toy in the garbage can and sat down. I didn't feel like a dominant male right now.

When Dad got home that night he poured himself a drink.

'Lots of calls?' I said.

'Lots,' he said. 'And I found out who gave CBS the picture.'

'I have a pretty good idea,' said Mom.

'The producers of the show got hold of a list of all our research students,' Dad said. 'They called up a bunch, until they found someone willing to say something negative. It was Susan Wilkes.'

'Her?' I exclaimed. Creepy Susan, who looked at Dad with adoration and nodded at everything he said? 'I thought she loved you!'

'She did,' Mom said coldly.

I stared at her, startled. 'Really?'

218

Dad sighed and actually looked embarrassed. 'Sarah, is this necessary?'

'She was heartbroken Dad didn't love her back,' Mom said. 'So this was her revenge.'

The second weekend of October there was a big storm, and the winds brought down a lot of dead branches from the elm in our back yard. When Mom and I took Zan outside the next morning, he got really excited. He scampered around, gathering up all the smaller branches, and dragging the bigger ones, and arranging them into a mound.

'Do you know what he's doing?' Mom said in amazement.

'What?'

'He's building a nest!'

'Really?' I'd read about how chimps made nests in trees. It had surprised me, because it seemed so unlikely – something birds and squirrels did, but not chimps.

Mom nodded. 'Absolutely. Go get your camera.'

When I came back, Zan was still fussing around with the branches. I snapped some photos as he climbed up and flopped down in the middle of his nest, half hidden.

'This is incredible,' said Mom. 'Chimps in the wild start doing this around one year old. Zan's never *seen* a nest. No one's *taught* him to do this. But he does it anyway.'

'How, though?' I said.

'It must be genetic,' said Mom. 'It's all there in his brain. No matter how hard we try to raise him as human, he knows he's a chimp.'

It made me happy, to think that there were parts of Zan we couldn't touch.

I took lots of pictures for Mom. She said Dad wouldn't be interested, but for her own research – studying the difference between chimp and human behaviour and development – this was important data.

That night, while helping to clean up after dinner, Zan jumped off the sink and walked over to the wall and stared at something. After a couple of minutes I went to him, to see what he was looking at. It must've been pretty interesting to take him away from his beloved washing up.

What? I signed.

He kept staring. As far as I could tell there was nothing there.

Then, without warning, Zan bounded back to the sink, jumped onto the counter, and grabbed the dish soap. He'd tricked me! He'd set me up! He gave a shriek of delight and sent out a spray of soap, but I caught him fast and wrestled the bottle away from him – and tickled him until he was laughing so hard he couldn't even sign *more* any more.

CHAPTER 16

WEATHER CHANGE

It was the Halloween dance, the first one of grade nine, and when I found Jennifer in the swirl of light and sound and heat, I asked her to dance.

'I don't really feel like dancing to this song,' she said into my ear.

'That's cool,' I said. 'How about the next one?'

'I just don't feel like dancing right now.'

It was a lie. I'd seen her dancing earlier when I came in.

'You danced with Hugh,' I pointed out.

She seemed annoyed. 'So? You think you're better than Hugh?'

'No,' I said, confused. I didn't understand why she was being this way. I felt my face heat up, and was glad she wouldn't see it in the half-light of the hall.

'Are you mad at me?' I asked, which I instantly knew was a mistake. It wasn't a dominant male question.

'No. Why don't you ask Selena to dance. She loves dancing.'

'I don't want to dance with Selena. I want to dance with you.' The next song had just started up, and it was really good. I smiled and tried to take her hand. 'C'mon!'

She frowned and pulled away. 'I'm not your *chimp*, Ben. You can't just order me around. Or tie me up.'

She looked past me and smiled and waved. 'Hey, Shannon! Jane!'

Somehow this upset me even more than the chimp comment. Like I'd been dismissed; like I wasn't even there. For the first time, I felt angry with her, and it wasn't a small anger. It was big and hot. What had *I* done wrong? What more was I supposed to do to please her? She started to walk off and I felt my fury swell and push at me, and before I could stop myself, I said, 'Why are you being such a *bitch*?'

She stopped and turned to me with a look of real disgust in her face, and then she just walked off.

The music pounded and my heart pounded faster and for a split second I wanted to pull her back, but I didn't. All the anger gushed out of me and I felt sick – and totally ashamed.

I could see Jennifer talking to Shannon and Jane, shaking her head. Then Jane looked my way, and I turned and walked for the darkest part of the hall. Everyone was going to hear I'd called her a bitch at the dance, and everyone would think I was a jerk, and now Jennifer would never like me. I'd gone and crashed Project Jennifer.

I saw Hugh talking with David, and jealousy surged through my veins. So it *was* Hugh she liked. Hugh was my rival. In a fight, male chimps went first for the toes. They'd bite them off. That immobilized their opponent. Then they'd go for the fingers, so he couldn't grab and hold. Then they'd go for the face, to maim, to bloody his eyes so he couldn't see. And last, they'd go for the scrotum to castrate him – so he'd bleed to death. That, I'd read, was what chimps did to each other in a life-or-death fight.

It scared me even thinking like this, and I didn't want to be here any more, so I left the hall fast, found a pay phone, and called for Mom to pick me up.

Zan knew right away I was sad.

Saturday morning when I went into his bedroom to get him dressed, he looked at me really intently. Maybe it was my face. I'd been up a lot of the night crying, and probably looked crappy. Or maybe it was my hoarse voice. He kept coming up to me and stroking me and signing, *Sorry*. He thought he'd done something wrong.

Zan good, I signed to him.

He looked at me. I don't know what he thought of that: *Zan good?* He knew food was good and ginger ale was good and tickling was good, but I'm not sure we'd used good in any other way yet.

Could he understand that people could be good too? He gazed deep into my eyes, like he could see all of me. It was such a kind look, it started me crying again, and Zan frowned and

223

put his face closer to mine and touched my tears and tasted them and seemed very surprised.

Come hug, he signed. *Tickle hug*.

And after we'd had a good long hug and tickle, he pulled away from me and signed, *Hide now*.

He covered his face with his hand, peeking, which was his way of asking for hide-and-seek. He was trying to cheer me up. I shook my head and signed *No* a few times. He brought me over some of his favourite dolls and put them in my lap. Then he sat down on top of me and patted me a lot.

He knew how I felt.

Sometimes brothers don't need to say anything.

School was torture. If I'd been more confident, I could've carried on with the dominant male routine and been un-apologetic.

Sure I called her a bitch. Big deal – she deserved it.

But I couldn't do it. The moment I arrived at school on Monday, I just felt like a cockroach. I felt like I should be scuttling around into corners and under desks so nobody would step on me. Whenever Jennifer came into my peripheral vision, I looked away.

Wednesday after school, David and I were in the changing rooms after cross-country practice. We were the first back from the run, so were alone. David took a plastic bag from his locker and passed it to me. He seemed uncomfortable, even a bit sorry for me.

'This is from Jen.'

I opened up the bag and saw the ABBA album I'd given her for her birthday.

'She loved that album, man,' said David.

I chuckled bitterly. 'What did she say about me?' I'd always been too afraid to ask, but there was nothing to lose any more. 'Not just now, but in general, you know, over the last year.'

David shrugged.

'She must've said *something*.'

'She thought you were a nice guy, fun to hang out with. Stuff like that.'

'A *fun* guy,' I said. 'Wow, that's exciting. We made out, you know!'

He said nothing.

'Did you tell her about the logbook?' I demanded.

'That big book with her name on it?'

'Yeah, that one.'

He grimaced. 'Sort of.'

'What'd she say?' I asked.

'Jane said it was creepy.'

'You told *Jane* too?' I said in horror.

'She's always over at our house!' David said. 'She's like an evil stepsister. I just told Jen you had this book where you wrote stuff about her. It looked like a pretty thick book, man. I mean, *Project Jennifer*? It looked like you were running an experiment on her.'

'It wasn't an *experiment*,' I muttered angrily, but the words stung. *Had* I been treating it like an experiment? Was she my little chimp, just like she'd said at the dance?

'Thanks a lot for wrecking everything,' I said. 'Thanks a million.'

'What'd I wreck?' he said, sounding annoyed for the first time.

'I thought me and your sister, you know . . . *had* something.'

'It's not like you were going out,' he said.

'Yeah, because she can't till she's sixteen!'

'I don't think she would've wanted to anyway,' he said.

I stared at him hard. 'Really?'

'She said you weren't a good kisser.'

I pretended to get something out of my locker, so he wouldn't see my burning face. 'Like she would know,' I said. 'Like she's been kissed a million times.'

'She said you guys had no chemistry.'

I looked at him, stunned. 'She actually told you that?'

'Well, not *me*,' said David. 'But I overheard her talking to Jane.'

'No chemistry, huh?'

He winced and shook his head. 'Sorry, man.'

'I thought we did. *I* did, anyway – for her, I mean.'

David pulled his dress shirt back on. 'She likes Hugh.'

It was like getting punched in the stomach. I sat down on the bench and fussed with my shoes.

'They've known each other, like, for ever,' David said, as if this somehow made it easier for me. 'She was pretty torn up when he started going out with Kelly. I think she was trying to make him jealous. And then, when they broke up . . . you know.'

'Uh-huh,' I said.

I felt dazed by how pointless it all was – all the work and observation and thinking. The lists and the daydreams and the plans. None of it mattered. I could be in a magazine and on TV. I could be funny and give her compliments and presents. I'd tried to do it right. Scientifically. But it didn't matter.

Because of chemistry. Was that what really made it work, even between people? I knew animals used chemistry. They worked on hormones and smells and tastes. That's how they decided who to mate with. And I guessed humans were just the same. No matter how hard I tried, without the right chemistry, I was screwed.

'She's a pain, anyway,' said David. 'Honestly, it's for the best. Cheer up, Tarzan. Hey, Jane likes you, big time.'

November: it was dark when I woke up for school and dark when I came home. It was always cloudy. The sun, when you could see it, was a dingy forty-watt bulb.

At school, I tried to make myself scarce. I started bringing a bag lunch so I wouldn't have to eat in the dining hall. Just the idea of walking in was horrible; I imagined everyone turning to look at me. I ate in one of the empty classrooms. David and I didn't talk as much any more. He wasn't mean to me, but he didn't seek me out, and I avoided him too. Seeing him just made me think of Jennifer and the whole humiliating business. Cross-country season ended, and I tried to work hard on my school work. That would please Dad, at least.

Towards the end of the month, one Wednesday after

school, I took the bus to the university. I had a project on Japan, post-World War Two, and our school library was pretty lousy. Dad had said he'd help me take out some books at the university.

I got to the campus early, and as I approached the psych department I saw a single guy standing outside the entrance with a sandwich board sign that said:

ARE HUMANS HUMANE?

He was handing out leaflets to whoever would take one. Not many would. He looked a bit like Peter, only whacked out. I took one of his leaflets as I passed him on the steps, and stuffed it into my pocket. I wondered if he was there because of Zan.

Dad's office was on the second floor, and as I approached I saw his door was closed. Through the tall skinny window, I noticed Professor Godwin. Dad was sitting behind his desk, and Professor Godwin was standing in front of it, talking. Dad nodded. I couldn't hear what Professor Godwin was saying, but there was something about Dad's expression, the way his body was arranged, which made me think Professor Godwin was giving him a hard time.

I suddenly felt sorry for Dad, which wasn't a feeling I had very often. I didn't want to keep watching – and I didn't want Professor Godwin to see me either. Jennifer had probably told him about the dance, and he'd hate my guts now.

I turned round and headed back to the stairwell, planning to go downstairs and buy a chocolate bar from the vending machine. Maybe it would fall on me and crush me and end my misery.

On the stairs I ran into Shira Mavjee in a lab coat. She worked with Zan twice a week, and she was always very nice and patient with him, even when he was in a bullying mood.

'Hi, Ben,' she said with a smile. 'Here to see your dad? Isn't he in his office?'

'Yeah, but he's still busy.'

'You want to see some rats?' she asked. 'They're pretty cute.'

I shrugged. 'Sure.'

'C'mon.' She led me down to the basement labs. Other white-coated students and professors walked up and down the long hall. It smelled unpleasantly of chemicals.

'Did you see that guy outside the building?' I asked her.

'He's been here a couple of days.'

'Do you think he saw the learning chair on TV?'

'Doubt it. He's always demonstrating about something. Last week it was clear-cutting trees. I think he did nukes too.'

I felt a bit better. Maybe it wasn't about Zan at all. Shira led me into a big room with rows of rat cages along one wall.

'What are you doing with them?' I asked.

'It's a cognitive response experiment,' she said. 'It's one of your dad's, actually.'

'Really?' I said, surprised. Dad had never talked about this.

Looking deeper into the lab, I caught a glimpse of Ryan Cross, Dad's star grad student, leaning over some kind of big glass case with a stopwatch. He operated a series of lights, and watched what was happening inside.

'Ryan's timing the trials,' said Shira.

I wasn't happy to see Ryan, after the way he'd treated Zan,

and he didn't look too happy to see me either. He didn't even say hello.

'I didn't know Dad was working with rats again,' I said.

'Project Zan isn't the only show in town,' said Ryan. 'And if I was a betting man, I'd say these rats are going to be more important to science than your chimp.'

I wished Zan had taken his whole finger off – maybe his hand too.

Ryan looked at Shira. 'He shouldn't be down here.'

'What's the big deal?' she said.

'It's a university lab, not a daycare,' said Ryan.

Shira frowned and shook her head at him. 'He's just going to look at the rats, Ryan.'

Ryan gave a hollow laugh. 'Just make sure he doesn't let them all out. By the way, 23-D isn't going to pull through.'

'Who's that?' I asked.

'One of the rats,' said Shira. 'It didn't respond well to the meds.'

Ryan had a needle in his hand and was going over to one of the cages.

'What are you doing to it?' I asked.

'Euthanizing it.'

'Killing it?'

'It suffers less. For its own good.'

Hard to imagine the rat would agree with that.

'They sometimes have seizures because of the drugs,' Shira explained, 'and then strokes, and then they're paralysed, like this one. It can't feed itself.'

After injecting the rat Ryan reached in and grabbed it by the tail and put it in a blue plastic bag, knotted it, and chucked it into a bin.

'It just goes in there?' I said dully.

'Well, normally there's a memorial service and hymns,' said Ryan, 'but we're a little pressed for time.'

Even Shira laughed. I didn't want to look at the rats any more. I didn't want to see them all in their cages, row after row.

'My dad's probably waiting for me.'

'See you later,' said Shira.

I headed back upstairs, and in the corridor passed Professor Godwin. He looked at me and gave a curt little nod and said, 'Ben,' but there was no warmth in his voice. He knew. He hated me.

Dad was waiting for me in his office.

'Is that guy outside the building here because of Zan?' I asked.

'He mentions him in his leaflet,' Dad said. 'But he's a campus crackpot. He'll move on to something else in a couple of days. Nukes, or free love, or polygamy. The SPCA wrote us a letter, though. They want to visit our house to make sure Zan's being treated humanely.'

'He is, though,' I said.

Dad shrugged. 'It's just a nuisance, nothing more. Now, you wanted to get some books out of the library, right?'

'I didn't know you had a rat experiment going,' I said.

I guess I'd always assumed that even if Dad didn't spend much time personally with Zan, he was still totally devoted to him, or to the *project* at least. I didn't like thinking Zan had to share his attention with rats.

'Rats are very interesting animals,' Dad said. 'We can learn a lot from them.'

Greg Jaworski came back from Berkeley in early December. He spent lots of time at our house, observing Zan with Mom and the students. And he spent even more time down at the university with Dad, watching the latest video footage. There were hundreds of hours of it.

Whenever Dad got home from work, he seemed even quieter than usual. I wondered if maybe he wasn't getting along with Jaworksi, or maybe Godwin was angry with him for the bad publicity over the 60 *Minutes* piece. But when I'd ask Mom if anything was wrong, she just said Dad was preoccupied with the project, and that he and Greg had a lot of material to collate and prepare for the big grant deadline in early January.

Still, I couldn't shake the feeling Dad was worried, and I didn't really understand it. Zan was still learning two new words a week. He'd even made his first three-word phrase a couple of days ago: *Drink more water*. The vocabulary wall-chart in our kitchen was getting pretty impressive. There was no way we could get turned down for the grant again. We had so much more data, plus this hotshot American scientist working with us now. When he went back home after three weeks, he didn't take two suitcases of videotapes with him this time.

I was glad when my classes ended for the holidays. My report card arrived a couple of days before Christmas, and my marks had improved. I wasn't getting As or anything, but mostly Bs and some Cs. Dad barely seemed to care. He glanced distractedly at the report card and said, 'Good, Ben.'

At school I'd gone from dominant male to low-ranking insect. I had no social life, and now, even though I'd been working hard in class, I couldn't even please my own father.

CHAPTER 17

SLOW LEARNER

At breakfast, Dad wasn't reading the newspaper, and Mom wasn't talking much. I could tell she was angry at Dad, really angry. She wouldn't look him in the eye, and she was super polite and formal whenever she asked for something. *Could you pass the butter, please? Thank you very much.* Zan was in his suite with the students, so it was just the three of us around the table.

It was four days after Christmas.

A feeling of dread began to expand in my stomach, and I could barely spoon down the last of my cornflakes.

'What's going on?' I asked finally.

'There's no easy way to tell you this, Ben,' Dad said. 'We're shutting down the project.'

Right away I looked at Mom. I didn't know why; maybe just to make sure it was really true. She was staring at the table.

'But why would you do that?' I demanded.

I saw Dad's chest rise, then fall. 'Zan's not learning language.'

It was like being told something so obviously untrue, you didn't know what to say.

The sun won't be coming up today, Ben.

Your mother and I are aliens from another planet. Sorry.

Again I looked at Mom, shaking my head. Dad might as well have been from another planet. He wasn't making any sense.

'Who says?' I said. 'Who says he's not learning?'

'Greg and I have gone through the videotapes—' he began, but I cut him off.

'So it's *Greg* who doesn't think he's learning?'

'We've watched the tapes together and it's clear Zan's mimicking us. He's very clever, Ben, there's no question. He watches us signing, and he watches for our cues—'

'*Cues?* We don't give him cues!' I protested.

'Oh, we do, Ben. You might not know it, but we do. It's very subtle, but our body language, our faces, our hands, they all give him clues about how he should be replying. Watching the tapes in slow motion, it's very easy to see. And because we know what the answer should be, we're more likely to get it.'

I shook my head. 'I don't understand.'

'It's like this,' Dad said. 'I show him a toy, and he signs *toy. I* know it's a toy, so I'm more likely to *see* him sign *toy,* even if he hasn't – not properly anyway. I put it down in my logbook, but it's unreliable data.'

'We should've been doing double-blind tests,' said Mom.

'What're those?' I asked.

'You use two people,' Mom explained. 'One person shows

Zan the object; the second person doesn't even see the object, but only watches Zan when he makes the sign. So that second person isn't expecting any particular answer. That way it's completely impartial.'

'Zan tricked us,' Dad said.

'*He* tricked *us?*' I said. 'We treat him like a human baby and pretend we're his real family, and *he's* tricking *us?*'

Dad said, 'Ben, control yourself.'

'Richard, he's upset,' said Mom.

'Losing his temper is not going to make it any easier for him,' said Dad.

'Zan talks to us all the time,' I insisted. 'He asks for things. He learned two new signs last week!'

Dad nodded. 'He's learning *words*. He's not learning *language*.'

'What's the difference?' I said.

'There's a pretty big difference, Ben,' said Mom gently. 'Language is how we use and organize words. Grammar. Syntax. Symbolism.'

'It's a very complicated thing, language,' Dad said. 'And when I said "tricked", what I meant is he imitates us. He wants to please us. He tells us what we want, so he can get what he wants. Food. Drinks. Hugs. Rewards of all kinds.' He grimaced. 'That's one of the many fatal flaws in the experiment.'

'No,' I said. I thought of Zan lying in the back yard telling me about the birds. I thought of him trying to comfort me when I was crying. I thought of him talking to his toys. 'He tells us what he's *feeling*. He talks to himself! He's not doing that to please us! Isn't that language?'

236

'Those are very good questions, Ben,' Mom said. 'I'm not sure your father has taken them into account.'

'Zan knows certain signs, there's no doubt about that,' said Dad impatiently. 'The question is, he's not meeting the definition of language I set out in the experiment.'

'So give him more time,' I said. 'He's only one and a half! You said this was supposed to go on for years. How come he has to learn so fast? Two words a week isn't fast enough for you? Maybe he's a slow learner, like me.' I was shouting now. 'How smart does he have to be before you love him?'

There was a silence and I saw Mom look away. I thought her eyes were filled with tears.

'This,' said Dad calmly, 'is not about love, Ben. It was never meant to be. I'm not punishing Zan, I'm just saying he's not learning language, and likely never will.'

I was desperate now, talking fast. 'So just . . . just *fix* the stuff you were doing wrong. Stop the rewards, and do those double-blind things.'

'There're other problems too. And the most important thing,' said Dad, 'is that Greg has lost faith in the project.'

'What does Greg know?' I said. 'He's hardly spent any time at all with Zan! Not compared with the rest of us.'

'He's watched the footage over and over,' said Dad. 'He's correlated it with the data we've collected.'

'Greg's wrong!' I couldn't believe I'd liked him at first. 'Why can't he be wrong?'

'He's one of the most pre-eminent scientists in his field.'

'Better than *you*?' I said tauntingly, wanting to hurt him. 'Better than Professor Tomlin?'

'I'm not a linguist, Ben. He is.'

'Get someone else,' I said.

'It's not so simple. Without Greg, any possible money from the US dries up. And there's virtually no hope of getting our big Canadian grant.'

I thought of all the months of work that had been going into the application. 'But you're going to apply, right?'

He shook his head. 'There's no point. The experiment's contaminated. We've contaminated it with our mistakes. We've been turned down once before. A second rejection would be very damaging.'

'For who?' I said.

'For my reputation as a scientist,' said Dad. 'It's best to wind down the experiment quietly, publish our findings, which are fascinating in themselves. But the outcome was not what I'd hoped for.'

Outcome. Another one of Dad's icy cold words.

'So no more money for the project,' I said.

He shook his head. 'We still have enough to get us through the spring.'

I felt myself start to shake. 'OK. But we keep Zan, right?'

Mom and Dad looked at each other.

Mom said, 'We're looking into our options, Ben.'

'Don't lie to him,' said Dad. 'We can't keep Zan here. All the money that paid for his handlers, the equipment, the food – we just won't have it.'

'So? He can still live with us. His food isn't so expensive. It's not like he's an elephant or anything.'

'And who's going to look after him?' Dad asked.

'We all will. *I* will.'

Dad shook his head. 'When you're at school? I'm at work all day, and your mother has her own work to do. She's got to finish her thesis. Zan requires a full-time caregiver. An *army* of caregivers.'

'Well,' I said, struggling, 'there's got to be some way—'

'Zan's not a baby any more. He's getting harder to manage.'

I knew this was true. It wasn't just that he bit. It was his growing strength. He could rip cabinets off walls. Soon he'd be able to punch holes through them. I'd read Mom's books on chimps in the wild. With every month Zan would only get bigger and stronger.

'But he's part . . . part of our family,' I said. 'That was the deal. He belongs with us.'

Dad smiled at me, and it was meant to be a kind smile, but I hated it.

'When I was starting out as a scientist, one of the smartest things one of my profs told me was that you can't love your experimental subject. You just can't. It's a very hard lesson to learn.'

'He's not *my* experimental subject,' I yelled. 'He's *yours*. He's my little brother.'

Dad tried to take my arm, but I pulled away. 'Ben, he's not your little brother and never will be. He's an animal. He's a different species.'

'You wanted us to be a family. No one ever asked what I thought about this. Not at the beginning and not now. I say he stays.'

'It's not up to you.'

'He thinks he's one of us. You *promised* him.'

'That was necessary for the experiment.'

'You made him call you Dad,' I said. 'I can't believe you did that. You never wanted to be his dad. It was all just a game to you. A trick.'

Dad shook his head.

'He stays with us,' I repeated.

'No.'

'He stays,' I said again and started crying – and that made me mad. I wouldn't be weak in front of him. Anger, welcome anger, flooded me.

The hair on my body rose. I pushed back from the table so sharply the chair fell over with a *bang*, and the sound was like a trigger. My whole body tensed, ready for fight. I saw Dad's calm, controlled face, and I went for him, pushing him hard by the shoulders, once, twice, until he stood and tried to grab my arms to stop me. Feeling myself pinned filled me with rage. His hands closed around my upper arms.

I did what Zan would have done. I bit him.

My teeth went down hard, but hit his wedding ring instead of flesh. It gave him time to pull free. He shoved me backwards so hard I fell on the floor.

Mom hurried over to me, but I ran to the front door, grabbed my jacket, and went outside. I think she came after me, but Dad was shouting at her to let me go, let me blow off some steam.

I got my bike out of the garage and tore off.

I biked all the way down to the university. It was drizzling, but not too cold. In Toronto the roads would be piled with snow. It took over an hour, pedalling hard, almost no thoughts at all in my head except little shards and loops about Zan and Dad.

I knew the residence building Peter lived in, but that was about it, so I had to ask around before someone gave me his room number. He wasn't in. I didn't know what else to do, so I just sat down on the floor and waited. The hallway smelled like old shoes and beer. Finally Peter showed up, his army surplus satchel loaded down with library books.

'What's up, man?' he asked, looking surprised. 'How long've you been waiting out here?'

He let me into his room, which was small and cluttered, and a bit musty.

'Did you know?' I demanded.

'I had an idea, but I wasn't sure.'

'How come you never told me?'

I must have sounded really angry, because his eyes widened. He took a deep breath. 'I'm sorry, Ben. But it was kind of your mom and dad's job, not mine.'

He was right. And I wasn't really angry with him; it's not like he could've done anything to change Dad's mind. 'They say he's not learning language.'

Peter scoffed and shook his head. 'They're wrong.'

'They say we can't keep him.'

'How'd you get down here?' he asked.

'Biked.'

'Biked! You've gotta be starving. C'mon. I'll buy you a burger.' He led me down to the main-floor cafeteria where we lined up with a tray and he told me to get whatever I wanted.

'Onion rings?' he offered.

'No thanks.'

'Fries?'

'No thanks.'

'Green Jell-O?'

'OK,' I said.

'I was just kidding about the Jell-O,' he said. 'I really wouldn't eat that. That white whippy stuff on the top is made from gasoline or something. It takes six months to digest.'

I thought of Zan and how much he loved Jell-O, and put it on my tray.

We sat down near a window overlooking some huge rhododendron bushes.

'We've got to figure out how to keep Zan,' I said. Between bites of my burger, I rattled off everything Dad had said about why we couldn't keep him at the house.

'It's a big job,' Peter agreed.

'If I paid you, would you take care of him?'

'Ben—'

I talked faster. 'I've got quite a bit saved up. And then I'd figure out—'

242

'Ben, I'd do it for free.'

I stared at him. 'You would?'

'Well, I mean, I'd need to eat and pay for school. But there's a lot more to it than that. I couldn't do it all alone. You'd need more people, and then there're all the other costs.'

'See, I was thinking about maybe fundraising,' I said. 'We could charge for visits. Or school groups could come.'

'You're talking about a kind of zoo?'

'Or renting him out for commercials.'

Peter blew out a big breath. 'Well, that's a whole other can of worms. I mean, we put him in show biz and we're making him sing for his supper all over again.'

I remembered how Dad had turned down a couple of offers to use Zan in TV commercials. They'd wanted to put him in overalls and muddy boots and get him to walk around the kitchen and make a mess, and then show how you could clean up, even after all that, if you just used their amazing new kind of soap.

Even though the money was tempting, Dad had thought it would interfere with the experiment and the family stuff, and it would look like we were profiting from Zan instead of studying him. But that was all over now.

'I don't like it either,' I said. 'But it's better than him getting sent away, isn't it? You don't think Dad would send him to a lab, do you?'

Peter looked out the windows for a few seconds. 'I don't think so.'

'You won't tell anyone else about this yet, right?' I said.

He shook his head. 'I think a few people are picking up rumours. That robot, Ryan Cross, he seems to have some idea what's going on.'

I said, 'I just don't want everyone quitting on Zan right now. Dad says we've got enough money until the spring.'

Peter nodded. 'Bottom line, Ben – even if your dad had money, he doesn't want Zan around. He'll see it as . . . an embarrassment, you know. The experiment he lost control of. The one that got away. Come on, throw your bike in my trunk and I'll drive you home. Your parents are going to be worried about you.'

Mom and Dad fought that night.

They woke me up. My digital clock said it was past one in the morning. They were still downstairs in the living room, so I quietly made my way to the top of the stairs.

'. . . can't just make a unilateral decision like that,' Mom was saying. 'It affects me too.'

'You'll have had almost two full years with him,' Dad replied calmly. 'That'll give you ample data for your thesis, no problem.'

'Zan was more than a *thesis*, Richard. He was supposed to be a lifetime project for both of us.'

'It was a glorious idea, but it's not working, and there's nothing I can do about that.'

'There is. You're too impatient. You're not giving it enough time. Get rid of Jaworski and bring in someone else.'

'Greg was the perfect fit – you know that.'

'He has a very, very rigid view of language. He doesn't even have his own children.'

'So what?'

'So he has no first-hand knowledge of how children learn language.'

'He's done study after study—'

'Yeah, *studies*.'

'Which is exactly what *we* do, Sarah. Jaworski is respected.'

'*You're* respected.'

I heard Dad sigh, almost sadly. 'Not like him.'

Mom said, 'We moved our family across the country for this project, Richard. You left a good job at a good university. We left our friends behind in Ontario. We left our *families*.'

'No great loss there.'

'Not for you, maybe. Unlike you, I actually love my family.'

'They drive you crazy, Sarah. You're well clear of them.'

'Yes, the fewer people in your life, the better. People are so *inconvenient* to you.'

'What is it you want to *say*, Sarah?'

'You're shutting down Project Zan because it's more work than you imagined. Admit it. And I'm not talking about intellectual or even physical work. *Emotional* work. Zan wants relationships with us. He wants parents. He wants love. So what do you do? You walk away. If something's not the way you want, you just *walk away*.'

'This is absurd,' Dad said. 'You're talking about Zan like he's a human.'

'I'm also talking about your own son.'

245

There was an awful silence. Then Dad said, 'How many times do we have to have this discussion?'

'Richard, you didn't even want your own *child*,' Mom said.

I was taking these tiny, silent sips of air, and felt suddenly light-headed.

'I didn't want a child right *then*,' said Dad. 'We were in the busiest stages of our educations. A lot of men would've walked away. I stuck it out.'

'*Stuck it out*,' said Mom. 'That's really heroic. I was the one who put my career on hold so you could finish your PhD. You've had it your way always, Richard. You wanted this project, and now you're killing it. Don't you care how Ben feels about this?'

'Ben's upset, but this is not just about a boy and a pet. It's about my career. I started with nothing,' he said fiercely. 'Everything I got, I worked like hell for: the best marks, the scholarships. Jobs. And I am not going to let this experiment wreck my reputation. Ben'll get over it.'

'Maybe. But will he forgive you?' Mom said.

After that, their voices got too quiet for me to hear.

Even if Dad couldn't answer Mom's question, I had a feeling I could.

Through January and February I put Zan to bed myself whenever Mom and Dad let me. The students had no problem leaving a bit early. I liked giving Zan his bath and putting him into his pyjamas and grooming him while he drank his bottle.

Sometimes we looked at his favourite books, and sometimes I told him the story of his day. He'd groom me back, parting my hair, gently touching and removing bits of dried skin. He was always very calm, and loved having his hair combed as he lay across my lap.

He still wouldn't go to sleep on his own, though. He'd arrange his blankets and his toys the way he wanted, but he needed you to lie down right beside him. Sometimes he'd leave an arm across your chest.

I didn't mind. That was how they slept in the wild, in their tree nests, snuggled against their mothers.

As I lay there, I thought of ways to save the project, ways to convince Dad to keep it going. Peter and I were making a big list of ideas. Officially, Project Zan was still going ahead. None of the other students had been told it was ending. Dad said he'd do that later in the spring. I had a couple of months to change his mind.

It didn't take Zan long to fall asleep, but it was a trick to get away without waking him. Before, I used to get impatient, first lifting his limp arm clear, then shifting my body away inch by inch, getting one leg down on the floor, then another, sliding my torso clear. Sometimes he'd wake up with a shriek and I'd have to start all over again.

But these nights, I stayed with him until I was sure he was deep asleep. I liked the heat of his body. I liked the faster beat of his heart against my own. A couple of times I even fell asleep myself and Mom had to come and wake me.

Once she let me sleep the whole night through with him.

When I woke up, Zan was already awake and gently grooming the back of my head. He didn't seem surprised to see me in his bed, but he was certainly happy, and as I'd opened the curtains and let the sunlight in, I felt good about myself.

I felt like I'd kept him safe.

CHAPTER 18

THE LAST SIGN

In early March, Mr Stotsky gave us a creative writing assignment. We'd been reading a collection of short stories that used all sorts of different descriptive techniques, and now we were supposed to write a piece about some part of our daily lives.

I started writing about a typical Sunday morning with Zan. It was fun; there was so much to describe and explain, but three paragraphs into it I started thinking about all the words I was using, and how easy that made it.

I had so many.

Zan had only sixty-six. I knew each of them by heart. At my desk I wrote them down on a fresh piece of paper. It didn't seem like much to work with.

I started my piece again. I decided I would only use Zan's words. I would try to tell the story of his morning in the only way he could tell it.

It took me quite a long time.

Up! Up now. Come give hug. Hug. Tickle! More tickle.

Drink! Sweet drink. Now!

No clean. No clean! Hug! Hug!

Gimme drink. More. Eat, drink. Good. Me eat. Hurry! Me eat. Banana! Apple. Gimme sweet. Hurry you. Milk good.

Where baby? My baby! Mine! More hide. More hide baby! Where baby? There baby! Baby drink. Eat baby eat! Baby! Mine!

Look book. Dog. Brush. Ball. Red ball. My book. Mine.

Out! Hurry! You me out! Now! Out!

Shoe on. Hurry shoe. Ball. Me ball.

Play sand. Bucket mine bucket. Hurry! Give shovel. Hide. Hide toy. Where toy? Me look. Me look. Where toy? There toy! More hide toy.

Listen. Listen bird. Bird eat. Listen. Me drink. Gimme sweet drink.

Come tickle. Kiss. Tickle hug. More. Up hug!

I called the piece 'Sunday Morning'.

A week later, when we got our assignments back, my teacher put it face down on my desk. When I turned it over, I saw that he'd written '*Stop messing about*' and given me a C–.

That night I took it home and asked Mom and Dad to read it.

'It's Zan's vocabulary,' said Mom.

'I understand that,' Dad said impatiently, draining his whisky. 'But you're not a chimp, Ben. This is gibberish. What're you trying to prove?'

He was right – I *was* trying to prove something. Something that might help change his mind.

'You're saying he's learning *words* but not *language*,' I said. 'So maybe the problem is the words we're teaching him. He does pretty well with them, but how much can you say with sixty-six words? You said it yourself. *Gibberish*.'

'The amazing thing,' said Mom, looking at it again, 'is how expressive it is.'

'Maybe with more words,' I said, 'and *better* words, I mean, more verbs and stuff, his sentences would—'

'Ben, if you look at the raw data – and Greg and I have, over and over – you'll see that mostly Zan uses the *same* very few words, and he uses them over and over again, for emphasis, for demands. There's very little variation. He'll just never have the grammar or sophistication to do anything more than this. I'm sorry, Ben, but that's the truth.'

A few weeks later, Peter and I did an evening shift together. Zan was getting impatient for his dinner, bouncing around his suite. He ran right up to the small, locked refrigerator, thumped on it, and then signed:

Open food box.

Peter and I looked at each other, and I said, 'Did you see that?'

It wasn't just that he'd used a three-word phrase – a complete sentence too! It was that he'd never been taught the word for refrigerator. So he'd just gone and made one up on his own!

'It makes total sense. *Food box*,' said Peter.

'He's never done anything like that before,' I said.

'It's a creative use of language!'

I felt this swelling of happiness and hope inside me. Maybe *this* was the kind of thing that would save Project Zan. A breakthrough! Could this change everything?

We told Dad right away, and he seemed interested.

'Zan did it three times?' he asked.

'Three times he called it a food box,' Peter said.

Dad pursed his lips and nodded thoughtfully. 'Does it constitute an abstract use of language, though? He saw the fridge, which to him is just a box.'

'We've never called it that,' I pointed out.

'But he's familiar with all sorts of other boxes,' Dad said. 'Like the fun box.'

'But that's an important distinction too,' said Peter. 'Knowing that there can be many different *kinds* of boxes.'

'I'll note it down and give Greg a call,' Dad said. 'Get his take on it.'

'He just needs more words, Dad,' I said, 'more time, then he'll be able to put them together better!'

Zan had made up his own word – this was more than just memorizing or mimicking. If that wasn't language, what was?

But I got the sense it didn't matter to Dad. It was like he'd already decided the project was a failure, and nothing would change his mind.

Early in April, I told Mom and Dad all my ideas about how we could keep Zan, assuming the project was really going to be cancelled.

They both listened without saying anything, which freaked me out a bit, because I was so used to Mom, and especially Dad, interrupting me.

'I want to show you something,' Dad told me.

He got his attaché case from the hall and pulled out a newspaper clipping. It was a story about some woman in the US who had a twelve-year-old pet chimp. The chimp had been in commercials for soft drinks and fast-food chains. He'd even been on a TV show as a wacky sidekick for a pizza delivery guy.

According to the news story, a repairman came over to fix the dishwasher, and the chimp decided he didn't like the repairman. He attacked him. He mauled the guy's face, crushed his hands and might have killed him if the chimp's owner hadn't started stabbing her own pet with a steak knife. Then the cops came and shot the chimp dead.

'They're not pets, Ben,' said Mom gently.

I shook my head. 'Zan would never do anything like that.'

'Look what he did to Ryan,' Dad pointed out. 'That was with baby teeth.'

'I bet this other chimp wasn't raised like Zan,' I said. 'Maybe he wasn't treated well. Peter said they beat show-biz chimps if they don't behave. Anyway, when Zan bit Ryan, it was because of that stupid chair of yours. Ryan deserved it.'

'How about Joyce Lenardon?' Dad said.

That took the wind out of my sails. Joyce hadn't done a thing to provoke Zan into biting her. That's what had made it scary; it seemed really sudden and unpredictable.

'The fact is,' said Mom, 'we can't keep a chimp in our house.'

I looked at her. 'But I thought you . . . you loved him.'

Mom just smiled at me, sadly and kindly. 'I'm a scientist too, Ben.'

'It's better for everyone,' Dad said.

'Not me,' I said. 'And not Zan.'

Dad made the official announcement at the next Sunday meeting. I was allowed to attend.

He told everyone Project Zan was being shut down. There were lots of questions. There was confusion. There were some tears.

Dad sat placidly in his armchair. 'Despite all that he's learned, despite his proficiency and the occasional flare for creativity, Greg Jaworski and I are not convinced he's learning human language – or ever will. But he's taught *us* a great deal, and for that we're very grateful to him.'

'What will happen to him?' asked one of the students.

'Well, technically Zan is the property of the university, and they, like me, understand that Zan belongs to science.'

The phrase made me feel sick to my stomach. Zan didn't *belong* to science. He belonged to his real mother, but we'd stolen him and raised him to think he belonged to us.

'That means,' said Dad, 'that we were eager to find a good home for him elsewhere. Not a zoo. Not the entertainment industry. But a proper research institution.'

'Not a biomedical lab,' Peter said.

Dad looked at Peter in surprise. 'I would never transfer Zan to a biomedical lab.'

'So no invasive procedures?' Peter asked.

Invasive, I knew, meant getting stuck with needles, or cut open.

Dad shook his head. 'Siegal University in northern Nevada has a primate institute that is very well regarded. I've been talking to them about Zan and they're willing to take him on.' He paused and looked around the table. 'And they do not conduct any kind of biomedical experiments. Zan's new home will be a very, very good one.'

'So the university's sold Zan?' I said.

Dad looked over at me. 'Yes. It's a standard transaction with animal test subjects.'

With every mention of Zan's new home, I felt like the walls of my chest were collapsing until no air was reaching me. Some of the students were looking at me, so I stared at the carpet.

'What kind of facility is it?' Peter asked.

'Well, I can tell you, the chimps have twenty-five acres of land and more facilities and professional support staff than we had here. Zan would also have company. They've got some adolescents as well as some adults. And the director, Jack Helson, is very knowledgeable. Zan will be in good hands.'

No one said anything.

'Now, I just want to assure you all,' Dad said, 'that none of this has anything to do with your performance on the project.

Project Zan was not a failure, ladies and gentlemen. This is science. A pursuit of the truth. It's not wish fulfilment. It's not fantasy. It told us the truth and we have to accept that. Now, as it happens, I have a relatively new experiment underway, and it's likely to get a great deal larger very soon. I'd be happy to welcome any of you as research assistants, if you're interested.'

'The rats,' said Peter.

'Correct,' Dad said. 'It promises to be a very fruitful project.'

It was Monday, mid-April, beautiful outside, but everything was colourless to me. In two weeks, Zan would be going to his new home. I didn't care about school. Sometimes I didn't even bother handing in my homework. I became a clock watcher. I didn't talk to anyone. Jennifer started looking like someone I'd known a long time ago. A few times David tried to talk to me, but it made me embarrassed, like he just pitied me. I didn't talk in class. I stayed out of people's way.

When I got home from school, Peter was outside with Zan. When he saw me through the sliding glass he waved me out.

'What's up?' I said.

He smiled. 'I'm going with him.'

It was like the blue in the sky, the green in the trees, had suddenly come back a bit. 'You mean to Nevada?'

He nodded. 'I told your dad I wanted to keep working with Zan, and I applied to grad school at Siegal. Your dad wrote a letter of recommendation for me. And he helped me put together a proposal for working with Zan, to see if he'd teach the other young chimps to sign. I guess Jack Helson has all sorts of projects going on down there and he seemed to think this would fit in with some of them.'

'Dad *helped* you?' I said.

'A lot.'

I didn't want to like Dad right now, but I couldn't deny he'd done a nice thing, a good thing. Zan wouldn't be alone. He'd have his favourite friend with him. It wouldn't be me, but it would be the next best thing.

Peter grinned. 'So after I finish up the term here, I'm heading down to Reno.'

My throat suddenly felt thick. 'You'll look after him,' I said.

Peter looked me straight in the eye. 'Why do you think I'm going down there? You think I'm crazy about Nevada? It's desert.'

'You love him too, right?'

He exhaled through his nose and nodded. 'I sure do.'

I hugged him hard, pressed my face into his musty jean jacket so he couldn't see my face get all red and snotty and crumpled.

'Thanks, Peter,' I said, and when I could talk properly again, I said, 'I wish I could come, too.'

'It's all right,' he said. 'Things are going to be all right.'

Three days before Zan had to go, he learned his last sign from us.

It was the sign for his own name. He'd always understood it when *we* made it. He knew it meant we were talking about him, or to him. But it was a tricky sign to form – probably a bad choice on our part.

But that day, in the sandbox, he made it.

He took his hand and zigzagged it across his chest and made the Z.

Zan, he said.

I smiled and nodded and signed it back to him several times, and he seemed very pleased with himself and started using it in all sorts of phrases.

Zan eat. Zan drink. Zan play.

It was like we'd just given him his name – and now we were taking it away from him.

PART III

The sign for *love* is very similar to *hug*. You just cross your wrists and place them over your heart.

That was not a word on our teaching lists. It never got written on the big wall chart in our kitchen.

We dressed Zan in our clothes, and fed him our food, and let him sleep in our beds. We told him to call us Mom and Dad and brother.

He lived with us and trusted us, and we lied to him every day. We fooled him into thinking we were his real family, and that we would always love him and take care of him. We did this so he'd perform all his tricks for us.

But later, when his tricks weren't useful any more, we locked him in a cage, and got rid of him.

CHAPTER 19

DR HELSON

Trying to pack for Zan when he was around was hopeless. I'd put some of his favourite things in a suitcase, and he'd come and grab them out and run off, wanting me to catch him and tickle him.

In the end we had to wait till he was asleep and then I moved through his room like a thief, selecting things. On his bed he was all wrapped up in his favourite blanket, with his pig and his cow and his GI Joe action figure. For a few seconds I tried to wiggle them away so I could pack them, but in the end, I just gave up and settled down beside him and slept the night there.

The next day at lunchtime, when Mom put the tranquilliser in Zan's milk she started to cry, and she couldn't stop. Dad was worried she might upset Zan and he wouldn't drink the bottle, so he told her to go upstairs.

Nearly two years ago they'd tranquillized Zan's mother so Mom could take Zan. Now she was putting him to sleep so she could abandon him.

Dad finished pouring the milk into the bottle, gave it a good shake, and passed it to me. 'Why don't you give it to him, Ben.'

'You do it,' I said. 'It's your show, Doctor.'

His eyes had so little warmth. He offered the bottle and Zan took it and drank eagerly, pausing only right at the beginning, probably because he noticed the taste.

He must have thought it was weird we hadn't put him in his high chair first, so he climbed up onto me and drank his bottle on my lap. I held him close, looked over the top of his head, and felt like a traitor.

I held him till he'd finished, and held him as he got very quiet and still. He fell asleep in my arms.

The doctor had given him a big dose. It was supposed to be totally safe, and would keep him asleep for eight hours. Just to make sure, we had a backup dose packed for the flight.

'Let's go,' Dad said.

Mom came down, her eyes all red and swollen, and we got into the Mercedes. We'd packed our own bags the night before too, and they were already in the back. The drive to the airport didn't take long. No public airline wanted a chimp bouncing around, so the university had paid for a private plane. The last of the Project Zan money.

The plane was waiting on the tarmac. It was little, with two propellers and not much room in the cabin. A little door separated us from the two pilots in the cockpit. Mom held Zan in her arms, wrapped in a blanket. No one talked much.

It was my first time on an aeroplane, and I should've been excited, checking everything out, but I didn't enjoy it. After we took off I looked out of the window and saw the island and then the water and then we climbed above the clouds and it was like we were in some nowhere land.

About an hour into the flight it got really bumpy, and though I was scared, part of me thought it would be good if we crashed, because at least we'd be all together. And then I wouldn't have to hand over Zan and say goodbye, and see the look in his eyes as he realized we were leaving him behind.

My mind kept shutting down then. I couldn't think beyond that moment. It was like nothing could possibly exist afterwards.

The plane didn't crash, and a couple of hours later, we landed in Nevada. I carried Zan down the steps to where Peter was waiting for us beside a station wagon.

It was really good to see Peter. He'd arrived the week before and was getting settled.

'Professor Tomlin,' he said, shaking Dad's hand. 'Sarah. Hey, Ben, how's sleepyhead?'

'He's all right,' I said.

'Still out cold, eh? OK, let's take you guys out to the ranch.'

Ranch sounded good: big and clean and wholesome. The people who worked there would all love animals and just want to take care of them as best they could.

'So, it's going to be a bit of a change for Zan,' Peter said as he pulled onto the highway. 'I just want to warn you. It's certainly been a change for me.'

It was sunny and hot, but I didn't care about what was outside the car windows. Didn't care about the desert or the cactuses or the birdsong.

Zan, warm in my arms.

'This will go easier for Zan if we act as normally as possible,' Dad said.

In the back seat I shook my head in disgust. Maybe Dad could do it, because he didn't feel as much as me – he never had. Mom looked out of the window, silent.

The plan was, we were going to stay five days to help Zan settle in. Dr Helson had been against it. He'd said a clean break, cold turkey, was the best way to do it. Don't drag it out. But Mom had insisted, and Dad had backed her up. We'd booked a motel on the outskirts of town and would spend the days at the ranch with Zan. I got to miss a week of school.

'How do you find working with Dr Helson?' Dad asked Peter.

'He's very . . .' Peter paused. 'He knows a lot about chimps; he's been working with them a long time. And Zan will have company here, which is really good. Chimps form pretty close bonds.'

All I could think about was how we'd torn apart the only bonds Zan had ever formed in his life. Twice.

Outside: a long country road lined with power poles, going on for ever. The land looked hard and dry but there were a few trees and shrubs, close to the ground and kind of scraggly looking.

'We're just coming up on it here,' Peter said, and turned onto a dirt road. There was a little rise and then I could see the chain-link fencing, topped with tilted rows of razor wire. I felt a lump form in my throat.

'There's a lot of land,' said Peter, 'so Zan'll have plenty of space outside. I've been talking to Dr Helson about building a kind of elevated playground for them – you know, poles with rope bridges, and platforms they can climb, like a more natural forest environment.'

There were more trees and bushes now, and we were coming up on what looked like a farm. I saw a couple of barns, then a large concrete building with high barred windows on all sides. Beyond that was a pretty farmhouse with a white veranda and picture windows. It looked like something from a story-book. *Old Macdonald had a farm.*

It was late afternoon, the light starting to slant beautifully on the buildings and trees, making long shadows across the ground.

We parked on the gravel drive, and the moment I opened the car door I heard the chimps.

'That's the main colony,' Peter said, nodding at the big concrete building. 'There're thirteen of them right now. Feeding time, by the sound of it.'

I'd heard Zan make a ruckus when he was having a temper tantrum, but he was one little chimp. The sound of so many chimpanzees together made my knees weak. They sounded big, and they sounded powerful, and suddenly I felt like I didn't know anything about chimps at all. I didn't want to go in there.

Luckily, from out of the pretty farmhouse, an entire family was coming to meet us. A man and a woman and two kids, a girl about my age and a boy about ten or so.

Mom was carrying Zan now, still fast asleep. I grabbed his suitcase. I saw Peter glance at it and look kind of sick, but he didn't say anything.

'Richard,' said the man, striding towards Dad with his hand outstretched. 'Jack Helson, welcome.'

Helson was tall and thin, but broad shouldered. With his sleeves rolled back, his forearms seemed way bigger than they should have been, all bulgy muscle and vein. He had close-cropped hair, a high forehead and very intense green eyes. He didn't look much like a professor to me; he looked like a soldier.

Introductions were made out there on the gravel drive, and then he asked us to come inside and have dinner.

'What a little sweetheart,' said Dr Helson's wife, Barbara, looking at Zan. 'He's a good size.'

'He's a good eater,' Mom said.

'Bring him inside,' Dr Helson said. 'Lord knows, our house is no stranger to baby chimps.'

I liked the way he called Zan a baby. Like he was something vulnerable and worth taking special care of.

Mrs Helson said, 'He'll probably start to rouse in an hour or two, and then we'll get him settled. The other chimps will be sleeping by then.' She was big boned and had a pleasant face. I knew from Peter that she was a vet, so she was a doctor too, really. The boy, Winston, looked like a miniature version of his dad, with a near-shaved head and piercing eyes. Sue-Ellen, the girl, was sort of pretty, blonde and curvy, with a sunny smile.

The Helsons' house was nice. Their dining table was already set for us, and there were all sorts of prints hanging on the walls, historical etchings of apes and chimps. I saw Mom and Dad look at them appreciatively and could tell they thought Helson was a cultivated man.

Sue-Ellen brought out a play pen for Zan, set it up in a corner of the dining room, and expertly took Zan from Mom's arms and laid him down so he could sleep comfortably while we ate. I remembered that very first barbecue in Victoria, when Zan was just days old, and everyone had wanted to hold him and coo over him. For a weird moment I felt like we were safe and all together, but I knew it was a lie.

It was a good meal – Dr Helson liked to cook apparently – but I couldn't eat much. I kept glancing at Zan sleeping in his playpen, wondering where he was going to be spending the night.

'They're fabulous creatures, chimps,' Dr Helson was saying. 'Intelligent. Empathetic. Murderous too. They're no angels.'

'Neither are we,' said Mom.

'That's why we have so much in common,' said Helson, nodding. 'But we're much, much smarter. The mistake is when we allow our human sentimentality to contaminate the experiments.'

'I would agree,' said Dad.

Helson tapped his fork at the air. 'Our craving to anthropomorphize them is remarkable.'

Anthropomorphize. I'd heard Dad use that word before. 'What's that mean?' I asked.

'Pretending animals are human,' said Sue-Ellen, giving me a smile. 'That they'll act just like us.'

Her father chuckled. 'And I can promise you, they don't. But people have a great deal of trouble realizing this, especially with the young ones. Even the people who work with them. Fascinating psychological process, to watch it happen. The delusion can be therapeutic for some. I do quite a bit of work in that area.'

I had no idea what he was talking about, and he didn't elaborate. He seemed to like looking at Mom an awful lot. He addressed most of his comments to her, and once I thought he was looking down her blouse.

'But of course, all babies grow up, and that's when the problems begin.' Helson turned his gaze on me now. 'You've seen the movie *101 Dalmatians?*'

I nodded.

'Well, the movie was popular, and the dogs were adorable. All those little puppies. And apparently, after the movie came out, everyone wanted a Dalmatian. Now, as it turns out, these dogs have superabundant energy, and they're not ideal house pets. They destroy houses. So people started getting rid of them in droves. Pounds were glutted with them. I suspect many were put down. Fantasy can be a dangerous thing.'

I moved food around my plate. I got the point of Helson's stories, and I also got the sense he thought we'd messed up Zan.

'Have you spent any time with mature chimps?' Helson asked us.

'Briefly, at Borroway, when I got Zan,' Mom said.

'Ah-ha, and you?' he asked my father.

'Unfortunately not,' said Dad.

'Well, you're in for an education after dinner.'

I could tell Dad didn't like to be talked to like this. He probably thought he'd had more education than Helson, down here on his ranch in Nowheresville, Nevada.

'Excellent meal,' he said. 'Thank you so much for your hospitality.'

'Not at all,' said Helson. 'It's been a trying day for you. Now, Sue-Ellen and Winston, help your mother clean up while I take the Tomlins out to the colony.'

The night air was warm. Bugs pulsed over the fields. As we neared the big, ugly concrete building, I could still hear some hoots and pants and wails, but it was much quieter than when we'd arrived.

We reached a door. Not steel, not like a bank vault or anything. Just normal. Inside we went, Zan still asleep in Mom's arms, though starting to stir. I carried his suitcase.

The smell came first: humid, intense. Nothing as bad as the pigpen I'd visited once on a class trip. But right away you knew you were in the presence of big animals.

Helson switched on a single, very dim light. All around the perimeter of the room were big cages, separate but connected to each other with tunnels. I was aware of dark shapes within the cages.

An incredible noise suddenly came at us, hoots and shrieks and barks and cries, rising to a crescendo that hurt my ears.

'Not too used to visitors after dinner,' said Helson.

Inside the cages the great shapes stirred. Some stood on two legs, some pressed their bodies right against the bars, arms raised; and a few of them howled, their vast mouths all teeth and red gums. They were massive. Their faces and hands and fur were much darker than Zan's. They were not beautiful. Zan was just a baby and I was terrified for him.

Peter was beside me, and I felt his hand on my shoulder. 'It's OK,' he whispered in my ear. 'They just like making noise. They're not so bad. I'll introduce you properly tomorrow.'

'We'll put Zan in here for now,' said Helson, leading us to one of the smaller cages in the corner of the building. 'It's sealed off.'

A cage.

Not a room, but a cage.

There was a concrete floor with a drain in the middle, nothing else.

Helson unlocked the door and swung it wide.

I looked at Mom, who held Zan swaddled in his favourite blanket.

'Bring him in,' said Helson. He smiled, but sounded impatient.

Reluctantly Mom went inside. I followed her with my little suitcase. The moment I walked through the cage door, I felt queasy. The cage was about ten feet by ten. I could see there was a tunnel, but the gate was locked for now.

In the next cage over were two big chimps. One sat very still, watching. The other was banging against the bars and hollering.

Helson nodded at Zan. 'Take his clothes off,' he told Mom. 'Why?' she asked.

Helson chuckled and waved a hand to the next cage. 'Do you see any of the others wearing clothes?'

'He's grown up with clothes,' Mom said, frowning.

'The other chimps won't accept him,' said Helson simply. 'Take them off.'

Zan was still asleep, and I helped Mom gently lift his T-shirt over his limp arms. I pulled his shorts down over his legs. That left only the diaper. I undid the clasps and pulled it off. It was warm and damp. Zan looked so much smaller now, so much more vulnerable, and I kept swallowing so I wouldn't cry.

I opened Zan's suitcase and started taking out some of his things.

'No,' said Helson, fixing me with those piercing eyes of his. I'd been in the middle of spreading Zan's favourite fleecy blankets on the floor. 'There won't be any of that here. Do you think chimps use blankets in the wild?'

'But Zan wasn't raised in the wild,' said Mom. 'He grew up with blankets and a bed.'

'So I understand,' said Helson. 'But that's not the way my chimps live. We don't pretend they're humans here. They're chimps and they live like chimps, and there's a lot more dignity in that than dressing them up in children's clothes. The sooner Zan realizes he's a chimp, the better. Now lay him down on the floor.'

272

I looked at all the things I'd packed for Zan in his suitcase. His GI Joe and his duck and chimp and cow: his babies. He loved these things. I looked at Mom, wanting to hear her protest.

Mom said, 'Dr Helson, surely, for the sake of easing his transition, he can have a couple of his favourite blankets.'

'And his GI Joe,' I said. 'He likes that one best.'

Helson exhaled impatiently. Dad, who was standing outside the cage, nodded. 'I see no benefit in traumatizing Zan on his first night,' he said.

The two men looked at each other. 'One blanket, nothing more,' said Helson.

I wanted to hit him. I wanted to hurt him.

'That's his favourite,' Mom said to me quietly, nodding at the one I'd already put out. She carefully laid Zan down on it. I folded it over him. Mom headed out of the cage. I closed up the suitcase and as I stood, I looked at all the people on the other side of the bars: Mom. Dad. Helson. Peter.

'We can't leave him here,' I said.

No one replied. I looked at Peter and all my fury flew towards him. 'He won't be happy here. You could've told us it would be like this. You saw this place. It's just a zoo!'

'Young man, listen to me,' said Helson, and his severe voice made my eyes snap to his. 'You may not like the look of these cages, but I can assure you, my facilities are as good as it gets in this country. The chimps have large cages, space to play outside, and they have company. They're well fed and have the best vet in the state looking after them. That would be my wife.

And they don't have people sticking needles into them and injecting them with hepatitis.'

I looked down at my shoes, my heart pounding, so much noise in my head.

Mom came back inside the cage and leaned her forehead against mine. 'He's right, Ben,' she said. 'There aren't a lot of places willing to take a chimp, and we tried to find the best one. I really think this is it.'

'I'm staying with him tonight,' I said.

'Not in the cage,' said Helson. 'If anything happens to you, I'm liable.'

'Zan would never hurt me,' I told him angrily.

Helson chuckled. 'They're full of surprises. Especially when under stress.'

'Outside the cage, then,' I said.

'Ben, you're not sleeping outside the cage,' said Dad.

Mom looked at him. 'Let him, if he wants.'

The way she said it, the way she looked at Dad, I knew he wouldn't argue.

'Suit yourself,' said Helson. 'Hard floor. It won't be comfy. No room service here. And stay away from the other chimp cages.'

'I've got a sleeping bag in the back of my car,' Peter told me. 'I'll get it out for you.'

After I got settled outside Zan's cage, Mom and Dad said goodbye, and Peter drove them to their motel. I lay there very still. I didn't want to upset the other chimps, most of whom seemed to have calmed down and gone to sleep.

I did not sleep. I kept my eyes on Zan, who was starting to stir more and more as the tranquillizer finally wore off. It seemed to take him for ever to wake up properly. Or maybe he was awake and it was just taking him a long time to figure out where on earth he was.

'Zan,' I called out to him softly. I didn't want to get the other chimps going.

Eventually he lifted his head. His eyes met mine. He gave a happy pant-hoot and scampered clumsily over, dragging his blanket with him. He settled down in front of me, right against the bars. They didn't seem to freak him out yet. He probably didn't understand what they were. We touched each other through the bars, stroking each other's hair and hands and faces.

Where shirt? he signed, noticing for the first time he wasn't wearing any clothes.

No shirt, I replied.

He didn't seem upset. He'd always hated his diaper, and getting dressed. Maybe he'd actually be happier naked.

He signed, *Zan eat*.

Peter had left me with some food and water, figuring Zan would be hungry if he woke up in the middle of the night. I had several chunks of something that looked like meat loaf, and Zan took them eagerly as I passed them through the bars. If anything, he seemed excited, like this was all a fun adventure.

In, he signed, inviting me inside.

No.

You in.

I shook my head and signed *No* again.

He looked around at his cage, this time with more concentration.

Out. You me out. Now out.

No.

Hurry out!

I tried to distract him by tickling him through the bars. This seemed to work for a bit. I'd kept his favourite GI Joe toy stuffed in my pocket, and passed it to him, and he tucked it under his armpit and pulled his blanket around him more. I wished I'd kept more of his toys on me so he could make his protective circle, but Peter had taken the suitcase back to his place.

I was worried Zan was getting upset, so I talked to him as I groomed him. I started telling him the story of his day, and flying on an aeroplane, but he wouldn't remember any of that, and anyway it was such a sad story I couldn't keep going.

So I made up another story – I told him about how, when the sun came up, we would go out and play and there would be trees and plants and branches and we would have lots of tickling and hide-and-seek.

I just kept telling this over and over, my voice getting slower and sleepier, until his eyelids drooped and we fell asleep together, side by side, touching through the bars.

CHAPTER 20

THE RANCH

I was woken by the sound of the big chimps hooting and shrieking, and a voice saying, 'Rise and shine, mate.' I squinted up from my sleeping bag to see a big guy uncoiling a long hose down the walkway.

'Time to clean the cages,' he said. He sounded Australian. 'I'm Marcus. You must be Ben, right?'

The other chimps seemed to know what to do. They moved through the tunnels into other cages while Marcus hosed down the floors, washing yesterday's food and urine and faeces down the drains.

Light poured through the high barred windows and Zan looked around properly for the first time. He stared and stared at the other chimps. I wondered what he was thinking. He'd never seen another chimp before in his life, except for pictures of himself. But those pictures were always beside photos of me and Mom and Dad and Peter. He was one of *us*. Not one of *them*. Finally he turned to me and signed: *Black dogs*.

Not far from our house in Victoria there was a huge black Rottweiler and that was pretty much the biggest animal Zan had ever seen before now. I didn't know how to tell him he was the same – or even if I should. Maybe it was better he figured it out in his own time.

Marcus saved our cage till last and I quickly pulled Zan's blanket and toy through the bars and urged him to one side so Marcus could hose down his floor. There wasn't much to clean up. Zan was pretty interested in watching the water swirl down the drain. Then he walked over to the water and had a pee, hooting with delight.

I couldn't help laughing. I was just glad he was happy. I still wasn't used to seeing him naked, though. He looked so small and young compared to the others. And he already looked less like one of us.

Once Marcus was done, another person came to help feed the chimps their breakfast. While all that was going on, Peter arrived with Mom and Dad. They'd brought me an Egg McMuffin and orange juice from McDonald's.

'How was your night?' Mom asked, hugging me. Dad put a hand on my shoulder.

'It was OK,' I said. 'He woke up and stayed up a long time, but he didn't seem too scared. He calls the other chimps *black dogs*.'

'Hah!' said Dad. 'The power of cross-fostering.'

Soon after, Dr Helson and his wife arrived. I guessed their kids had gone off to school.

When they unlocked Zan's cage, and I went inside, he was so excited he nearly strangled me, hugging and kissing me. Dr Helson watched us with a rueful smile. Mrs Helson wanted to examine Zan, but it took a while to get him off me. She had an excellent, reassuring manner with him, and he let her poke and prod him.

'He's a very healthy little chimp,' she announced.

'That's good,' said Helson. 'In a chimp colony, the weak can be victimized. The faster we integrate him, the better chance he has of being accepted. We'll introduce him to Sheba later today. She lost her own baby four months ago.'

'What happened?' Mom asked.

'One of the other males bit its face off,' said Helson matter-of-factly.

I looked at him in horror.

'A mother typically takes care of a chimp for at least five years,' Mrs Helson explained. 'It's a big-time investment for her, and she won't have any other babies during that time. We'd bred her with Maxwell, because they seemed natural mates.'

'Zeus got jealous,' Helson went on, looking at my mother. 'He thought if he took the baby out of the equation, he'd have a chance of mating with Sheba and producing his own off-spring. Not that they always know who the father is anyway. A female in oestrus tends to be quite generous. She'll mate with many males.'

I wished I hadn't eaten breakfast; the aftertaste in my mouth was making my stomach churn.

'Will Zan be safe with Sheba?' I wanted to know. 'I mean, that other baby . . .'

'The other baby was very small, quite defenceless,' said Helson. 'Zan's much bigger. I suspect it'll be an altogether different proposition. Here's Sheba.'

He pointed a couple of cages over. Sheba was tall and rangy, chewing happily on a big piece of the chimp loaf and a head of lettuce.

'I'll be very interested to see if her maternal instinct kicks in with Zan,' said Dr Helson.

The way he said it – 'very interested to see' – made it sound like another experiment, and one that might not turn out very well.

'Sheba's gentle,' Peter said to me. 'And Maxwell.' He nodded at an even bigger chimp that was in the cage with Sheba. 'He's a sweetheart. Very patient, and nurturing too.'

'But not strong enough to save his baby,' I said.

'We introduced Zeus too early,' said Dr Helson. 'That was a miscalculation.'

'And these are our boys,' said Mrs Helson affectionately, as we walked to the next cage.

They still looked pretty big to me, at least two or three times Zan's size. 'They've lost their tail tufts,' I noted. 'So that makes them at least five?'

'Very good,' said Mrs Helson, giving me a smile. 'Igor is six and Caliban is seven.'

'I'll be working with these two on signing,' Peter said. 'And I'm pretty sure Zan will play a big part in teaching them.'

I'd already known that Peter would be working with the other chimps too, but it still gave me a pang that he wouldn't just be taking care of Zan.

A couple of other chimpers, Sven and Patricia, came in to take Igor and Caliban out for their morning walks. In their hands they held neck collars with long chain-link leashes.

'Take them to the south paddock today,' Helson instructed them. 'We'll let Zan have the east field to himself, just for now.'

'Thank you,' said Mom.

I was watching as Sven and Patricia went into the cage and attached the metal collars to the chimps. Igor and Caliban seemed used to it, and barely protested. It made them look like giant, oversized dogs – but to me, mostly, they seemed like prisoners. Helson ushered us out of the way as they headed from the building. From a rack on the wall, each chimper took a long pole.

'What're those?' I asked.

'Cattle prods,' said Helson. 'Everyone carries one when they're working with the chimps. Safety policy.'

I looked at Peter. Something else he hadn't told us.

'Zan doesn't need a cattle prod,' I said. 'Or a collar.'

Helson said, 'Don't underestimate his strength. And remember, my fellows are a lot older, and a lot stronger. Zeus here is 175 pounds and seven times stronger than me.'

So this was Zeus. The one that had bitten off the baby's face. Sitting, eating, he didn't seem so monstrous. But I guess I must have gotten too close to his cage, because he suddenly leaped up, all shoulders and arms, and jaws wide and fierce. He

281

ran on two legs to the bars, shrieking. I jumped back, my heart beating so fast and hard, I worried I'd faint. Mom stepped back too. Helson and his wife, I noticed, held their ground, as did Dad and Peter. Watching me, Zeus filled his mouth with water from the spigot near the floor.

'Look out,' Helson said.

Too late. Zeus sprayed the water, drenching me.

'He's asserting his dominance,' Helson explained. He took a scraggly towel from a hook on the wall and tossed it at me. 'You're small, and you looked scared, so he knew he could get away with it. You'd never try anything like that with me, would you, Zeus, old boy?'

Helson stood very close to the cage, close enough that Zeus could easily have reached through and grabbed him. But Zeus did nothing, just dropped to all fours and shambled back to his food.

I patted myself dry with the towel. 'At least he doesn't share a cage with anyone else,' I said with relief.

Mrs Helson seemed surprised. 'Oh no, he's quite sociable. He's our alpha male. But he feeds alone. The others know there's no point being near him at feeding time. Unless they want to get smacked and wait for his seconds.'

Peter, Mom and I took Zan out to the east field to play. Dad had things he wanted to discuss with Dr Helson. When I saw Peter putting the collar on Zan, I started to object, but he glanced at me and shook his head.

And I knew, in that moment, that Zan was no longer mine.

Not that he'd ever *belonged* to me, not like a cat or dog – but now Peter was about to take over as the most important person in his life. In some ways he had been for months. No one spent more of his waking hours with Zan.

Once we were inside the fenced field, Peter took off the collar, and we played with Zan. He loved all the space, and the trees, and the fallen branches, and the little pond that Helson kept stocked with fish. In some ways, it was better than what he had in our back yard, and I began to wonder if he'd be happier here.

Dad joined us later with a picnic lunch, which we all ate on the grass together, big blanket spread out. My throat still felt like it had a fist clenched in it, but I ate some food, trying to smile and be cheerful for Zan.

Afterwards, Zan didn't want his collar put back on, and as we neared the chimp house, he held back, pulling against his lead. Peter let him come up into his arms, and we carried him into the building.

Helson was waiting for us. As Peter took Zan back inside his cage, Zan started crying and very nearly climbed out of Peter's arms, but Peter laid out Zan's blanket and his GI Joe toy and got Zan interested in a game of hide-and-seek. He hid the toy at the far end of the cage and as Zan scampered over to claim it, Peter crept out and locked the door. It was a dirty trick, and Peter knew it. He didn't look happy.

I noticed that in the next cage, Sheba was sitting alone. Helson pulled a lever and the gate between the two cages slid up.

Then we waited.

It was a long wait. First they just ignored each other, and then, after about half an hour, Sheba walked through the tunnel into Zan's cage. It was the first time I'd seen Zan so close to another chimp, and he looked small and defenceless.

When he saw Sheba enter the cage he stood up on both legs and displayed. Chest thrown out, arms high, hands slapping at his chest, he shrieked and hooted.

'Excellent,' said Helson.

I felt kind of proud of Zan's bravery, but scared too. I didn't want him provoking Sheba into a fight. Sheba didn't seem very impressed by Zan's antics. She sniffed around his cage and then caught sight of his blanket.

'This should prove interesting,' said Helson.

Sheba picked up the blanket and rubbed it in her hands. Zan took a few steps closer and very urgently but clearly signed:

My blanket. Zan blanket.

This meant nothing to Sheba. She held the blanket and rubbed it against her face; she seemed to enjoy its softness. Zan shrieked impatiently.

Sheba threw the blanket at him, which shut Zan up – until she picked up his GI Joe, his baby.

Sheba held it quite tenderly in her hand, and I was hopeful, wondering if she was remembering her own little baby.

Zan signed, My baby. Give baby!

'No,' I whispered as he scampered closer to Sheba, hand outstretched, shrieking.

Sheba sniffed at the toy and crushed it in her hands. The

plastic pieces fell to the floor. Zan flipped out. When he ran to gather the pieces, Sheba caught him by the arm, picked him up and threw him across the cage like a stuffed animal. Zan hit the floor hard. Sheba was walking towards him swiftly, and she did not look happy.

'Do something!' I shouted at Helson.

Swiftly Helson opened the cage door and went inside, holding a cattle pod.

'Sheba,' he said. 'Cage.' And he pointed, with the cattle prod, at the tunnel.

Sheba's eyes were on that cattle prod. She obviously knew what it could do. She turned and walked, slowly, back into her own cage.

'Seal it off,' Helson told Peter.

Peter pulled the lever, and then I rushed inside to check on Zan. I held him. He was shaken, but he didn't seem badly hurt.

'She could've killed him!' I said.

'She could've, but she didn't want to,' said Helson calmly. 'She was just annoyed. It may be too early for Sheba to nurture again. One never knows in captivity. Many females lose their nurturing instinct altogether. Once I saw a mother tear the arms off her own newborn.'

I didn't know how much more I wanted to hear from Helson. From Mom's books, I already knew chimps could be brutal with each other, but could also be kind and loving. They shared things. They taught each other how to use tools. Mostly they were very tolerant of the babies. But Helson's view of chimps seemed altogether darker.

'I think we should keep Zan alone at least another night,' Peter said.

'I'd agree with that,' Dad said.

'Can't you introduce him to some of the younger ones first?' Mom asked. 'Caliban or Igor?'

'It's important he has an adult to look out for him,' said Helson.

'What about Rachel?' Peter suggested.

Helson considered this. 'Her ranking's too low to lend him much status, but she might take to him. We'll see.'

They wouldn't let me stay with Zan another night. I had to say goodbye to him through the bars. We signed for a bit. We'd never taught him *tomorrow*, so it was hard to explain I was coming back. At home, he took it for granted that every day when he woke, we'd be there. It was all different now. He didn't even have his favourite toy.

'He'll be OK,' Peter said to me. 'He's tough. The way he stood up to Sheba. That was something.'

'He's a survivor,' Helson said, and I felt vaguely grateful to him. 'We'll see you tomorrow. Not first thing. Come mid-morning. It's important he starts making the transition.'

Making the transition meant getting used to being without us. For good.

It smelled like chocolate cake when we arrived at the chimp house next day, around ten-thirty.

'It's Sam's birthday,' Peter explained to me, nodding to one of the male chimps in the colony. He was a distinguished-looking fellow with a greying beard. 'He's twenty, our oldest.'

Two of Helson's research assistants, Marcus and Patricia, had bought one of those big square supermarket cakes and were dividing it up. All the chimps could smell it and were getting really excited.

I went straight to Zan. He came to the bars and we touched each other and kissed.

Out hurry out, he signed.

He wanted to get back into that field and play again.

Yes, I signed back to him, and said, 'Soon,' because we'd never been able to teach him that sign. For Zan everything was *now*.

Fish, he signed, which made me smile, because Peter had just taught him that one yesterday when he was watching the fish in the pond.

Fish, I signed back and nodded. 'Soon.'

Patricia was bringing the first piece of cake to Sam. Each cage door had an opening in the middle, about twice the size of a letter slot, so the chimps could reach out and get their own food.

I noticed that Sam's cage was sealed off from the others for now, probably so he could enjoy his birthday cake in peace. Looking around the chimp house, I noticed that the two other chimps who'd been hanging out with Zeus had quietly left his cage so they wouldn't have to compete with him for their fair share.

Zeus stared hard at Sam, at the cake, at Patricia bringing him the cake.

When Sam had the cake in his hand, Patricia and Marcus and Peter started singing 'Happy Birthday to You'. We all joined in, and were about six words into it when Zeus gave such a shriek that I actually jumped. He rattled the bars of his cage.

'I guess he wants his cake now,' I said, leaning close to Peter so I could be heard.

'Actually, he wanted it first,' Peter said. 'They usually feed the highest-ranking chimp first so no one gets upset.'

I watched as Zeus strode powerfully through the tunnel into Sheba and Igor's cage. It was right next to Sam's but was, of course, sealed off.

'Better get him some cake fast,' Patricia said.

But before she even reached the slot, Zeus had given Sheba a hard smack across the chest. She cowered in submission, but Zeus kept at her.

'Why's he doing that?' I exclaimed.

'He's ticked off,' said Marcus. 'He's taking it out on Sheba – Zeus! No!'

But Zeus barely looked over. Instead he turned on Igor and displayed, his hair shooting out. I knew from all the time I'd spent grooming Zan that chimp hair was surprisingly long. When it stood out, it made the chimp look double his size. Zeus was huge now, a monster from a movie.

Igor displayed too, but without as much conviction. Zeus went for him and bit him on the arm, then the toes, like he was trying to chomp them off. Marcus started unravelling the water hose towards the cage.

'Call Helson!' he called to Patricia, and she ran for the phone.

I went over to Zan, who was watching all this, wide-eyed. I crouched down next to him and his hand reached out through the bars and clutched mine.

Marcus was about to start hosing down Zeus when Helson came in with a shotgun.

'Step back!' he told Marcus, then shouted: 'Zeus. Down!'

Zeus spun on him, in full fight mode, mouth wide.

The look on Helson's face was almost as scary. His eyes had narrowed to slits, and his lips were pulled back so you could see all his teeth meeting in a deadly grimace. It was the face a soldier might make before running someone through with a bayonet.

I watched, unable to turn away, Zan's hand clenching mine so hard it was painful. Igor and Sheba, I noticed, had taken off through the tunnel.

'Down!' Helson shouted again at Zeus.

Zeus spat at him.

Helson pulled the trigger. By now I could see it wasn't a real shotgun but a pellet gun. The shot hit Zeus mid-chest and barely fazed him, though a little blood matted his fur. He displayed again. Helson shot again. Then a third and fourth time, until at last Zeus staggered back, weary and wounded. To my surprise Helson opened the cage and walked in. Zeus fell down on all fours before him.

'Down, Zeus!' Helson shouted.

Zeus bowed his head and extended his arm, wrist limp in submission.

'Good,' said Helson. Over his shoulder he shouted, 'Get me

the dart gun. We'll need to sedate him to dig out the shot.'

The chimp house was rank with fury and fear. It was unlike anything I'd ever smelled: the sweat and pheromones of a dozen terrified animals and humans, all mixed up. I turned to the wall and threw up my breakfast.

Later that day we took Zan out to the east paddock again – just me and Peter and Mom and Dad. Zan played in the low branches of the trees, tried to catch the fish in the pond. He seemed happy. Maybe he thought this was just a new home for all of us. He wasn't crazy about the cage part, or the other chimps (or *black dogs*), but he liked being outside.

'We can't leave Zan here,' I said. My insides felt empty of anything but anger. 'The other chimps are awful. They'll kill Zan.'

'The paperwork's been done, Ben,' Dad said. 'Siegal University owns Zan now.'

'You've seen some pretty harsh stuff,' Peter said. 'It's been hard on me too. I mean, before Project Zan, I knew nothing about chimps. And Zan taught me about *baby* chimps. The bigger ones are different, I know.'

'I hate them all,' I said. 'Zan has nothing in common with them.'

'He will, though,' said Mom.

It surprised me, coming from Mom. It was the sort of thing I thought Dad would say. But Mom's face was kind when she said it.

'He'll learn he's one of them, and they'll accept him.'

Peter said to me, 'The other chimps, they really are OK. The second day I got here, one of them died. It was Petra. She was kind of the matriarch. She'd been around the longest, and she'd been sick for a few months, and when she died they let her lie in her cage for a while. It was Mrs Helson's idea. She thought it was good for the others to be able to see her dead, and say goodbye. Well, it was Jack's idea too. He wanted to see what they'd do to a dead body.'

'Probably hoping they'd eat it,' I muttered.

Mom was listening closely. This was the kind of thing she'd been interested in all along.

'What happened?' she asked Peter.

'It was amazing,' he said. 'Some of the other chimps wouldn't go in at all, but almost all the females did. And they tried to wake her, lifting her arms and stuff. Some of the younger ones filled their mouths with water and tried to put it in hers. Then after a while they just sat around her and groomed her, and they were crying. They were making their sad faces and pant-hoots and stroking her fur.'

'Grieving,' said Mom.

'Absolutely,' said Peter. 'They care about each other. It's hard for some of them, because they came from all sorts of different places and families, so it's difficult for them to feel loyalty. But when they do, it's phenomenal to see.' He looked at me. 'So don't write them off as monsters yet.'

'Yeah, all right,' I murmured.

'What about Helson?' Mom asked, looking at Dad and then Peter.

'He's a bit weird. He doesn't take no for an answer. He's strict, but he knows how to take care of the chimps.'

'It's better than medical research,' Dad said.

'Way better,' Peter agreed.

I looked at Zan, swinging from a low branch and hooting for me to join him. He still liked to keep us close. 'I don't think he's safe here.'

'I'll take care of him,' Peter said.

'Jack said we can come back in the summer and visit, and see how he's doing,' Mom told me.

'Really?' I looked at Dad. He didn't say anything.

'As soon as school gets out,' Mom said, 'we'll come back. That's just two months.'

I nodded, feeling a little better.

The next day Helson agreed to introduce Zan to Rachel. She was eight years old, large and squat and one of the quietest chimps in the colony. Peter said she was sort of like Zan because she'd grown up with a human family for ten months – one of Helson's cross-fostering experiments. Language had no part in it. He just wanted to see what it did to the chimps – and the people, especially the woman, who wasn't sure she wanted to have children of her own.

After the humans were finished with Rachel, they'd returned her to Helson, and she had a hard time fitting back into the colony. She was OK with a few of the chimps, but was mostly a loner.

We got her in the cage next to Zan and opened the tunnel.

Just like the first time, the two chimps ignored each other in their separate cages for a good long time. But then, to my surprise, it was Zan who walked through the tunnel to Rachel.

He sat down a few feet away, and every so often shuffled a little closer.

Rachel avoided even looking at him. But when she finally did, Zan signed to her.

Come hug.

Rachel sat still. I swallowed, remembering what Sheba had done to Zan.

Come hug tickle, Zan signed, very slowly and clearly.

No reaction from Rachel.

Slowly, his head bent low, Zan walked on all fours to Rachel and touched her hand. She let him. Before long she was touching his fingers, grooming them.

Zan crawled up into her lap.

I held my breath.

Rachel put one arm around Zan, and they stayed like that for the rest of the afternoon.

On our last day we saw Zan in the afternoon. He'd spent the night in Rachel's cage and there hadn't been any problems. Peter was really happy about that.

'We'll leave them together for a few more days, and then introduce an adult when we think it's safe.'

'OK,' I said. I wasn't really taking much in, because I knew in less than an hour we'd be leaving for the airport.

'He's a survivor,' Peter told me. 'He'll be fine. I promise you.'

I truly believed Peter would do everything he could to take care of Zan. But it seemed pretty obvious that Helson was running things. Could Peter ever go against his wishes?

'You've got the suitcase, right?' I said.

Peter nodded. It was in his apartment. Helson wouldn't allow the blankets and toys in Zan's cage any more, but Peter said he'd try to let Zan play with them when they were outside, just the two of them.

We took Zan for one last walk to the field. We thought it would be easier. This way we wouldn't have to say goodbye to him in a cage. Zan and I played around in the low branches and looked at the fish, and pretty soon it was time to go. Peter made sure to have a treat ready for Zan so we could slip away one by one. He'd brought ginger ale and cake.

Dad shook Peter's hand. 'Thanks, Peter, for all your help on this. I'm sure it won't be long before I'll be addressing you as Doctor.'

Peter chuckled. 'Thank you, but that's a ways off yet.'

I'm not sure Zan even noticed Dad leaving the paddock.

Mom had a good tickle with Zan and then she too slipped away.

'This isn't gonna be easy, man,' Peter said to me.

'I know.'

'Remember, you're coming back in eight weeks.'

'Can I call you? So I know how he's doing?'

'Absolutely. Your dad and mom have my phone number. Any time, honest, just call me.'

His eyes looked moist, and I knew that if I saw him cry I'd

start bawling, and then getting away from Zan would be hope-less. I looked at Zan, eating happily. I didn't want to trick him into running off somewhere, like that time in the cage.

I went over and we had a good hug and tickle, but I didn't say goodbye.

Then Peter got him interested in some horses Helson kept in the neighbouring field.

I walked fast for the gate. I felt like a great rip had opened up inside me, from belly to breastbone. I hadn't known such pain was possible.

I didn't talk to my dad all the way to the airport or on the plane home.

I wasn't going to talk to him for the rest of my life.

He'd just left my little brother in a cage.

CHAPTER 21

MAY AND JUNE

In Zan's bedroom: his bed, perfectly made, the drawers still stacked with little shorts and sleeveless shirts. In the kitchen: the fridge, emptied of yoghurt and milk and ginger ale and vegetables and meat; the cupboards empty, no need to keep them locked now. In his playroom: the red table and chairs. Lined up on shelves were his toys, but not the favourite ones he'd circle around himself every night – they were in the suitcase, in Nevada, in Peter's apartment, while Zan slept in his cage.

It was bizarre going back to school after that week in Nevada. It was like being a tourist in another country. It had nothing to do with me. All these kids walking around and sitting at desks and listening to teachers talk about stuff that wasn't the least bit important. I wondered why anyone bothered to show up at all.

I wrote another English assignment using only Zan's

sixty-six words, just to piss Dad off. Mr Stotsky actually gave me an A– and said I'd achieved something quite poetic. I didn't give a damn. I muttered. I stared. I skulked.

Weirder still: I was popular again.

Even though Dad had refused to talk to reporters, the local paper had put together a story about how Zan had been shipped off to some university in the States. They printed a really cute picture of him sitting on my lap asking for a drink. So most kids at school knew he wasn't living with us any more.

First day back, David Godwin came up to me and slapped me on the shoulder and said, 'Sorry, Ben, about Zan. I think the whole thing stinks. It wasn't my dad, you know. He wanted to keep it going, but your father seemed pretty determined to shut it down.'

The girls were the nicest. Girls I didn't even *know*, in all grades, kept coming up to me and telling me how sorry they were that Zan was gone.

How could they do that?

He was like a kid brother to you!

Why couldn't he stay?

It's so unfair!

Some said they really missed him. Even though they'd never *met* him, they felt like they *knew* him, just reading about him and seeing his pictures. Knowing he was gone made them so, so sad. A couple of girls even started crying and threw their arms around me.

I'd just mumble and shrug and sigh.

It wasn't like I was putting on an act.

But I'd given them a drama that was impossible to resist.

It almost made me laugh. I was a dominant male again. Finally I'd become the mysterious, stoic man with the wounded past.

Even Jennifer gave me sympathetic little smiles in the hallway. But not even my renewed alpha status could bring her back to me. We had no *chemistry*. I knew a lot more about chemistry after the ranch, watching chimps, seeing who had power over whom.

Jennifer and Hugh were all over each other. They were holding hands in school for everyone to see, kissing in the hallways.

'I thought she wasn't allowed to date until she was sixteen,' I said to David.

He rolled his eyes. 'Mom and Dad reconsidered. They think she's mature enough. And Hugh being older, I guess that helped.'

The pain was a pale echo of what I'd felt leaving Zan behind at Helson's.

Now that Jennifer and Hugh were going out, I didn't see her very much with Jane and Shannon. They weren't necessary to her life any more.

One day after school I was waiting at the bus stop and Shannon came up and said, 'I'm really sorry about what happened with Zan. It must've been awful.'

She sounded completely sincere, and I remembered that time we'd talked about Zan last year at the rugby party, and how interested she'd seemed. I felt like I was seeing Shannon through a new lens, undistracted by Jennifer's nuclear glow. I could see how pretty she really was, how kind her eyes were.

'Yeah,' I said, 'thanks. It was really hard.'

And then I said something I'd never said before, even though I'd always known it.

'But I'm going to get him back.'

That night, I came downstairs from doing homework to get a drink. Mom and Dad weren't in the living room or kitchen, but I heard their voices faintly from Zan's suite. The door was ajar and I walked closer to listen.

'It'd make a super family room,' said Dad. 'Finishing the basement seems daunting, and I hate basements anyway. We'd have room for a TV and the hi-fi. And even a separate home office for you.'

'I don't know if I'm ready to talk about this,' I heard Mom say.

I walked in, and they both turned in surprise. I saw Mom give Dad a kind of disgusted look, like she couldn't believe he'd even brought the subject up, with me in the house.

'I bet you could fit lots of rats in here too,' I said to Dad. 'You could stack three or four rows against that wall probably. Keep an eye on them. That'd be handy.'

'We won't be doing anything to this room until you're ready,' Dad said.

'I'm not going to be ready,' I said, and felt my heart start pumping hard. I'd started to like that feeling, that drumbeat of anger. 'Because Zan's coming back.'

'Ben—' Dad began.

'How much did you sell him for?' I demanded.

He had his unflappable, psychologist face on. 'I didn't make those arrangements, Ben. It would've been the university.'

'But how much?'

'There's no purpose to this discussion. Zan *cannot* come back here to live with us.'

I looked at Mom. 'Do you know how much they paid for him?'

'I really don't, sweetie.'

I said, 'I've got money. All that money you paid me.'

'That wouldn't be enough,' Dad said.

'So you *do* know how much he cost?'

'Thousands, Ben.'

I tried to do the math quickly, but couldn't. 'OK. If you never paid me my allowance again, would that be enough?'

'Ben . . .' Mom began sadly.

'The only real issue here,' Dad said, 'is that Zan is not coming back. Where would we put him? He can't sleep in a normal house any more. We'd need to build cages, concrete walls. Even if I had all the money in the world I wouldn't do it. It'd turn our home into a prison – and we still wouldn't have the space or staff Helson does. Zan's better off there.'

'We could buy the field behind the house.'

Dad looked at me carefully. 'Ben, I'm concerned about you. I really don't think it's healthy to dwell on this.'

'No, it's healthier to *forget*, isn't it? Just make people disappear.'

And I walked off.

That night Mom cried. A lot.

I set my alarm for six so I could call Peter before Mom and Dad were awake. I went downstairs and took the living-room phone on its long cord into the laundry room, and closed the door. Peter was an hour ahead and I knew he liked to get up early.

'How's Zan?' I asked right away.

'He's doing all right,' Peter said. 'Yeah. Helson's decided he wants me to work with him and this other family.'

I didn't understand. 'You mean to *live* with them?'

'No, no, just in the mornings. I take him over and he spends an hour with them. I'm like the babysitter and teacher and interpreter.'

My jealousy was instant. Zan had another home, another family?

'Do they have kids?'

'No. That's the point, sort of. They're, um, well, the man and woman are both in psychotherapy and they're having problems with their marriage and Helson wants to find out the effect Zan has on them. This couple lost their own son nine months ago, so Helson wants to see if Zan helps them grieve.'

I didn't care about them and their dead son. I hated them, having Zan in their house when he should have been in mine.

'Are they nice to him?'

'Mostly. Zan seems to like it. I mean, he likes being in a house again. He likes the chairs and carpets and beds, and he gets to drink from cups. Anyway, that's a little side project of Helson's. In the afternoon I take Zan back to the ranch and work with his signing. And I'm slowly introducing him to Igor and Caliban so I can see if they'll sign together.'

'Does he seem happy?'

'He's doing OK, Ben, really.'

'Has Zeus hurt him? Or Sheba?'

'No. They keep them apart. But he and Rachel are really close.'

'That's good.' He had a mother, sort of.

'And how are you doing, my man?' Peter asked me.

'Dad wants me to see a therapist.'

'What?' Peter exclaimed.

'He doesn't think I'm dealing with things well. He thinks I'm too angry.'

'Don't go, man,' said Peter. 'That's all crap.'

'Mom wants me to go too.'

'*They* should be going, not you. Anyway, these therapists, what do they know? They'll fit you into some diagnosis and put you on pills. Happened to my cousin. Used to be energetic and creative and now he just sits in a chair, watching TV with the sound turned down.'

I chuckled. 'Really?'

Peter laughed. 'No. But you're fine,' he said to me. 'You don't need a therapist. Your heart is normal. You're entitled to be as angry as you want.'

I wasn't sure it was good advice, but I loved him for giving it to me.

I rode my bike around a lot, just to empty out my head. Sometimes bits of things would circle around. Just words. Sometimes Zan's words.

Go. Go, go. Hurry.

There dog. Go dog.

Tree. Apple tree.

Water. Dirty. No drink.

Look. Listen.

Bird.

Bird eat. Eat bird eat.

Listen bird.

When I rode, I was kind of hoping I'd run into Tim Borden and Mike and their gang. I wanted to see how deep my anger was, how hot it would burn if Mike provoked me. I wanted to display. I wanted to hit. Toes. Fingers. Face. Scrotum.

All I cared about was the end of the year, so I could go down to visit Zan.

I dreamed about him all the time.

In my dreams I carried him everywhere. He wanted to be held, so I held him. I didn't put him down once. We walked and walked, and when I sat, he sat on my lap, and we signed and I read to him and showed him pictures from his favourite books. Sometimes we just listened to the sounds the world was making.

'How long is this appointment?' I asked.

'About an hour,' the therapist said.

He was a colleague of my father's, so I already thought he was a jerk-off, even if he did have friendly eyes. I'd promised Mom I'd go. But I'd only made the promise so I could piss off Dad.

I took a magazine from my knapsack and started reading. I wasn't really reading. I was just looking at the pictures and turning the pages every once in a while.

'Ben?' said Dr Stanwick.

I looked up. 'Yeah?'

'Do you want to talk?'

'Not really.'

'Do you want to be here?'

I shook my head.

'Why not?'

'Because it was my father's idea. He thinks I'm having problems because I miss Zan and want him back. I think most people would be upset if they saw their brother locked up in a cage.'

'You see Zan as your brother?' Dr Stanwick asked.

'Sure.'

'Did you consider him human?'

I sighed. 'He's a *chimp*. But I still loved him. Dad didn't.' I shrugged. 'He didn't even want *me*. He wanted rats.'

'Do you feel he cares more about his work than you?'

'Is this how it's going to be?' I said. I didn't like being rude to him, because he seemed like a nice guy.

'What do you mean?' he asked.

'You asking me questions and me answering so you can write a report for my father.'

'I'm here to see if I can help *you*, Ben.'

'You can't help me,' I said. I felt the anger coursing through me again.

Dr Stanwick said, 'If you'd prefer, you can just talk and I'll listen. Whatever you want to talk about, that's fine.'

'I can save you some time,' I said. 'Because I know my father'll want to know what we talked about. Tell him I hate him.'

The therapist said nothing, just watched me.

'Tell him, "Screw you, screw you and screw you."' I wiped my nose. I was crying. 'You can write that down,' I said, pointing at his pad. 'Write it down and you can do a graph or something.'

On the weekend, I helped Mom do the grocery shopping at the Cordova Plaza. As we passed the pet shop she stopped to admire a puppy in the window.

'Check out this guy. He is so cute,' Mom said. 'I had a cocker spaniel when I was young.'

'I don't want a dog, Mom,' I said.

'Who said anything about getting a dog?' she replied with a shrug.

It was nice of her to try; she wanted to distract me, make me feel better.

'We're still going to visit Zan once school gets out, right?' I asked her.

'Absolutely. A road trip to Nevada. It'll be a blast.'

'Will Dad come?'

305

'Just you and me, I think.'

That suited me fine.

'Do your parents know we talk so much?' Peter asked a couple of weeks later.

'No.'

'They will when they get the phone bill.'

'I'll worry about that later,' I said. 'How's he doing? How's he getting along with this new family?'

'Well, they decided to stop seeing him.'

'What happened?' I asked, worried.

'Helson's calling it a therapeutic triumph. The couple were able to grieve properly over their son, they learned more about themselves, and now they've decided to get divorced.'

'Wow. That's a triumph?'

'Helson was pretty excited.'

I twisted the phone cord round and round my wrist. 'So is this what he's going to keep doing with Zan – loan him out like a teddy bear?'

There was a hesitation on the other end of the line. 'I don't think the couple liked Zan. He tormented their cat.'

I couldn't help smiling.

'I mean, Zan *loved* the cat,' said Peter. 'It's just that he tended to stroke it and hug it kind of hard. Also, he bit the woman.'

'Badly?'

'Three stitches, antibiotics, nothing on what he did to Ryan.'

Part of me was glad. Zan was mine, ours, and I didn't like

sharing him. I also didn't think it was good, introducing him to all these new people and then just taking him away – and I told Peter so.

'I agree,' he said. 'He seems a bit down now that it's over. He likes living like a human. He misses it. But it might be for the best.'

'How?'

'Well, now he can really try to fit in here, and I'm having some success. I had him and Igor in the same cage for an hour or so.'

'And?'

'They just ignored each other. But they didn't fight!'

'That's good?'

'It's progress. I take him out every day to the field, and we talk and play. And he's still learning signs. He knows *harmonica* now.'

'Harmonica?'

'He loves the thing. Loves listening to it, loves playing it.'

We talked a bit more about what was going on up here, and he actually told me to do my best at school, which I didn't like.

'You're a smart kid, Ben.'

'I'm not smart.'

'You are. Don't waste it, man.'

I wished I could believe him.

'I wanted to tell you something about your dad,' Mom said.

I was half asleep when she came in and sat at the edge of my bed. It was a Saturday night, and Dad was away in Vancouver at a conference.

'Why?' I mumbled.

Mom's breath smelled strongly of wine, and I wondered if she was a little drunk.

'I just thought it might help.'

I'd seen the therapist three times now. I kind of liked it. I'm not sure if it was helping me, but it felt good to talk, and he didn't seem to mind what I said, or how angry I got, or if I swore or cried. I wondered if Dr Stanwick called my dad after every session and made a report. I didn't care.

Mom said, 'He was the first to hold you when you were born. I was wiped. I was shaking so hard I was afraid I'd drop you. So the nurse got you all wrapped up and passed you to Dad and he got to be the first. He said you were totally awake. Your eyes were completely focused on him, on his eyes. He held you like that for a long time, and you just looked at each other and he said your name over and over again. He loved that.'

I turned my face to the wall. 'Dad never told me that story.'

'Well, it's not the kind of thing Dad talks about.'

I snorted.

'Your dad's a very . . . controlled person,' Mom said. 'He keeps it in. He doesn't show what he feels very well. Or often enough. I think the way he was brought up . . .' She hesitated. 'There wasn't much money, which isn't the end of the world, but I'm not sure he got enough love either. Your dad grew up very self-sufficient. He wanted to do well, and he did. His work means a lot to him. Too much maybe.'

I didn't know what to say for a while. I wasn't quite sure what Mom wanted.

'So I'm supposed to forgive him now?' I asked. 'Because he had a crappy childhood, and he loved me for ten minutes when I was a baby?'

'He loves you *now*, Ben, and you know it.'

I didn't know if I believed her.

'I'm a slow learner,' I said. 'Just ask Dad.'

At the end of May the school held the last dance of the year. I didn't know why, but I went.

I slow-danced a lot with Shannon. Maybe she felt sorry for me. Maybe she honestly liked me. With her arms around my neck, she pressed herself close, and I could feel her breasts. I felt myself stiffen between my legs.

'You want to go upstairs?' I asked, surprising myself.

She nodded.

In the darkness, Jennifer was already up there with Hugh, necking. I made sure to shove against her knees as I passed with Shannon, made sure she looked up and saw me.

Shannon and I found a place in the shadows and kissed. I was hungry and thirsty for her mouth and tongue and I could tell she liked it too, and pretty soon our hands were on each other, necks and cheeks and shirts, and a terrible thought came into my head.

I thought: *She likes me so much, I could* control *her. I could make her do anything I want.*

For a crazy moment I thought I was going to cry, because I

knew you couldn't really control anyone or anything. You couldn't *make* people like you or love you, no matter how hard you tried to please them, no matter how much you wanted it. And sometimes, the people who *did* love you got taken away, and there was nothing you could do about that either.

But I forced these thoughts away and kept kissing and touching her until we were parched and breathless and a teacher came up to clear us all out of the gallery.

June was beautiful. In Toronto it always went from winter to summer in about two weeks, but here in Victoria the spring started in February and went into May and everything was all green and flowery and smelled good.

Just two more weeks of school and then Mom and I would be driving down to visit Zan.

One night at dinner Dad said, a bit gruffly, 'There's no way Helson would've allowed this visit if it weren't for your mom.'

'Because of her research?' I said. I knew she wanted more information about how Zan was adjusting to the chimp colony, after being cross-fostered with humans.

'Let's just say he likes your mother's company,' Dad said.

There was a twisted edge to his voice that I wasn't used to hearing. I said nothing, just looked from Dad to Mom.

Mom seemed surprised. 'I can't see Jack Helson caring for anyone's company but his own, frankly.'

'He flirts with you,' Dad said. 'He has a reputation.'

I remembered now the way Jack Helson kept looking at Mom.

Mom shrugged. 'Well, he holds no attraction for me, I can

tell you. I'm going so I can see Zan.' She almost smiled. 'You're not jealous, are you, Richard?'

Dad ignored her and turned to me. 'Ben, I'd like you to stop calling Peter so much. It's expensive.'

He must've gotten the phone bill. 'But it's the only way I know what's happening with Zan.'

'It's useful to me too,' said Mom, 'hearing how he's fitting in.'

Dad said, 'You've been calling him three times a week. Once is enough, OK?'

'OK,' I said. 'OK.'

I called Peter the next morning, early as usual.

'He's been having a bit of a bad patch, Ben. I'm not going to lie to you.'

Zan and Rachel were still getting along, and they shared a cage at night, but apart from her, the other chimps weren't accepting him. Part of it was Zan. He didn't *want* to fit in. He liked spending time with Peter outside the chimp house, but that was about it.

'But you said last time he was making progress,' I said, confused.

'Sometimes there's a kind of delayed thing,' said Peter. 'Helson says he's seen it before. They're OK for the first little while, then they freak out. Maybe we were delaying it with Helson's human therapy experiment. I thought it was a stupid idea myself, but he's technically my thesis supervisor, so I can't really say no to him. Anyway, Zan's gotten kind of . . . antisocial.'

'What do you mean exactly?'

'He doesn't seem to enjoy as much,' said Peter. 'He's not eating so well. He pulls out the hair on his arms a bit.'

I swallowed. 'Why would he do that?'

'Helson said it's common. It's a trauma reaction. It passes. He, um, also rocks by himself sometimes.'

I remembered that film I'd seen last year, that tiny chimp in a tiny cage, hugging himself and rocking and rocking, desperate for any kind of contact and comfort. The rip in my chest started opening up again.

'What about Rachel? Doesn't she hug him?'

'Yeah, when Zan lets her, but sometimes he just wants to be alone.'

'He misses us,' I said.

'I'm there with him every day, Ben. I'm taking flak from Helson because I'm carrying Zan around everywhere and feeding him by hand. He just wants to toss Zan into a cage with the other adolescents and be done with it.'

'What would happen?' I asked, horrified.

'They'd fight, they'd scream, but then Zan would finally realize he's a chimp and get on with his life. That's Helson's theory. Not a big fan of babying.'

'We'll be down in two weeks,' I said.

'I know. Helson's pissed off, though. He thinks you'll just set him back.'

I didn't care about Helson. I needed to see Zan, but it killed me to think my presence might hurt him.

I fought to keep my voice steady. 'Do you think I shouldn't come?' I asked.

'You come,' he said. 'You need to see him.'

'Does Zan need to see *me*?'

'I can't think of anything in the world that would make him happier,' said Peter.

Before falling asleep that night, I worried about Zan, and when I woke up, I worried about him some more.

I crashed and burned on my final exams. I had hardly opened the books. I'd told Mom and Dad I was studying, but I wasn't.

Report cards came two days before Mom and I were to leave for Nevada.

Dad said, 'Your marks can't be very pleasing to you, Ben.'

I took a deep breath. 'The data is correct, Professor Tomlin. I am unexceptional. Project Ben was a failure. But don't worry. I'm sure there's somewhere you can send me.'

He looked at me, and there wasn't any anger in his eyes, only sadness. He exhaled, and then stabbed me with a smile. 'Well, it's been a tough term. I hope you and your mom have a good time in Nevada.'

I wanted to say something to him.

Sorry, or something like that.

I felt my hands twitch, like they wanted to sign, like they wanted to say the thing my mouth couldn't.

But no words came.

CHAPTER 22

CH-72

Mile by mile, the heat grew as we drove south, until it was almost better to keep the windows rolled up, to keep out the searing wind. Dad's Mercedes didn't have air conditioning. We tried to leave early in the mornings and find a motel by four.

The trip was so different from the one Dad and I had taken two years ago, crossing Canada. This time I sat up in front with Mom the whole time and we talked and talked and our words filled the car. I loved it. Away from Dad, Mom seemed different, younger, happier – freer somehow. We talked a lot about Zan, how we felt when he first arrived, and how our feelings about him changed week by month by year. We talked about the things he'd done that made us crazy and made us love him, and the things that made us shake our heads in amazement.

When Mom and I listened to the radio, sometimes we sang

along together, so loud once that we didn't hear the siren of the police car that was trying to pull us over for speeding. The cop was pretty harsh with Mom when he first came to the window, but she was so apologetic and pretty and charming that within three minutes he was chuckling, and he let us go with a warning and wishes for a great vacation in Reno.

I had my birthday on the road. I turned fifteen, and that night at dinner the waitress brought out a cake with sparklers on it and everyone in the diner sang 'Happy Birthday to You'. It was the best birthday ever, because I knew I'd be seeing Zan the next day.

We pulled onto the gravel drive of Helson's ranch around ten-thirty in the morning. Peter must have heard our car coming, because he emerged from the chimp house to meet us. He looked different. He'd cut off his beard, just leaving the moustache, and it made him look younger and handsomer, but also kind of vulnerable.

He opened his arms to me and I gave him a big hug. Then Mom surprised me by hugging him too and giving him a kiss on the cheek – something I'd never seen her do around Dad.

'I've got Zan in a cage by himself,' Peter said. 'I figured Rachel might get a little jealous, so I moved her to the other side.'

As I walked into the chimp house, my stomach did gymnastics. What if he'd forgotten me? What if he thought I was a traitor for leaving him?

All the chimps set up their usual din when we entered

the building. Zan was in the corner cage, and as I slowly approached the bars, he turned.

He stared for a moment, motionless, expressionless, and for a second I thought:

It's happened. He's forgotten me.

Then his eyebrows shot up and his lips pulled back in a smile to reveal his lower teeth. He raised himself on his legs and ran to the bars.

His hands greeted me instantly. He pursed his lips for a kiss and I let him shower my cheeks, and then I kissed him all over his forehead and face.

Come tickle! he signed. *Hug! Hug!*

I pushed my hand through the bars and tickled him as much as I could. He didn't smell like us any more. Not our soap or shampoo or food. He smelled clean, but more like a real animal. It didn't matter. All that mattered was being here.

'I missed you, Zan. I missed you so much,' I said aloud. I didn't even try to sign it because my feelings were in such a hurry.

Out. You me out. Open now!

'Can he come out?' I asked Peter. 'Or can I go in?'

'We'll bring Zan out after lunch.'

The way Peter said it made me realize these were Helson's rules, but I didn't care right now. It was so good just to be beside him, and we talked and laughed and played through the bars. He greeted Mom warmly too, and they spent a long time grooming.

Though he still seemed small compared to the other chimps

316

in the colony, I could tell he was bigger now, in the face and chest and legs especially. His skin was a bit darker too. Just two months. He looked pretty healthy. Peter had been taking good care of him. I checked Zan's arms and saw a few mangy patches where he'd pulled out his own hair. It didn't look too bad. But then Zan smiled and I noticed one of his upper teeth was missing.

'What happened to his tooth?' I asked. It was too early for him to be losing baby teeth.

Peter nodded uncomfortably. 'Bit of a run-in with Zeus.'

'Helson put them together?' Mom said, aghast.

'Part of his acclimatization regime,' Peter replied. 'Zan and Rachel are very friendly now, and that's great, but the ideal would be to introduce another male into the mix. I've been working on Caliban and Igor slowly.' He rocked his head side to side. 'Limited success so far, but I'm still hopeful. It's early days. But Helson's more of a tough-love guy. He wants Zan integrated faster. So he started bringing in some of the other males, sometimes two at a time. Mostly it goes OK – if everyone just kind of stays out of everyone else's way. Other times, there's trouble.'

'Doesn't Rachel stand up for him?' I asked.

'She does, but her status is fairly low, and she's not that strong, so she backs down pretty fast if she's ganged up on. Anyway, Zan's still wary of the other males and he usually gets as far away as he can, against the bars of the cage. He turns his back on them, which they don't like – it's insulting. But Zan doesn't know that. So he just stares out of the bars.'

Like a prisoner, I thought, wishing I could take him a million miles away.

'One day Helson let Zeus in,' Peter continued, 'and Zeus watched Zan for a while, and then just walked over and gave him a smack. Zan's face hit the bars, and his tooth got cracked right in two. We had to remove it.'

My eyes watered just thinking of it. I looked at Peter's cattle prod, and imagined shoving it into Zeus's chest and zapping him until he fell over. Why would anyone pick on someone so small?

The chimps suddenly all hooted and we turned to see Dr Helson entering the building with Sue-Ellen.

'Sarah, lovely to see you again,' he said, shaking Mom's hand – and holding it a little longer than I thought was necessary. I was watching him more carefully now, after what Dad had said. 'And, Ben, hello there, young man. I'm sorry I didn't come out to greet you. I was on a long-distance call.'

'We were just noticing Zan's missing tooth,' Mom said directly.

Dr Helson shrugged. 'A baby tooth. It'll come back.'

'Perhaps it's not wise to have Zeus and Zan in the same cage yet,' Mom said.

I could tell Dr Helson didn't like this at all. He seemed to stand a little taller and his nostrils flared.

'Strange as it may sound, Zeus was doing Zan a favour. Zeus was asking for an acknowledgement of his superiority, which is natural and right in a colony. It's also Zeus's way of saying *Snap out of it*. And after that slap, I noticed Zan didn't spend as much time staring meekly through the bars. Wouldn't you say, Peter?'

'He's a little more active now, definitely,' said Peter.

'Your Zan's just having a good long sulk,' Helson said, looking from me to Mom. 'It's not good for him, and it's upsetting the harmony of my colony. He needs to adjust. Faster the better. Now, I hope you'll have dinner with me tonight.'

I noticed Mom hesitate a second before saying, 'That would be lovely, thank you.'

'I'm off early tomorrow for a conference in Florida, so it's my one chance to visit with you properly. Barbara's getting back tomorrow and Peter knows the ropes. They'll be able to answer any questions you might have for your doctoral dissertation, Sarah.'

'Thank you very much,' said my mother. 'I'm sure it'll be a very productive visit for me.'

That afternoon after lunch, Peter took Zan out to one of the fields with me and Mom. Sue-Ellen came along. School was out for her too. She'd grown up with chimpanzees and was completely comfortable around them. She was patient and gentle and respectful – and it made me think her father couldn't be a complete monster, or where would she have learned all this? Zan really seemed to like her.

Mom had brought her notebook and was observing Zan and asking Peter all sorts of questions. Sue-Ellen and I mostly played with Zan in the shade of the few trees.

'He's such a darling,' she said. 'Caliban and Igor are sweethearts, but they have nothing on Zan.'

I wondered if she was just trying to be nice, but she seemed genuine. She'd learned some signs on her own, so she could talk to Zan. She was quite pretty, a bit short maybe, but I liked watching her breasts move under her halter top. I wondered if she was interested in me.

At the end of the afternoon Peter had to put the collar on Zan and walk him back to the chimp house. Outside his cage Zan gave me a hug, squeezing his arms around me so tight it started to hurt.

'I'll see you tomorrow,' I told him, but if he understood, he didn't believe me. He clung to me even tighter. 'Zan,' I said. 'Let go! You're hurting me!' And I actually gave him a thump on the back to get his attention. I'd never hit him before.

'Zan!' said Peter, and lifted the cattle prod.

At the mere sight of the prod Zan whimpered and stopped squeezing me. I didn't like to see him threatened like that – or that Peter was the one to do it – but I was glad Zan let go. He was a lot stronger than I remembered.

Sorry, he signed to me. *Sorry*.

Sorry, I signed back, and stroked his arm and shoulder.

We tickled a bit more. I wanted to show him I wasn't angry. And after a while, he seemed happy enough to jump up onto Peter and get a piggyback into his cage.

That night at dinner I think Dr Helson tried to get Mom drunk. He kept filling her wineglass. This time, Zan was not in a cot beside us. Peter had not been invited. It was only Helson, me, Mom, Sue-Ellen and Winston.

Just like last time, Dr Helson had cooked the meal. It was pork – from one of the pigs on his farm, he told us. Apparently he had all sorts of animals on it. He wasn't just interested in chimpanzees.

The food was excellent. And I didn't want a single bite of it.

Back at the motel later that night, I said to Mom, 'I don't want Zan to be here.'

'I know,' she said. 'But I think this really might be the best place for him, Ben.'

'Right! He's already lost a tooth. Next it'll be a toe, or maybe Zeus'll just bite his head off. Dr Helson wouldn't care.'

'I don't like him either,' Mom said.

'Put an eye patch on him, give him a white cat to stroke, and he could be a Bond villain.'

We laughed and it felt good, but it didn't change the fact that Zan wasn't safe, and one day he could get hurt. Or worse.

We only had three more days at the ranch, and Mom and I both wanted to spend as much time with Zan as possible. Peter had taught Zan about eight new signs, and Zan certainly didn't seem to have forgotten any of his old ones.

I was glad Dr Helson had disappeared for his conference. I hated him, his tall arrogant body and cold green eyes. The way his alpha male gaze settled on my mom – and then on me, like I was some newborn chimp he'd like to destroy so he could mate with my mother and make more of his own offspring. *Good riddance, Dr Helson.*

That morning, one of the other handlers brought Igor out to the field with Zan, and they seemed to be getting along pretty well, playing in the trees and breaking off low branches to make nests.

'He's a strange hybrid,' I heard Peter say to Mom. 'I mean, he tries to sign with the other chimps. He'll sign before he'll vocalize. He tries it with them, and sometimes he gets really angry when they don't understand, and there's a showdown and it gets physical. He's no coward. I've seen him stand up to pretty much everyone, except Zeus. Him, he just ignores, but I think it's fear.'

'We taught him too well,' said Mom. 'To be a human.'

Peter nodded. 'And it's harder for him to fit in like that.'

I felt suddenly really sad. We'd made it impossible for him to be what he was. Making him human made it easier for us to care for him and teach him – and maybe even love him. But now, could he ever be loved by chimps?

Later, when I told this to Sue-Ellen, she said, 'Rachel loves him, and I think he loves her too. They sleep together, all cuddled up, just like a mother and baby. You watch, tonight after dinner. And I think he and Igor are starting to get closer. He just needs to learn how to play, chimp-style, a bit more. It's rough stuff. We wouldn't like it.'

We were walking past one of the other paddocks where some of the older chimps were playing. They liked to bite each other and throw each other around.

'If they did that to us, they'd kill us,' I said.

'Yep.'

'Is that Sheba?' I asked, pointing.

She nodded.

'What's wrong with her? Her bum's all swollen.' It seemed enormous, like two fleshy red lobes.

Sue-Ellen looked at me, smiling faintly. 'That's not her bum. That's her genitalia.'

'Oh,' I said, feeling foolish.

'That's what happens when the females are in oestrus. It shows they're ready to mate.'

'And does she?'

'Oh, all the time. Lately she seems to like Rex best. That's why we've been putting them in the same paddock. They usually have a go at it, around this time.'

We stood there by the fence, watching, waiting for them to *have a go at it*. I felt the day's heat on my hat, my face, trickling from my armpits down my sides. I glanced over at Sue-Ellen, saw the faint sweat rings on her T-shirt and suddenly felt a deep surge of desire. It was kind of awkward, waiting for chimps to start mating, standing a few inches away from a girl, but I was pretty curious too.

Rex came sniffing around Sheba, but after fifteen minutes nothing much seemed to be happening and Sue-Ellen laughed and said, 'Another time, I guess.'

'Another time,' I echoed, half disappointed, half relieved.

* * *

On our third night, Peter had Mom and me over to his place in Reno for fondue. He lived in a little apartment building not far from the university campus. He was on the top floor, but he had an air-conditioning unit in his window and it was going full blast, so we were pretty comfortable.

Mom had brought the best bottle of wine she could find at the liquor store near our motel. The store was called the Liquor Barn and seemed to sell mostly whisky and beer.

We all sat down around the wobbly table and stuck our bits of bread and meat into the fondue pot. When Peter served the wine he poured me a full glass and winked.

'Helson's gonna make an alcoholic of me,' he said. 'Some of the days on that ranch . . .'

I was so much happier here than I had been at Helson's dining table. For the first part of the meal Peter wanted to know about us and what was going on back in Victoria – about my school and what happened to Jennifer, and who was Shannon, and was that going anywhere, and was I going to keep going to Windermere? Normally I might have been self-conscious answering around Mom, but things felt different somehow, with just the three of us – or maybe I'd just had lots of practice talking about myself with Dr Stanwick.

Afterwards Peter asked Mom about her research and when she'd submit her dissertation. He asked a little about Dad and his rat experiment.

He and Mom finished the bottle of wine pretty fast, and then Peter got out some cold beer.

Holding his bottle, Peter looked from side to side, a bit

nervous, like the guy who gives James Bond secret information before getting fed to sharks in the next scene.

'There's stuff going on here,' he said.

I sort of giggled, and so did Mom.

'What do you mean?' I asked.

Peter wasn't smiling. 'It's hard for me to figure out because I'm so new, and people aren't sure they can trust me yet. I'm not sure I can trust them either.'

'You're sounding a little paranoid, Peter,' said Mom.

'I know, but just listen. I think Helson's star is falling at the university. Some of the stuff he does here is kind of, well, way out there. He's done these experiments with pigs and electroshock.'

I swallowed, thinking of the other night's pork.

'And there's this thing with gibbons he's got going in another barn, putting newborns in total isolation for the first week of life and studying the results.'

'I can't imagine they're good,' said Mom.

Peter shook his head. 'His experiments aren't attracting much funding, and I know for a fact his budget got cut back last year. He was hoping to make a lot of money renting Zan out to all these people – he calls them his *patients*. He's not a licensed psychotherapist but a lot of people like to get counselling from him.'

'There's a lot of weird people out there,' I said, and tried to help myself to a beer, but Mom caught my hand and put it firmly on the table.

'Anyway,' said Peter, 'I don't think Helson's had any other

requests for Zan. In Manhattan, maybe it'd be huge, you know, chimp therapy, who knows. In rural Nevada, no.'

'What's worrying you, Peter?' Mom asked.

I looked at Peter. 'You don't think he's going to *sell* Zan?'

'Look,' said Peter, 'this could get me into a lot of trouble, but . . . Helson got a letter from the Thurston Foundation.'

'Who're they?' I asked, looking from Mom to Peter.

'They do biomedical research with animals,' Mom said.

Now I remembered: the newborn chimp in the isolette, rocking to comfort himself. *That* was the Thurston Foundation.

'They're really bad,' I said.

'One of the worst,' said Peter. 'They do a lot of drug trials, for hepatitis and tuberculosis and other things. Make Helson's ranch look like a five-star resort.'

The smell of the cheese fondue suddenly seemed sour and nasty. 'Why's Helson getting letters from *them?*' I asked.

'Helson's sold a couple of his chimps there in the past,' said Peter. 'A long time ago. He keeps it quiet.'

'I think we're all getting excited about nothing,' Mom said. 'Helson got a letter from the Thurston Foundation – so what? It could be about anything.'

Peter was silent. Mom looked at him. I couldn't stand it any longer.

'Did you *see* the letter?' I demanded.

'I *have* the letter,' said Peter. 'This morning I arrived at Helson's the same time as the mail van. I was just closing the gate behind me and the guy handed me a stack of mail, and I said I'd take it up to the office. The letter was right on top.'

326

He stood up and went to his bookcase and pulled an envelope from between the books. He let it dangle between two fingers, like it was contaminated.

'I haven't opened it,' he said.

'That's good,' said Mom. 'That's illegal, opening someone else's mail.'

'A federal offence, they call it down here,' said Peter.

He put it down on the table. We all stared at it.

'Have you got a kettle?' Mom asked.

'Right over here,' said Peter. 'Have you done this before?'

She shook her head. 'How hard can it be?'

We boiled water in the kettle and carefully swished the letter through the steam. Then, with a butter knife, Mom tried to prise the envelope open along the seal. It took a surprisingly long time. She did a great job, leaving only one little tear.

She pulled out the letter. It was a single piece of paper, thick and creamy. Across the top was the green logo of the Thurston Foundation, which looked very space age – a brain and atoms swirling around it, like they were going to single-handedly perfect the human race.

Dear Dr Helson

RE: CH-54, CH-37, CH-72

With reference to our recent correspondence, please find enclosed our offer of purchase for the above-cited chimpanzees.

*We can offer the price of $30,000, half upon signature of this
agreement, half on the receipt of said healthy chimps at our facility.*

As discussed earlier, you will bear the cost of their transportation.

There was some more stuff, and then a signature.

'So he's selling three chimps,' I said dully.

'Trying, anyway,' said Mom. 'Do you know which ones,
Peter?'

Peter looked back at the top of the letter. I felt a terrible
dread building in me.

'CH-54 is Igor. CH-37, that's Caliban. And CH-72.
That's Zan.'

We talked and talked.

Mom said, 'He promised Zan would never be used in
biomedical experiments.'

'Did Richard get it in writing?' Peter asked.

Mom took a breath. 'I don't know.'

'If it's not in writing, it's no good, is it? I mean, in a court
of law?'

'What if *we* offer to buy Zan?' I blurted out.

'He'd be suspicious,' said Peter. 'He'd think we knew
something.'

Mom said, 'Would he? He knows Ben's heartbroken and
wants Zan back. Could be as simple as that.'

Peter thought for a moment. 'Helson's been working
chimps for twenty years. He can read people just like they can.

He can practically *smell* your thoughts. The guy's uncanny. Scares the hell out of me. Anyway, he wouldn't sell Zan to you.'

'Why not?' Mom asked.

Peter said, 'He needs Zan to sell the others.'

'Why?' I asked.

'Zan's the youngest. He's the most valuable. He's fresh, young, untainted. They can use him the longest. The other two are older. Zan's the prize. Helson won't sell him alone, I can almost promise you.'

We talked into the early hours of morning before we decided what to do.

We would steal Zan.

CHAPTER 23

STEALING ZAN

'This is crazy,' Mom murmured.

We killed the headlights as we pulled onto the long driveway, crept slowly along the gravel in the moonlight for a few minutes, then pulled over, way before we could even see the farmhouse or other buildings. Through the open car windows the air was perfect body temperature. Cricket chatter rose from the fields. It was 3:22 in the morning. We'd spent a whole day preparing for this.

Mom and I got out of the car, and closed the doors silently, then started down the drive, walking on the grassy verge so our footsteps were soundless. Our cold hands touched and she gave me a quick encouraging squeeze. Thank goodness the Helsons didn't keep any dogs at the front of the property, or they'd have been all over us by now.

Peter had wanted to come with us, but Mom had said no. If Helson figured out he was mixed up in this in any way, he'd probably get booted out of university – or worse.

Ahead I could make out the low outline of the chimp house. In the farmhouse all the lights were out. Good. The chimp house would be locked, as would all the cages. The keys were kept in the shed just behind the chimp house, and the rusted padlock didn't close properly.

Getting to the shed was scary because it meant sneaking right past the farmhouse. I hoped the Helsons were deep sleepers. I thought of Sue-Ellen in her bed. She wouldn't want Zan to be sent to a lab – or Caliban and Igor either, but I couldn't do anything about them right now.

We reached the shed and I was grateful for the big moon. I slid the broken padlock from its clasp and eased the door open. Peter had oiled the hinges yesterday, because normally they gave a terrible shriek, but right now they made barely a sound. From the darkness wafted the smell of oil and straw and rust. I pulled a small penlight from my pocket (bought at the gas station near our motel) and carefully turned it on. Near the door, high on the wall, was a big metal cabinet. Mom opened it up and, while I held the light steady, went through the rows and rows of keys on hooks. Luckily, Helson was an orderly man, and they were all labelled.

Chimp house. Got it.

Cage #8. Got it.

We closed the shed door behind us and moved towards the chimp house. The moonlight let us guide the key into the lock. Slowly, so slowly, we swung open the door, just enough so I could slip inside.

331

We'd agreed that only one of us would enter. Less noise, less smell, less chance of rousing the sleeping chimps. It was pitch black, but I dared not use the penlight. Cage eight was nearest the door, and Peter, before his afternoon shift ended, had made sure Zan was in it, alone. He'd made up some excuse about Rachel being crotchety and it being best to split the two of them up. I'd felt a bit bad, because I'd seen how attached they were to each other.

My outstretched hand touched the bars of the cage. I felt for the door, and the lock. Every second I took was a second longer the chimps might sense me. And then there'd be a godawful racket to wake the entire ranch. I slid in the key and turned. Pulled the lock free.

I swung the oiled door open, and for a horrible moment wondered:

What if someone switched the chimps, and I've just opened Zeus's cage?

My last memory would be of something grabbing my arm and pulling. Teeth in my face.

I crouched and stared, willing my eyes to be chimp's eyes, to bring light to the darkness.

Zan was sleeping not four feet from the door. I could have gone in and picked him up, but I didn't want to startle him. He might give a hoot. I waited for a moment, hoping he'd sense me. *Wake up.* I took a deep breath and silently blew against his head. He murmured and turned. His eyes opened, then widened. He stared.

I made the sign, *Quiet.* It was one he understood, though he'd never used it himself.

Then I made his name. I crossed my chest with the Z and then pointed at him.

You Zan! Come now.

For a moment he just sat motionless, and I worried he was too bewildered and scared to move. From some of the other cages I heard movement. Shadows shifted in my peripheral vision.

If Zan panted or shrieked we were sunk. We'd be caught.

Then Zan came.

He ran to me and leaped into my arms so fast I nearly toppled right over. I stood, and walked towards the pillar of moonlight at the main door. Then I was outside.

'All right?' whispered Mom.

I nodded.

We walked back towards the car as quickly as we could. I held Zan tight. He kept pulling away and looking around in the dark and giving soft surprised pants, then kissing me on the cheek.

We reached the car and got in. I sat in the back with Zan. I tried to get the seat belt on him but he kept jumping around.

'Just try to keep him back there,' said Mom, starting the engine.

After a few minutes I got him sitting on my lap and talked to him softly as he looked out of the window. His body was still small but I could feel the new strength in him; he was heavier too.

I was shaking.

'Mom,' I said, 'what's going to happen?'

'I don't know, Ben.'

I wondered if she was shaking too. I heard a police siren in the distance and wondered if it was coming for us. But it faded away soon enough. We were way out in the middle of nowhere, heading northwest. Darkness towered solid on either side of the road. We were like a spaceship, hurtling across the universe. We were like those astronauts in *Planet of the Apes*.

Before long, we'd crossed the state line into California, which was good. In movies it was always good when you crossed the state line – if you were a criminal, anyway. That way it would take longer for the law to find you. It was still pretty early, and Helson's staff usually didn't open up the chimp house until seven o'clock.

We saw a gas station, and Mom went in and bought some diapers, some cheap shorts, and a T-shirt with a picture of a slot machine on it.

I tried to get the diaper on Zan, but after going without them for months, there was no way he was putting one back on. He seemed pleased, though, to have shorts and a T-shirt again.

Pants, he signed. *Shirt!*

'Should we call Dad?' I asked, looking at the glowing phone booth outside the gas station.

'No,' Mom said. 'We'll be home soon enough.'

We drove. After a while Zan fell asleep against me, and I didn't move in case I woke him. Before long I was asleep too. When I woke, it was six-thirty and beautiful, the sun rising up over rocky hills.

'Are you tired?' I asked Mom.

'Getting there,' she said. 'I'm good for another few hours. Then we'll stop somewhere for breakfast.'

We didn't go into a restaurant. We bought stuff at a gas station and ate in the car. We didn't want anyone seeing Zan, if possible. Now that he was awake, I was a little worried about how he'd behave. Mostly he was pretty good. He could stare out the window for a long time, the wind in his face, just hooting and signing at all the things he saw. He'd never spent much time in a car, so this was all new, and I think he loved it. We'd filled the back with all the blankets and favourite toys from his suitcase – his own moving playroom.

Once, he crawled into the front seat and put his hand on the wheel. He didn't turn it or anything, but Mom slowed right down and pulled over. We were both very strict with Zan and told him he had to stay in the back.

Sorry, he signed, and felt bad enough that he actually let me buckle him in for a while. Fifteen minutes later, when he wanted out, it took him about two seconds to figure out how to undo the buckle.

Registering at the motel wasn't too tricky. Mom just left me and Zan in the car while she checked in at the office, and then we carried Zan in, all wrapped up in a blanket like a big baby – and double-locked the door.

We bathed him. Mom said it was like the scene in the Bible where Moses parts the Red Sea. Huge waves and water everywhere, people getting doused and drowned. Mom and I both ended up soaked. But afterwards Zan smelled a lot better, though he still didn't let us put a diaper on him.

When Mom went out to buy us some food for dinner she got a bunch of new clothing for Zan, since he was going through it so fast and we had no way of cleaning it. Mom was fantastic. I knew she didn't want Zan ending up in a lab either, but I got the feeling she was doing this mainly for me.

We didn't talk about what would happen when we got home.

We just talked about getting there.

The next day we drove through Oregon and Washington and reached Port Angeles. We took the last ferry over to Victoria.

It was very late when we pulled up in the driveway, and Zan was so excited I thought he was going to knock himself out trying to get out of the car. He obviously hadn't forgotten our house.

Mom took a deep breath, gripping the steering wheel for dear life.

Lights were on inside, so I knew Dad was home, and awake. I watched the front door, waiting for it to open.

For a second, I hoped . . .

I hoped it would be like the first time Zan came to us, and Dad would rush out and be happy to see him. And then we'd all eat pizza on the living-room floor while Zan slept.

The front door didn't open.

We all got out of the car and went inside. Dad was sitting with a drink in his hand. He looked at all three of us. He didn't seem the least bit surprised.

'Jack Helson called,' he said wearily. 'He wondered if I knew anything about the robbery.'

'Robbery?' I said, horrified by the word. It had been ricocheting in my head the whole drive home, but Mom and I had never said it aloud.

Dad nodded. 'You stole his property.'

The idea of Zan being owned, being property – I hated it.

'God, Sarah,' Dad said, slamming his glass down so hard I thought it'd shatter. 'What the hell have you done?'

'He was going to sell Zan to a lab!' I said.

'The Thurston Foundation,' Mom said. 'We saw the letter.'

'He showed you this letter?' Dad said.

'We opened it.'

'You opened his confidential mail?'

Mom nodded. 'We did. Because Peter had a hunch he was planning on selling Zan. And he was right.'

'Peter's involved in this too, is he?'

Mom said nothing.

'What Jack Helson does with Zan is not our concern,' Dad said.

'It is too!' I shouted.

'It *is* our concern,' Mom echoed. 'We have obligations to Zan. The understanding with Helson was that Zan would *not* be used for biomedical experiments.'

As all this was going on, Zan was charging around the house, skidding on cushions, and swiping books out of the shelves and then climbing higher to get at the next row. I think he may have pooped somewhere. He scampered into the kitchen, and I heard the fridge door opening and things hitting the floor.

337

With disconcerting calm, Dad said, 'Ben, get him under control, and put him in . . . his room.'

I left Mom and Dad to fight this out and went to Zan. He was sitting contentedly on the floor amid a pile of food, scooping yogurt out of the tub with his fingers.

Hide, I signed. *Play.*

That caught his attention.

Come, I signed, leading him into his suite.

Inside, he looked at his bed for a few seconds, like he couldn't quite remember what it was for. He was used to sleeping on concrete now. Then he leaped up onto it gleefully.

From the shelf he took down his old toys and arranged them around himself in a circle. It seemed such a simple, easy thing. Just a few little scraps of material and bits of plastic in a ring, and he felt safe. But I knew he wasn't, not yet. Maybe not ever.

All the way home, I'd let myself fantasize.

It would be like this:

Zan would live with us, and be my younger brother. We'd play in the back yard. We'd climb trees together. We'd watch the birds eat seed from their feeders. We'd throw leaves at each other and chase and tickle each other.

I never thought: *Who will take care of him when I'm at school and Mom and Dad are at work?*

I never thought: *How will we keep him safe? Keep him from hurting other people and himself?*

Brush teeth, I signed.

Where toothbrush? he signed back.

He remembered *toothbrush*, even though he hadn't used one

in months. I went to the little bathroom to check, and found one. We kept plenty because Zan liked brushing his teeth a lot, and tended to chew off the bristles after a couple of weeks.

I gave him the new toothbrush and watched him go at it. He hadn't forgotten.

Through the dark window he looked outside at the back yard.

Out. Play.

I shook my head, and he let me pick him up and put him back on his bed, encircled by his toys.

He didn't smell very good; he needed another bath.

I lay down beside him. Putting my arm around him, I could feel his heart beating against my hand.

I fell asleep on his bed, curled against him.

CHAPTER 24

ZAN AT HOME

Zan and I slept late, even though I'd forgotten to close the curtains. I think it was the breakfast smells coming from the kitchen that finally woke us: bacon and toast and coffee. Zan still looked a little confused by the room and his blankets and toys, and he was bewildered enough to let me get a diaper on him, and then a clean set of clothes, which were really too small for him now. We had a good game of hide-and-seek and tickle-hug and then went into the kitchen to get something to eat.

Dad and Mom were already there, and Dad was saying, 'Helson's being reasonable. He won't call the police if we return Zan right away.'

I guess they hadn't really settled anything last night. Through the doorway to the living room I saw someone had slept on the sofa. I didn't think it was Mom. Dad rubbed wearily at his temples when he saw Zan.

'There's got to be another option,' Mom said.

Zan let me slip him into his high chair (also too small for him now), and I started putting all his old favourite foods in front of him. No chimp loaf for him, not today – not ever again if I could help it.

'Helson's perfectly within his rights,' Dad said, 'even if he wants to sell Zan.'

I had an idea. 'What if we told the university here what Helson was going to do – sell Zan to the Thurston Foundation?'

Dad shook his head. 'Why on earth would a university be upset about legitimate scientific research?'

'You *know* the kinds of things they do at the Thurston Foundation,' Mom said, slapping some burned toast on his plate.

'Sure,' said Dad. 'I also know they've produced a lot of very useful biomedical data. And drugs that've helped thousands of people. We use animals to advance human science. It's completely acceptable. It's only a very small group of people who protest it. Ben, if you had a terrible disease, and I could use Zan to find a cure, but it would kill him, there'd be no hesitation. I'd sacrifice Zan's life in a second, to save yours.'

I didn't know what to say. It meant Dad cared about me, but it wasn't really the answer I wanted.

'I don't want Zan to be sacrificed at all,' I said quietly.

Dad pushed his burned toast away and looked at Mom hard. 'This isn't easy, and you've made it harder, bringing him back. But if Zan isn't returned, you're going to destroy your career, Sarah – and seriously harm mine.'

Mom said, 'Maybe you should worry less about your career and more about your family – because that's going to be in serious trouble too if you don't do the right thing.'

I'd never seen Mom look so seriously, and so coldly, at Dad. It was riveting, and terrifying too, because it was the kind of look one chimp gave another. It meant: *Only one of us is going to win this, and it's going to be me.*

'The *right* thing?' said Dad, with a frustrated laugh. 'And what exactly would that be, Sarah?'

'He's an animal, you're right,' said Mom. 'And we use them all the time. We eat them. We inject them. We kill them. Zan's not human. But we *taught* him he was. We raised him like a child. Our child. And we have responsibilities to him now, Richard. We do. We can't just abandon him to the Thurston Foundation.' Her voice was hoarse. 'It is wrong.'

There was a knock at the door, and my heart lurched. I thought: *Police. The County sheriff with the big gut and gun on his belt, spitting tobacco juice on my shoe.*

'It's all right,' said Mom. 'It'll be Peter.'

'Peter?' I said in astonishment, and at the sound of his name, Zan started hooting.

'Jack Helson flew him out to bring Zan back,' Dad said.

I ran to the door and threw it open for Peter. The taxi was just pulling away.

'Hey, man,' he said, looking exhausted.

'Come in, come in,' said Mom.

I grabbed his suitcase and dragged it into the front hall.

Peter looked at me. 'You know why I'm here, right?'

I nodded. 'But you're not really going to take him back, are you?'

'Hell, no,' said Peter. 'But Helson doesn't know that, and it got me a free ticket home. Is that bacon I smell?'

We got him seated at the breakfast table and I helped get him a big plate of bacon and eggs and made sure his toast wasn't burned.

Dad let Peter eat for a few minutes and then said, 'If you don't take Zan back, you're ending your academic career at Siegal – maybe everywhere else too.'

Peter shrugged. 'I want what's best for Zan.'

I smiled. Mom and I had another ally.

After breakfast we all went outside into the back yard so Zan could play while we talked.

'There's no escaping the facts,' Dad said. 'Zan is Helson's legal property, and if we don't return him, we'll be guilty of theft.' He looked at Mom. 'And mail fraud, if he finds out. You can go to jail for that too.'

'Helson wants money, right?' I said to Peter.

'Definitely, yeah.'

'So the university here won't buy him back?' I asked Dad.

'Not a chance.'

I swallowed. 'Well, if they won't buy him back, I will.'

Dad sighed. 'OK, let's just say that's possible. Let's say you can come up with ten thousand bucks and buy Zan back. We own a chimp. Then what?'

We'd already talked about this. We'd need a new, stronger

building to contain Zan. We'd need to feed him, and hire people to work with him. We'd need more land to give him proper room to play. Buying Zan was one thing. Taking care of him, paying for him for the rest of his life – that was something else.

'It would mean a total change in our lives,' Dad said. 'And I'm not willing to make that change. It's not what I want, and I doubt it's what your mother wants either.'

I looked at Mom. 'Mom?' I said.

She shook her head slowly.

'But we stole him together! We wanted him home!'

'I'm sorry, Ben. I don't want him to go to a biomedical lab, but he can't stay here for ever.'

'I'm kind of with your parents on this one, man,' Peter said, surprising me. 'You want Zan. I know. But there's something you couldn't give him up here. Other chimps.'

'Like they were so great,' I said sarcastically.

'He does need them, though,' said Peter. 'He needs companionship. He needs to be among his own kind. He was starting to integrate. I think Helson just expected too much too fast. But it would've happened.'

I turned to look at Zan in our tree. I remembered how frightened he'd been, the first time I'd held him to the lowest branch, waiting for him to cling and go swinging. It had taken him a long time to want to climb a tree. Now he went as high as he could go.

Wild chimps lived in trees. They lived in jungles. They lived in colonies. They hunted and shared and killed, just like us.

It was hard for me to say, but I did: 'We could send him back to Africa. Give him back what we took.'

'Utter fantasy,' scoffed Dad.

'Oh, Ben,' said Mom. 'I don't think that's even an option. He'll never be a wild chimp.'

Peter nodded. 'I don't think he'd make it. It'd be like dumping you in the jungle, Ben – how long would you survive?'

'So what's left?' I said. 'A zoo?'

I didn't much like that idea, but anything was better than seeing him disappear inside a lab for ever.

'No,' said Peter. 'A sanctuary.'

From his pocket he fished out a pamphlet. I recognized it from the William Eckler talk we'd gone to together.

'There's this place in Florida,' said Peter. He passed me the crumpled leaflet. There were buildings with cages, just like at Helson's. But there were also islands and wooden bridges and high platforms and ropes to climb.

'Looks like a zoo,' I said, with a shrug. 'What's the difference?'

'No experiments, for starters. Not even sign language experiments. The chimps are fed, cared for, enriched, but basically left alone. It's their home.'

'Where do the chimps come from?' Mom asked.

'All sorts of places,' Peter said. 'From the entertainment industry when they aren't young and cute any more. From people who bought them as little pets and then figured out they were too big and strong. From biomedical labs too, when they've used the chimps all up.'

'I doubt they *buy* the chimps, though,' Dad said.

'I don't know,' said Peter.

We'd brought Zan all this way, all this way home, and here we were talking about how to send him away again. It seemed so pointless and stupid and cruel.

Even if I *could* buy Zan back, even if I won – I'd lose.

I'd lose Zan.

Later in the afternoon, when Zan was having some quiet time with Peter in his room, and Mom and Dad were out getting groceries, I took Peter's pamphlet and dialled the number of the sanctuary in Florida.

Someone picked up. There was a lot of background noise. It sounded like a kitchen. Pots clanging. I heard the hooting of chimps. I guess with the time difference, it was dinner in Florida.

'Hello?' said a woman's slightly harried voice.

'Hi,' I said. 'I was wondering if you wanted another chimp for your sanctuary.'

'Who's calling, please?'

'My name's Ben. I have a chimp – well, I *used* to have a chimp but he's . . .' It felt so awful to talk about Zan like this. 'He's going to be sold to a biomedical lab for tests.'

'Do you know which one?'

'The Thurston Foundation.'

'Uh-huh,' she said, in a way that told me she knew all about it, and what went on inside.

'I don't want him to go there,' I said. 'Can you help him?'

I heard her sigh. 'How old are you, Ben?'

'Fifteen.'

'Where's your chimp right now?'

'At home, in Victoria, BC. But he's owned by Siegal University.'

'Jack Helson?'

'Yeah. He's supposed to go back.'

'Look, we don't buy chimps, we don't have the money. And we don't rescue them either. We don't go charging in and break them out, you understand?' she said bluntly.

'Yes, ma'am, sure,' I said.

I heard her sigh again, like she felt bad about something.

'What we do,' she said, 'is offer a home for chimps that people don't want any more.'

'But if I *could* get him, would you take him?'

'If you got him legally, *owned* him, yes, we would talk about it. Absolutely, Ben.'

'OK,' I said. 'Thanks.'

'Good luck,' she said.

'I'm going to buy Zan back and give him to that sanctuary,' I said.

Peter had just come into the kitchen after putting Zan to bed, and we were all cleaning up after dinner.

'Buy him with what money?' Dad asked. 'Come on, Ben, be sensible. From that letter it sounds like Helson wants at least ten thousand dollars.'

'I've got three hundred saved up,' I said.

347

'I've got fourteen hundred,' said Peter.

I turned to him. 'You'd do that?' I said.

He tousled my hair. 'It's a good cause, sure. My needs are few.'

'So that's one thousand seven hundred,' I said. 'We could do some kind of fundraiser for the rest.' I didn't know much about raising money. 'What if we called that reporter, the one who did the last story about Zan, and said we needed donations to buy him back? I bet—'

'No,' said Dad, with such force that I gave a jerk.

'Why not?' I demanded.

'If this becomes public, it could be very embarrassing for the university here. Some bleeding hearts will think it was cruel and negligent. It'll make Helson look like a monster, and the Thurston Foundation too. Then we've got people suing each other for defamation. Not to mention the fact that we've actually got a *stolen* chimp on our hands. No. The chimp goes back with Peter. I assume Jack Helson made arrangements for a private flight, Peter?'

'He's waiting for my call,' Peter said.

'Oh, we'll call Jack Helson,' said Mom firmly. 'And we'll make him an offer to buy Zan.'

Dad turned to Peter. 'I think we need some privacy to discuss this, Peter, if you don't mind.'

'Sure, yeah, of course,' said Peter, and he headed upstairs to the spare room.

Dad must have seen the determination in my face, because he didn't ask me to leave. No way was I missing this conversation.

'You actually want us to buy Zan?' Dad said to Mom, dumb-founded. 'With whose money, Sarah?'

'We have some savings.'

'Nowhere near enough,' Dad said.

'We can borrow.'

'Have you seen interest rates right now? We're in a global recession, Sarah. It's not prudent.'

'To hell with prudent,' Mom replied.

'I didn't grow up rich like you.'

'Well, you're making up for it now,' said Mom. 'A fancy private school, and a new Mercedes in the driveway.'

'I'll pay it all back,' I pleaded with Dad. 'Every summer job I have, I don't care how long it takes. It's just a loan. It's really, really important to me.'

Dad looked at me then. He *really* looked at me, and for a long time. Then he nodded. 'OK, Ben. OK.'

I did something I hadn't done for ages. I hugged my father.

'I'm sorry,' he said. 'I truly didn't want you to get hurt like this.'

'It's OK,' I replied.

We patted each other on the back. I thought I felt his shoulders tremble, but probably it was just me. After a bit, Dad cleared his throat and turned to Mom.

'It's risky. If Helson figures out you read his mail and presses charges, you could go to jail.'

'He can't prove anything,' she said. 'I'll chance it.'

'Well, then, let's give good old Jack a call,' said Dad.

* * *

Dad made the call from downstairs. Upstairs, Peter, Mom and I pressed our ears to the other phone. Mom's hand covered the mouthpiece so we wouldn't be heard.

'Jack, it's Richard Tomlin.'

'Good evening, Richard. Peter arrived this morning, I hope?'

'He did.'

'Tell him I'll charter him a plane for Thursday. And, Richard, I'm going to ask you to take care of that cost. In the interests of maintaining good relations between us.'

'I understand, Jack. But I have a business proposition I want to discuss with you as well.'

There was a short pause. 'What's that?'

'We'd like to purchase Zan.'

'What makes you think I'm willing to sell him, Richard? He's a valuable addition to my colony.'

Liar! I had to turn my face away for a moment, I was breathing so hard.

'I know it's an inconvenience to you, Jack,' Dad said, 'but it's my son. Ben's heartbroken, or Sarah never would've taken Zan like she did. It was wrong, Jack, no question, but I was hoping you might see your way to selling Zan back to us. I'm willing to reimburse you for what you paid the university – and compensate you for all your expenses, of course. Peter's airfare and so forth.'

Helson's laughter rang over the line. 'Richard, please. What I paid for Zan was a joke. Your department was eager to unload him for five thousand. Zan's value is far greater than that – even if I were *considering* selling him.'

350

'I can offer ten thousand,' Dad said.

Dad knew the Thurston Foundation had offered $30,000 for three chimps. He also knew that Zan was the most valuable. So why was he offering only ten? And then I realized it was a bargaining ploy. I hoped it wouldn't backfire on him.

Helson said abruptly, 'Not interested, Richard. Now, please, tell Peter he's flying back Thursday with Zan. And tell him to come with his tail between his legs. No doubt he played a part in this fiasco.'

'We'll pay you fifteen thousand for Zan,' Dad said. 'But that's as high as we can go, Jack. It's a very good offer.'

I waited, breath snagged in my throat, for the yes. It had to be yes now.

'Richard,' said Dr Helson, 'you and I both know that there are numerous institutions that are always eager to acquire chimpanzees. Zan's unique in that he's very young. That sweetens any deal if a buyer's looking for more than one chimp.'

He was talking about Igor and Caliban. He was saying that the lab was willing to take three because Zan was so valuable. Without Zan there might not be a deal at all.

'Jack, it was our understanding you wouldn't be selling Zan to a biomedical institution.'

'Who said I was?' Jack replied calmly. 'I was just giving an example.'

I hated him. He knew we didn't have any proof – none that we could admit to. I wondered if he knew we'd opened his mail. He must've suspected it, after we took off with Zan

351

in the middle of the night. I felt sweat prickle under my arms.

'What price are you looking for, Jack?' Dad asked, sounding impatient.

'For Zan alone? Oh, I imagine it would be in the range of twenty thousand.'

'That's a great deal of money,' my father said.

'Zan's an extraordinary animal.'

I could hear the aggression now in both their voices. It was like being back in the chimp house and seeing two males face off. In a colony there was only one alpha male, but here there were two. I could almost smell their pheromones, transmitting themselves over the phone lines. I had no idea what would happen next, and I saw defeat for Dad. Twenty thousand was too much.

'Tell Peter Thursday, then,' said Helson, 'and—'

'We'll pay twenty thousand,' Dad said.

I almost squeaked in surprise. I looked at Peter, amazed. Mom squeezed my arm.

'I didn't know you were so well-heeled, Richard,' said Helson. 'Are you sure you have the means?'

'Yes. But I'll need a couple of weeks to access the funds. You draw up a legal transfer of ownership, and we can proceed from there.'

'You have ten days, Richard, no more.'

'That should be fine,' said Dad. 'Thank you, Jack.' And he hung up.

When we all ran downstairs, Dad was pouring himself a stiff drink. He looked pale.

'I'm a complete ass,' he said. 'I don't know what I was thinking.'

'No,' I said. 'You're the alpha male and you didn't submit!'

He croaked a laugh. 'Where are we going to get twenty thousand?' he said, looking at Mom.

'We can ask my family for a loan,' she said.

'No,' Dad said, with a firmness I didn't understand, but I got the feeling there was a lot of pride tied up in it.

'We only have a few thousand of our own savings,' Mom said, and after a pause added, 'But there's a very shiny new car in the driveway.'

I watched Dad. The day he got that car he was probably the happiest I'd seen him in the past year. He wouldn't part with it.

He actually chuckled. 'It's covered in chimp hair now,' he said. 'But we should get something for it. Once I pay back the car loan, though, we're only looking at five thousand, maybe.'

'You'd really sell the car?' I said.

He shrugged. 'Who needs a Mercedes? But we're still at least ten thousand short.'

'Fund-raising might be the only way after all,' said Mom.

Dad shook his head. 'We can't be part of that, Sarah.'

'You don't have to be,' Peter said suddenly. 'We can give William Eckler's organization a call and bring him on board.'

'Would he help us?' I asked.

Peter shrugged. 'It's what he lives for – why not?'

'But they don't have any money, surely,' said Mom.

'No, but they can collect donations once the word gets out.'

Dad poured everyone else a drink, except me. 'We've only

got ten days. How do you spread the word in ten days? More important, how do we make sure the universities don't lose face?'

'Make it all about me and Zan,' I said. 'I go to that reporter and tell him I'm trying to buy my chimp back. Because I miss him and he's like my little brother, and I'm afraid *one day* he *might* end up in a lab. I'll say I want to send him to a sanctuary where he'll always be safe.'

'It's a hell of a story,' said Peter. 'Everyone loves a good story.'

'People loved Zan, Dad. They'd give money. We'd have our money in no time.'

Dad looked only at Mom as he said, 'You know how risky this is for us?'

She nodded.

Dad took a deep breath. 'It could ruin us.'

The next morning, Peter got in touch with William Eckler, and he agreed to help us out.

The rest was up to us. To me, really.

It started well. I called the local reporter and told him my story over the phone. He came out to the house and talked to me and Peter, and a photographer snapped us all playing happily with Zan. When they ran the article two days later, they included the address and phone number where donations could be made.

The next day CTV and CBC sent camera crews out to do a story, and three local radio stations wanted me to come in and talk about Zan and why I wanted him back and why I was afraid he might come to harm. I never mentioned Jack Helson by name, or the universities or the names of the labs. I tried to keep what I said as general as I could.

Donations started coming in.

In three days we had $2,000.

Some of Dad's old students came back for free to help us look after Zan.

In five days we had $4,000.

Dad went and sold the Mercedes and drove home in a used Toyota. 'They say they last for ever,' he said.

Sometimes envelopes just came through our mail slot. A ten-dollar bill from Tim Borden – I'd always known he had a good heart. Fifty from a local school for the deaf, whose students had once visited and signed with Zan.

One day I was in the kitchen when I heard the mail slot clunk. When I opened the unmarked envelope there was thirty dollars in cash and a handwritten note saying, *For Zan, from Jennifer.*

I opened the door and saw her in a station wagon as it pulled out of the driveway, driven by big hairy Cal. We just had time to wave before the car turned the corner.

The next day Shannon and her mother drove by to make a donation too. While Shannon's mom talked to mine, I took Shannon out back and introduced her to Zan, who was with a couple of student volunteers. Luckily, he seemed to like Shannon right away, and her expression was sheer delight as Zan hugged and tickled her. Then we went back inside and talked a bit in the kitchen. Before long her mother called out from the living room that it was time to go.

'Thanks, Shannon,' I said, and I kissed her on the mouth. She looked happy, and I felt a surge of something between us that made me think: *chemistry*.

The donations kept coming.

After eight days William Eckler called and told us we had ten thousand.

And the story kept spreading. It had already been covered in a couple of the big Canadian papers, and then the Associated Press did a story that got picked up all across the United States.

On the day before Helson's deadline, we'd raised $12,000, and only had to use $8,000 of our own. Tomorrow we'd wire the money to Jack Helson, and Zan would be ours.

Peter and I were outside with a couple of other students, signing and playing with Zan. I felt great. Ten days ago, everything had seemed so desperate, but we'd done it.

Around three o'clock I heard the sound of a car pulling into the driveway. I went around to see who it was. It was Dad, home early. The moment he stepped out of the car I knew something was wrong. He looked grey.

'What's wrong?' I asked.

'Let's go inside,' he said.

In the living room with Mom and Peter, he told us.

'Helson's not selling. He wants Zan back. He saw a piece in the paper implying he was *planning* to sell Zan to a lab. So he's just issued a statement to the press, saying he never had *any* such intention. He claims he wants to continue his language studies with Zan and other chimps. He said his chimp was stolen by its former owner, and he's suing us for defamation. He wants Zan on a plane with Peter by Sunday or he'll pursue all his legal options.' He nodded at Mom. 'Including pressing charges against you for theft.'

'What can we do?' I asked.

'Nothing,' said Dad. 'Zan has to go back.'

CHAPTER 25

JUNGLE

I'd never been camping in my life, and had no idea what I was doing. I filled a knapsack with food cans and a can opener, some plastic cutlery and a cup, a Thermos with water. Extra clothes. Zan's blanket and a few of his toys. I had three hundred dollars in cash.

I wished I knew how to drive – not that it would've done me any good. Mom and Dad were out with the car, getting tranquillizer drugs for Zan. Peter was at the radio station doing another interview, trying to set the record straight about Jack Helson and Zan and all the accusations and charges flying around.

In four hours Zan was going to board a plane that would take him back to Helson's ranch.

Come out. Play, I signed to Zan.

I think he was surprised I was leading him to the front door instead of the back. Outside, I took him by the hand and walked to the garage. I climbed on my bike, slung the knapsack over my shoulders, and then held out my arms. Zan hooted with excitement and jumped up onto my lap. His long arms went all the way around my back, underneath the knapsack.

I pedalled hard. Out onto West Saanich Road, towards Beaver Lake.

It was a crummy plan, and I knew it, but I had no other. Beaver Lake became Elk Lake and all along the western shore was parkland. There were paths and picnic areas in some of it, but mostly it was pretty dense forest, and that was where I was taking us.

I could not take him back to Africa, but I could take him into a forest on the outskirts of Victoria. And maybe he'd be safe there. For a while, anyway.

It was a weekday, around two o'clock, and the roads were almost deserted. We only passed a few cars. I hoped no one would notice Zan, clinging and hooting and panting. I'd been a bit nervous he'd try to jump off, but if anything he held me too tight, afraid maybe, because he'd never been on my bike before.

I was worrying about the entrance to the park, where the cars came in and out. That was where we were most likely to be seen. Get past that bit, and I could veer onto one of the forest paths.

In fifteen minutes we were at the entrance – no cars in sight. But coming towards us was another bicycle, and on it was Tim Borden.

I tried to pretend I didn't see him, but he called out.

'Ben!' And then again, 'Hey, Ben! Is that Zan?'

He'd turned and was following me and I knew it was no good. I rode a ways into the trees before I stopped, just so no one else would see us.

'What're you doing?' Tim asked.

'Just taking Zan out for a ride,' I lied.

'I heard about what's going on,' he said. 'About him having to go back.'

'Yeah. Thanks for the money you sent. You'll get it back.'

He shrugged like he didn't care. He looked at my bulging knapsack.

'You're running away,' he said.

'Yep.'

'Into the forest?'

I sighed. 'That was the idea.'

He nodded. Zan hooted pleasantly at him, and Tim hooted back. They'd always seemed to like each other. Zan hopped off my bike and climbed onto Tim. Tim giggled.

'Man, he's getting strong, huh?'

'Stronger than us. And he's only two.'

'I know a place,' said Tim. 'Deep in. There's even a creek so you'd have fresh water.'

I looked at him hard, wondering if I could trust him – and knew I could.

'Show me?' I said.

We cycled until the path disappeared, then dismounted and walked our bikes. Zan stayed close to me, sometimes on my back, sometimes at my side, but never straying far. He'd never been among so many trees before and I think it freaked him out. There were all kinds – pines and oaks and chestnuts. Mostly I didn't know their names. I caught Zan, from the corner of my eye, signing to himself. *Tree. Bird. Listen. Bird. Big tree. Water.*

Water. We'd reached the little creek.

'Thanks, Tim.'

'No one comes here. You got food?'

'Not much. Enough for a day or two.'

I had this idea that when the food ran out, I could sneak off to the concession stands near the beach and buy burgers and fries until my money ran out.

'I can bring you guys food and stuff,' Tim said.

'Really?'

'Yeah!'

'Here, I've got money.' I pulled some bills from my pocket and handed them to him.

'Just tell me what you need and I'll bring it to you here.'

'We might move around a bit,' I said.

'Well, if you're not here I'll just hang it up' – he looked around – 'on that tree over there.'

'OK,' I said. 'Tim. You won't tell anyone, right? Not even my parents, OK?'

'No way,' he said. 'This is cool. You're doing the coolest thing. So I'll see you tomorrow.'

He stuck out his hand and we shook, and then he was off.

It suddenly felt like real wilderness. I couldn't hear people or cars or anything. Zan seemed content, as long as I wasn't more than ten feet away. He would swing from trees and collect broken boughs and make them into a big nest. Then he'd get bored with that and start on another nest.

It was warm, and the light coming through the branches dappled everything and made it beautiful. I felt hopeful. We could live here for ever. We had each other. As long as we stayed warm and had food, why not?

As the afternoon went on, the sounds changed. Different bugs, different animals and birds scuffling around. Things could sound really big in the undergrowth. Two tiny birds sounded like cougars and scared Zan and me half to death.

We ate some food and had some quiet time, grooming each other and signing.

Darkness was coming on and, even though it was summer, it started to cool off. Probably I should've brought more blankets. I'd ask Tim for some tomorrow. I'd make a list and gradually I'd get everything right. We'd be all set up.

Night came faster in the forest, because of all the trees.

We had a little more food and some water from the creek, and then Zan arranged his blanket in his nest and we cuddled up together at the base of the tree. It was really, really uncomfortable. There were mosquitoes. I whispered stories to Zan. I told him the story of our day, like I used to.

It got darker still, until I could barely see. I was cold. Even with Zan smushed against me I wished I'd brought my own blanket. I hadn't thought to bring a flashlight either. More things for the list.

After a while, I couldn't see anything. I wondered if Zan could.

We clung to each other. I think Zan was as terrified as I was. All through that night we woke up and listened to noises. I had no idea what kind of animals made those noises. You could get all sorts of things around here. Snakes. Black widow spiders. A cougar had been sighted once, I remembered that.

I lay there and felt desperate. What the hell was I doing? We couldn't stay out here for ever. I wasn't Tarzan.

Slowly the light came back.

I was exhausted, Zan asleep in my arms. With the dawn, my confidence returned a bit. Maybe we could do this after all.

We ate. We drank from the stream. I didn't even bother to change Zan's diaper, just took it off. He didn't want pants or a shirt on either.

We climbed trees. I marvelled at how fast and easy it was for him. I was in his world now. He was the dominant species, and I lagged behind. I couldn't go as high as him; I didn't know where to grip and pull. My arms and legs, my toes and fingers were feeble compared to his.

I tried to see the forest as he saw it. Hear it as he heard it. I couldn't. Chimps were our closest living relatives and I could often guess what he was thinking, but sometimes he was half brother, half stranger to me.

Mid-morning came and we heard new sounds. Zan caught them before I did. He gave a series of low pants.

Regular cracklings. Footfalls.

And then human voices.

Tim had said nobody came out here.

My bike was laid flat under a screen of branches. My knap-sack too.

I took Zan's hand and led him behind a big tree. There was laughter, a shout, and then a bang, which made both of us jerk. A second bang. More laughter.

Quiet, I signed to Zan.

I peered round the trunk and saw three kids. It took me a moment to recognize Mike. He and his two friends were taking turns with a gun, shooting at squirrels and stuff. It was a BB gun, like the one Tim had.

'There's the little bugger,' said Mike, and he took a shot at something.

I hoped they would just wander off, but they were coming closer.

Zan gave several low hoots of fear.

'What's that?' one of the kids said. 'Over there!'

I held Zan's hand. He hooted louder.

I was afraid they might start shooting at us, so I said, in as low and manly a voice as possible: 'Just some people hanging out over here, man.'

Maybe they'd think I was a crazy, dangerous hippie drifter, and get freaked out.

'Come on,' I heard one of Mike's friends mutter to him, like he wanted to get going.

But I heard footsteps coming closer, and then Mike walked round our tree, giving it a wide berth, the gun crooked under his arm. He stared at us.

'Look at this!' he crowed. 'It's chimp boy and his chimp!'

The other two cautiously emerged from round the tree.

Zan curled back his lips with displeasure and gave a warning hoot.

'Looks like little Ben's gone native,' said Mike.

'Just leave us alone, Mike,' I said. I was scared, but I tried not to show it.

'Your dad's not around to save your ass this time.'

He still had the gun pointed in our general direction. He shouldn't have stepped any closer, but he did. If he'd thought Zan would forget being hit by a rock, he was wrong. Chimps had long memories. They carried grudges. They were just like us.

Loyal too. Zan saw Mike take another step towards me, and he stood on both legs and displayed. All his hair stood out, all two inches of it, and he shrieked and struck the air with his long, powerful arms.

I saw the fear on Mike's face as he took a step back.

'Better beat it, Mike,' I said. 'He's strong.'

I said Zan's name several times, and told him to come.

But he wouldn't come. He stood there between me and Mike, showing his teeth.

'All right, all right,' said Mike, and he quickly lowered his gun so the muzzle pointed earthwards. He took a step backwards and, as a parting gesture, snarled at Zan.

Zan leaped at him. I don't know what made Zan do it. Maybe it was the snarl; maybe the gun reminded him of a cattle prod. But he threw himself at Mike, knocked him over, and bit his foot right through his sneaker. Mike cursed and screamed. I saw blood. Zan tried to bite him again.

I ran forward, snatched the BB gun, and whipped it into the trees.

'Zan!' I shouted. 'Stop!'

I pulled at all his muscle and fury, and I knew I couldn't stop him, not if he didn't want to stop himself. Then he spun at me, and his eyes blazed with a pure animal rage I'd never seen before. I was afraid he might actually bite *me*. But instead he whimpered and jumped into my arms.

'You are so friggin' *dead*!' shouted Mike. His eyes looked crazy as he staggered up.

I whirled and ran towards a tree with many low branches.

Up, I signed to Zan. *Climb*.

He climbed, and I climbed after him. I glanced back to see Mike looking around for his gun.

'Where is it?' he shouted at his two stunned friends. 'Get me that frickin' gun!'

Zan climbed fast and high. Even at that moment, I marvelled at him. I didn't dare look down.

I heard the crack of the gun, then a second crack, and felt a searing pain in my bum. I swore.

'*Yeah!*' shouted Mike from below. 'More coming your way!'

I tried to climb round to the other side of the tree, where the branches were bushier, but they were also farther apart and they slowed me down. I heard a few more shots, but they missed. I was hoping Mike couldn't get a clear aim any more.

I glanced up and saw Zan, crouched on the branch above me, giving me encouraging pant-hoots.

I reached up to his branch and got a grip with both hands. then started looking for a foothold. The crack of the gun, and the pain in my bare right arm came at the same moment. It hurt so bad that my right hand lost its strength and slipped. I dangled, my left hand holding on, but I could feel its power failing.

Zan grabbed my left hand. He held me in place, and his grip was so tight I felt my fingers breaking, actually breaking, and I screamed with agony, screamed for him to let go, even though I knew I'd fall if he did.

He didn't. He held me tight. He pulled with all the might of his little body. With my right hand I flailed around for a hold and finally found one. Zan helped pull me up onto his branch.

I looked at my hand and retched in pain and disgust. It looked like a weird swollen red and purple glove, the fingers bent at odd angles. I cried. I couldn't help it. I'd never known such pain. Zan was looking at it too, and stroking it and my arm, and signing, *Sorry, sorry, hurt*.

'What the hell're you doing?' someone shouted from below.

Through the branches, I saw Tim Borden approach Mike. Mike let his gun drop a little.

'Just a few potshots,' said Mike.

'Tim!' I called down to him.

'Ben? Is Zan up there too? Are you guys OK?'

'My hand's busted.'

I saw Tim turn on Mike. 'You freaking nutcase!' He

snatched the gun from Mike's hand and pointed it at him. 'Get going before I load your ass.'

'Take it easy,' said Mike, backing off. 'No big deal.'

'Go!' shouted Tim.

With his two friends, Mike hurried off.

'You need help getting down?' said Tim.

'Maybe.'

He hid the gun under some brush and climbed up. We sat there together for a while. I saw Tim look at my hand and then look away without saying anything. I didn't feel too good. I felt like if I moved my hand, I'd puke.

'You were on the news last night,' Tim said. '*The National*. Boy disappears with pet chimp. People are looking for you. They had this one guy calling you a fugitive from justice.' He chuckled.

'Dr Helson?' I asked.

He nodded. 'Tall and thin, like those crazy training sergeants in the movies?'

'Sounds like him,' I said.

'You're in the morning paper too,' Tim said. 'Everyone feels sorry for you and Zan. You're sort of a hero.'

The throbbing in my hand was getting deeper and meaner.

'I think I better get home,' I said. I felt about six years old.

Together, Tim and Zan helped me down from the tree. It took a while. And then there was the long walk through the woods. We left the knapsack and the bikes. When we reached the parking lot, there was a pay phone, and Tim called my house.

'They're coming to pick you guys up right away,' he said after he hung up.

And then we just sat down and waited.

Zan had broken every finger in my hand, even my thumb.

He couldn't help it. He was just so strong.

But he'd saved me from breaking a leg, and probably my neck. He'd probably saved my life

I was in the hospital two days as they X-rayed my hand and discussed what was best, and how successful they might be at repairing the damage, and then they decided I needed a little operation. I got put to sleep, and when I woke up, Mom and Dad and Peter were all there. My left hand was so wrapped up it looked like I was wearing an oven mitt.

'Where's Zan?' I croaked. My mouth had never felt so dry.

'Good news,' said Mom with a smile. She took my good hand and pressed her cheek against mine. After all the bad hospital smells, her perfume was so good.

'He doesn't have to go back to Helson's,' said Peter, beaming.

'What happened?' I asked, trying to sit up.

'The power of the media,' said Dad, helping me. 'It saved us in the end.'

After interviewing Helson, a reporter had somehow gotten hold of the letters between him and the Thurston Foundation. All about which chimps Helson was offering for sale, which ones the Foundation wanted to buy. There were letters haggling about the price, until the last one we'd seen, where the Foundation had made its final offer.

They showed that letter on TV from coast to coast.

Helson was still insisting these letters were just *discussions*. No formal agreement had ever been reached, he said, and he was not doing anything that wasn't within his legal rights. But it made him look like a liar.

And, thanks to William Eckler, the news station also showed some footage of the lab where Zan might end up. They showed the cages and the little baby chimps banging their bodies against the bars.

Apparently the newspapers and the TV stations received a ton of phone calls and letters.

And the next day, Helson issued a statement. He said that, given my personal attachment to the chimp, he was willing to return him to me.

I wondered how the reporter got those letters. Did someone at the Thurston Foundation leak them, some researcher sick of seeing the suffering of the chimps? Or was it closer to home? Was it Sue-Ellen, who'd grown up with Caliban and Igor, and was starting to love Zan? Maybe she'd gone into her dad's office one night, stolen the letters and given them to the newspaper. I guessed we'd never know. I was just so grateful it worked out.

Five days later we bought Zan back from Helson for one dollar.

The last night Zan was with us, I put him to bed. I lay beside him with his blankets and toys and brushed his hair for a long, long time, and I told him the story of his life.

'Here's the real story,' I told him, 'because maybe no one

else will ever tell you. Your real mother lived in a lab and she had you in a cage, and she loved you and fed you until Mom came along and stole you. And Mom brought you here. And we gave you a room and a yard and food and pretended that you were a real human and a part of our family. Dad pretended to like you. Mom was really fond of you right away, and then she started loving you for real.' I paused, because this part was hard to admit. 'I didn't love you at first, Zan. I thought you were weird, and I guess I was jealous, and sometimes I didn't want you at all. But that didn't last long. You were my little brother. I really felt that. That was never fake.'

I don't know how much he understood. He understood a lot, much more than he could sign.

But I think he was asleep long before I finished.

CHAPTER 26

SANCTUARY

Another private plane, more sweltering country roads, flat land on all sides. Zan asleep on my lap, in the back seat.

I still had a cast on my left hand. The doctors had X-rayed it a couple more times, taken off one cast, reset a couple of fingers, put on a new cast. They talked about how, maybe, I'd never regain full use of my hand, my thumb especially. It might not work too well any more. It was funny, because chimps had weak thumbs too. Look at them, and you could see how short they were, compared to their other fingers. Often they used just their fingers to pick things up. I didn't mind if I had a chimp hand. Zan's hand.

When we first pulled up at the sanctuary, my heart felt sick, because it didn't look much different from Helson's ranch. Fences and big outbuildings with bars and high windows. But beyond the fences I could see five islands in large ponds, and in the trees I saw the dark outlines of two chimps, playing. Driving

372

closer, we passed fields where there were huge wooden walkways and shaded platforms and ropes and planks with more chimps playing on them. Some of them looked pretty young, still with their white tail tufts, not much older than Zan.

The woman who ran the sanctuary was named Margaret Inverness, and I liked her right away. She came out from the office in jeans and T-shirt, and when she greeted us I realized she'd been the person I talked to that first time on the phone. Mom and Dad and Peter were there, but it was me she looked at most as she showed us around the grounds and main buildings. Zan slept in my arms.

There were still cages where the chimps slept and ate. When we arrived it was lunchtime and the volunteers were feeding them. They loaded trolleys with all sorts of drinks and fruits and vegetables and yoghurt and other things, and the chimps could reach through these slots and just take what they wanted. Every cage had its own trolley. It was sort of like a rolling cafeteria.

Above the cages were lofts where the chimps liked to sleep, and above those were bigger caged areas where they could also play and sleep together if they wanted. They had blankets and toys and all sorts of things to stimulate and comfort them.

I watched the volunteers as they fed the chimps, and they really did seem to like them. They talked to the chimps and joked with them. The chimps were all ages and sizes. One guy kept clapping his hands to get a volunteer's attention and she always seemed to know exactly what it was he wanted.

There was a cage ready for Zan, and they let us put in his

favourite blankets and toys and anything else we thought might make his transition easier.

'Now, there's some paperwork,' said Margaret.

We went into her office. It was a single piece of paper we had to sign. Mom and Dad read it, and so did Peter.

'What this says,' Margaret told me, 'is that once you transfer Zan to us, we will never release him. You understand?'

'I think so,' I said. Zan was beginning to stir in my arms.

'That means we don't let anyone have him. Not a scientist or a zoo or a lab. Or you, Ben. You understand that, right?'

For a second I couldn't say anything. 'Yeah,' I said. 'Sure.'

'So even if you change your mind and want Zan back, you can't have him.'

I nodded, and Dad signed the papers.

We spent three days at the sanctuary, trying to make it easier for Zan. Or maybe it was to make it easier for us. It sure helped me to see that it was a good place for him, filled with people who really loved the chimps and wanted the best for them.

I hoped it helped Zan too, us staying on a few days.

On the last day, we left him in one of the play areas. We were all on the other side of the fence. That was one of the things about the sanctuary. There was no human–chimp contact unless the chimps were sick. You could touch them through the bars and groom their hands and backs if you knew them well enough. But there'd be no more teaching, no more signing. Zan was allowed to be just as he wanted.

'I bet he teaches some of the young ones signs,' said Peter. 'I bet he does.'

'Maybe he will,' Dad said.

Then, one by one, we slipped away.

I was last.

Zan came over for a tickle and hug through the fence. A couple of other young chimps were bounding around on the play apparatus and Zan kept looking over his shoulder to check on them. One hooted impatiently at him, and Zan looked at me one last time, then turned and scampered off.

I watched him go, and hoped that one day he'd forget he was ever human.

A couple of nights later, after we got home, I dreamed about Zan.

We were talking, signing.

Our hands, flying to speak.

I didn't understand how his vocabulary – or mine – had grown so much. There were no words we couldn't say to each other, and I felt such joy to be talking to him, the way I'd always wanted to, all those months he'd been one of us.

The sanctuary's OK, isn't it? I asked.

I like it, he said. *The food is excellent. If anything they give us too much.*

I wish you could've stayed with us.

A house can't hold me, he said. *I'm going to get a lot bigger and a lot stronger. Probably smelly. I'm pretty rambunctious, too. I break things. It's fun, you should try it some time. That time I ripped your kitchen cabinet off the wall – that was very satisfying.*

I never knew if you were angry or happy when you did that.

I was having a ball, he replied.

I liked it when you bit Ryan, I signed.

Zan gave a little pant-hoot. *That was satisfying. But we can have big tempers. It's not safe for you to be around us.*

You'd never hurt me, I signed.

Your hand.

Well, it's pretty messed up, but you did save my life.

But I could hurt you, worse, another time, he told me. *We're not like you. We do things.*

I took a breath.

Will you forget about us? I asked.

We have long memories.

It was hard for me to sign the next bit, but I did:

It's probably best if you do. Forget about us.

That's up to me, he said.

It wasn't fair what we did to you, Zan. I'm sorry.

He shrugged. *I liked the yoghurt. You don't get that in the wild.*

I thought of something I'd said aloud to him many times, whispered to him as he fell asleep in my arms. But I'd never signed it, because Dad had never thought it was useful or important to teach him. For Zan, that phrase had never existed.

I signed it now.

For a long time Zan's hands were still, and I felt I'd said too much. I knew what I wanted him to sign back – but how could I expect it? We'd stolen him. We'd cheated him. We'd used him. We'd abandoned him. We'd told him to be something he wasn't – a human – and then told him to go back to being a chimp. He should have hated me.

Zan's hands moved. With his index finger he touched his breastbone. Then he crossed both wrists over his chest, and finally pointed at me.

He made the B sign over my heart.

He did it twice.